Night's End

Night's End

Jackson Compton

VANTAGE PRESS
New York

This is a work of fiction. Any similarity between the names and characters in this book and any real persons, living or dead, is purely coincidental.

FIRST EDITION

All rights reserved, including the right of reproduction in whole or in part in any form.

Copyright © 2008 by Jackson Compton

Published by Vantage Press, Inc.
419 Park Ave. South, New York, NY 10016

Manufactured in the United States of America
ISBN: 978-0-533-15517-0

Library of Congress Catalog Card No.: 2006904016

0 9 8 7 6 5 4 3 2 1

Thank You

I would like to thank my test readers, Alicia, Stan, Anne, and Roni for their time and patience during the writing process. I would also like to thank Vantage Press for all of their hard work.

This book is dedicated to the memory of David Gemmell (1948–2006). The inspiration from your moving novels will be missed.

Introduction

My love for books started out as a punishment. I forget exactly what I had done to anger my dad, for there were many things being a headstrong child, but he was as mad as I ever remember him being. He told me to get into the car, and I did so reluctantly. I knew that I had crossed the line and now was on my way somewhere where my dad could kill me without witnesses to see my grizzly fate, at least that is how I remember feeling at the time.

Instead of my impending demise, we drove in silence to a local bookstore where he bought a copy of *Treasure Island* by Robert Louis Stevenson and handed it to me. He told me that I was to read a chapter a day, and that he would discuss it with me afterward. The last thing that I wanted to do was read a book when there was TV to watch and video games to play.

Halfheartedly, I read through the first chapter and found that I could not put the book down. I have been an avid reader of Science Fiction, Fantasy, Horror, and Ancient Histories (anything having to do with swords) ever since. Looking back on that single act of punishment, which was really an act of love on my dad's part, was a defining point in my life that set me on a path of discovery. I believe that with every book read has come inspiration, imagination, and knowledge, and that knowledge in turn is power, and that power allows one to control his destiny.

So to my dad, Robert, I thank you for showing me the path. I hope you enjoy the similarities that rubbed off on some of these characters for whom you were the inspiration.

Night's End

Prologue

The child crept slowly from the hearth where the embers of the fire flickered and glowed. He held the scalding kettle carefully away from his body in his outstretched hands. Steam from the tea whiffed and danced about his dark face, causing his short curly black hair to stick to his forehead above soft brown eyes. Pursing his lips, he blew the strands of hair out of his eyes, scattering the vapors in the wake of his breath. He continued toward the table at a slow and meticulous pace, watching for obstacles along the way.

The cottage door burst open and was slammed shut by a young man, looking like an older version of the boy carrying the kettle. The child froze, staring wild-eyed at his brother. The older boy fell back against the door breathing heavily after throwing the board latch into place, securing the door. He tried to catch his breath. A startled woman emerged from the pantry carrying utensils and some cups. Her shock was apparent upon seeing the older boy's expression.

"Deetric?" she half said, half gasped.

"Momma, it's been spotted near the village. The Magistrate told me to spread the word and then get inside."

Deetric flung himself from the door and began checking the window latches that had already been secured with the coming night. The shocked mother dropped the utensils and rushed up the creaky wooden stairs to check the windows on the second story. It was commonplace to be locked indoors before sunset and it was even more commonplace to know that whatever you did for safety, it was never enough.

The child sat the kettle in the center of the table on a worn piece of narrow wood and dashed across the room, climbing into the lap of the elderly grandmother who was sitting near the fire in an old rocking chair. She pulled the frightened child close, wrapping him in her shawl as she stroked his hair with coarse-withered hands. Whispered reassurances to the child did little to conceal her own growing fright.

"It will be all right, Tadley," she cooed. The child's focus was on his brother racing back and forth across the room, making preparations. His gaze turned at the sound of his raven-haired mother who raced down the stairs with a soot-covered lantern and a leather flask of oil.

"Deetric, where's your father?" she asked, trying to keep her voice from becoming frantic after setting the lamp on the table. Deetric had picked up a hatchet and an axe and positioned them near the hearth for quick reach.

"He's riding with Baron Keltch and his men. They were chasing one of them already out of its grave tonight. I'm not sure if it's the same one seen near the village. He sent me home before dusk in case he was gone all night. I ran into the Magistrate on my way home. I was able to pass the word to some of the families before returning," Deetric said as he readied a knife from the sheath on his belt.

The mother pulled her shawl tightly around herself and plopped at the foot of the grandmother's chair. Tadley reached down and put his small arm around her neck, giving her a squeeze. She returned the gesture by rubbing and patting his small hand, her eyes working busily over the closed door and windows. Deetric was still breathing heavily from his race to the village. Running a hand through his dark sweat-drenched hair, he too watched the door.

An unsettling silence fell on the household as they strained to listen. The nighttime sounds of birds and insects haltingly abated. The only sound heard in the common room was that of racing hearts and the occasional crackle of the burning wood in the brick fireplace. The cottage occupants held their breath as if by doing so, this night might end that much sooner. Unfortunately, the night decided to stay.

Rolling hoarse laughter shattered the silence. Deetric slowly reached across and picked up the axe. He pulled it close to his body to try to keep his hands from shaking. Again there was the menacing laughter. A deep ominous bellow echoed, rocking the dirt foundation of the small cottage, and a throaty voice followed.

"Where has everyone gone?" Laughter followed again. "Come now. These straw walls can't keep me out. Is there no one home?" Another bout of humorless laughter followed. Silence. Several moments passed. "What have we here?" the voice boomed in mock amusement. A scream issued forth from a woman, possibly only a few houses down the street. The scream was answered by several more coming from the same direction. Again the laughter rolled, blending a bass with the high octave of screams through the audience of night. More shouts erupted, this time nearer the cottage. The frightened mother placed her arms around the legs of the grandmother and buried her face into the folds of her threadbare dress. Tadley wrapped both arms around his mother's neck, clinging to her while the grandmother clutched him around his small waist.

The screams shifted to sobs and the night swallowed them up. Deetric wrapped his hands around the rounded axe handle, squeezing it so tight that his knuckles turned white. The air became an oppressive thing that pushed down the occupants of the small cottage and the room began to smell of decay and sulfur. Faint tendrils of what looked like dark green-colored smoke crept under the door. The creeping tendrils moved along the floor of the household, carrying the decaying stench. The tentacle-like smoke appeared as a living shadow that was perpetually seeking, searching and always finding.

Deetric moved closer to the door, catching a stronger whiff of the noxious fumes that watered his eyes and turned his stomach. He became extremely ill and collapsed onto his knees using the axe handle as a crutch to steady himself from toppling over. The crying women winced and gagged as the retched smell burned their eyes and throats.

The tendrils worked their way around the room affecting everyone to some degree. The concentration focused on the small figure whose face was buried into his mother's hair. The vapors set into his lungs and he gasped for air gripping his mother's neck with an inhuman strength. She choked and tried to pull his small hands free but to no avail. Spots blurred her vision as she fought desperately for a breath of air. Tadley's body shook with spasms and his face contorted into a wrinkled mess with bulging eyes. The grandmother screamed for Deetric to help as she fought frantically with feeble hands to try to free the mother from the child's choking grasp.

Tadley's childish features were replaced by that of a hideous visage. His dark skin had paled to an ashen gray and his small frame bloated under the onslaught of spasms in his muscles. He gurgled and wheezed in pain as he squeezed the life from his limp mother. Deetric reacted by trying desperately to free his brother's grip and then finally resorted to harsher measures. Deetric swung the hatchet and hacked at the tiny limbs that held such unearthly and deadly strength. The child wailed out with a very human cry as Deetric, staring through tear-streaked eyes and howling in throaty disgust, severed the last arm and kicked the child away from the unconscious form of its mother.

"Momma!" Deetric yelled, trying to wake her. She choked and swallowed the air greedily while clutching at her bruised throat. Deetric held her close as the life seeped back into her body. He watched the sprawled form which used to be his brother shake and flop haphazardly on the floor.

Its whimper was a mixture of the cries of the former child and the unholy roar of some kind of demon. Deetric pulled his mother and grandmother into the stairwell and backed up slowly, putting as much distance as they could between them and the altered sibling.

The ghastly smell and oppressiveness of the air began to thin. The echoing laughter began to fade away as the tendrils sought elsewhere. Deetric had moved the family to the second floor landing and the women held each other and wept for the loss of the child.

Slowly Deetric crept back down the creaking stairs. He held the hatchet poised over his head, ready for an attack. Tadley had rolled onto his stomach and was attempting to stand up by propping himself up on the bloody stumps of his arms. Deetric moved cautiously, avoiding the entrance door, and stood over the ashen form of his brother. The child's malicious look sent a cold chill up his spine causing him to shake worse than he already was. Murderous eyes followed him as he edged his way closer to the prone form. Spit and bile hung from the distorted gray chin jiggling back and forth as the child made an attempt to stand. Deetric jumped and landed on the back of the struggling form pinning it to the floor. It wielded the strength of a full-grown man and nearly knocked Deetric off his feet in the struggle.

Deetric brandished the hatchet in both hands over his head ready to strike. Recognition appeared on the small face of the child and for an instant its hate-filled eyes cleared.

"Deet? Don't hurt me," a small voice said from the grotesque mouth. Deetric hesitated and watched the terrified face looking back at him. He slowly lowered the hatchet and stepped off the back of his brother. The prone form stayed still and watched Deetric slowly back away.

The mangled child made another attempt to get up but collapsed back onto the blood-slicked floor. Tadley looked up pleadingly at Deetric.

"Help me, brother. Please!"

Its already hideous face contorted and tears welled in its red eyes. Deetric set the hatchet on the stone floor and straddled the form. Reaching around his brother's waist, Deetric gently gathered his brother from the floor. The small form went limp in his arms as he raised him to a standing position. Deetric stood Tadley on his feet and the boy looked up at him.

Tears flowed down Deetric's face and a horrible shame filled him. He bent down to embrace his brother. Tadley wrapped his bleeding stumps around Deetric's waist and both brothers wept.

"I'm sorry," Deetric heard Tadley whisper and the child squeezed him in a deadly embrace. Deetric struggled and looked down into the red eyes and saw the evil grin on the face of the thing that had been his brother.

Tadley's horrific beam turned into a scowl and he sank his teeth into Deetric's chest ripping out a massive chunk of flesh. Deetric screamed and struggled to get away but Tadley held him fast even though they both were becoming drenched in sticky blood. Again Tadley sank his jagged teeth into Deetric's torso tearing another strip of flesh and muscle. Both figures became as one in crimson and the struggle appeared as some strange exotic dance until Deetric's bloody body arched back with his arms hanging near the ground quite dead. The creature continued to ravenously gorge on the fleshy tissue of the body it still clutched.

A loud thump came from the barred door shaking the walls and loosening freed dust into the air. Another loud thump and the wood cracked and splintered as part of the door ripped from the lower hinge. A face poked through the broken door.

"Deetric!" the peeking face cried out.

Thud. Again something hitting the door as it broke away from the remaining hinge to crash to the floor.

Several armed men ran through the doorway carrying various weapons. The creature hurled the limp body at the entering men, trying to scatter them so it could make a break from the cottage.

It was successful in doing so but was stopped as a spear impaled it through the backside. The creature that had been Tadley wailed and grasped at the tip of the spear poking through its chest. He tried to pull it out as he flailed his way outside of the cottage. Several men grabbed the long spear and lifted Tadley off the ground. Struggling furiously, the creature slid down the shaft of the upraised spear. When it reached about midway, two other men grabbed the spear point end and leveled it off. Tadley was caught midway on the spear shaft and the men held him off the ground so he could go nowhere. Tadley flailed, trying to free himself, but without hands it was to no avail. The group of men carried the child away from the row of cottages on the cobbled street toward the town square.

Orders were shouted and doors opened as hysterical crying and angry shouts filled the area around the square as cautious people filtered in. A scaffold and platform had been erected with several makeshift planks in the form of crosses and were covered with restraining devices.

The group carrying the spear stomped through the wet streets and up the stairs onto the scaffold. They lashed the spear suspended between two of the posts. Two other men clambered onto the scaffold each carrying a wrapped bundle. The women cried and held each other and cursed the gods for their betrayal. The somber-faced males unwrapped the two squirming bundles and held them outstretched before them. The hideous gray masses of flesh gurgled and spewed. Wrinkled faces hissed and the bodies shook convulsively. Each infant was tied to the remaining posts and left dangling. Tadley continued his own struggle trying to free himself from the spear that held him fast. He kicked continuously through the empty air. Although his hunger was somewhat sated, it had not the strength to aid in an effort to escape. He was just too small, yet he continued to struggle with all his might.

The crowd parted for a robed man leaning heavily on a staff. The old man entered the square and approached the platform. The shouts of remorse somewhat abated and only the sobs of the town's women could be heard. He approached the three restrained figures and looked them over. His gaze passed them over for several minutes before he finally turned around to address the expectant crowd.

"My friends, these evil fiends must be stopped! They have once again returned to our village to terrorize our homes!" he yelled with a passion that defied his age. He shook his balled fist angrily and contorted his face. He did his best to try and control his rage.

"These creatures have preyed on us for far too long. Look what they do for amusement," the old man said turning around to point at the struggling figures in the torchlight. "They damn our children to this fate and it must be stopped! We can no longer be victims of these foul beings. We must act!" the old man yelled through clenched teeth.

"What can we do?" came a male voice from the crowd. The old man searched for the speaking figure. The aged man located the questioner as he spoke again. "They're too strong for us. We can barely deal with our children when they have been changed, let alone those monsters that have been ravaging our homes. What are we supposed to do?" the man said with murmurs of approval from others that had gathered.

"Sunlight kills," offered a man in the crowd.

"Only the young ones," someone else added. The dark sky was already turning a deep shade of purple, announcing the coming of morning. "These creatures have been around for as long as anyone can remember. Some of them even walk in the daylight. I know that for some of them, that's the only time they come out."

"It's true," the old priest conceded nodding his head, "but there has to be another way to rid them," the old man said, scratching his stubbled chin in thought.

"Baron Keltch has sworn to rid us of them. He and his soldiers are hunting for them as we speak," another man offered.

The robed man broke from his reverie and looked toward the direction Keltch and his men had ridden off to. His look turned sour as he said, "Keltch had done more harm than good with his personal vendetta." The crowd murmured at the statement.

The sky lightened and traces of orange rimmed the purplish-blue. The squirming figures became more agitated as the darkness fled. The old man pulled a leather-bound volume from the inserts of his robes and opened it to near the middle of the book. He paced in front of the crowd in a ritual that had become all too familiar. He began reading passages that were clearly already memorized.

"It says in the Great Tome to love our children for they are the future of our world. The Tome also says that there is no greater sin than that which hurts and defiles a child. These monsters make a mockery of the word of the Tome by acts that we believe to be inconceivable. These demons rob us of our loved ones and our future." Closing the book with a slap, the old man pointed a finger at the struggling forms. "These creatures are no longer our children, they are shells that house the demons that torment us. We must have faith that reason and light will see us through our desperate times!"

As if on cue, the sun rose above the horizon line and soft golden beams bathed the scaffold. The creatures wailed and struggled in their bonds as the light touched their pallid skin. The grayness changed to coal-black as the light penetrated the newly formed creatures. Chunks of blackened flesh fell onto the ground as smoking ash. The inhuman cries subsided, but the hiss and crackling of the disintegrating bodies continued to issue forth.

The crowd mourned and whispered their last good-byes while others could not watch and turned from the nightmarish scene. As the last of the flesh was burned and the bones crumbled, the old man nodded and stepped slowly from the scaffold, leaning against his staff. Once again the priest looked more like his age and moved through the crowd at a slow pace. The mourners parted for him then moved to fill his wake.

Morning light filled the square and slowly the crowd began to thin. Many left flowers and trinkets on the scaffold in remembrance of their loved ones. Some gave silent prayers to whichever gods they believed in and others cursed the gods for allowing such suffering. All of the mourners thirsted for vengeance that never seemed forthcoming.

1

Baron Keltch drew back the reins on his horse, slapped back his visor with a gauntleted hand, and searched for something lurking in the surrounding darkness. The other riders stopped short, extending their torches, trying to pierce the enveloping night. The foot soldiers fanned out around the horsemen with torches and lanterns trying to add to the brightness.

"Over there!" someone yelled. Keltch spurred his horse and rode in the direction the shouting men were pointing. A silhouetted figure stood bathed in the waning moonlight. Keltch knew the form without actually seeing who it was. He had been at this cat-and-mouse game long enough to know his enemy. Keltch had been trading punches with this particular creature for years. Out of the main four who terrorized the land, this monster was the one he hated the most.

Keltch was only a boy when his father was slain at the hands of the evil creature known as Flange. He spent the rest of his childhood training and learning the arts of war with his uncle, in hopes of conquering this foe. For the past twenty-some years, he had spent his time hunting all the elusive Undead, but Flange in particular. Years had passed with nothing happening to tip the scales in his favor. The creatures would come and go and sometimes be gone for years at a time, but usually one or two of them stayed around to terrorize the people. It was only recently that all four had been seen lurking near the village.

Flange had returned, after an extended leave of some years, to play the fox that constantly led Keltch's hounds on a chase. The only thing Keltch could say in favor of Flange is that at least he was not like his siblings. The others rarely left the village alone. Flange chose mostly to avoid the village people and only hunted those who were brave or foolish enough to pursue him, and Keltch always led that pack.

The horses tore across the ground from the clearing onto a path that entered the wooded area where Flange had last been seen. The men on foot did their best to try and keep up with those who were mounted. Not everyone in the village could afford a horse or the upkeep that comes with it. Keltch had rounded up forty men and only four had horses.

Baron Keltch pulled the reins again and looked through the foliage for the evading creature. The mounted riders fanned out as the footmen filtered between the horses with torches blazing. Those carrying weapons hacked at the tall grass and saplings, trying to clear a path. Keltch watched as the men scattered and searched.

A cry of surprise echoed off the trees and a horse reared and threw its rider to the ground. The flung torch quickly started a fire on a dry scrub of brush. The rider stood on shaky legs, dusted himself off, and looked for the horse that had run off. The unseated rider hollered for some of the footmen to help put out the fire. Kneeling down, he reached near the blaze and retrieved the fallen torch. As he brought it up, a smiling shape stepped from behind the closest tree. The figure bathed in torchlight looked like any other man. The stranger's face was handsome and his frame was slight. But on closer inspection, the dark clothes and boots were decades out of style. The most disconcerting factor was the orange light reflecting off the ashen face and black-silver hair.

Terror gripped the heart of the rider and he was not dissuaded by the charming smile on the person who faced him. The rider reached for the sword at his side, but was intercepted by a lightning-quick response as the creature lunged forward and held the man's arms pinned against his side. The rider struggled, but was held firmly in place by the smiling fiend. An icy chill filled the man's limbs where the creature's hands clutched him. He began to shake under the cold burning touch. The creature lifted the man off the ground and leaned forward, whispering in his ear.

"Not yet, my friend. You will get your chance to kill me soon enough, but I prefer that the chase last a bit longer, just as your master does." And with that, the creature moved so fast that the man saw only a blur as it let go and disappeared through the trees.

Breathing heavily, the man picked himself off the ground and tried to rub the numbing chill from his bones. The footmen arrived and stomped out the blaze that was spreading around the rider.

The rider's horse wandered back and nudged his shoulder with its muzzle. Stunned, he slowly came to his senses and staggered about. He fumbled with the reigns and clumsily mounted the horse.

"It's over there!" shouted a footman. The other riders, including the Baron, led the way as the footmen hurried in their wake. The shaken rider was careful to stay toward the rear of the group. Once the footmen ran past the bewildered rider, he pulled rein and cut back in the direction of the village. After having such a close brush with living death, he decided that he never wanted to be that close again.

The chase continued for the next several hours while the pursuers were led in circles around the surrounding countryside. Shadows began to form as the sun climbed into the morning sky.

Flange could feel his power ebbing as the day began replacing the night. His strength of twenty men soon became that of just one. His ashen skin pulled taut against his body, resisting the sun that threatened to destroy him. Flange knew this was the time he had been waiting for. *What better way to humiliate an enemy than by doing it in your most weakened state?* Flange felt feeble, a state he was not used to. His legs felt quivery and his arms grew leaden and awkward. He laughed aloud and stepped from the protection of the trees. The pursuing men were tired and worn out from the night's excursion but by no means were they depleted. Flange stepped into the clearing just opposite of Baron Keltch and his men. He strolled forward with the grace of a nobleman, stopped and gave a long and lissome bow with outstretched arms.

The Baron shouted orders and the foot soldiers charged forward, crying out for vengeance. The marauding group cleared about half the distance to where Flange was standing as he finally straightened from his bow, continuing to smile his wickedly charming smile. The mass of armed men closed the distance in a matter of seconds. Flange placed his left hand across his right hip onto the hilt of a sheathed, slightly curved sword. He bent his knees slightly and smiled with glee.

The first charging man, carrying a club banded with strips of iron, drove forward as fast as his legs would carry him, trying to clobber Flange with a clumsy overhead swing. Flange waited till the last possible moment and sidestepped the attacker, bringing the sword from its sheath with a resounding cling. Flange spun on his heel, bringing the blade up perpendicular to his body and level with his waist. The man realized his mistake all too late, as he ran past Flange, catching the outstretched blade across his belly, opening up his innards. The stunned men stopped and looked at the gaping wound in his stomach and the dangling entrails that spilled forth.

Flange paid him no mind as the next attacker rushed to meet him. He brought the sword up in both hands and deflected a blow while cutting with the same stroke. The attacker dropped to the ground in two separate pieces as two other men reached him attacking with a sword and a mace. The man with the mace struck with an overhead blow.

Flange brought his weapon up to block the mace while the other man struck him in the torso, sinking the blade in his unprotected side. Flange grimaced in pain as the blade stopped by bouncing off his pelvic bone and sunk into his spinal column. Flange knocked the mace from the attacking soldier's hand and followed with a backstroke, severing the man's head. The other attacker yanked at the protruding blade, trying to dislodge it from Flange's body. Flange took the opportunity to hack the man's struggling limbs off as he tried to free his weapon. The soldier screamed in pain and staggered away in shock.

The armless man bumped into the first attacker who was desperately trying, to no avail, to staunch the wound in his stomach with his hands. The first attacker slipped on the bloodied grass, losing his balance and spilling his intestines onto the ground. The armless man tripped and fell on the other scrambling prone soldier.

Flange smiled through bloodstained teeth and yanked the protruding blade free form his body. Quivering and shaking, he fell to his knees as thick black-colored blood oozed from the gashed rip in his side. He tossed the blade aside and stood slowly to his full height and prepared for the next attack.

Before the main mass of soldiers intercepted him, a volley of arrows raced at him from a hastily assembled line of archers. If it had been night, he could have easily avoided the shafts, even catching them on a whim. Unfortunately in this weakened state, two arrows pierced his chest, sinking to the fletching. Another arrow tore through the thin flesh in the palm of his right hand between his thumb and finger. The archers were unable to send off another volley of arrows before the main group of soldiers collided with the creature.

Flange turned his right hand out and swatted the nearest man in the head with the arrow that was jutting from it. It buried itself deep into the side of the soldier's neck, breaking the shaft off from Flange's hand. Keltch lost sight of the creature as his men swarmed it.

Flange swung his blade in a wide arc, mowing down anyone within its deadly radius. His grimace only widened as he swung, striking down his enemies and kicking those missed by the sweeping blade. Bodies fell around him, and soon he began tripping over the sprawled forms. He deflected, stabbed, and climbed atop the carnage he was creating. The higher the bodies stacked, the further he climbed up the pile. Spears pierced his arms and axes sliced open gashes in his legs. Still the men came. And still the men died.

Flange felt himself breathing heavily, a state he was unused to. *After all*, he thought, *if I am not a living thing anymore, why should I be breathing at all?* Yet his breath came faster and faster. His arms could barely lift his blade to defend himself as the horsemen closed on him. Circling, the three horsemen wearily eyed the defiant creature that stood atop the mound of carnage. The trio attacked.

Flange deflected the blows from a spear and a lance with his sword. He stabbed his blade deep into the meaty mound beneath his feet so the sword flicked back and forth like a pendulum. He grabbed a displaced spear at his feet and threw it at the closest horse. The shaft pierced the animal in the neck, causing it to rear and topple over, pinning the horsemen beneath it.

Another rider charged up the hill of bodies, trying to reach Flange with a lance. The horse had difficulty climbing the sprawled forms and tripped, throwing its rider and dropping him in front of Flange near the sword swaying out of the bodies. The rider lunged for the sword in an attempt to retrieve it. He grabbed for the blade as Flange pulled it free from the bodies being used as a sheath, and in the process sliced off the unlucky man's fingers. The figure recoiled as Flange drove the blade through the man's sternum. Yanking his sword free, the creature kicked the dying man from the pile, causing him to crash at the foot of the other horseman.

The rider leaped from his saddle and grabbed his fallen comrade, hoisting him over the saddle before climbing onto the horse himself. Yanking the reins and kicking the horse into a gallop, the burdened rider fled away from the mound of death.

Baron Keltch moved his horse forward and drew his sword. His face twisted into a scowl and he prepared for a charge. Flange raised his hands into the air and began laughing, twirling his sword around in a loose arc. The Baron yanked his reins and stopped, eyeing the undead creature. Flange knelt and wiped his blade onto the clothing of the man he was standing on, eyes locked with the Baron's own. Flange sheathed his blade in the scabbard at his waist and placed his hands on his hips.

"I win again, Baron. How many does this make that I have killed now? Two hundred? Is it three hundred? I have lost count over the years. I even had to start the count over when you took your father's place trying to kill me. Are you keeping up with those you send to their death? I would keep track for you, but I have little need to." Flange paused, waiting for a response from Keltch. "How long can we prolong this little game of ours? I, personally, can do it forever. Unfortunately for you, mortal, you cannot. It is just a matter of time before you become too decrepit for the chase."

Keltch lowered his weapon but continued to glare at his enemy. "I guess I could make you like me, could I not? Then we could keep the game going for an eternity. You are worthy and have enough anger in you to keep you going forever," Flange said, and gestured thoughtfully as if he was actually considering it. "We are just opposite sides of the same coin, are we not, Baron?"

"I'm not playing a game with you, devil! I'm nothing like you," Keltch said evenly through clenched teeth. "How can you consider murder a game?" Keltch fumed, shaking his sword at him.

"Murder?" Flange said in a mock hurt tone. "Murder?" he repeated again and gestured with his hands as though he would faint at such a notion. "It is not murder if they willfully come to their deaths. Would you prefer that I raise the whole lot and send them home just as if they were alive? Would it be murder then if I brought them back?" Flange said as he pretended to ponder the question.

"You could, but you wouldn't dare," the Baron said flatly.

"Oh? Why would I not?" Flange said, still acting as though he was surprised.

"Because you hate being Undead," Keltch stated.

"And what makes you say that, my good nemesis?" Flange said continuing his charade of astonishment.

"Because in all the years that we have been warring, I have never heard of you ever using your abilities that way. You're a monster, Flange, but nothing such as your siblings or the she-wolf."

Flange's voice took on a hard edge and his handsome face shifted into a scowl as he whispered, "You know nothing about me other than what I want you to know."

"I know this much, if you wanted to create others like yourself or raise these poor souls, you would be doing it instead of talking about it. Maybe you don't have the power to do it. I can't say for sure, but this 'game' as you call it has been going on long enough for me to see that." Keltch sheathed his sword. Flange quietly scratched his chin in thought. "I still owe you for the murder of my father, Flange, and I will find a way to destroy you for that." The words caused Flange to shake away his reverie.

"Your father died fighting on the battlefield playing the same game that you and I are playing now. I guess tonight we have another stalemate," Flange said, narrowing his eyes.

The sun had cleared the treetops and Flange's pasty gray complexion looked even more unnatural in the filtered sunlight. The Baron nudged his horse closer to the pile of bodies, only a short distance between the two enemies. Keltch leaned forward and said, "It's only a game to you and your ungoldly kind, but not to anyone else." He spat at Flange but it fell short, landing on the body in front of him. Keltch pulled the reins about and kicked his horse in the flanks to leave the clearing.

Flange broke the protruding arrows from his chest and licked the blood from the wound in his palm. He watched Keltch slowly disappear into the woods. As the Baron moved through the trees, Flange leapt from the mound and glanced at his handiwork.

Bodies were strung all around the meadow, leading to the pile where he had stood his ground. His breathing became nonexistent once more and with a quick smile, the earth yawned beneath his feet and swallowed the ashen creature. The meadow returned to its peaceful state and the only sound to be heard was that of the morning birds, chirping crickets and the buzz of gathering flies.

2

"He killed them all, all but four of us," Keltch whispered, more to himself than to the daughter who was dressing the nicks and scrapes that he had acquired riding through the thickets during the pursuit of the undead known as Flange. The blank stare and numb automation of her father bothered the young brunette woman. She watched the horror from earlier this morning play out in the expressions of his face. "It's all a game to him. And what's worse is I'm playing along with him. No matter how much I deny it, he is right. I'm caught up in something started so long ago." He let the sentence trail off and his brow furrowed as he rested his aged bearded face in the palms of his hands.

Kate fought back tears as her father's eyes brimmed and glistened, threatening waterworks of his own. She hugged him fiercely and then picked up the tray she was using to doctor his wounds and removed it to the kitchen. She put away the items and retrieved a wet cloth soaked in cool water, and returned to the living area of the grand cottage. She laid the cloth across her barrel-chested father's forehead as he leaned his head back against the headrest of the chair.

"It'll be all right, Father," Kate said, patting his thick coarse hand. "You and your men will get them soon enough."

"No, Katie. It has been years and the only thing that has been accomplished is nothing but death for those who follow me." He patted her hand and closed his eyes. Kate watched her father fall into a restless fitful sleep. She covered him in a crocheted woolen blanket and kissed him lightly on the cheek. This did little to comfort him in his sleep.

Kate removed her apron from her slender waist and laid it over a wooden stool near the kitchen entrance. A knock on the entrance door startled her vigilance over her father. She slid the bolt back and opened the door a crack. The old priest stood holding a worn leather-bound book and rapped on the door with his walking stick.

"Where's your father, child?" the priest said.

"He's resting. Please come back later, or I'll have him meet you when he wakes." Kate made an attempt to close the door but was halted by the old man's staff, jabbed between the door and the casing. She gave the priest a fierce look and opened the door, freeing the staff.

"He'll see me now, child," he said sternly. Kate was a woman and resented being called anything else, even from a holy man. She reluctantly opened the door and invited the priest in.

"Please have a seat over there and I'll bring you something to drink." She gestured at a chair near the entryway. Turning away before receiving a response, she walked hurriedly into the next rooms.

Keltch snored in his chair, finally finding some peaceful slumber. She hated waking him, especially after a hunt, and reluctantly did so. Gently shaking him, she leaned over and whispered to him, "Papa, Papa, wake up." The rhythmic snoring was broken as the Baron grasped for breath and cleared his throat.

"What is it, Katie?" he said rubbing his eyes. "Is there a problem?"

"No, Papa. The old priest Iesed is here and demands to see you. I have him in the entryway. I was going to get him something to drink while I woke you."

"Good girl. I'll join him shortly." Keltch squeezed her hand to reassure her and prepared to climb out of his chair. Kate went into the kitchen, poured a glass of mild brandy and brought it to the old priest.

Iesed had risen from the offered chair and met her halfway in the entryway. "Where is your father?" he demanded in a less-than-cordial tone. She attempted to hand him the drink and to tell him that her father would be here shortly, but stopped, stunned, as the priest slapped the crystal glass from her hands, smashing it on the brick floor. Kate's alarm turned to anger as her face twisted into a scowl. Before she could react, a booming bellow shook the walls.

"Iesed!" Kate turned to see her father angrily storming across the cottage. Again he bellowed, "Iesed!" The Baron Keltch was quite a large man with the strides to match it. Five quick steps brought him in front of the inconsiderate priest. "You had better have a damn good reason for your actions in my house! And you had better have an even better reason for the way you're treating my daughter!" Keltch raged.

"We have to talk," the priest said, trying to show that the larger man did not intimidate him.

"That's not good enough!" The flustered Baron grabbed the priest by the front of the robes and lifted him off the ground. The loose garment slipped up over the priest's head and Keltch twisted the opening, burying the priest's head somewhere in the folds. The startled look on Kate's face turned to astonishment, and she tried her best to keep from bursting out laughing.

Keltch raised the bundle up in one hand and opened the front door with the other. Kate raced to the door to see where her father was off to. The muffled complaints of the priest went ignored as the large man strode around the side of the cottage to the pens and stable in the rear.

Kate did her best to keep up, all the while wondering what in the world would possess her father to take up these measures. It was strangely exciting but also brought out a tinge of fear in her. She rounded the cottage in time to see her father shaking the robe viciously, not unlike beating a dirty rug. He flicked the priest from his garment and the old man fell, wearing next to nothing, into a feed trough on the other side of the corral fence.

"Now!" bellowed the huge Baron as he dusted his hands off, "it seems to me we have a more appropriate place to talk in accordance to your manners, wouldn't you say?" Kate could not believe her eyes and she stared with her mouth agape. The priest, a man of the church, lay sprawled in the rotting muck that the pigs were eating. Kate could not decide what was funnier, the look of utter astonishment on the priest's face or the look of grand satisfaction on her father's.

The Baron gently folded the robe and laid it over the top rails on the fence. "Now Iesed," the large man said as he placed his left foot on the center rail and leaned over the top one. "You can bathe in the water trough over there," he gestured behind the priest, "and if you still feel like talking afterward, feel free to knock on the door. But I suggest if you do, you better be on your best behavior, or there will be more of the same." The Baron turned away and strode toward his astounded daughter, wearing one of the most rare things he ever had, a smile.

* * *

Kate watched the priest bathe in the water trough and try his best to dry off before slipping his robe back on. The priest was thankful that his tome had been preserved when it fell on the ground near the fence. He made an effort to make himself as presentable as possible before he started his trek to the front door. He rapped gently on the door.

"I wonder who that could be at this time of day?" The Baron feigned surprise as he slapped his cheeks with the palms of his hands, and his eyes became big and round looking much like an innocent overgrown child with a beard.

Kate burst out with giggles until tears rolled down her cheeks. The Baron joined in the laughter, and they held each other for a long time. Laughing times were few and far between these days and they cherished the moment as long as they could.

The priest knocked lightly upon the door again. "Katie, would you be so kind as to let the pious priest in, please?" Keltch said in a most proper voice.

"Why of course I would, Father dearest," she said in her most angelic voice while giving a gentle curtsey.

"I'll be in the study, my dear."

The Baron stepped from the kitchen and into the other room. Katie did her best to wipe the smile from her face and paused, trying to regain her composure before opening the door. A somewhat humbled priest stood before her with a look of embarrassment on his face. She smiled as if greeting an old friend.

"What can I do for you, Brother Iesed?" she asked. The old man played along.

"If you would be so kind to alert the Lord Baron Keltch that I would beg a word with him at his most utter convenience. I would appreciate it." The words from the priest sounded sincere enough, but the look in his eyes betrayed his true feelings. Katie chose to ignore the look and continued to play the good host.

"My father is expecting you. I'm to show you to him." She smiled brightly and led the way through several rooms to the study. The walls of the room were covered in ceremonial weapons, shields, and plaques of coat of arms. The Baron sat behind a huge oak desk topped with loose parchments and quill pens.

Kate entered the room, still playing the part, and led the priest to a chair opposite of the enormous desk where she motioned for him to sit. "Father, Brother Iesed has requested an audience with your Lordship." She smiled gaily and curtsied. The Baron nodded. She turned around, facing the priest, and clasped her hands together in front of her. "Would you care for something to drink, Brother Iesed?" she asked, still smiling. He shook his head.

"No, child, thank you anyway." Her smile faltered at the mention of being called a child, and for a brief instant, she could see a look of satisfaction on the wrinkled face of the priest. She curtsied low and left the room.

"What's your business here today, Iesed?" The Baron grumbled, no longer wanting to play the good host. The change in mood offset the priest and he sat up straighter in his chair. He cleared his throat and gathered his thoughts. The priest was still shook up from his ordeal in the trough.

"I came to deliver a message from the Magistrate." The priest gripped the staff that lay across his lap and nervously rolled it across his knees.

"And what message is that?" the Baron asked, already becoming bored with the conversation. The staff stopped rolling and the priest leaned forward.

"The Magistrate has hired a group of travelers who claim to be able to rid us of our undead problems," the priest stated. The Baron laughed and slapped his hands on the tabletop.

"You mean he's hired Stakes?" the Baron said and continued to laugh. The priest kept his composure as the Baron continued with his fit of laughter. "You would think he would have learned the first time when that group of charlatans took his money and ran. By the Gods! Stakes!" the Baron mused.

The name "Stakes" was originally given to a group of undead hunters who believed that wooden stakes driven through the heart of the undead would kill them for good. Unfortunately for the hunters, no one told the undead creatures that stakes would kill them. As luck would have it, the hunters were found killed by their own sharpened pickets through their own misled hearts. It was an extreme example that they were very wrong. The name "Stakes" had been given to would-be undead hunters in the region ever since.

"And how much is the Magistrate paying?" the Baron mused. Now it was the priest's turn to laugh. The Baron eyed him suspiciously.

"The Magistrate hasn't paid a penny."

"Well, good for him," the Baron added.

"The Lords of the lands are paying for it," the priest said smiling.

"What?" The Baron slammed his hands down on the tabletop, bolting upright from his chair. The priest leaned back in the chair after claiming the upper hand.

"That's right, Baron. The Magistrate decreed that the price is to be met, and to cover it; he has ordered the landowners to pay a percentage according to holdings. That makes you the one putting up most of the payroll," the priest said matter-of-factly. The Baron dropped to his chair and slumped back with his head resting against the wall.

"How much do they want?"

"Five thousand gold coins. Half in advance for supplies," the priest stated and Keltch winced.

"That's ludicrous. You really don't believe these Stakes are going to pull it off, do you?"

The priest shrugged and said, "Well it can't be any worse than your campaigns as the self righteous, self-proclaimed protector. And at any rate, at least it will be their men going to the slaughter house and not our sons like you prefer to use."

The Baron's face turned blood red and his pulsing veins showed. "The soldiers under my command know the risks and are paid accordingly. Any man who joins the hunt knows the risks," the Baron said in a dangerous whisper. The priest smiled nervously.

"How many people did you let die this morning, Keltch? How many have died altogether?" The priest's words mirrored Flange's own from earlier in the morning, "How long do you plan on continuing your little game?"

The priest's last sentence caused the Baron to snap. He leapt from his chair and grabbed the edge of the enormous desk and flipped it up into the air. The desk tumbled over the priest's head and crashed into the opposite wall, sending the decorations flying. The wide-eyed priest squirmed in his chair, knowing he had gone too far. The Baron grabbed the old man by the throat and hoisted him from the seat. He gasped, choked, and fought, to no avail, to escape.

"Father! Father!" Kate shrilled at the top of her lungs, "You're killing him!" She rushed into the room and latched her arms around one of his, trying in vain to pull the priest free. The Baron looked at his daughter as if seeing her for the first time, and then back to the blue-faced priest. He let go, dropping the robed man to the floor. The priest gasped for air and did his best to scoot across the floor away from the angry man. Kate ran to the priest's side, yanking him to his feet, half dragging him from the room. Keltch stared out of the window. Kate sat the bewildered priest in a chair in the entryway but the old man shooed her away saying he was all right now. He stood rubbing his throat and staggered to the door. Kate opened it and apologized for his near-death experience at the hands of her father.

"Iesed!" Keltch bellowed as he rounded the corner into the entryway. The old priest was already backing out of the open front door. Kate froze, unused to her father's angry outburst. "You tell that damned Magistrate he'll get no money from me! You tell him, when those Stakes fail, not to come running to me! I am finished with this whole mess!" The priest continued stumbling backward away from the cottage, wild-eyed and stricken.

Keltch stood framed in the doorway; scarlet-faced as a demon, and slammed the door shut. Kate looked at her raging father, seeing a side of him that he never allowed shown in her presence. She looked at him pleadingly, even fearfully. He turned away from her dumbstruck expression and stormed off to another part of the cottage, cursing all the way. Kate cautiously left the entryway, entered her bedroom, closed the door, and wept.

3

The orchestra of night sounds echoed around the clearing in the forest. A gentle breeze caused the long silky strands of hair to dance in the wind. The brooding figure, Flange, was perched on a rock with his long slender arms hugging his knees close to his chest, his chin resting on his knees. The Baron's words stung him, and struck a chord in his soul. The words continued to rattle around in his head.

I am only a monster because I was made to be one, he thought. Flange tried to shake the sensation of emotions that flooded him. It had been a long time since he felt anything, and the strength of the emotions threatened to overwhelm him. Doing his best to shrug the troubling thoughts off, he stretched his arms and legs out.

Flange thought about the way he was responding to the Baron's words and recognition dawned on him, causing him to laugh out loud. *I actually like the old Baron,* he thought. *Why else would I go to such terrible lengths to impress the man with my feats?* A tingling sensation broke his reverie.

An ethereal shape cleared the ring of trees that encompassed Flange. The silhouetted shape was surrounded by reaching tendrils, like translucent, dark green floating octopus hovering around the semblance of a man. The tendrils interlaced the air in random directions, seeking always to touch. The figure soundlessly moved ever closer, and the odorous tendrils snaked past the reclusive Flange, who was sitting with his back to the creature.

"Go away, Barcus," Flange said simply. Barcus' stench always gave him away to his siblings as well the villagers. Flange had smelled Barcus from nearly a mile away, and knew that a visit would soon be upon him. The figure slowed, and Flange continued to ignore it. The haphazard tendrils began focusing on the sitting figure.

"Is that any way to treat your brother?" the approaching figure said.

"You stopped being my brother centuries ago," Flange said, not looking in the direction of his sibling. "Now leave me in peace."

Barcus stopped, standing near Flange, and folded his arms across his chest. The menacing figure stood almost a full head taller than Flange, and was more thickly built in stature. Barcus' hair was close-cropped and he wore a matted beard in sharp contrast to Flange's long straight hair and clean-shaven face.

"Nice wound you have there, brother," Barcus said, pointing to Flange's side. Flange continued to disregard the imposing relative. Barcus noticed the sword and scabbard hanging from Flange's belt. "I've never seen the make of a blade like that before. You must have traveled some distance to acquire it," Barcus continued his probing after receiving no response; "I liked your handiwork last night." Flange turned, looking over his shoulder at the waiting sibling.

"As opposed to your handiwork I suppose?" Flange said with each word dripping venomous disgust. "What drives you to create others of our own that can't survive?"

"You know that each of us have different gifts, and a different way to sate the bloodlust that drives us," Barcus said flatly. "You are no different than me."

"Oh, I beg to differ, I am different than you. I find no sport in killing babies, Barcus, and you seem to revel in it." The standing figure just shrugged at the accusation, turning slightly away. "We've had this conversation before and I don't intend to have it again. What do you want?" Flange snarled. The figure stood silently for a moment.

"You were gone for some time, brother, almost too long. How can you stay away from Haven for so long and keep the madness at bay?" Barcus questioned. Flange did not answer. Barcus tried a different approach. "It has come to our attention that you have found another piece in the puzzle."

"Oh, really? And how do you figure that?" Flange said leaping from the boulder, faster than a human mortal could blink, into a reserved stance before his massive brother.

"Well, brother, if you can so easily shrug off the madness, why else would you return after being gone for several years?" Flange did not respond immediately. He let his fierce eyes bore into Barcus' own.

"What I will tell you, Barcus, is I have returned to find my lair desecrated in violation of the agreements that we are supposed to have. Would you like to explain that? And on top that, you want to know about my research?" Flange venomously spat. "What, pray tell, gives you the right to know anything about what I have been doing or might be doing?" Barcus stood in silence, digesting the words.

"I did not destroy your lair. I had no part in it," Barcus stated quietly.

"Oh, I know who did it. I'd recognized Sasha's claw marks anywhere. And knowing that Sasha did it, then I also know that our darling sister put her up to it," Flange said, grimacing each time he said Sasha's name.

Barcus remained silent then said, "I know you have multiple lairs. We all do. Nothing of importance was found there. You are obviously keeping the items somewhere else." The truth of the matter was that Flange did have many lairs scattered throughout the land. Some of the lairs were decoys that could easily be found, while others would never be.

"That is not the point, Barcus, and you know it. You are nothing but an agent of our sister. You are no better than Sasha is," Flange said through gritted teeth, his eyes flaring in anger. Barcus shrugged once more and looked away from those hate-filled eyes.

"Our goals are the same, and we should work together to accomplish them," Barcus said lamely, locking gazes with the shorter sibling. Flange let out a laugh and scoffed.

"Our goals are not the same, and you will not get any more information from me," Flange said, shouldering past his daunted brother.

"Brother, I was very impressed with your stand against the Baron's men yesterday. I would not have been so bold to make such an attempt in a weakened state," Barcus stated.

"Now that does not surprise me coming from a baby killer," Flange spat, as he continued to put distance between his malodorous brother. Barcus fumed and flung his tattered cloak over one shoulder.

"Brother, I liked your stand so much that I decided to immortalize those who fell at your hand." It was Barcus' turn to have a wistful laugh. Flange stopped dead in his tracks.

The mist clinging to the base of the trees swirled and parted as lumbering shapes broke through the veiled darkness. More stumbling shapes staggered through the trees. The raised dead wandered into the clearing, tottering and bumping into each other. Those with missing legs or arms dragged themselves along the ground. Flange could see the livery worn by the soldiers of the Baron. These were the same creatures he had killed the day before. The groaning and howling of the damned shattered the normally quiet sounds of the forest.

"What have you done, bastard!" Flange yelled. "You know the agreement. My kills are not to be raised by anyone!"

"It seems that we have no more agreements where you're concerned, brother. I raised them because we can use them. It is a waste for you to kill them and let their corpses rot in the burning sun. They will serve a purpose once again, but this time as my retainers," Barcus said, and strode away from the shaken Flange. Anger swept through him, and his sword left his scabbard in a resounding "cling." An unearthly howl escaped his dead lungs and he waded into the ranks of the raised dead, hacking and slashing the decaying forms, trying to kill them all over again.

* * *

"Please, have a seat, gentlemen," the Magistrate said, motioning the three men to the vacant chairs across from his desk, and then reseating himself. The Magistrate's gray clothes matched the color of his eyes. He quickly sized up of the three men as they sat.

The first man was older than the others, probably by a good twenty years. His tall, lanky form was covered in a simple blue tunic tied at the waist with a piece of raveled hemp rope. The older man had his hands folded within the long sleeves of his woolen tunic. The Magistrate was a bit nervous, being unable to see the man's hands, but his concern lessened realizing this man was a priest, not unlike Iesed. The silver beard on the priest's face was long and unkempt, and his balding pate reflected the sunlight coming from the window. Immediately the Magistrate wondered if his own balding head did the same, and reflexively pulled the tucked-in crusher from his belt, and placed it on top of his head. If the priest noticed the intent of the action, he paid it no heed.

The second man was short and well built, wearing worn leather armor with a long-sword at his side. The warrior's eyes were deep-set, dark, and very fierce. The Magistrate could see this man was a veteran, possibly from some of the wars that had raged in the East for decades. This man was obviously the leader and his presence was overpowering. He removed the leather headgear and turned the chair around, straddling it facing the wrong way, such is the method with most warriors. He dropped the helmet in his lap after seating himself.

The third man was more of a mystery. He was more a boy than a man. The Magistrate guessed his age to be short of twenty. Although he did not have the appearance of being a large man, he did have the potential of becoming one. The handsome youth had clear, intelligent eyes, and his movements were as graceful as a cat. The boy's leather clothes were worn but neat. A floppy, wide-brimmed hat sat over long coppery hair. The headpiece looked somewhat ridiculous, but the bandoleer of various daggers over one shoulder and surrounding his chest offset any mocking thoughts. The young man's eyes searched the Magistrate's. The Magistrate did not see a resemblance to any of the men, but he knew that looks could be deceiving.

"I am Magistrate Burgman, and on behalf of the village of Klevia, I welcome you," the Magistrate said, gesturing in the sign of welcome. The men across him each nodded and made the sign of thanks.

"I am Jorth, former Captain of Kellien's Regulars." He motioned to the tall old man on his left. "This is Simil, Priest of the order of Sugoth." The older man nodded without smiling. Jorth motioned to his right, "And this is Sprig." The youth smiled as if remembering some private joke.

A servant entered the room carrying a tray of fruit, nuts, and a lead crystal pitcher with four matching glasses. "Some refreshments, gentlemen?" The Magistrate said, motioning. The men graciously accepted, drinking the wine that was poured and nibbling from the tray of food. The Magistrate watched as the men ate in silence, and chuckled to himself as the young man slipped several pieces of dried fruit into the pockets of his jerkin.

When the Magistrate was sure the men had had their fill, he summoned a servant to remove the tray and bring in several rolled parchments. The pleasant smile that the Magistrate had been wearing disappeared as he thought about the task at hand.

He steepled his fingers together on the desk before him and spoke. "Gentlemen, these are grave times for our village and the surrounding countryside. Undead creatures have plagued this area since before my great-grandfather's time. We've made many attempts to be rid of them, but to no benefit. Baron Keltch has made himself the self-appointed protector of the area, but I fear he has only sent hundreds of men to their deaths in the attempt. This is not sitting well with the people of the village anymore. I am searching for a way out of this situation and your troop was highly recommended. We thank you for your quick response to our dispatch."

Jorth nodded, stroking his bearded chin in thought.

"Tell us what you know of the creatures, and be as specific as you can, Magistrate," Jorth said. The youth pulled out a leather-bound book and an inkwell. He removed a stylus from under his hat and from behind his ear, hidden by his hair, and dipped it in the inkwell. The Magistrate sat for a moment in thought.

"We have dispatched many of the zombies and skeletons that have been created. They're easy enough to kill. It is the four siblings that are the real concern. They are unlike the other Undead and are more than likely responsible for the creation of the lesser ones. The zombies and skeletons are not free-thinking creatures. They are usually controlled, and those not under any control usually wander around aimlessly, searching for living flesh to devour.

"Those creatures are fearful of the sun, and can be killed easily enough. But the four siblings are not like the rest of them. They're free thinkers and they live to terrorize. The four are unique in appearance and mannerism. It was understood that the four hated each other, but they made some kind of agreements, and staked out separate territories respecting each other's claims.

"They are rarely seen together except for the two women. They seem to have a partnership of some kind. Rewella is the one most rarely seen. In fact, no one is really sure what she looks like anymore. The she-wolf is named Sasha, and is probably Rewella's eyes and ears. Sasha is a ruthless killer with a savage temper. She kills anything in her path and is known to travel sometimes in the daylight.

"Barcus seems to be the one who likes to terrorize the village most of all. His shadow can seek out living beings and change them into Undead without killing or actually touching his victims."

An uneasy glance was exchanged between the warrior and the priest. If the Magistrate noticed the exchange, he continued as though he had not. "Barcus' power seems to affect the very young, old, and the weak. Just yesterday, he affected three of our children during the night. After such transformations, he leaves the creatures to wreak havoc so that we must kill our own. We believe he is fearful of the sun because he's never been seen during the day. He always attacks after dark, during curfew.

"The last creature is Flange. He has never been seen in or near the village, and it's believed that he is not capable of raising undead creatures, for none have ever been seen near or around his sightings. We are not sure what his abilities are other than strength and resistance to sunlight. However, he is a killer. He and the Baron seem to be having a secret war with each other. Flange has killed anyone who has sought him out, except the Baron. He's been seen day and night. He is quite resistant where the others are not. Flange killed almost forty men yesterday in a clash with the Baron. The families went to recover the bodies today only to find them a mile from where they were originally killed."

"Originally killed?" the priest asked.

"Yes. It appears that one of the foul creatures raised the bodies, and Flange was so furious that he destroyed them once again." The Magistrate finished and leaned back in his chair. The warrior scratched his chin absently. The priest cleared his throat and removed his hands from the folds in his tunic.

"It's been awhile since we fought those kind of creatures that can turn the living into the Undead," the priest said to the warrior, who nodded, still stroking his coarse beard.

"I've only heard of such a thing," the youth said, envisioning.

"We've fought such creatures, but seems like ages ago," Jorth said aloud, but more to himself. He shook the moment of nostalgia, "We shouldn't have any problems as long as the payment we agreed upon is met," Jorth said to the Magistrate.

"The fee won't be a problem. It is being taken care of as we speak," the Magistrate said.

"It just may be a problem, Magistrate." Everyone seated turned to the voice of the man who had entered the room. The priest Iesed leaned his staff against the wall and sat his creaking body into an empty chair. He looked at the men, who were carefully gauging him.

"Explain yourself, Iesed," Burgman said.

Iesed exhaled a breath that he seemed to be holding, and let his eyes settle on the Magistrate.

"Keltch humiliated me and refused to pay his mandatory share for the services of these gentlemen. In his exact words, he refuses to pay for a bunch of 'Stakes' as he termed it," the old priest said, digging some dried mud out of his beard. "Something has to be done about that man, or he will be the death of us all," the old priest said with a sigh, and he shrugged.

"He cannot refuse. It would mean risking loss of all his entitled lands," the Magistrate stated.

"You tell him that!" Iesed fumed, sinking further into his chair.

"You were able to collect from the other landowners?" the Magistrate asked.

"Yes. Keltch was the only one to refuse," the old priest said, trying to calm his temper.

"How many coins?" the Magistrate asked.

"Two thousand, seven hundred and thirty-six. It has already been delivered to the treasury," Iesed said.

"Is it enough?" the Magistrate asked the warrior, with a look of hope on his face.

"We won't be able to rid all four for anything less than the amount agreed," the warrior interjected. "One, maybe two at best."

"It will have to do," the Magistrate said. "I will have these contracts redrawn for the specifics and the new price."

"That sounds good. The only question now is which one do you want us to hunt?" the warrior asked.

The Magistrate leaned his chair back against the wall and folded his hands, thinking. After a moment of silence, he looked at the old priest with resignation and said, "It might as well be a toss up, but I think Barcus is the first one to be brought down." Iesed nodded in agreement. The three men shook hands with Burgman, and left the building to make preparations. Iesed removed himself from his seat and sat in one of the vacated chairs near the Magistrate.

"Do you think they can pull it off, Iesed?" the Magistrate asked the old priest. The old man shrugged and said, "You had better hope so, because if they fail, things are going to become very messy around here."

* * *

The door to the Magistrate's office closed as the three strangers strode with purpose to the stables. They spoke in hushed whispers as they walked.

"I don't like this, Jorth. We haven't fought creatures like this in a long time. It's hard enough to bring down one creature such as that, but four?" Simil said unsure of the outcome.

"You heard the Magistrate, they weren't able to come up with the full amount, so we will get rid of this Barcus character and be off," Jorth said.

"What if the others intervene or seek revenge?" Sprig asked, trailing the two men.

"I don't think it will happen. If what he said is true, then there is no love lost between the four," Jorth replied.

"What if he is wrong? What if everything he told us was just guesswork? I find it hard to believe that one of them, let alone four of them really exists," Sprig spouted off.

The priest stopped and spun on his heels. He grabbed the youth's leather jerkin near the throat and hoisted him up and back. The sudden action caught the usually nimble man off guard forcing a step or two backwards on the balls of his feet.

Anger filled the older man's eyes, and his wrinkled features turned bright red. Through gritted teeth, he said, "Listen up boy, and listen good. These kinds of creatures *do* exist and we know it from first-hand experience. They're not like those mindless creatures you've had a hand in. Zombies and skeletons are lesser Undead. They may be dangerous, but they're nothing compared to the freethinkers of the greater Undead. Look at me and look at Jorth. I look to be his senior don't I? Well, guess again. I'm actually five years younger than he is." Some of the anger left his voice, and he let go of Sprig's jerkin. The boy inhaled a breath deeply, holding his bruised throat, and stared in shock at the normally docile priest.

"I'm sorry. Please forgive me, Sprig. I'm so very sorry," the priest said sorrowfully, his eyes begging for forgiveness.

"It's all right, Simil. How come I've never seen any of them?" Sprig asked, still rubbing his neck.

Jorth answered the question. "They're rare, Sprig. We've only encountered the greater kinds a few times in the past twenty years. Our initial encounter led us to become Undead-slayers."

"What exactly happened to you, Simil?" Sprig ventured, watching the man carefully. The priest hesitated as if trying to remember a forgotten distant horror. From somewhere embedded deep within the priest's memories came the woeful tale. Speaking barely above a whisper, Sprig had to lean closer to catch every word the older man was saying.

"I was a young acolyte of The Order, about the age you are now. I was administering to the wounded of Kellien's Regulars during the wars with the Vagrians in the East. Our soldiers pushed the enemy out of the land and we were quick to pursue the defeated army back into their homeland. Most of our men had never seen the strange lands of the East, and we were ignorant of their traditions. The Vagrians have an order of mystical priests, known as 'The Keepers of the Dead.' We knew not that this order communed with the dead, or that they were responsible for the upkeep of the burial grounds and chambers.

"The fleeing Vagrians tried to hide from our army, and they did so in a massive network of catacombs on the edge of one of their fallen cities. Our men continued pursuit and followed the fleeing men into the underground chambers. Our soldiers soon lost interest in chasing the enemy because of the abundance of great wealth that had been buried with the dead. Soon, our soldiers were opening the sarcophagi and looting the treasures within. They reveled in the violation of the corpses.

"The mystical priests tried to stop our pilfering soldiers, but most of them were slain in the attempt. Those that survived began making nuisance attacks on the army from hidden alcoves and recesses in the walls. A band of fifteen veterans, including Jorth and myself, broke off from the main group of men in pursuit of the mystical priests. We followed them for hours down the passageways. All the while, we could hear a chanting echoing from behind the walls.

"The honeycomb of passageways ended in a huge stone room lighted with torches, and filled with several large sarcophagi on a raised dais on the opposite end of the room. The chamber was full of gold. Our group stood in awe and extinguished the torches we were carrying to save them for later use. Many of the men began filling their packs and satchels with the golden items that were neatly set about the room.

"I myself do not believe in personal wealth, but even I was tempted by the riches before me. I approached the dais and walked to the stone steps up to the largest sarcophagus. It was solid gold and encrusted with thousands of gems, some the size of your fist! I saw one in particular that caught my eye. It was a soft blue that matched the robes of my order. I believed it would make a fine offering to my temple when we reached home.

"I found an ornamental dagger and set at prying the gem from its setting. As I did so, the entrance into the chamber disappeared as a stone slab fell, sealing us in. The soldiers began to panic and tried desperately to free the slab. Others tried to find another way out of the chamber. I continued to pry at the gem on the lid. I struggled, and with an enormous burst of my strength, the gem popped loose, falling off the dais and sliding across the floor.

"My exertion left me winded and I slipped and fell to the stone floor. I heard the shouts as my eyes swept past the dark ceiling and the top rim of the sarcophagus next to me. Before I could react to the ruckus at the other end of the chamber, I heard the scraping of stone and the lid visibly moved above me. I was terrified. I froze and was unable to move."

The priest stopped, and Sprig could see that he was reliving the nightmare all over again somewhere in his head. After a moment, Simil continued. "I heard the lid fall off the sarcophagus as it crashed onto the dais stonework. Shriveled skeletal hands grasped the lip of the sarcophagus and pulled the bulk of its body upright. I saw a misshapen skull with glowing eyes surveying the room. I could hear the shouts turning into terrified screams all around the chamber. The Undead figure stood, and continued to gaze upon the room.

"I tried to scoot on my back away from the creature. His gaze crossed mine, and I could see a hint of a smile pulling at the corners of its twisted hellish mouth. It leapt at me, and landed on my chest. Its frozen touch burned my skin, and I cried out, suddenly growing weak. I closed my eyes and spoke a silent prayer.

"The weight on my chest disappeared, and I opened my eyes to see that Jorth had knocked the creature clear of me, and was chopping at it with his long-sword. I reached into my satchel and retrieved a vial of blessed water and removed the cork. I raised myself to my knees and splashed the contents on the creature. It screamed and writhed in agony, and began to smoke where the liquid touched it.

"My actions were enough to buy us some time. Jorth helped me off the dais, and we ran to the stone slab that blocked our exit. Chaos had erupted in the chamber as skeletal creatures attacked the remaining members of our group. The continuing screams echoed off the chamber walls, and bodies littered the floor. Jorth saw one of the mystical priests staring out of a hidden alcove, but before the man could turn and run, Jorth hurled a dagger and dropped him. The body fell through the hidden exit door, blocking it open. Jorth pushed me in the direction of the door, and he fought his way back to his remaining men. I spiked the door open and lit a torch. It was only then that I noticed how wrinkled my hands were in the flickering light. Jorth was dragging a wounded man while three other soldiers fought a retreat toward the door.

"I could see that the passage inclined with a gentle turn toward the right. I held my torch aloft and led the way while the remaining men kicked the spike loose, letting the door swing shut. Jorth passed the wounded man to the three soldiers, and waited near the door to see if the creatures would pursue. We walked the incline following the passage until it ended at a door.

"When Jorth caught up with the rest of us, we tried the door. It opened onto a ledge directly above where the main force of our army was looting the catacomb. Jorth yelled to the startled men, and they helped us down. Everyone stared at me with horrified looks. I knew I felt strange, but I was not completely sure what had happened to me. I felt an ache in my bones and I was so very tired. Jorth ordered the force to leave the catacombs immediately, and we fled.

"We camped in a clearing in the woods on the outskirts of the burial area, setting up a double watch. I pulled my shaving mirror from my satchel and stared at the face of a stranger. That devil of a creature had aged me. I had been in my prime and it made me an old man." The priest pulled his sleeves to his elbows, and showed the white blotches scarring his arms. "These are from its touch."

Sprig stood open-mouthed, listening to the tale in grim fascination, but eventually made his mouth work to ask, "Is that why you hunt them? Because of what they did to you?"

"They are evil, unearthly creatures. That is enough of a reason, Sprig," the priest said, pulling his sleeves down and losing his hands within the folds.

"Too bad you didn't get the stone," Sprig said. The priest nodded his agreement.

The trio continued toward the stable. Jorth had been silent during the tale, but his face continued to show signs of reliving the events. When the group reached the stable and checked their mounts, Jorth finally spoke, "After the wars, Kellien's Regulars disbanded, leaving most of the men unemployed and homeless. Many of the soldiers decided to go back to the catacombs to loot its treasures once more. I was adamantly against such folly, but the fools decided that what happened to us was only a ploy we made up to keep them from the treasures. Those men were stupid, greedy bastards," Jorth snorted and spat on the ground with a curse. "I had no say-so anymore because I was no longer their commanding officer. Some two hundred men left and never returned.

"We eventually went to find them, and we did. All the men were impaled on spikes surrounding the catacombs. Each face was frozen in terror. We left that place to keep the same from happening to us."

"What happened to the three surviving men from the chamber?" Sprig asked, checking his saddle and stowing his stylus, inkwell, and leather-bound book in the saddlebag. Jorth exchanged glances with Simil and said, "The wounded man died only a few days later. The other two deserted before the orders to disband were given."

"Oh, I see," the youth said with a tone of disappointment. Sprig mounted his horse and pulled the reins. The other two men finished checking their mounts and saddled also. "Now what?" Sprig questioned.

"We bring in the troop and send some Undead back to hell where they belong!" Jorth said, spurring the horse's hindquarters, and rode off leading the way.

4

Thousands of beautiful inverted porcelain faces shone in the reflections of the multifaceted cut gem. The lovely and petite woman lowered the huge stone, which she had been looking through, away from her alabaster face. The action caused the refracted images to shrink, change, and fade in the surrounding light. The raven-haired beauty dropped her gaze from the stone and smiled at her reclining companion. The room was comfortably furnished and illuminated by an uncanny light without a visible source.

"Where did you find this, Sasha?" the smiling face of chiseled perfection asked. Rewella's smile pleased the chestnut-haired woman. Sasha mimicked the smile opposite her.

"I felt the power within. It's a piece of the puzzle isn't it?" Sasha asked, avoiding the question.

At first glance, Sasha carried a similar beauty to that of Rewella, but a second glance revealed Sasha's form was larger, and her shape differed in an odd way from that of a normal woman. She was wearing a loose tunic cinched at the waist with a silk tie and wore no shoes. Sasha's face contained sharply angled features, and was extremely attractive. Her nose was slightly upturned to a gentle end. Her ears were larger than normal and rose to a point instead of rounding out like normal ones should. When she smiled, her canines were noticeably longer and shaped like ivory stilettos. Her fingers were long and slender, ending in sharp talon-like nails.

Sasha launched herself from the couch and knelt before Rewella, smiling, eyes expectant. Rewella reached over with her free hand and tenderly stroked Sasha's thick hair. "Yes, I'm sure it is. I'm not sure what combination to try with the other items, but I'm sure it will be useful," Rewella said smiling, and placed a light kiss on the kneeling women's forehead. "Now, where did you get it?" Rewella questioned again. Sasha's smile grew larger and her dark eyes shone.

"I found it in one of Barcus' hidden lairs," Sasha said, grinning.

"Oh, really?" Rewella mused, "It seems that my brother has been holding out on us. Not good for him is it, Sasha?" Sasha smiled, shaking her shaggy mane "no," and kissed Rewella gently on the lips. Sasha rose from her kneeling position, standing before Rewella, and ran her long fingers through the thick tussle of jet-black hair. Sasha smoothed out the silky strands and stepped away from Rewella.

Sasha interlaced her long fingers together, raised her hands over her head, and stretched. She deeply exhaled as the vertebrae in her back raised and popped. She undid the knot in the silk tie that was keeping the tunic cinched around her shapely waist and shrugged the garment off onto the floor. Her arms and legs lengthened and thick coarse hair covered her body. Sasha's ears perked up, and her upturned nose stretched into a jutting snout. She stretched her body once more and turned facing Rewella. Sasha's dark eyes were replaced by a set of reddish-yellow feral eyes.

In a guttural voice, Sasha asked, "What do you want me to do with Barcus?"

"Nothing. I will deal with him myself. I want you to find out what Flange is up to. Keep a close eye on him. He may have found the missing pieces we need," Rewella said tapping her lips rhythmically with a delicate digit.

"And if he has?" Sasha throated expectantly.

"Do what you can to secure them and let me know if he goes into Haven," Rewella said and embraced the lupine form before her. Sasha's furred shape leaped onto all fours and bounded away, unleashing an unearthly howl as she went.

Rewella studied the gem in her hand. *This is only a minor piece,* she thought, *but it may have its uses.* She studied the glinting light for another minute or so and then sat the gem on the table. "What are you up to, Flange?" she contemplated out loud. Flange's return made her very nervous. "If he has the necessary items, he would have already made the attempt by now," she continued to ponder. She shrugged and dismissed the thoughts. There were other things yet to learn.

Rewella loosened her clinging robe and laid it carefully over the back of the ancient chair. She moved gracefully into the center of the room and closed her eyes. Her flawless face took on a less serene look as she concentrated. Her shapely naked body began to quiver and convulse. The spasm ended abruptly and her body burst apart. Thousands of spiders landed on the floor and scurried from the room. All that remained of the porcelain woman was the neatly folded discarded robe.

* * *

Baron Keltch rode at a gentle trot toward the village, letting the warm sunshine bathe his face. He was in no particular hurry to reach his destination.

Earlier that morning, one of the Magistrate's messengers delivered a sealed parchment. The letter demanded an audience with the Baron at the Magistrate's office at the noon hour. The Baron laughed, wadded the message up in both hands and tossed it over the messenger's shoulder. The messenger turned, without a hint of expression on his face, mounted his horse and rode back toward the village.

The Baron scoffed at such a summons, and yet on a second thought, he grabbed his broadsword and traveling gear. "I'll be back shortly, Katie," Keltch yelled into the interior of the cottage. Kate was still upset and had made herself scarce for the last few days. The Baron waited a moment for a reply. His heart sank when a response was not forthcoming. He closed the entry door and locked it with a heavy brass key. A servant readied his mount and Keltch loaded his saddlebags with necessities. He stroked the mare's finely brushed mane and double checked the harness and saddle.

When the inspection met his specifications, he mounted the vigorous beast and cantered past his cottage trying to catch a glimpse of Kate through the dusty lead crystal windows. His heart sank even further when he did not see her.

It was shortly after noon when Keltch arrived at the village stable. He dismounted and called to a waiting stable boy. "Here lad," the Baron said, tossing a coin through the air as he dismounted, "Take extra care with her and there will be another just like it when I get back." The excited child snatched the coin from the air and quickly pocketed it in his threadbare pants.

"Yes, sir," the boy said, gratefully grabbing the reins.

"Treat her nice," the Baron said and winked. He good-heartedly ruffled the already tussled hair on the boy's head, and left the stable.

Keltch did nothing to shake the riding dust from his traveling clothes. Instead, he waited until he entered the Magistrate's office, and then went to great lengths to dust himself off in the spotless entryway.

"You're late, Baron," the irritated Magistrate growled when Keltch entered the building. "Come here so I can introduce these gentlemen to you."

"Am I? Oh, you mean for your summons?" The Baron clapped the dust form his hands, completing the annoying gesture and dismissed the waiting men with a nonchalant glance. "I'm not here for your meeting. I'm on personal business and only stopped by your office as a courtesy."

The Magistrate's face contorted, turning scarlet as he stood clenching his hands into fists. "A courtesy? Surely you are overstepping your bounds?" the Magistrate said, his anger growing. The small group was assembled around the Magistrate's desk, including Iesed, and watched the exchange in silence. The Baron eyed each one with open contempt, ignoring the Magistrate's comments.

"So, these are your Stakes? They sure look like fearless Undead Slayers. Why I bet the boy alone here could take them on all by himself," the Baron said in a mocking tone, adding a mirthless laugh. The youth stabbed a venomous look at the Baron and eased his crossed arms so his hands were in easy reach of the knives circling his bandoleer.

"That is enough, Keltch!" the Magistrate snapped.

"That's Baron Keltch to you, Magistrate," the Baron spoke evenly in a low dangerous tone.

"Are you here to pay the debt that you have been charged with?" the Magistrate barked.

"To these revelers?" the Baron sneered, "I think not!"

"Then you are a Baron no more, Keltch. I hereby proclaim your lands and title are forfeit," the Magistrate said coolly, keeping his gaze even.

"You cannot . . ."

"I can, and have if you refuse the debt!" the Magistrate bellowed cutting off Keltch's stammering reply.

"Those lands have been in my family's possession for over a hundred years. You think I'm going to let some sniveling bureaucrat take away my holdings? You're wrong, dead wrong." Keltch's words took on a deadly edge, and every man in the room did not doubt his sincerity. Still, the Magistrate was resolute.

"How many men have died under your command in your personal war with the evil one, Flange? How much closer are you to vanquishing that creature or his siblings? You've proven not to be part of the solution to this village's problems. In fact, you've only become another problem. I see no other solution; your lands are forfeit, Keltch. Now get out and attend to your personal business so we can attend to ours," the Magistrate finished, and sat back down at his desk.

Keltch was furious, and his arms trembled as he shook with rage. Iesed flashed a wry smile at the defeated Baron.

"I'll kill you both!" Keltch spouted, his broadsword left its sheath, and he charged through the entryway into the office.

The silent trio of men sitting together reacted reflexively to the outburst. The youth rolled from his chair, coming up into a squatting position with two daggers in hand. The warrior's own long sword leaped into his hands, and he lunged to intercept the mass of furious rage that was barreling through the room. The older man seemed to pull an iron mace from thin air and dropped into a defensive stance.

The charging Baron started a stroke intended for the Magistrate's neck but was deflected by the clash of the warrior's sword. Keltch and Jorth stood face to face locked, both exerted forces against the other's blade. Each fighter gauged the other. Both men were about the same height, build, and age. The Baron struggled and forced the blades to the side, and then shouldered the warrior away from him. Jorth staggered backwards toward the desk, but maintained his defensive posture blocking access to any would-be victims.

Iesed had moved into the corner behind the desk, trying to put as much room between the enraged Baron and himself. He was extremely frightened, and his old frame shook as he fought to control it. The Magistrate's own hand gripped the handle of his ceremonial saber at his side, but he made no attempt to draw it.

Keltch stepped back two paces out of swords-swiping range, taking in the odds against him. The warrior lowered his sword, but stayed on his guard. Keltch took another step backwards nearer the entrance door. He lowered his weapon and sheathed it without taking his eyes off the persons in the room. "You can forfeit my title, but you'll never get my lands. You think you have a problem with the Undead lurking around here now, just wait and see what happens if you or any of your men shows up on my doorstep. I'll kill every last one of them!" the ex-Baron said through clenched teeth. He turned on his heels and was through the door.

"By the Gods, that man has an ego!" the Magistrate yelled, slamming his fists on the desk. Iesed, finding relief in Keltch's exit, located his chair and slumped down, breathing heavily. The warrior returned his long sword to its sheath and watched the closed door. When he was sure that Keltch was not going to return, he sat down. The youth returned the daggers to the sheaths on his bandoleer, retrieved his fallen floppy hat, and rested it on his head. The priest's mace disappeared just as quickly as it had appeared, lost within the cassock of his robe. The Magistrate, blood still pulsing through the veins in his ears, slowly took his seat. It was a moment before anyone broke the silence.

The Magistrate found his senses and said, "Well, thank you gentlemen for your quick responses. That was quite unexpected."

"Not by me," Iesed said, patting his racing heart. The Magistrate gave him a scornful look, but the intended gesture was lost on Iesed, who was too relieved to notice it.

"Lucky for you, Magistrate, that he didn't spill any blood, or we would have had to charge you extra for it," the warrior said and chuckled, showing huge teeth and a crooked smile that stretched across his bearded face. The Magistrate did not see the humor in the situation.

*   *   *

Night fell and the fog rolled across the forest like a thick blanket engulfing the ground. The nightly ritual of securing doors and windows in the village was completed before dusk. An uneasy silence fell around the desolate streets.

An acrid smell filled the air, and a hulking shape slipped through the mist, almost a part of it. An ethereal form darkened near a whitewashed building. Smoky tendrils reached out, weaving through the air, probing though the crevices and cracks of the building. The creature stood stock-still and deathly quiet, waiting for the sound that was music to his ears.

A woman cried out and began screaming. Barcus smiled and relished the sounds as they filled his Undead ears. His eyes fluttered closed as the ecstasy filled him, somewhat sating the blood lust that always arose. He bellowed a robust laughter that echoed through the night. Barcus could feel the terror he was causing, and sense the negative energy of the Undead he had just created.

The tendrils searched the rest of the house for another easily converted person. They located an ancient woman and began tearing away at her will. She fought desperately, but in the end was changed into the shadow of the likes of her creator. Again the ecstasy flowed into Barcus' being through the outstretched tentacles. His laughter raged again, filling the night.

Barcus felt the impact before he had a chance to discern the intruder. His mind was too filled in the zenith of sensations. An iron mace swung down and impacted into the side of his skull, caving it in. A blood-curdling moan escaped his lips and it turned into a crescendo of a wail. Barcus flung his head back, the mace protruded from his caved skull with the handle jutting forth. He lunged and grabbed Simil by the robe, jerking him close to his massive body. Simil attempted to pull the stuck mace free, but let go of it in favor of trying to dislodge himself from the crushing grip. It was no use. Barcus' hug squeezed the life from him, and the flailing only caused his breath to escape all that more rapidly.

Barcus felt the life-force ebb from the struggling priest and he hurled the broken form to the ground before him. The lancing pain was unbearable, and Barcus yanked the mace free from his dented head. He held it up high and then brought it down with a smashing blow. He continued repeatedly pounding the still figure that had been Simil.

"I heard it over here!" A shout sounded from the other end of the village. Barcus dropped the gore-covered mace, closed his remaining eye, and focused. The tendrils were whipping uncontrollably and Barcus attempted to suppress the thrashing. After a moment, they calmed and settled, focusing on the fallen form, penetrating it. An eerie red glow filled Simil's eyes and his body mechanically raised itself from the ground along with the gore-covered mace. Barcus wrestled with the pain coursing through his body as it disoriented him. He staggered from the building, unsure where he was. Shouting voices neared, and Barcus maneuvered the newly created Undead between him and the approaching men. The zombie of Simil staggered toward the source of the adjacent commotion.

"Simil! Simil! Where are you?" a panicked voice yelled, searching through the concealing mist. Sprig saw the lumbering shape of the priest moving toward him and he ran to greet him.

"Look out, boy!" Jorth yelled. Sprig looked up in time to see Simil's swinging hands and the mace swish past his face. Sprig dropped onto his back and rolled, returning to his feet in a defensive crouch. He reflexively pulled out two daggers.

The mist parted enough for him to actually see what had been done to the priest Simil. The creature's arm did not work quite right, and Sprig could see that they were broken in several places. Even so, the creature still managed to swing the mace fairly accurately. Sprig rolled to the right, avoiding a crushing blow, ending up in a crouched position ready to spring.

Jorth hurriedly cleared the distance and struck the creature across its outstretched arms, severing one limb and opening its entrails. Jorth, on the back swing, decapitated the head, and the body crashed to the ground, unmoving. Jorth turned toward Sprig who was still crouched and very much in shock.

"Are you okay, boy?" Jorth asked, trying to keep his voice low.

"That couldn't have been Simil!" The realization of terror finally hit Sprig. "What did those bastards do to him?" Sprig slowly raised himself from his crouch. Jorth was staring into the shrouded darkness in front of them. A deep growl drifted from somewhere near the two men. Sprig spun around, hearing the sounds echoing off the nearby walls.

Jorth lowered his center of gravity, sword ready, and continued to scan the curtain of fog. A bounding form parted the whirling mist and streaked through the air, crashing into Jorth and knocking him to the ground.

"Jorth!" Sprig screamed. The wolf-like creature ripped its ferocious claws across Jorth's chest, tearing his breastplate clean off. The creature buried its jaws into the soft belly and Sprig could hear the cracking of bones. Jorth's face contorted into a grimace and blood sprayed from his squeezed mouth. The wolf creature yanked at the exposed entrails and crunched more bones. It was eating Jorth alive.

Anger filled Sprig's limbs and he launched himself at the beast. The creature was by far faster than the springing boy, and sidestepped easily. The youth crashed into the ground, just missing his intended target. The beast snarled and bared its blood-dripping fangs.

Sprig was on his back but still held his daggers in hand. He struck out with both blades and pierced the side of the she-wolf with one of them. The beast jumped to the side and growled at the prone figure. Blood flowed freely from the wound. Sprig saw intelligence in those eyes, the same eyes that were staring intently at the daggers in his hands.

"You don't like silver, huh, she-bitch?" Jorth gurgled as he arched his back and rolled to his side, facing the she-wolf. Jorth spat blood in her direction, and his eyes rolled to the back of his head. Collapsing, he lay still. Sprig assumed a protective position over the fallen warrior's body. A slight smile formed on the wolf's mouth and it spoke in a harsh guttural voice. "I'll be back for you, little one. I'll rip your still-beating heart from your chest and feast on the marrow of your bones." The smile lengthened. Then she turned and disappeared into the murky night.

Sprig stood for many minutes, waiting to see if he had been tricked, but after a few moments, she did not return. Eventually he lowered his guard and checked Jorth's body; he was dead. The misshapen form of the priest caught his eye. Sprig's legs gave way and he collapsed near the bodies. Tears filled his eyes and he wailed uncontrollably for the two men who accepted him and raised him to be a man. Numbness set in and slowly the tears subsided.

A glint on the grass near Simil's body caught Sprig's eye. He wiped the tears away, thinking it was a play of the light on his watery eyes, but the image remained. Slowly, Sprig reached forward and his fingers closed around the item on the grass. It was cold, heavy, and with smooth edges. He held the gem before his face. Its color matched Simil's robe.

Sprig absently slipped the jewel into his jerkin and picked himself up from the ground. He felt his way around the buildings and eventually wandered toward the stable where the rest of the troop was camping out. He could hear the shouts and crying from the building behind him, but he did not care. Everyone that meant anything to him was gone, again.

*　　*　　*

Barcus struggled to free his mind of the pain radiating through him. It was no use. The village disappeared behind him and his tendrils searched the way for him. The woods thickened around him. "Where is it? Damn it! Where's Haven?" Barcus howled, trying to beat back the pain threatening to overwhelm him. The faint tendrils searched the air and ground around him. The tendrils focused on something behind him, and he spun to face the pursuing enemy.

The foliage parted and Sasha leaped before the bewildered Barcus, who unsteadily readied for an attack. Sasha stood on her hind legs and cradled her side with both hands. Crimson stained her hands as blood flowed freely from her wound. "Sasha! Call upon Haven! I can't locate it. The pain's too gr . . ." Barcus bellowed and fell, not finishing his request. Sasha looked over her shoulder and smelled the air.

"We're not being pursued," she growled hoarsely. She looked down at her side. Her lips pulled back from her sharp teeth into a tight grimace. "This is a night of surprises," she lapped the sticky maroon substance from her stained hands. Blood continued to ooze from the gash in her side. For the first time, Sasha actually noticed Barcus' face and burst into throaty laughter.

He was quite a miserable sight to behold. His head was no longer symmetrical. The right side of his head and face were a crater. The right eye was missing somewhere within the mess of gray matter. She continued her guttural laughing. What a sight! No living creature could survive such a wound.

"What's so damn funny?" Barcus raged from his sprawled position on the ground. His misshapen head could no longer convey the emotions that he was trying to get across. Sasha laughed harder at his attempt. Barcus' tendrils lashed out at her, snaking harmlessly around her, trying to reach within.

Barcus was a huge imposing figure, but Sasha in her lupine form was nearly a head taller than he. Barcus gave up his effort to lash out at her in favor of requesting her help. "You have to find Haven, Sasha. I'm in no condition to locate it," Barcus slurred. Sasha noted the plea in his voice. Her laughter subsided into a husky chuckle.

"If you can't find Haven on you own, I can't help you. You know the rules," Sasha said without malice.

"Damn the rules! This has nothing to do with them anyway! Concentrate, find it, and take me there!" Barcus demanded, and then wailed as the pain overtook him. He was attempting to stagger to his feet, but fell down with the tendrils whipping about the air. Sasha noted the pathetic form and debated leaving him there to his fate. She thought better of it. The sun would be up soon and in his condition, he would never survive it.

Sasha stood over the sprawled form and hoisted Barcus across her shoulders. She winced at the pain in her side that continued to bleed freely. She leaped over a fallen tree trunk and broke into a run through the trees carrying the groaning form. *Rewella is not going to be pleased about this*, she thought, ducking the branches flying past her face.

* * *

Sasha entered the lair she shared with Rewella and dropped Barcus unceremoniously to the stone floor. She panted heavily, sucking in quick breaths, holding her wounded side. Barcus struggled to right himself against the wall. Sasha smelled the air, scanning the room.

"Where are we? Is this one of Rewella's lairs?" Barcus asked, his vaporous tendrils searching through the area around him.

"She's not here at the moment," Sasha said in a more feminine voice as her body reverted to its womanlike form. Her tall, lanky figure crossed the room to a washbasin. She grabbed a wet cloth and dabbed at the seeping wound that continued flowing from her side. Her face twisted into a scowl at the pain but she would not cry out.

Barcus scanned the room warily trying to take in the details though the pain he was experiencing kept him from comprehension. He was disoriented and weak, but this location sparked a memory somewhere in his mind. The room was filled with ancient and beautifully carved furniture and the walls were covered in decayed tapestries. This room looked familiar, like one from the manor he had known as a boy. "Where are we, Sasha? This place no longer exists. It was destroyed hundreds of years ago," Barcus said, his voice barely above a whisper.

Sasha ignored Barcus' ramblings, as she stood naked over the basin, cleansing the wound in her side. Something about her manner did not seem right. Barcus had seen Flange wounded and on one occasion he himself had been. Their wounds oozed a thick substance for a short time, but eventually healed. Sasha's wound looked like any other human's. Recognition dawned on him as he continued to watch her. "You're not truly one of us, are you?" Sasha did not take the bait and continued to ignore him.

His tendrils felt the air around her and lapped across her body. Barcus wondered how her essence could radiate Undeath, yet he could not sense a living life force in her. "Is that why you wouldn't take me to Haven? You can't find it on your own, can you?" Barcus fell silent as another wave of pain washed over him. His teeth ground together, and his body shook on the stone floor.

Sasha turned, seeing the flailing figure, and a smile escaped her lips. She not only enjoyed his pain, but reveled in it. Her own pain forgotten for the moment, she stood over the twitching body. "Of course I'm one of you, Barcus. You know that each of us is different in some way. I just happen to bleed."

She applied pressure to the wound with a tattered towel. She smiled outwardly at the twitching form of Barcus, but fear gripped her heart on the inside. She had never been wounded before, and now that she had, it made a crack in her deception. Sasha wrapped the towel around her waist and retrieved a robe to cover her naked body. Barcus' eye rolled to the back of his head and he lay moaning. Sasha seated herself on a couch, careful not to get any more blood than necessary on the ancient fabric. Her mind was filled with puzzled thoughts. *No blade has ever hurt me before,* she thought. *He said it was silver and it cut me like a knife going through warmed butter.*

Sasha suddenly looked around the room. Her gaze fell on a silver mirror placed on a vanity. Up off the couch she went purposely to the table. She carefully reached out to touch the dull silver handle and was quite relieved when it did nothing to harm her. She picked up the mirror and held it up to look into the fogged reflection.

She tried to open up her senses like Rewella had taught her. The silver took on a sinister feel to it. She saw it as something stronger than steel, and many times more deadly. The mirror fell from her hands, and the glass portion of it broke all over the floor. Sasha had the distinct impression that if that mirror handle had an edge, it would have cut her hand off.

She cradled the hand that had held the mirror close to her chest and looked down at the blood-soaked towel wrapped around her. This was not something that Rewella had warned her about. For probably the first time since she had been created, she was afraid. The sensation gnawed away at her and she began to pace the stone floor between the couches.

A spider crept slowly across the floor. Its multifaceted eyes searched the room, first at the sprawled form of Barcus and then to the pacing form of Sasha. The spider was joined by another, and then another. The corner of the room bustled with the activity of thousands of spiders crawling over each other forming a mound. The mound grew taller and the form began resembling a woman. In a blink of an eye, the mass of arachnids became an anthropoid form of the porcelain lady, and she stepped from the shadows of the corner.

Sasha sensed the presence and picked up the carefully draped robe and raced toward the corner where Rewella was emerging. Rewella slipped gracefully into the garment and then, acting surprised, noticed the wound in Sasha's side as if for the first time. "What happened, Sasha?" she asked, concern dripping from her sweet voice. She pulled the she-wolf to her in a loving embrace. Sasha's eyes looked as if they were going to overflow with tears, but they did not.

"I've been wounded," Sasha said, looking down at her side. Rewella reached inside the blood-stained robe and carefully undid the wrapped towel. She probed the wound gently, yet her gentle caress still caused Sasha to wince. The bleeding continued unabated. When she finished her observation, Rewella carefully wrapped the towel and tucked it around Sasha's waist.

"How did it happen?" Rewella said, looking into Sasha's watery eyes.

"I was stabbed with a weapon. A dagger, I think," Sasha replied.

"What was it made out of?" Rewella questioned. Sasha looked down at the floor and hesitated.

"I'm not sure. It looked like any other steel dagger," Sasha said looking back to Rewella. Rewella searched Sasha's face for a moment, saying nothing. Sasha became uncomfortable under the scrutiny, and turned away toward the opposite corner where Barcus lay. She thumbed in that direction and said, "Barcus is wounded also. He took a swipe to the head. It's cratered." Sasha smiled and giggled. "He looks quite ridiculous."

A tiny smile crept to the corner of the petite set of full red lips of the Porcelain Lady. "Did Flange do it?" Rewella asked.

"No, some supposed Undead Slayers did it," Sasha said, not sensing the trap.

"So where was Flange while all this happened?" Rewella asked, the smile disappearing from her face. Sasha fidgeted slightly.

"I'm not sure. I haven't been able to locate him," Sasha said nervously.

"Did he go into Haven?" Rewella said to herself, crossing the room to stand over the stricken unresponsive form of Barcus. She gave his ribs a gentle kick and his eye opened, circling around, trying to focus on the looming figure.

"Rewella, take me to Haven. Sasha couldn't. She's not like us," Barcus whispered. Both the women exchanged glances. Rewella looked back at the pathetic figure.

"Sasha did not take you to Haven because of the agreements we have," Rewella said. "You know that any of us or a newly created Undead must find Haven on their own. Those are the rules we agreed on, remember?" Barcus' eye focused on Rewella's face and his tendrils sought her out.

"If the agreements still stands, then why did you send Sasha to ransack Flange's lair?" Another look was passed between the two women.

"Did Flange tell you that?" Rewella asked.

"Yes," Barcus said simply.

"He's making it up," Rewella said with a dismissive gesture.

"No, he's not. I have my agents just as you. I know that she did it, just as I know she looks for his other lairs almost every day. Even though I can't move around in the daylight like she can, doesn't mean I don't know what's going on," he said looking back and forth at the two women, who fell silent. "You violated the agreements; both of you. I did also by raising his kills, but I'm sure you're already aware of that," he said. Rewella nodded and kneeled before Barcus, who had managed to pull himself against the wall into a sitting position.

"You are right. The agreements are broken on all ends except on Flange's," Rewella said. Another spasm of pain swept over Barcus, and he shook violently. Rewella caressed the caved portion of his head with slender delicate fingers. Barcus had become incoherent once more. Rewella stood and crossed the room to stand before Sasha, questions written in her eyes.

"He knows that I'm different because of my wound and the fact that I cannot call upon Haven. Although I was able to convince him that even though we all have separate traits, that we are still the same kind of beings. Your excuse about the agreement covered why I did not take him to Haven." Rewella nodded in understanding.

"I think it is time to pay Haven a visit. Don't you?" Rewella said, looking over her shoulder at Barcus. "Are you too weak to carry my brother?" Rewella asked, grinning. Sasha straightened and her form darkened as she became lupine once more. The towel wrapped around her waist loosened and fell during her transformation. Rewella picked it up and re-wrapped it around Sasha's waist, tucking the end in. She kissed Sasha's hairy cheek and hugged her gently, trying not to aggravate the seeping wound. Sasha took four elongated steps to Barcus and hoisted him up. She draped his body over her shoulder and turned to Rewella.

Rewella had already moved to the darkest corner of the room and raised her arms above her head. She began chanting in a rhythm and pitch that would have burst a normal human's eardrum. The shadow of the corner became darker. She motioned for Sasha to follow and the group, swallowed by the unnatural shadow, disappeared from sight.

* * *

It was still several hours before dawn and the fog in the forest had somewhat abated. A shadow along a gnarled and twisted tree trunk lengthened, turning darker than its surroundings. Two shapes seemed to appear from an unseen passage under the tree. The two figures, upon closer inspection, were actually three. The larger of the two forms was carrying another person. The figures left the woods and moved silently into the clearing near an enormous fairy ring. The smaller of the figures moved to the center of the patch of mushrooms and raised its arms. The larger figure followed shortly after, still hefting its bundle. A small vibration rumbled across the area, and the grass swayed like a ripple in a pond from a cast stone.

The ground opened up beneath the waiting figures and consumed them. The night was still once more as the ripples subsided, leaving the ground once again undisturbed.

A shadow detached itself from a nearby tree and carefully glided to the spot where the figures disappeared. The figure stood in contemplation for a moment then turned from the spot, careful not to step on the mushrooms, and merged with the shadow from whence it had come.

* * *

Sasha watched Rewella enter the circle of luminescent mushrooms. Sasha had tried many times to transport herself to Haven, but was unsuccessful in her attempts. Rewella and the other siblings could move freely to Haven under the right conditions, but not Sasha. She was not like the others, and that secret was one Sasha and Rewella planned to keep from the brothers.

Sasha thought back to the first time she was brought to Haven. It was well over a hundred years ago. She was barely eighteen when a petite woman approached her in the dead of night. The woman radiated power and Sasha was drawn to her at once. The Porcelain Lady, who was not that way then, offered Sasha immortality if only she would do her bidding. Sasha had no doubt in her mind whatsoever that this woman could fulfill such a promise.

Every night for many months, Rewella appeared after dusk. She would embrace the young girl and talk of a place of great power with an unlimited source of possibilities. This place could change the reality around you with the right combination of items. Sasha was dumbfounded. Any promise to leave the miserable life she had would do. Rewella unfolded a plan to deceive her siblings, who were also like her, yet each one was different.

When Rewella was sure that Sasha was ready, she led the eager girl from the village into the forest. Rewella opened a passage in a shadow, and told Sasha to walk into it, which she did without hesitation. As she passed into the shadow, her world grew dark and extremely cold. She cried out and fell into a fetal position hugging her legs trying to keep the fleeting warmth in her extremities. Sasha felt hands grasping her frozen form, pulling her from the ground. The petite form of Rewella knelt, cradling her head in her lap like a baby.

"I'mmm freezzzing," she said through chattering teeth.

"I'm so sorry, child. I had no idea that would happen to you," Rewella said, concerned, and held her close. The night air was warm and humid. It took a few minutes for her to stop shaking and to regain her footing. Rewella waited patiently for the girl to warm sufficiently. When she was no longer trembling, Rewella led her to a spot in the clearing in the forest.

Sasha shook off her thoughtful trance as Rewella entered the center of the fairy ring circle. She followed and stood next to Rewella as she began concentrating. Sasha again thought back to her first trip to Haven.

The iciness left her limbs and Rewella led her by the hand to a circular patch of mushrooms in the clearing.

"This isn't going to feel the same way, is it?" Sasha asked in a small-frightened voice. Rewella thought for a moment and shook her head slightly.

"I don't know. Here, wear this necklace and I'll hold you close just the same," Rewella said and placed the trinket around Sasha's neck.

The earth trembled for a moment, and Sasha could feel the soil under her feet shift and her feet sank. A moment of panic swelled in her. *I'm going to be buried alive!* She thought. The ground gave way and she watched the night sky disappear from view. She closed her eyes and held her breath. The soil was cool but nothing like the frigid temperature she felt passing through the shadow. A sensation of falling caused her to grasp Rewella tightly. Her dangling feet touched solid ground and she continued to hold her breath, believing she was trapped in the earth. Rewella untangled herself from the flailing grasp and stepped away. "You can open your eyes, Sasha," she said.

Sasha stood still and slowly opened her eyes. A faint light illuminated the surroundings. Sasha looked above, searching for the hole they would have fallen through only to see a stone ceiling. Slowly her eyes swept the room and rested on a circle etched in gold, silver, and other metals, on the floor. It radiated an aura of power. Symbols and shapes ringed the outer edge of the circle. The surrounding walls were covered in some type of pictographs.

Sasha walked slowly toward the circle, trying to make some sense of the designs.

"I'll be back shortly, Sasha. Until then, look but don't touch. Stay off the circle," Rewella said, and vanished. Sasha nodded, but was too caught up in her surroundings to really pay attention to what was being said to her. She continued to walk around the circle, noting the grooves and hollows in the floor.

Sasha was unsure how much time had passed when Rewella stepped into the light carrying a wooden case. Sasha had not heard nor seen her enter, but was not surprised by the entrance. Rewella placed the case on the floor and opened the lid. Sasha's eyes lit up at the gems and gold items Rewella removed from the case.

"What are those for?" she asked, kneeling next to Rewella, who was carefully setting the items in an orderly fashion on the floor around the case.

"Each one of these items radiates a power of some kind and extent. Can you feel it?" Rewella said, holding out a gem for Sasha to take. Sasha held the gem up to the light.

"It's beautiful, but I can't feel anything but the texture," Sasha said handing it back.

"When I am finished with you, it will be one of your abilities," Rewella said, straightening her back and placing her hands on her hips. "You will be stronger, faster, and have senses that no other living person has." Smiling, she reached across to Sasha and gently caressed her cheek. "Are you ready to become immortal?" Rewella asked. Sasha smiled and stood up.

"What do you want me to do?" Sasha said.

"For a moment, nothing. I need some time to prepare for your transformation," Rewella said, standing up and taking Sasha's hand. "Do you see the walls with the pictures carved in them?" Sasha nodded. "Each set of pictures is a type of formula. Each formula requires certain items of power. Do you understand?" Sasha nodded again. "The items, used in unison on that Circle of Power, over there, will alter a person. That is how I am going to give you immortality, without making you Undead. Do you understand?" Sasha shook her head vigorously. Rewella released her hand. "Okay. I need you to stay clear of me until I'm ready for you." Sasha moved away from the Circle of Power and the loose items on the floor.

Sasha watched Rewella walk to the walls and study them. Rewella retraced the raised and etched runes with her hands, and occasionally looked over at the items she brought into the room to make sure she had everything she needed. When she was satisfied with her inspection, she chose several pieces and placed them in select places on the circle. Many of the items fit in precise shallows on the circle. Carefully, Rewella arranged the items to her satisfaction and stood clear of the circle. She turned toward Sasha and gestured. "It's ready, child. Remove your clothes and come take your place in the center of the circle. Be careful not to touch the metal lines that are etched or topple the items I have placed."

Sasha obeyed, removed her clothes, and stepped gingerly into the center of the circle. After a moment of silence she asked, "What happens no . . ." A scream erupted from her lips as a blinding light arced from the metallic lines and coursed through her. Her high-pitched squeal turned into a hoarse, low-pitched howl, and her form shook, silhouetted against the blinding light.

Sasha fell to her hands and knees as the black lightning discharged from her body back into the metallic lines that they originally had come from. Sasha's body shrank into the form of a wolf. Feral canine eyes stared at the figure across the room and it panted with its tongue hanging out.

"This is a crucial moment for you, Sasha. You have to remember who you are," Rewella said in a soft reassuring voice. The wolf watched her cautiously. "Sasha, do you know who I am? Do you recognize my voice?" The wolf slowed its panting and laid down in the circle. "Sasha, you are going to have to will yourself back to what you were. Can you do that? Place an image in your mind of how you remember yourself." The wolf stretched its paws and sat, as if pondering what it was hearing. It reared back on its hind legs. Its limbs elongated and its jaw shrank a bit. The thick coarse coat covering the wolf thinned.

The lupine form stood on two legs and stared down at its almost-human hands. Sasha continued to concentrate and her form became more like herself. "Sasha, do you know me?" a voice asked. Sasha looked at the women standing before her. Sasha slowly nodded her head "yes."

"What happened?" a throaty voice asked. Sasha clamped her hand to her mouth, startled by the sound.

"It's okay, Sasha. When you revert back to human form, it will pass," Rewella said reassuringly. Sasha closed her eyes and rolled her head back. After a moment, the rest of the hair on her body disappeared and she stood naked and very much human. She opened her eyes and sighed in relief.

Rewella led her from the circle and handed back the discarded clothes. "The hard part is over, Sasha. I will have to set up some other combinations on the circle to give you full abilities, but you can rest for now," she said.

Sasha dressed herself, noticing that her clothes were much too tight. She also knew she was towering over Rewella, who smiled.

"You've grown a bit, my lovely," Rewella said and led her to a corner. "Rest here until I'm ready for you." Sasha laid on the stone floor and fell almost instantly into a deep slumber.

Rewella looked at the circle. The items she had used to change Sasha were gone; destroyed by the process. Rewella picked up several new items and went about the task of placing them around the pattern on the circle. She completed the task and watched the sleeping form. A frown creased Rewella's face. She removed a vial from her case and popped the cork. She poured the contents onto several of the items that were already placed on the circle. Liquid silver dripped out into beads. Afterward, she corked the vial and hid it back in the case.

Rewella stood over the sleeping girl and caressed her cheek lightly. Sasha stirred and smiled at her benevolent benefactor. Rewella noticed that Sasha's ears were slightly pointed and her canines had lengthened.

So much for looking completely human, Rewella thought, and reached out and helped Sasha to her feet. "This time, we are going to add to the deception that you are one of us and give you the senses you need to search out other items that can be used in the Circle of Power," Rewella mentioned with a sweet smile.

Sasha hesitated for a moment and concern filled her face. "Will it hurt like it did earlier?" Sasha asked anxiously.

"Your body will resist most anything now. It shouldn't hurt at all. I have used the circle on myself several times with no ill results," Rewella said, still smiling. The reassuring look filled Sasha with confidence. She strolled purposely to the center of the circle. After about a minute, the black lightning struck her again. This time she did not cry out or fall to the ground.

The items vaporized and the lightning jumped back to the metal etching on the floor. Sasha walked from the circle, staring at the items stacked around the open case. "I see what you mean. The gems radiate an unnatural light. I can feel a purpose." Her preternatural eyes scanned the walls. "I can see purpose here also, but I can't make sense of it other than it is magic."

"That is all you will need to know to suit my purpose. It is time to lay a surprise for my dear brother," Rewella said, embracing her newly created creature.

The trio appeared in Haven and Sasha brought her mind to the present. Sasha had been here many times since her first venture into these halls, but not of her own accord. Rewella or Flange had always accompanied her and the sensation of suffocation never bothered her after the change.

Sasha dropped Barcus onto the stone floor. He made no sound as his tendrils drifted randomly around him. Sasha wondered if Barcus' tendrils came from the circle, or if he had become present during his change into an Undead creature. It was not a topic Rewella openly shared. Sasha winced and grabbed at her side. The towel was soaked and completely crimson. She flung the drenched towel to the floor and used her robe to try and staunch the wound.

"I'll be back shortly," Rewella said, not waiting for a reply, and disappeared. Sasha looked at the crumpled form and straightened him out with a swift kick to the ribs, rolling him over onto his back. She held her side and allowed a low deep howl to escape her lungs. The wound continued to burn and bleed freely.

Rewella returned in a matter of minutes carrying a small exquisitely decorated chest with a dull iron lock. The chest was placed on a dark wood table near the Circle of Power. Whispering an indiscernible phrase, Rewella removed her left index finger. The bone, attaching to the knuckle, was carved into the shape of a key. She carefully inserted the bone-key into the lock. With a gentle turn, the lock was unfastened, falling free of the chest. Rewella reattached her digit to the exposed knuckle and worked her fingers as if making sure it was placed properly.

Sasha crept to the table, examining the chest. She was sure she had never seen the chest before, but that did not surprise her in the least. Sasha was Rewella's ward, but that did not mean she shared all of her secrets with her. Rewella removed a silver dagger from the chest and placed it on the table.

Sasha, reflexively, stepped back away from the table. Rewella paid no heed, and continued to remove gems and several colored vials of various natures. Sasha watched Rewella intently as she prepared her inventory, often scanning the walls for the formulas that only she understood. Sasha could feel the aura of power emulating from the objects. One object of interest stood out from the rest. It was the gem she had stolen from Barcus' hidden lair. Rewella was obviously intent on using it in the rituals.

Rewella glanced over her shoulder to her waiting accomplice. "I am going to try to restore Barcus, before I get to you. Your wound is superficial compared to his," she said, and gathered the items into the folds of her arms, kneeling before the circle. She placed the items meticulously into the niches, adjusting angles accordingly.

When Rewella was satisfied, she motioned for Sasha to pick up the limp form of Barcus and place him in the center of the circle. Sasha grabbed the slumped form with one arm and carried him to the circle, careful not to step on the items Rewella had arranged. She dropped Barcus with a thud onto the stone floor, and leaped from the circle in one bound.

Several minutes passed, and Sasha was growing impatient. "Is this going to work?" she asked. Rewella continued to stand, locked in place, watching the etched lines of the circle. She did not look at the pacing lupine.

"Only if he is not too far gone. He shouldn't be. I've worked with far worse." A smile, just a hint of one, crept across her face as if recollecting the experience.

Sasha was insistent. "What if using the circle will eventually deplete it of power?"

Rewella turned from her vigilance, smiling, and said, "You're starting to sound like Flange, my sweet." Sasha's face turned scarlet at the mention that Flange and she could share the same thought. Sasha's temper flared.

"You don't know for sure do you? It is a plausible possibility, Rewella. Don't think for a minute that just because I'm your underling, that I can't think for myself. My concern comes not from any teachings of Flange, but from the fact that this place may not have an inexhaustible source of power," she snarled.

As Sasha finished her sentence, Rewella's raven hair began to sparkle. Their locked gazes separated as both turned to watch the black lightning do its work on the slumped figure. Barcus convulsed and twitched as the blue-black sparks coursed through his body. His tendrils snaked about with a life of their own, trying to escape the lightning's wrath. The sparks dimmed and the lightning leaped back into the metallic etching.

Wispy smoke whiffed from the struggling Barcus and dissipated in the air above the circle. As in all the other previous instances, the items used in the process were destroyed. Barcus clambered to his hands and knees. His downturned head snapped up when the seeking tendrils touched the staring women standing before him. "Wha-what happened to me?" Barcus said and rocked back on his haunches, balancing himself. His right hand reached up and felt for the eye that he could not see out of, and jerked his hand away in surprise after feeling the crater in his head. Barcus looked at Rewella for answers. "Who did this to me?"

Rewella moved discreetly to the circle and helped Barcus to his feet. Sasha was amused at the ingenuity. With a slight alteration of the formula, Rewella removed his memories from the last few hours. Barcus was obstinate, "Who did this to me, Rewella?" Rewella's face became solemn.

"Our own blood did this to you," she said.

"Flange? Flange did this to me?" Barcus thundered.

"In his own way, he did. He's angry with you for raising his slain assailants, and he worked with the Undead Slayers that the village hired to destroy you. Sasha followed him to your lair, and he destroyed it. He also stole this gem." She removed the gem from her robe that Sasha had stolen from Barcus' lair, and held it out to show him. "Sasha attacked him trying to retrieve your stolen property, only to be wounded in the process. The Undead Slayers fell on you after Flange tipped them off. I found you wounded and brought you to Haven to try and help," she said, pausing to let her words sink in.

Barcus looked down at the ground in thought. Suddenly, his head snapped back up. "You're positive Flange is responsible for this?" Barcus asked. Rewella nodded in return.

"How else could Sasha have been hurt like this?" Rewella said motioning to the still-bleeding wound in Sasha's side. "I used some of my most prized items to save you. Can I use this gem of yours to help restore Sasha?"

"Of course," Barcus said, bobbing his grotesque head, stroking his uneven beard, "Do what you must." Barcus slipped into a thoughtful silence, his tendrils rested their constant seeking.

Rewella turned back to the table with her back to Barcus. A knowing smile passed between the two women. Rewella slipped the gem she had acquired from Barcus into her chest and replaced it with a similar one. She removed the silver dagger from the table and moved to the circle. Rewella knelt down and slipped the dagger into a crevice in the etching and placed the gem into a shallow of an intricately carved rune. "I'm ready, Sasha. Take your place in the circle," Rewella said, standing from her kneeling position.

Sasha crept to the center of the circle, careful to avoid the items, especially the silver dagger. She waited, holding her side, trying to stem the crimson flow. Sparks leaped across the dagger and arced across, striking Sasha's wounded side. She roared in pain, doubling over. The dagger melted away, joining the silver and gold that made up the etching, and the gem crumbled into dust in the shallow recess.

A blackened scorch covered where the gash had been in her side. Sasha probed the cauterized area and wrinkled her nose at the smell of burned fur. *It smells almost as repugnant as Barcus himself,* she thought. The area was tender but the bleeding had stopped. Sasha was satisfied with the results and leaped gracefully from the circle to stand next to Rewella.

The trio watched each other in silence for several moments. Rewella broke the silence. "What are you going to do?" she asked in a small voice. Barcus' baritone laughter echoed through the chamber.

"What do you think I'm going to do? I'm going to rip that traitorous bastard apart!" Barcus yelled. He strode purposefully to the corner of the room, his form became wispy, and he vanished as the shadowy corner swallowed him up.

The two women both laughed and fell together into an embrace. Sasha stroked Rewella's cheek with her lupine hand. "That was brilliant! I had no idea you were going to do that to him," Sasha praised, quite amused by the turn of events.

"You haven't seen anything yet, my pet," Rewella assured.

5

"Look, I don't care if the rest of the troop is leaving. I was one of the signers of the contract, and I am going to fulfill my end of it!" Sprig shouted angrily, leaning over the Magistrate's desk, jabbing a finger for emphasis. The Magistrate leaned back in his chair, sizing up the youth.

Sprig had spent the morning burying his two mentors in a cemetery, with Iesed presiding over the ceremony. Sprig showed no sign of emotion while the service was being conducted. He could not, being surrounded by people he did not know. The troop said their good-byes and decided to leave the area at once. Sprig, angry at their cowardice, cursed them. He gathered his meager belongings, and left the group without a second thought.

"My dear boy, you are only going to get yourself killed along with your friends. They have failed, and the contract is null and void," the Magistrate said, seeing no more reason for the debate. "It's over. Go find yourself a young lass and a place to settle down far away from this ill-fated place."

The Magistrate stood, and walked around to the front of his desk. He grabbed Sprig's arm and led him to the door. "You have a lot of heart, son, but there is nothing more you can do."

Sprig pulled away and stopped himself from being dismissed. "I don't care about the contract. You can keep your damn money! They killed my friends, my family. I will find a way to avenge them," Sprig pleaded.

"Your friends were veterans, were they not? Now they are dead, and if you are not careful, you will be too," the Magistrate said, with no hint of malice.

"What about the Baron? Surely he would help?" Sprig said in desperation, causing the Magistrate to get angry.

"That fool will be the death of us all! He'll get you killed just like all the others who have followed him to their doom. Mark my words, boy; any alliance with him might as well be a pact with the Undead, and I'll have no part in it," the Magistrate fumed, hurriedly making for the exit, taking Sprig by the arm and dragging him with him. "Good day, Sir." The Magistrate pushed Sprig out the door and closed it behind him before he had a chance to refute.

Sprig stared at the closed door, rubbing his shoulder where the Magistrate had nearly jerked his arm out of its socket. He placed his hand on the doorknob, prepared to burst back through to argue his case, but knew it was futile. He did an about-face and marched purposefully to the stables.

The remainder of the troop had left earlier that morning. Sprig did not really care for any of the other members of the troop. The group was composed of the camp followers that trailed behind the army. After the war, the parasites tagged along with Jorth and his company for protection. Most of them did little work, and Sprig was surprised that Jorth allowed them to stay. Sprig summarized that the allowance was because Jorth never had to cook another meal for himself. For all the good they were worth, Sprig would have had them scattered to the four corners of the world. His heightened dislike for the troop suddenly made him ashamed. Jorth could have very well left *him* alone to die. Uneasiness crept over him as he remembered that day.

The bright sunshine promised an early spring by melting the hard-packed snow. Sprig and several other village children played in the nearby woods. The group had split into two teams, and each were doing their best to steal the others' designated flag. This game of "Capture the Standard" lasted a good portion of the afternoon. Sprig, using his agility, had made three of the five captures for his team. Now it was his turn to guard his team's home base. He was scanning the underbrush intently for the enemies of the other team, and so he was not first to locate the smoke.

Some of the older boys were shouting and Sprig could not make out what was being said. He left his position slowly, wondering if he was being tricked into abandoning his post. Then he saw the smoke coming from the direction of the village. His cautious movement turned into a reckless run. His team's base was located farthest away and he was last to clear the woods.

The village was consumed in flames. Men on horseback rode through the streets carrying livestock, grains, and some of the village's women. Sprig could see bodies lying in pools of blood everywhere. Most of the children had broke cover and ran terrified to try and find their families. The riders ran them down and killed them.

Sprig was frightened, but also furious. His eyes searched the village and fell on a discarded hoe very near him. A horse sped past his hiding spot; the rider was dragging a person behind it. Sprig leaped from his concealment, running to the hoe and hoisted it up like a sword.

Another rider saw the boy, pulled his reins about, and kicked the horse in the flanks. Sprig saw the charging horse and the rider's intent. Sprig straightened to his full height and let the hoe drag the ground behind him.

The rider raised his sword and leaned over the left side of his saddle, positioning himself to make an attack on the boy. Sprig's heart pounded but he stood his ground. The horse's hooves dug into the ground, tearing up the earth in its wake. The rider cleared the distance quickly and made for a swipe at such an easy target. As the rider's arm began its swing, Sprig dropped to the ground and snapped the hoe up in front of him. The hoe's dull blade bounced across the rider's shoulder, hitting him in the side of the head, and then fell down between the horse's legs. The hoe tripped the barreling horse and caused it to crash, skidding across the ground, pinning the rider underneath.

The rider groaned and tried to push the crippled horse off his pinned legs, to no avail. Sprig strode forward, calmly and cool. The rider watched the knife-wielding boy approach through squinted and tear-filled eyes. The bandit started to beg for mercy, but before he could stammer a few words, the boy cut his throat.

Sprig turned at the realization of the heavy silence around him. The rest of the brigands had ridden away, carrying off what they could. Sprig sheathed his knife and searched for any of his people that might have escaped. Everyone he found was dead.

Sprig laid the bodies side by side in the center of the village, except for his parents, whom he placed a little ways off. The wood buildings and grass huts continued to burn out of control, but he paid them no mind. Sprig counted the dead and made a mental note of who was missing: seven women. Sprig had not accounted for the burning structures and would not be sure until the blaze died down so that they could be searched.

Sprig decided to make a sweep around the perimeter of the village to see if anyone was hiding. He found two more bodies, both young women, who had been taken into the woods, raped and then murdered. Disgust welled inside of him. The violated forms shocked him back to his senses and he began to cry. He located two linen sheets and gently wrapped the two bodies. He carried them to join the rest of the dead and laid them on the end of the row. Twenty-nine bodies lay carefully together and two more off to the side.

Sprig located a shovel and dug a hole wide enough to be able to lay his parents together. He shook the dust from his hands after packing the dirt on the grave. He turned from the scene and walked into the surrounding woods.

Sprig spent the next two days gathering wood. He built a huge funeral pyre near the row of the slain. The village structures had burned themselves out, leaving only smoldering traces of ash. Sprig was sure that everyone had fled the buildings when they were torched, and he had found no other bodies on his wood-gathering venture. The pyre was a rough circle with a diameter of nearly fifty feet. Sprig dragged the bodies onto the heap of wood. It was late afternoon on the second day after the attack when his task was completed. The sun was nearly down when he lighted the tinder. The fire quickly spread and the circle blazed.

Sprig, suddenly exhausted after his effort, let his legs give way, and he crumpled to his knees. Tears stung his eyes and the blinding firelight flickered across his face. His anguish and sorrow escaped his throat in a mournful cry. After some time, Sprig blinked away the tears and stood, slowly backing away from the fire. He started to make a run for the fire, intent on joining his loved ones, but the sound of horses neighing stayed him. He spun with his hunting knife in an outstretched hand.

Several men wearing soldiers garb stayed together at a respectful distance. Sprig watched them cautiously. A large bearded man dismounted from a barded horse, his breastplate clanking against his mail shirt as he stepped to the ground. Sprig sheathed his blade and lowered his eyes to the ground. The warrior stopped just short of the boy. In a voice that was surprisingly gentle, he said, "Are you okay, lad?" The warrior reached for the child's chin and tilted his head back. The boy raised his tear-filled eyes to meet the warrior's own.

"They killed everyone," his small voice spoke, "I think they took some of the women." The child searched the man's eyes and saw compassion and understanding.

An older man without armor stepped from his horse to join the warrior. He made the sign of protection at the funeral pyre and began a prayerful chant for the dead. The other riders joined the prayer. Tears streamed down the boy's face. The warrior pulled the child close and stroked his hair with a gauntleted hand. The boy cried uncontrollably and the warrior tried to soothe the bewildered child.

"You did good, lad. They would be very proud of you for the way you took care of them," the warrior said, patting the boy on the back. The child drew back and looked into the larger man's eyes.

"I couldn't save them. I tried, but I was too late." The warrior was at a loss for words. The priest had finished his requiem and readied for the warrior's orders.

"Take the 'Sprig' and put him in one of the sleeping wagons and I'll get the trackers up here so we can find the trail. I want the bastards responsible for this found and killed," the warrior said in an authoritative tone. The priest led the bewildered Sprig to one of the wagons in the caravan.

"When was the last time you ate, my son?" the gentle priest asked. The boy shrugged. "I'll find you some food. Rest for now, if you can." The child nodded and lay on the waiting cot, closed his eyes, and fell asleep.

The memories Sprig was reliving vanished when he entered the stable. His mind turned to the business at hand. A stable boy was grooming a mare. Sprig stopped next to the horse to admire the effort.

"You do good work."

The stable hand smiled and continued brushing the horse's mane. Sprig opened a pouch of coins from his leather belt and handed a silver coin to the stable boy. The boy stared at the coin, unable to discern its origin, but silver is silver, and he quickly pushed the coin deep in his trouser pocket.

"Your horse has been fed and groomed. Are you going to leave it here for another night?" the stable boy asked.

"No. I'm leaving this evening," Sprig replied. A look of shock passed the boy's face.

"You're not riding after curfew are you?" the boy said, mouth agape.

"I hopefully won't be traveling far. Do you know where the Baron lives?" The boy hesitated, but his tongue loosened when Sprig produced another silver coin.

"Follow the road on the west side of the village. You will pass through a wooded area. When you clear the thickets, his house is less than a mile away. His cottage is very grand, with stables and servant quarters. You can't miss it. He usually has some type of guard patrolling around the area and you will probably run into them before you find his house," the boy finished and then added, "Good luck," and made the sign of protection. Sprig mirrored the image.

"Thank you," Sprig said, and led his waiting horse from the stable.

* * *

Sprig started his horse at a trot and he was well out of sight of the village before kicking his mount into a run. The wooded area gave him chills. The dense canopy of limbs and leaves made the area seem like night had already fallen. He clung low on the horse to keep from inadvertently knocking himself off by low hanging branches. Cursing, he pulled his horse to a halt. The trail was littered with debris. Sprig dismounted and tied the horse to a nearby branch. He scanned the underbrush for any signs of hidden persons and closed the distance to where the debris was scattered.

Several tree trunks had been dragged to block the path, and leaves had been scattered to cover the footprints. "Pretty poor excuse for covering your tracks," Sprig said out loud so anyone near could hear this. "What kind of brigands are you? This setup wouldn't fool anyone."

"Who are you calling brigands?" A man appeared on the opposite side of the debris, on the path. He was dressed in leather with a mail shirt and a metal skullcap. A short sword hung in a scabbard at his side. "What business do you have on the Baron's lands?" the man inquired.

Sprig took several steps in the man's direction. "My business is with the Baron. Who are you to stop me?" Sprig said, adjusting his arms to be able to pull his knives easily.

"I have my orders to keep anyone from entering the estate," the man replied. Another person ran down the trail behind Sprig, startling his horse.

"He's alone," the newcomer said.

"We've been following you since you entered the woods. We thought you were a scout for the Magistrate's guards. The debris was hastily placed to slow you so we could check to be sure. Please escort your mount through here." As the man finished, four others appeared from the brush on either side of Sprig. All of them carried bows, short swords and were covered in soft leather armor.

Sprig untied his mount and led it through the opening the four men created after moving the trunks. Once past the debris, the trunks were replaced and the woodsmen disappeared into the thicket. "Who are you?" the man asked. Sprig searched the man's eyes for any hint of malevolence. He saw none.

"I'm one of the 'Stakes,' at least that's what the Baron called us," Sprig said.

A smile crept onto the man's otherwise stoic face. "The Baron doesn't like Stakes. What do you want with him, lad?" the man said, much more personally. The two walked further up the path to the man's waiting horse.

"I have news for the Baron and a proposition for him," Sprig said mounting his horse.

"I could hear a lot of bellyaching coming from him because of this. You had better hope that the Baron's in better spirits than he has been, or I'll never hear the end of it. Come on, lad, let's get back before the sun goes down. No one should to be out in the woods, or anywhere else for that matter, after dark." The man mounted his hidden horse, and led the way at an easy trot.

The woods thinned and disappeared altogether after nearly half an hour of riding. During that time, the man said nothing more to Sprig. The countryside was beautiful. Wildflowers bloomed and dotted the field in flamboyant colors. It was hard to imagine such a place as this being plagued with Undead, but an underlying hint of tragedy hung in the air, making the hairs on his neck stand on end.

The trip allowed Sprig's thoughts to wander back to when he first learned that his newfound family were Undead Slayers. His guardians, Jorth and Simil, told him that the wars in the East were the first exposure that they had with the Undead. Sprig could make little sense of what they were saying, and was never really exposed to it when he was a child in their company. He was always resentful for being left behind with the camp followers when the two men landed a slaying job. They would leave for a few days and return with some coins or supplies for payment.

Simil began his instruction on how to read and write. Sprig immediately excelled at the task and had read Simil's entire library within the first few years. The books excited him and taught him how to think, but he longed to learn the weapons of Jorth the Warrior. He practiced daily with kitchen knives from the chuck wagon. When the quartermaster took his grievances to Jorth about the constantly missing utensils, the tide turned for the best.

Jorth presented Sprig with two throwing daggers and a bandoleer that could hold several more. The warrior wanted to know what the youth had taught himself and asked for an exhibition. Sprig went through the routine and motions he had practiced. Jorth watched in silence.

When Sprig had finished, he waited for a response. Jorth rubbed his bearded chin thoughtfully. "That's all pretty and such, but how do you ever intend to use that on someone who's trying to kill you?" Jorth said. Sprig stood, confused, and sheathed the daggers in the bandoleer. "Okay, boy. I'm going to kill you. What are you going to do about it?" Sprig laughed at the notion, but his laughter died in his throat.

Jorth pulled a long hunting knife from his boot and lunged at the boy. Sprig ducked and leaped to the side. He held the bandoleer wrapped around both his fists, daggers still sheathed.

An evil smile stretched across the warrior's bearded face. He did not say a word as he dropped into a stance and prepared for another attack. The warrior lunged, and the attack left a trickle of blood on Sprig's right forearm.

He really means to kill me, Sprig thought. He lowered himself and held his hands wrapped in the bandoleer before him. Jorth lunged again. Sprig popped the bandoleer up and crossed his hands, entangling Jorth's own. He let go of the bandoleer and pulled the sheathed blades free. Jorth shook the entangling leather from his hands and lunged for the boy again.

Sprig dropped into a crouch, and let the warrior step toward him, making a strike. Sprig swung between Jorth's parted legs, and leaped up, turning. Sprig reached around Jorth's head with his left hand and rested a knife's edge under his neck, biting into his throat. His right hand placed the other blade's point just behind Jorth's right shoulder blade. "Are you seeking your death, warrior?" Sprig spat angrily. Jorth raised his arms slowly so Sprig could see over his shoulder, and then he released his knife, letting it clatter to the ground.

"You win, boy," Jorth said, raising his hands up over his head, "lower your blades." Sprig did not budge.

"Do you want me to complete the test, Jorth? Do I need to draw your blood? Is that what you are looking for? I can, and have."

"You're talking about the horse rider in your village. He was not among those laid on the funeral pyre," Jorth said in understanding.

"That's right," Sprig said, "I slit his throat after tripping his horse. I have no regrets about it, and would do it again. Is this what you wanted to prove by your test, to see if I would kill someone if my life depended on it? Well guess what, I already have and will do so again if need be. Do I pass your test?"

The warrior nodded, or tried to. Sprig pulled the blade across the warrior's throat, drawing a thin line of crimson. The warrior held his breath, careful not to move even after Sprig withdrew his blades. Sprig knelt down, ever watchful of the warrior, and picked up the bandoleer, which he placed over his head, letting it drape over his left shoulder.

The warrior removed the gauntlet from his right hand and carefully caressed his neck. His fingers were sticky and stained red. Blood oozed its way down his shirt collar. Sprig took note of the action.

"Blood for blood," Sprig said, showing the trickle running from his forearm. Jorth nodded in acceptance.

"I expect you to report to my tent every morning at sunrise. Your formal training's just begun," Jorth said with a hint of a smile. He executed a short bow and left. Sprig's legs buckled and he nearly collapsed to the ground. He had not expected Jorth to pull such a stunt, and he was even more surprised with himself for following through the way he did. Sprig was pleased with himself.

Those particular thoughts brought a smile to his face, but soon faded in the knowledge that Jorth and Simil were now dead, and he was alone again.

Sprig scanned the horizon. A plume of gray smoke billowed in the distance. "There's the Baron's home," the man said, gesturing into the distance. Sprig took mental notes of any markers that were near for future reference. Uneasiness moved up his spine the nearer he approached the cottage. *What if the Baron turns me away? Or worse yet, what if he refuses me shelter and I have to contend with the creatures of the night by myself?* These questions flashed across his mind as the details of the cottage came into view.

The sun was setting low in the sky, nearly completing the day. The man leaned close and said, "Stop here. I'll go prepare the Baron for your arrival." The man spurred his horse and rode ahead.

Sprig watched as a barrel-chested person left the cottage and conversed with the rider. Sprig could not hear the exchange between the men and kicked his horse gently in the flanks to move it forward. The two men seemed to be in a debate, and they did not notice the youth approach, but Sprig could tell that the conversation was not in his favor.

"Your orders were not to let anyone through, let alone a Stake!" the Baron yelled. The man was assuring him that he was acting on good faith, when Sprig interrupted.

"Excuse me, Baron."

Both men stopped conversing and turned toward the youth. "I would like to help you rid this land of these hell-spawned creatures." The Baron took a moment to size the youth up and then laugh.

"You? What would I want to do with a charlatan Stake? What makes you think I would need a whelp like you? What's wrong, did Barcus kill your friends off, boy?" Keltch chided. As angry as Sprig had been made, all he could do was nod. The Baron stopped, as if reconsidering. "Be off, boy, before the spirits of the night come for you."

"Sir, you can't leave him out here. The sun is already beginning to set," the rider pleaded, "Sir, he is only a boy," the man added.

"Bah! He knew the risk coming out here. Let him find his own way back to the village. He'll be back there before those bastards come a knocking," the Baron said dismissively.

"He most certainly will not!" a woman's voice said from the doorway of the cottage. "Father! What has gotten into you? What about hospitality, Father? He is surely a weary traveler and deserves the right of hospitality like anyone else, does he not?" the woman said in an authoritative tone.

"He's a Stake, Katie!" the Baron said, as if that explained it all.

"Father, you deny him hospitality, and I will never speak to you again," the distraught woman said. Sprig was sure she was serious. The Baron must have thought so too because he gave in.

"All right. He can stay until dawn, and then he must leave. He can stay in the barn with the rest of the animals."

"Father!" the woman shouted.

"In the barn, Katie, or he leaves this instant!" The Baron was quite resolute. She closed the cottage door behind her and walked out to greet the young man.

"I'll show you where you can stay," Kate said, smiling at the youth.

"Mengrig can show him where to stay," Keltch said. Kate glared at her father. Sprig dismounted and greeted the lovely woman. Sprig removed his floppy hat, and bowed, kissing her hand gently. She smiled, amused at the gesture and led the youth toward the stable. Keltch dismissed the gesture with a low growl. "Get back to your post, Mengrig!" Keltch barked, throwing his hands into the air, storming into the cottage and slamming the door. Mengrig made a salute to the lady of the house and the young man she escorted. They both waved as he rode back toward the outlying woods.

"Thanks," Sprig said, placing his floppy hat back on his head. "My name is Sprig," he said, somewhat shyly.

"Sprig? What kind of name is that?" Kate said lightheartedly. Sprig reddened.

"Well, that is what Jorth called me when he found me. My real name is Almondo. I haven't gone by that since my family . . ." he trailed off, not finishing. Kate could see the pain flash across his face and decided not to dwell upon it, she tried to divert his thoughts.

"My name is Kate. And that of course was my father," the bright-eyed woman said, "So what should I call you?"

"Sprig is fine. At least I'm used to it anyway. I really do need to talk to the Baron, Kate. It is a matter of great importance to me," he said pleadingly.

"Not tonight, Sprig," Kate said, letting the name roll of her tongue. "I think I like Almondo better," she concluded, trying to keep the mood light.

"I hope it can wait until morning," Sprig said watching the sun drop below the horizon.

"Let me work on him tonight. He will give you better audience tomorrow," she said, entering the stable. "I suggest you sleep in the loft. It will be warmer up there and dryer. I will bring some linen sheets and something for you to eat. There are empty stalls on the end for you to bed your horse. I'm sorry that we have no one here to take care of your horse, but it is near curfew, and the other servants are indoors for the night," she informed him, waiting for some questions.

"Thank you. You've been very kind to me. Is there anything I can do to repay your hospitality?" Sprig questioned.

"Just stay out of Papa's hair until tomorrow," Kate said with a smile. She gently squeezed Sprig's hand and turned from the stable. "Make yourself comfortable. I'll be back shortly." Sprig smiled and nodded. Kate ducked out the door and returned to the cottage. Sprig removed the saddle and harness from the horse and led it to an empty stall, latching the door behind it. Sprig dipped into a barrel of oats and scooped out a bucket for his horse.

When his horse was fed and prepared for the night, Sprig stretched his tired frame and dropped to a relatively dry spot of straw. He closed his eyes, taking in all the sounds surrounding him. A clinking sound could be heard from somewhere near. Sprig figured it was the smith hammering on some last-minute work. He heard the creak of the barn door and the rustle of straw. Sprig pulled himself to a sitting position and waited for the returning Kate. She rounded the stalls carrying a wicker basket and a bundle of linen under her arm.

Sprig stood and removed his hat, dropping it to the straw pile next to him. Kate sat the basket down and spread the linen on the ground. She motioned Sprig to sit, and she placed the basket on the center of the sheet. "Is it all right to join you?" she asked.

"Of course. You're very welcome," Sprig said, smiling broadly, truly glad of the company. Kate sat, and spread colored linens, some utensils, and a plate. Sprig saw the solitary dish. "Won't you be eating?" he asked.

She smiled and said, "Father and I have already eaten. I was on my way to toss this food out to the farm animals when you showed. Lucky for you it doesn't have to go to waste." She scooped out the beef and potatoes onto his plate and handed it to him. He accepted gratefully and began eating. Kate removed a wine flask from the basket and poured two cups. She handed one to Sprig, who pulled a quick draw. His face wrinkled into a grimace. Kate frowned.

"I'm sorry, Kate. I've never been one for spirits. It takes a moment getting used to it." He sipped the wine cautiously once more without making a face. Kate smiled at his pretended delight.

"We grow and bottle our own label here. My father drinks no other," she said with her smile slipping from her face. Sprig saw the reaction and stopped in mid-chew.

"Are you all right?" he asked. She searched his face and then lowered her eyes. Her voice took on an edge of melancholy.

"It's this business with the Undead beings. I fear it is killing him. Father's personal quest to rid this place of those foul creatures has turned against him. Did you know the Magistrate declared my father's title forfeit?" she questioned.

"Yes, I was there when it happened. He nearly killed the priest and the Magistrate. Jorth stopped him from doing so." Sprig choked on the words, mentioning Jorth. Kate could see the pain in his eyes.

"A messenger said that some of the Undead Slayers were killed last night. Was he among them?" she asked, barely above a whisper.

"Yes, he and Simil. They were my guardians."

"What about your family? Do you have any nearby?" Kate asked. Sprig was silent.

"My village was destroyed when I was just a kid. A raiding party of brigands killed everyone but me. Jorth found me several days later. He sent his soldiers to follow the raider's tracks to their campsite. They found the raiders nearly a week later, and he had them all hanged." Sprig stopped, remembering the ordeal. Kate sat quietly, watching the emotions play out on Sprig's face. He looked up at her with renewed determination. "Those undead bastards killed my mentors! I want the Baron to help me find them and destroy them!" he said through gritted teeth. "Please, talk to him. I'll do anything he asks." Kate was silent, digesting what she had learned. "Please," Sprig pleaded. Kate nodded.

"I'll talk to him," she promised.

"Katie! It's past curfew. Get yourself inside," Keltch's voice boomed from the cottage.

"I have to go. Take the sheets to the loft and make yourself a bed. Leave the dishes here with the basket and I'll retrieve them in the morning." Sprig stood and helped her up. She smiled and walked out the barn doors. Sprig shook the linen sheet and folded it up, tucking it under an arm. He watched her go and stood for many moments after he lost sight of her. He sighed deeply, grabbed his pack, and climbed the ladder to the loft.

The straw was dryer up there and Sprig spread the sheet out and unrolled a blanket from his pack. He removed his riding boots and placed them together near his belongings. He pulled his bandoleer from over his shoulder and dropped it on the sheet. He curled up under the blanket, wrapping his hand around the bandoleer. The conversation with Kate rolled around in his head. She was a lovely vision of a woman and like no other he had met. The day's ride had taken its toll, and Sprig sighed, letting his weary body relax. His thoughts raced and eventually calmed as they drifted back to the day Jorth had found him.

Sprig had been sleeping fitfully in a wagon. Jorth woke him up, giving him some fruit and a hard loaf of bread. "I've sent scouts and trackers ahead to try and locate the men responsible for this massacre. I've given them orders to have every one of them killed for their murderous deeds," Jorth said. Sprig held the uneaten food and watched the warrior.

"You're a soldier?" the boy asked.

"I was. Men still act on my authority. We still keep the peace," Jorth said.

"I want to go with them. I want to be the one who kills them all," Sprig said, his words dripping with malice. The warrior searched the determined child's eyes.

"I know what you are feeling, but it is better this way. By the time we reach the raider's camp, my men will have completed the task at hand," Jorth said. The boy's fierce eyes burned through Jorth. The boy was intent on having vengeance. Jorth patted the boy and said, "Eat, you'll need your strength," then he left the wagon to go about his business. Sprig sat for many moments, and decided to eat the food given to him. He chewed slowly, not tasting the juices of the fruit.

Sprig could feel the wagon lurch and bump on whatever road they were traveling. Eventually the rhythm rocked him back to sleep. The wagon stopped and he awoke from his slumber. Stretching his body, Sprig scooted to the rear of the wagon. He poked his head out of the hanging canvas and could see nothing of interest, but he could hear conversations near the front of the line.

Sprig leaped down from the wagon, landing lightly on his feet. He wound his way through the other wagons and horses to where the soldiers were congregated. Sprig saw the scouts reporting to Jorth. Smoke was billowing in the background. Sprig circumvented the mass of people and crept into the burning camp, stopping dead in his tracks. The trees were filled with swinging bodies. Sprig counted the bodies; fifteen men were strung up with coarse ropes. The spectacle reminded him of a marionette show he had seen in a traveling sideshow that passed through his village. He looked each one in the face and the horror of what happened to these men did not affect him. He only snickered at the swinging bodies, knowing they deserved a fate far worse.

Jorth saw the boy staring at the dead men. Sprig looked over his shoulder at the approaching warrior. "There's your justice, boy. They'll never harm another soul again," Jorth said.

"That's not justice," Sprig countered, "they should have been slowly tortured until they were begging to die. Even then, they should have been left alive for the carrion to feast on." Sprig spat on the ground. Jorth placed his balled fists on his hips, and an angry expression formed on his face.

"Justice has been done. It may not be as fitting as you would like to see, but it has been done in a mannerly fashion," Jorth said.

"Those bastards didn't deserve a merciful death. You should have let me do it!" The boy hollered. The warrior's face softened a bit.

"Son, you would never be able to live with yourself if you would have done it," Jorth said.

"Well I guess I'll never know now, will I? Where are the women they took?" Sprig yelled. The warrior rubbed his bearded chin.

"The missing girls were found violated and murdered near the raiders' camp. They have already been buried," Jorth answered. Both stood, staring intently at each other. Some of the anger left

Sprig, and his shoulders slumped. Jorth reached out and pulled him close.

"What am I going to do?" the boy said between sobs. "Everyone is gone." Jorth held him closer.

"I'll not leave you to the wolves, Sprig," the warrior said.

"My name is Almondo," the boy said, but Jorth could not hear through the sobs.

* * *

Sprig opened his eyes and squinted at the early morning light filtering through the cracks in the boards of the stable wall. He stretched and yawned groggily, scratching his chest. His hand brushed something just over his head. His mouth froze open, and he scurried back against the loft's wall. Two decapitated heads were dangling over the spot where he was sleeping; they were Jorth and Simil's heads. Horror and shock washed over Sprig, followed by anger. He realized he had pulled out his daggers reflexively. He took a quick look around the loft, but saw no one.

Sprig stood, slowly rising against the wall and slipped his boots on. The heads were tied together by each other's hair, and then tied to a rope. Sprig inched forward, waiting for the heads to speak or worse, attack. They both swayed in the morning breeze. He reached above the heads and pulled the rope toward himself. He carefully cut the rope and held the heads at arm's length.

Sprig could see that Jorth's head had been ripped away from its body by claws. Tears filled his eyes and he began to cry. "Bastards!" He moved to the ladder, holding the head before him. He worked his way down the ladder and went to the stall where his horse was stabled.

Unbuckling the satchel attached to his saddle, he pulled a large sack from it. He dropped the heads in the sack and exhaled, not realizing he had been holding his breath. Tears streamed down his cheeks. He tied the end of the sack in a large knot and bounded for the stable door.

The sun was filling the sky with early morning light as Sprig slammed the stable door open. He wiped the tears from his eyes on his sleeve and walked with determination toward the cottage. A shout from an incoming rider broke his stride. He watched the man leap from the horse and run to the cottage door and pounded on it. Keltch opened the door with sword in hand. Sprig ran to the men exchanging words.

"Are you sure it was him?" Keltch was saying.

"Yes, sir. He appeared out of nowhere on the trail nearly scaring my horse to death. He just stood there watching me. I saw his hand reach into the folds of his cloak and he bade me to come closer. I was frozen, but I saw myself getting off the horse and approaching him. He handed this scroll to me and said to give it to you." Keltch leaned the sword against the wall and grabbed the scroll being extended from Mengrig's hand.

Keltch stared at the seal on the wax and then broke the seal and slowly unraveled the parchment, eyeing it cautiously. Kate appeared in the doorway wearing a robe.

"What is it, Papa?" she said. Keltch read the message and then re-read it again.

Sprig cleared his throat. His eyes were red and swollen, and he was carrying a sack. Keltch hardly noticed him. Kate left the entryway with concern in her eyes. "Are you okay, Sprig? You look like you've seen a ghost," she said walking up to him.

"Baron," Sprig said with his throat clenching, "they were here last night." Tears again filled his eyes.

"What happened?" Kate said, wiping his eyes with her own hand. Sprig held the sack away from his body, and tossed it to the ground in front of Keltch. Keltch saw the bag but made no move to touch it. Mengrig picked up the sack, untied the knot, and looked in it. His face drained of color. He looked at the youth and then at the Baron. Keltch rolled the parchment and held it in one hand.

"What's in the bag, lad?" Keltch quietly inquired staring at the upset youth.

"The heads of my mentors, Sir," Sprig choked on the reply and new tears filled his eyes at the admission. "They were buried yesterday in a graveyard near the church in the village. I found their heads hanging above me this morning." Kate squeezed his hand reassuringly. A fierce look took hold of the youth's face. "Help me kill them, Baron! Help me end this nightmare! I'm only one man and I need your help. I will swear loyalty to you and do any menial task you tell me to, but just help me! Please!" Sprig pleaded.

Keltch surveyed the youth and found that he was seeing his own past reflected. The situation was not unlike when he found out his own father had been killed by Flange. Kate stood near the youth, still holding his hand. Keltch looked at his daughter.

"Katie, have the servants draw up a bath for the lad," Keltch said in a gentle voice. Kate led Sprig into the cottage. "Mengrig, get some sleep. Around the noon hour, I want you to take a cart with a team and three other men to the village. Find out where the bodies of these two men are, and bring them back here for burial," he ordered.

"What about the message, Sir? What does it say? Mengrig asked. Keltch unrolled the parchment and read the message again. It had not changed any in the last few minutes. It was a moment before he could speak.

"It's a message from Flange and he is proposing a truce. He wants to meet," Keltch spoke as if in a trance.

"Do you think it's a trick, my lord?" Mengrig asked. Keltch shook his head.

"He delivered it to you personally, so I don't think so. That's not his way," Keltch said in defense.

"What if it is a trick?" Mengrig persisted. Keltch smiled.

"Well then, I'll take the Stake with me for protection," Keltch said with a wink. He patted the soldier on the shoulder. "Get some sleep, man. You've got a lot to do today." Mengrig nodded and left with the grisly contents. Keltch rolled the parchment and tucked it in his belt. He picked up his sword and entered his cottage, closing the door gently behind him.

* * *

Sprig had bathed and was given some loose-fitting clothes while his were being laundered. Keltch had summoned him after he had eaten his fill of fried eggs and salted ham. Sprig felt uncomfortable sitting across from the large man who was so much like Jorth, yet different. Keltch thumbed the rolled scroll on the table. "Can you read, lad?" Keltch said. Sprig searched the man's eyes, looking for something he did not find.

"Yes, I can read," Sprig snapped.

"I thought so. You have the look of smarts about you," Keltch said, rubbing his bearded chin, much like Jorth would when he was thinking. Sprig scanned the contents and looked up at the Baron.

"Do you believe him?" Sprig asked. Keltch shrugged.

"I think I can actually say yes. He has no reason to lie to me. He could have killed Mengrig, but didn't," Keltch said.

"But why? Why would he want a truce with you if you two are having a war?" Sprig wondered.

"I don't know, lad. What I do know is that he is different from his siblings," Keltch explained.

"You almost sound like you respect him," Sprig said.

The Baron grew silent watching the youth, and then he said, "I suppose I do. It would be a great mistake not to respect an enemy. I hate Flange for killing my father and my followers. But I do respect him. I have never heard of him taking the life of someone who was not searching for his own. In truth, I have sent those men to their deaths because of my crusade against him," Keltch said, as the truth of the matter sank in. He watched the boy, who was hanging on his every word. "I'm sorry for you loss, lad. I wish things could be different for you," Keltch consoled.

"I'll manage," Sprig said indifferently. "What do you plan to do?" Keltch leaned back in his chair.

"I'm going to find out his terms," Keltch said.

"I'm going with you then," Sprig said. Keltch saw the hungry look in his eyes.

"I'm to understand that the she-bitch and the tentacled one are the ones responsible for the death of your guardians?" Keltch asked.

"Yes, I didn't see any of the others," Sprig said, wondering about his point.

"Flange was not responsible," Keltch said.

"So? He's one of them. He has killed your men and will probably continue to do so," Sprig said, just short of anger.

"Listen to me, lad, I am going to meet him tonight, and I am taking you with me. But I want no tricks out of you. This is a parlay only. Make no move to attack him and he will do nothing to us. Do you understand?" Keltch questioned. Sprig reluctantly nodded his head.

"Yes, sir," Sprig said. Keltch did not like the look in the boy's eyes.

"Swear it, lad," Keltch said evenly. Sprig stared at him. "I know you know what honor is, boy, now swear it," Keltch demanded.

"I swear. By all that's still holy, I swear it," Sprig said in resignation, knowing he would honor his word.

"Good, lad," Keltch said with a slight grin. Kate entered the study carrying some folded clothes.

"Your clothes are dry, Almondo," Kate said. Keltch stared at the youth.

"Almondo?" Keltch said, raising his eyebrows. Sprig was not sure if it was the look on the Baron's face that made him blush or the fact that Kate was holding his clean underpants.

"Sprig. My name is Sprig," he said jumping up from his chair and grabbing his clean garments. "I'm going to go change. Thank you for the cleaning," he said, bolting up the stairs to an empty room. Kate and her father exchanged glances. Both smiled.

"I like him," Keltch said, "even if he is a Stake." Kate leaned over and kissed his balding pate.

"He's a nice boy," Kate said, smiling cheerfully.

"That 'boy' is probably older than you are, Katie," Keltch said.

"Yes, Father, but he is still a boy," she said leaving the room, but not before giving a smile that made Keltch very uneasy. He knew she liked the boy too, but hoped she didn't like him too much. Keltch threw his hands in the air, and then unrolled the parchment once more. He would have to tackle one problem at a time.

* * *

Sprig checked his saddled horse. The stable hands were grooming his mount as he checked the saddle and harness to make sure they were secure. After completing that particular inspection, he then checked his horse's shoes. Keltch watched the meticulous care the youth took preparing for the ride. Sprig buckled his satchels after placing some supplies in them.

Kate strolled into the stable with the same basket Sprig had seen the night before. Her disposition brought a smile to his face and Kate reacted in kind. The Baron did not miss the exchange, and he frowned. His look went unnoticed by the two who eagerly watched each other.

Mengrig rode into the stable and dismounted his horse. The stable hands grabbed the sweating beast and walked it around the corral, cooling it down. A look of concern clouded his face.

"Are you sure you want to do it this way, my lord?" Mengrig asked. Keltch looked up from checking his own horse.

"It is what he asked for," Keltch said, cinching the saddle a notch tighter.

"What if it is a trap? I could have the men follow you at a distance, ready to aid if necessary," Mengrig said, knowing the Baron's mind was set. Keltch smiled and grabbed his friend's shoulder.

"We'll be fine," he said looking over at Sprig, "besides, I've got the Stake with me, and he could take them all on by himself." The couple stood together, still smiling at each other oblivious to the conversation. A sour look crossed Keltch's face. In a grumbling voice he said, "Or I'll use him for bait, then cut and run." The two were so caught up in each other that the threat skipped right off them. Keltch shook his head. Mengrig did his best to hide his smirk.

Keltch climbed up onto his horse and said, "Keep your wits about you, boy. You're going to need them. "We're off, Katie. I'll be back before dawn."

"Don't you mean both of you will be back by dawn?" she questioned with mock surprise.

"That remains to be seen," Keltch threw a look of distaste Sprig's way. Sprig sort of half smiled, unsure how to react. Kate produced Sprig's hat from behind her back. Sprig had been looking for it earlier that afternoon. He had left it sitting in the guest room that was given to him, and it disappeared shortly after. He figured it was possible a servant took it to have it cleaned or even burned. A ring of woven pastel-colored flowers circled the brim of the hat. Kate placed it gingerly on Sprig's head. The youth was at a loss for words but managed a quiet, "Thank you."

"Hold the fort, Mengrig," Keltch said, gently kicking his mount, and it marched through the open stable door. Sprig grabbed the reins, put a foot in the stirrups, and mounted his horse. He removed his hat long enough to give a sweeping bow, then placed it back atop his head, smiling. He kicked the horse's flanks and caught up with the Baron, who was loping toward the woods. Kate waved and called to them, wishing good luck.

The sky was becoming overcast as the duo entered the trail into the thickening woods. Sprig could catch a glimpse of figures moving through the trees. "We're being followed," he said quietly. Keltch nodded.

"My men will tail us through the woods, even though I told them not to. They are extremely loyal. But they also know that if I get a look at any of them, that there will be hell to pay. They'll stay just outside of where we can see them. If they know what's good for them, they will stay in the woods when we clear them." Keltch stared at the ridiculous garland of flowers resting on Sprig's head. "My daughter has it in for you, lad. Brigands could spot that colorful bouquet miles away." Sprig removed the garland from his hat and hung the circlet from the saddle horn.

Keltch smelled the air and said, "It's going to rain soon." Thunder rumbled off in the distance, as if answering his suspicions. Droplets of rain started to fall on the canopy of leaves. The riders occasionally felt some of the drops, but the dense canopy of leaves diverted most of the precipitation off of them. However, the ground was beginning to soften under the pooling puddles and the men slowed their horses. Thunder rolled across the sky, ever increasing in volume, and the rain began falling harder.

The saturated tree limbs, heavy with their watery contents, started pounding down on the riders in a steady flow. Sprig stopped his horse and dismounted. He fumbled with the clasp on his saddlebag and removed a black oilcloth cloak. He secured the clasp around his neck and pulled the full hood up over his floppy hat. Keltch also stopped to put on a watertight cloak.

Both men mounted their horses and continued along the trail. The steady rain continued to fall, occasionally drenching the men in open areas in the canopy of leaves. Thunder rumbled overhead and flashes of lightning streaked above the treetops.

"I don't like the looks of this storm, lad," Keltch said, pulling his mount to a stop. He eyed the air around him. "This is not a spring storm that will pass in a couple of hours. We may be in for this all night," Sprig nodded. The sky was already darkening, not only from the clouds, but also with the setting of the sun.

"Will he show in this weather?" Sprig hollered through the noise of the pounding rain.

"This is nothing that would affect him. I wonder if he even notices it," Keltch wondered, shrugging his shoulders and stroking his wet beard. "My concern is whether we will make it to the agreed place on time. When we hit the clearing, we're going to have to deal with the mud and it will slow us down considerably."

The sun was disappearing unseen behind the canopy. Flashes of lightning scorched the air over the riders. The thunder that followed nearly burst Sprig's eardrums. Rustling branches swayed overhead as the winds increased. Ground strikes of lightning burned orange where they splintered trees in the surrounding woods, but the subsequent rain doused the flames.

Sprig's horse panicked and tried to run, after a near miss of a bolt of lightning and blast of rumbling thunder. He yanked the reins and tried to steady his mount. He leaned over and stroked the horse's head, reassuring it with soft whispers that he doubted the animal could hear above the surrounding noise. The beast calmed itself and held its ground.

The wind roared through the trees, and falling branches and leaves swished past the riders crashing to the ground. Sprig heard the Baron yell something, but the wind swallowed his words. Sprig maneuvered his mount nearer the Baron. "What?" he yelled.

"I said, we will be coming out of the woods soon, and it is not going to be pretty. If you knew the area better, I would send you back to the cottage," Keltch yelled.

"I can handle it. Besides, I know you don't want me alone with your daughter," Sprig said in good humor.

"Katie can handle the likes of a Stake like you. And besides, I would make you sleep in the stable with only your mare to keep you company," Keltch returned, keeping up the good banter. Sprig laughed and steered his mount around a fallen limb.

The trees were thinning and the rain continued to drench the riders as patches of the gray sky were exposed. Fog spread around the trees obscuring the trail, and soon Sprig lost perspective and was unsure of the path. Keltch seemed to know exactly where he was, or at least gave the illusion that he did.

The only way Sprig knew that he had reached the clearing was from the increased rain that pelted him, and he was actually able to see the bolts of lightning that arched across the sky.

Sprig inched his mount nearer to the Baron's and yelled, "How much further?"

"About seven miles or so," Keltch hollered over the rumbling echo of the thunder. Sprig could feel his horse's hooves sink into the mud, and the effort it was taking to pull them out. The ungainly movements of his horse jerked him around in the saddle. The terrain did not seem to bother Keltch's monstrosity of a war-horse. In fact, the horse seemed to relish the addition of exercise. Sprig wished his own mount welcomed the task of trudging through the boggy ground. He could tell that his horse was getting tired and skittish in the angry storm.

Sprig lost himself in thought while his mount picked its way carefully across the exposed roots and slippery vegetation. He lurched in the saddle and grabbed for the saddle horn as his horse tripped in the mud. The horse tried to correct itself but staggered, spilling Sprig on the ground.

"Damn it!" Sprig cursed. He was covered in brown muck, still holding his reins, and tried to stand, only to fall back on his rear. His horse jerked as thunder clapped overhead, and it tried to run. Sprig hung onto the reins and was dragged across the ground. Keltch could hear that Sprig was cursing but the wind drowned out the blasphemy.

Sprig slid across the ground and his foot caught on an exposed root. The horse continued its canter, and Sprig was raised from the ground and stretched between the fleeing horse and the snaring root. His muscles pulled and his limbs stretched. The horse reared to a halt and stepped back a few paces. Sprig plopped face first into the mud. Keltch was glad that the activity of the storm masked his eruption of laughter. He would have been embarrassed if positions were reversed, and had no intention of rubbing the boy's face any further in the folly. After all, he was already covered in mud.

Sprig pulled himself up and stood holding onto the saddle horn. Keltch watched the lighting-illuminated boy throw a slime-covered leg over his saddle, and climb aboard the startled horse. If the boy was embarrassed, Keltch could not tell in the harsh lightning that disappeared just as quickly as it flashed across the sky. Both men continued cautiously along the trail before entering a less-wooded area.

Keltch reined in his horse and cantered up next to the mud-covered boy, "Flange said there is another clearing past these trees with several fallen tree trunks." Keltch yelled over the wind.

"I hope there is some shelter or some place we can hold a conversation," Sprig yelled in reply.

"Listen, lad. I want you to keep quiet and pay attention to our surroundings. I'll deal with Flange," Keltch shouted.

"Do you think Flange has an ulterior motive for this meeting?" Sprig hollered.

"There is always an ulterior motive with anyone. You may believe that he is going to betray us, but I don't think so. I'm actually more concerned about his siblings. They might want to crash the party, you never know," Keltch yelled. Sprig dropped his hood back and removed his hat. He let the cold rain rinse the filthy mud from his face, and he wiped his sleeve across his face, using it as a squeegee to get rid of the grime. He replaced his drenched hat, and pulled the hood of the cloak back over his soaked head.

Sprig scanned the trail, watching for the landmarks the Baron had mentioned. The trees continued to thin and the fog thickened, completely obscuring the ground. Keltch pulled his horse to a halt. "We best walk it from here, lad. The meeting spot is not far ahead, and I don't want a lame horse," Keltch yelled to be heard and then dismounted.

Sprig carefully slipped from the saddle and tested his footing before putting his weight on his legs. He wrapped the reins around his fist and led the horse next to the Baron's own. "The clearing is just on the other side of those trees. Keep your wits, because if there is going to be an ambush, it will happen soon enough."

Sprig reached into his cloak, pulling a dagger from his bandoleer, and tucked it into his sleeve with the handle jutting out. He was not sure if it would do any good against the undead Flange, but it seemed to hurt the she-beast, Sasha. He watched the wary Baron throw his cloak off his right shoulder, freeing up his sword arm. Keltch held the reins in his left hand while his right rested on the pommel of his sword hilt. Keltch radiated confidence and self-assuredness and Sprig wished he felt the same, but uneasiness crept over him and the stormy weather added to the restless feelings.

The turbulent wind tossed the tree branches in a chaotic display. Lightning, streaking across the sky, gave trees the appearance of threatening sentinels guarding the path. Sprig shivered, unsure if it was the cold from the wet or the fear that was welling up inside of him.

A streak of lightning struck a nearby tree, and a fire started that was quickly extinguished by the pouring rain. The sparse trees ended in a clearing made up of felled trees. Sprig could tell by the description that this was the meeting spot, but he saw no one. "What do we do now?" he yelled over the howling wind. Keltch surveyed the clearing.

"Tie your horse to that sapling, and then we wait for the bastard to show." Sprig did as he was told and secured his reins around a trunk. He whispered soothing words to his horse, trying to calm the already frightened beast. He patted the horse's cheek and offered it an apple that he produced from a saddlebag. The horse snatched it gratefully. Keltch tied his mount to a branch and then patrolled the perimeter. Both men stood together when he finished the task.

Another flash of lightning washed out the Baron's features and the thunderclap pierced both their ears. Sprig's horse pulled at the reins trying to bolt, but was held fast by the sapling. "I don't know how much of this my horse can take," Sprig shouted. Keltch nodded in understanding and continued to watch the surroundings.

The intermittent flashes of lightning illuminated the fallen trunks. A shadow lengthened during a particular strike on the other side of a group of fallen trunks. Sprig placed his left hand on the handle of his partially concealed dagger in his right sleeve. A figure stood silhouetted against the intermittent change between the darkness and the temporary illumination from the lighting—a figure blacker than the night.

A voice from deep inside of Sprig screamed to turn and run for his life. He held the voice in check by being unable to move at all. The sight before him in itself was not terrifying, but the power of its presence filled him with foreboding. The Baron moved cautiously forward to the waiting figure, crossing his arms over his chest in the gesture of "no arms will be used." The menacing figure watched as the Baron crept forward.

"I'm glad that you made it, Baron, regardless of the weather," Flange said when the Baron was standing in front of him. "I am sorry for dragging you out on such a night. If I would have known that the evening would turn so sour, I would have asked you for another time," Flange said in a rather polite voice that could be heard above the storm.

"Makes no difference to me, Flange. What do you propose?" Keltch said rather loudly to be heard over the wind.

"Baron, you may speak at a whisper. I will be able to hear you," Flange said.

"It figures," Keltch muttered under his voice. A smile spread across the handsome face of the Undead man.

"I heard that, Baron," Flange said with his smile spreading further. The Baron tried to hide his uneasiness.

"What do you want, Flange? Do you really want a truce? And if so, why?" the Baron questioned, speaking just under his breath. The smile disappeared from Flange's face.

"I wish a truce, Baron, because I no longer wish to fight you. Our game ends tonight," Flange said resolutely.

"I can't believe that a truce is what you seek. You live for killing. I've seen what you've done to my men," Keltch stated flatly. Flange was silent, watching the Baron. Sprig watched the muted exchange in detached wonderment.

"What do you know about my siblings?" Flange asked.

"They are heartless and cruel and kill without necessity. They've plagued this area for centuries," Keltch replied. Flange shook his drenched milky hair.

"That is not what I mean. What do you know about them personally?" Flange asked.

"Not much. You have been my focus all these years," the Baron declared.

"Only because I killed your father. If I had not, you would have surely vanquished my siblings and Sasha by now."

"Sasha's not your sister?" the Baron questioned.

"No. She was created later."

"By whom?"

"She is Rewella's spawn."

The Baron nodded in understanding. "I understood that the two were your sisters," he said rubbing his bearded chin.

"Almost, but not quite. Sasha isn't even Undead, and I found that out the hard way." Flange said as if reminiscing to himself. The Baron held the moment, waiting for more of a response, but when none was forthcoming, he said, "Why do you want a truce, Flange?" the Baron questioned again. "We've been at war with each other my whole life. You disappeared for a while and now you come back wanting a truce."

"If you knew more about the relationship that I have with my siblings, you would understand the implications. Let me try to explain. When we were created hundreds of years ago, it was apparent that each of us was different. We were created in the image of our selfish desires or at least that is what I believed at the time. We knew that we were different from each other and that we had contrary goals and beliefs.

"We also knew that we were powerful beings and that our ambitions would cause us to cross one another eventually. So, to prevent stepping on each other's toes, we set out to create an understanding that would be beneficial to each other. We created a pact with guidelines that would never be crossed. It seemed to work until recently.

"Rewella's ambitions overstepped those bounds created so many centuries ago. In a nutshell, things have changed because Rewella broke the agreement by ordering Sasha to ransack my lair. The final nail in the coffin, so to speak, was Barcus raising my kills. That part of the agreement is what I held as being most sacred, and because of that violation, I am no longer bound to abide by any of the agreements that we set up so long ago. That includes protecting them and their secrets," Flange finished.

"If that is the case, you are only calling a truce only to satisfy revenge on your siblings and their lack of honor," the Baron stated flatly.

"That may be true to an extent, but I have other reasons for a truce with you, Baron. I will help you end this rule of darkness from my siblings," Flange said, and a look of hopefulness filled him.

"Why now?" Keltch prodded, not really convinced. "After all these years of killing, why now?" Keltch took a step closer to Flange. A smile crept to the corner of Flange's thin-lipped mouth. *Now here is a man who is so blinded by his hatred of me that he is completely unafraid,* Flange thought. "Tell me why I should not kill you now?" Keltch said in a deadly tone.

A brief flash of lightning illuminated the stark features on the Baron's face that almost sent a chill up Flange's spine—almost. Flange's slight smile slipped as he considered his answer.

"To tell you that I am sorry for killing your father would be an outright lie. Next to you, he was the best hunter I have ever seen. His valiant effort to eradicate us made the game all that more fun."

The Baron's face twisted into a scowl of fury, only enhanced by the blinding forks of lightning.

"Answer my question," the Baron whispered. Flange watched with cold, amused eyes.

"Yes, all of this was a game to me. However, my perspective has been altered, and I may have found a way out of this situation for both of us. There are powers at work that even I cannot completely comprehend, but they are possibly the keys to ending our conflict," Flange offered. Keltch listened in silence. "A rift has formed between my brother and sister that is far from simple sibling rivalry."

"It was my understanding that you and your siblings staked out territories to keep from tripping over each other," Keltch said.

"Yes, that is true to some extent. But we each have our own agendas, and the means to carry them out. The one common goal is a race to unlock the secrets of Haven."

"Haven? What is Haven?" Keltch said, squeezing the water from his drenched beard.

"It is a place of great power. One of the unseen forces that has lent a hand in the creation of the Undead in this area." Keltch frowned at this puzzling prospect and ventured another question, "You mean this place is responsible for your creation?"

"Not exactly, but it does respond to our kind. I don't think its original purpose was intended for our use to begin with. I spent the last century trying to unlock its most complicated secrets. Some of those secrets are rather elementary but they always lead to more enormous questions.

"I have always thought that Haven was a place that was more than an instrument or a tool with which with to work. I have realized that it could actually be an entity of a sort, and that led me away on a search to seek the truth," Flange said, seeing Keltch turn the implication over in his mind.

Keltch noticed the pause and said, "So you have found out some information about Haven that changes your views on life? That changes nothing in my eyes. You're still the murderer of my father and of countless others. I don't give a damn about your Haven or what you can do with it. Now tell me why you want a truce? Are you worried your siblings are going to find out your little secret and they're going to become vindictive? Are you worried about having to fight too many fronts?"

Flange was silent. The tension had built between the two men and the Baron's hand strayed nearer his sword hilt. If Flange noticed the gesture, he did nothing to react to it. Flange dropped his shoulders in what looked like a sigh and broke his gaze with Keltch. He looked back to the expectant Baron. "Perhaps what I seek is a sort of redemption. I have a plan to rectify some of my actions, but I have no idea if it will even work. I need to start somewhere, and I wish to start by making peace with you. I can't alter what has happened in the past, but I can have an effect on the future. I no longer view you as an enemy. In fact, I never actually did. You were an amusement that helped me tolerate this dreary existence."

"Am I supposed to show you some type of gratitude for the honor of being a pawn in your amusement?" Keltch questioned sourly.

"No. I am not trying to be callous, Baron. I am trying to make you understand that I want out of this predicament. I wish to end this feud between us," Flange stated.

"If you're looking for forgiveness from me, you will never get it. Tell me this, how long have you had this realization? Was it before or after you returned and killed my men?" Keltch snarled. Both men stood drenched in the pouring rain watching each other in silence that followed. Flange broke that silence.

"It was your words that changed my outlook on the situation in addition to the actions of my siblings. Now I choose a different path and I want your understanding even if I can't have your forgiveness."

Keltch could not believe his ears. His childhood nemesis wanted a truce. The implications sent his head reeling. To have an end to the fighting even if it was not the end to his hatred of this murderous creature. This was not only a way out for Flange, but also a way out for himself. This was all too much, but how could he refuse? His reverie broke with new questions.

"What about your siblings? Are you offering your help to rid the land of them?"

"Yes, to an extent. If I can avoid direct contact with them, I would prefer it. They will find out about the truce, but not right away. If you agree, I can give you secrets of their strengths and weaknesses. I have too many preparations to make to be involved directly in a conflict with them," Flange said.

"Before I agree to anything, I want to see this Haven for myself," Keltch whispered.

"I'm not sure if that is even possible. I've never known of a mortal entering Haven before." Flange knew this to be somewhat of a lie, but he had never personally brought anyone to Haven other than Sasha. He had always believed she could come and go as she pleased.

"It is the only way you will get my cooperation in this venture. I want to see it for myself," Keltch said firmly. Flange nodded reluctantly.

"I'll see what can be done. I'll need some time to research. Give me two nights. Perhaps then the weather will be more permitting."

"Agreed," Keltch said, nodding his head. "Where do we meet?"

"A league from here is another clearing. The meadow is filled with an enormous ring of mushrooms. I will be waiting there for you at noon," Flange said.

"During the daylight?" the Baron questioned.

"Yes. it will be the safest time to go. Consider it a token of my pledge," Flange said and smiled with a lopsided grin that enhanced the handsome features of his face.

"And the boy?" Keltch said, jerking his thumb over his shoulder in the general direction of the waiting youth. Flange eyed the patient youth in his ridiculous floppy hat with its soggy drooping plumage.

"He is more than welcome to accompany you. However, he may not be able to enter Haven." The look from the Baron caused Flange to add, "You may not be able to enter Haven either, that remains to be seen. Nonetheless, bring him along. Consider it another token." Again Flange displayed his alluring smile. A chill crept across the back of the Baron's neck at the easiness of the display. The only other time he had seen Flange smile like that was when he was knee-deep in bodies, hacking people to pieces. He did not like the feeling that was left with him.

Sprig watched the quiet exchange, unable to hear what was being said. He wondered about the conversation and wondered even more when Keltch motioned in his direction. The creature's eyes locked with his causing his fear to be doubled. It was as if this being could see into his heart, even into his very soul. A shiver, not related to the cold rain, raced down his spine. The creature released his grip, when his gaze was averted, back to the speaking Baron. Sprig could not imagine how Keltch could tolerate the presence of such a being; let along hold a conversation with it.

Sprig wiped a drenched sleeve across his face. The exchange ended and the Baron did an about-face in the mud and strode toward the waiting youth. The creature seemed to fade into the mud, disappearing from view. Sprig had to convince himself that he had even seen the Undead man, for as quick as it vanished.

A flash of lightning temporarily blinded the young man, and when his vision returned, the Baron stood in front of him. "How did it go?" Sprig shouted over the pounding of the rain on the leaves and branches.

"It looks like we might have a truce," the Baron said almost inaudibly.

"What?" Sprig shouted. Keltch realized that he was no longer speaking to Flange and had to raise his voice to be heard.

"I said, we might have a truce, boy," Keltch barked, "Get the horses, lad. This rain is bad for my joints, and I long for a cozy fire and a mug of spiced brew." Sprig nodded and worked his way across the slippery ground to where the horses were tied. The Baron followed slowly behind the youth, careful not to slip.

Keltch looked over his shoulder where the Undead creature had stood and was unsure exactly what to think. Here was the opportunity he had hoped for, and it seemed too good to be true because the truce was not on his own terms. After all, he had always wanted to slay the creature for killing his father. Looking back on all of those who had died in his service fighting against Flange made him no different than a murderer. He was tired of the chase and the responsibility that came with it. It could all be over soon enough, and he had no doubt the Flange would keep his end of the bargain. That perhaps was Flange's most admirable trait in the eyes of the Baron; Flange was honor bound.

Sprig untangled the reins and led the war-horse to the Baron, who mounted the mighty beast. Sprig fumbled with the slippery stirrup and pulled himself onto the saddle. The Baron spurred his horse down the trail. Sprig kicked his mount and hurried to catch up, not wanting to be left behind in the dank woods.

The rain slowed as the duo entered a dense portion of the woods, and both men rode in silence. The fog thickened as a light mist shrouded the surroundings. Sprig could not make heads or tails of the locale. He began to question where they were. "How do you know where you are going in this mist?" Sprig asked. Keltch looked over at the wondering youth.

"You see that tree? Is there any moss on it?" Keltch said, pointing. Sprig steered his mount toward the tree. He stared at the trunk.

"I don't see any," Sprig said, examining the tree.

"Look on the other side, boy," Keltch said. Sprig leaned over his saddle to look at the other side of the trunk. A strip of moss ran up the tree. He turned around in the saddle toward the Baron.

"I see a strip that runs up the other side. What does it signify?" Sprig asked.

"Moss grows on the north side. That means we are heading in the right direction," Keltch said, matter-of-factly. Sprig eyed him suspiciously, not completely convinced.

"What you say may be fact, I won't dispute that. But how can you see the moss in this fog? I could barely see it right in front of my face," Sprig said.

The Baron laughed, continuing down the trail. When his chuckling subsided, he turned to the dismayed youth and said, "Listen, boy. This old girl knows the way home. It matters not where I am. She'll find the way home. All you have to do is let her take you there." Keltch patted the horse's neck with a gauntleted hand. Sprig knew it had to be something like that and was relieved that the Baron confessed instead of leaving him in the dark.

The rain changed to drizzle and the fog continued to engulf the area. Lingering flashes of lightning bathed the clouds in cobalt blue, but the thunder rolled many miles in the distance. The worst of the storm had passed to ravish lands elsewhere.

Sprig's horse whinnied, skipped a step, and threatened to rear. Keltch's horse also jerked its head back, pulling to a stop. Sprig cooed to his mount, trying to calm it. The fog swirled and a stretched black form leaped across the path before the horses. The creature touched all fours on the path and bound from the trail disappearing into the thicket of trees.

Sprig heard a "cling" as the Baron's sword cleared the scabbard. Sprig did his best to hold his mount steady with one hand

and drew a dagger with the other. Recognition dawned on him. *That was Sasha!* His mind raced at the prospect of Sasha fulfilling her promise about dealing with him later.

The Baron listened to the echoing silence around him. Sprig's mount eased its unsteadiness. Sprig felt a sharp burning sensation flare on his right hand, and he shook it vigorously, watching a dislodged spider fall into the fog. He sucked on the back of his hand where the reddened whelp had raised as the jolt of pain subsided.

"She's gone. Let's move," Keltch said sheathing his sword. Sprig was not so convinced and held his dagger ready, watching the fog around him. He kicked the horse's flanks and followed the Baron warily.

Sprig's uneasiness stayed with him until the two ran into Keltch's picket of soldiers. Mengrig was the first to materialize from the mist into view. He approached cautiously, continually scanning the shrouded fog that followed the dampened weary duo.

"How'd it go, Baron?" Mengrig said barely above a whisper, falling into step with Keltch as he dismounted and led his horse.

"Good. Almost better than I would have expected," Keltch said and followed it with a spasm of coughing. Concern filled Mengrig's eyes.

"Are you all right, Baron?" Mengrig questioned. The Baron hesitated, and followed the hesitance with a loud sneeze.

"It's this damn damp weather," Keltch explained. Mengrig nodded his head in understanding and grabbed the horse's reins from the Baron.

"I'll put her away for you, Sir," Mengrig said. Keltch mechanically handed over the wet leather straps wrapped around his fist. Keltch was more than willing to put away his own mount, and usually insisted on it, but the ride home had been miserable for the Baron with his aging body stiffening from the cold damp weather. Three more soldiers appeared on the trail approaching the three men.

Sprig was also tired and cramped from the ride. Horses were a luxury where he came from. They either belonged to soldiers or men of wealth. Jorth had given this mount to him as a gift, but he rarely rode it for prolonged amounts of time. He preferred to walk or run. Sprig slid out of the saddle and landed on poorly circulated legs that threatened to give way under the sudden weight. He staggered and flailed his arms, grabbing the saddle horn to keep from falling.

Seeing the display, Mengrig gave a short whistle and the two approaching men grabbed the reins of both horses and hurried toward the stable with mounts in tow. Sprig stretched his arms over his head and heard his vertebrae pop. He limped on his sleeping legs, trying to restore circulation. Removing his damp hat, he wrung the water from it and then snapped it out with a flick of the wrist and replaced it on his soaked head. The limp sides flopped down over his ears and face, but he did not care. He just wanted to get out of this dreary weather and into someplace warm.

The trio cleared the woods and Sprig could see the diffused glow of torches and lanterns, including those in the hazy windows of the cottage. Keltch began removing various articles of clothing in no particular order. Mengrig did his best to catch the garments and belts before they each hit the ground. Sprig noticed absently that the only items on the Baron, as he strode purposely to his cottage, were his trousers, boots, and sword. *The bare necessities,* Sprig thought.

Keltch threw open the wooden door and marched directly up the staircase. Sprig stopped in the entrance and removed his drenched cloak, hanging it on the coat rack near the door. He reluctantly removed his hat and plopped it on the crown of the rack, then kicked his boots off onto the entryway rug.

Sprig felt the polished wood under his palm as he pulled himself up the stairs. His eyes closed and he felt his way to the bedroom door. After a couple of wrong turns, he located the knob and entered his room. A soft embrace enveloped him as he fell forward and landed on the down comforter on the bed. The soft pleasantness of the bed mixed with his dreaming state. A smile worked the corners of his mouth and his face buried deeper in the plush pillow.

Sprig saw himself playing in a field full of wildflowers with insects buzzing lazily from colorful bud to colorful bud. He felt himself floating to his waiting doppelganger and merge, so he was viewing with its eyes. His outstretched hands moved over the cool silky petals, caressing each one he touched. He saw the red raised bump on the back of his hand, and rubbed it absently. He had forgotten about the bite, for it was not bothering him now.

He shrugged and continued to enjoy the beauty of his surroundings. The breeze was cool but the air was comfortable. He closed his eyes and breathed deeply, inhaling the fragrant vapors. Exhaling, he opened his eyes and surveyed the field.

The sun was shining brightly on his face and the flowers danced in a symphony of the wind. He smiled and chuckled out loud. A thought struck him. *I wish Kate were here to enjoy this with me.* As if on that thought, a shapely figure appeared across the field in front of him. He smiled as she walked casually through the knee-high field of wildflowers in his direction.

Sprig quickly picked a colorful bouquet and tied it together with a piece of leather he retrieved from his pocket. He carefully walked through the field, trying to avoid stepping on the flowers, but that was next to impossible. The approaching figure smiled at the gesture of being given a bouquet in the middle of a field of flowers. The couple stopped within inches of one another. Sprig, suddenly embarrassed, averted his eyes following the path of a buzzing bee.

"These are for you," he said reaching out with the bouquet. He dared a quick glimpse at her beautiful eyes and she smiled in response, accepting the flowers. Her fingers caressed his hand as they touched in passing, causing the hairs on his neck to stand on end as a result.

A spider fell out of the bouquet onto the ground. Sprig watched it crawl off to be hidden by some decaying leaves. Another one dropped, and then another one. His smile changed to a slight frown. Kate did not seem to notice and she gazed intently at Sprig, eyes full of love and softness. Sprig returned a smile trying not to let his distraction with the spiders ruin his moment here with Kate.

Another spider dropped to the ground. Sprig frowned and gently pulled the flowers from her grasp. He shook them gently, but no more arachnids fell out. He handed the flowers back to her waiting hand. He smiled as if from some folly.

"What's wrong, Sprig, don't like spiders?" a voice said that was unlike Kate's own. Sprig's smile faltered as ten or twenty more spiders dropped from the bouquet that Kate was holding. Her expression did not change, but the look in her eyes did. No longer were they filled with love, but with calculated malice.

Spring watched as the flowers fell in slow motion from her hands to the ground. The petals were interchanged with spiders.

He took two steps backward and watched the remaining flowers fall and she began to laugh.

Kate's lovely outstretched hands held nothing but spiders that climbed over and fell from her fingers. Her hands began to darken and twist in a misshapen way. Sprig took two more steps, backing away from the specter. The beautiful form that was Kate changed. Her unforgettable face shriveled and crackled, exposing decomposed flesh and bones, but still she laughed.

Panic overtook Sprig and he turned and ran across the field away from the horrific sight. The bright sunshine began to fade as clouds quickly obscured the sky. The field, just moments ago washed in flamboyant colors, was now turned into shades of ashy gray. The petals shrank and fell from the stems as the plants died and crumbled.

Sprig chanced a look over his shoulder to see if he was being pursued. At the center of the field stood the figure. Sprig had cleared enough distance that he could not see the figure clearly anymore, but a black circle spread from where she stood, engulfing the field. Sprig turned back around to focus on where he was heading. Her laughter rang in his ears as though she was right behind him, and this prompted him to run faster even though his heart felt like it would burst.

The incline of the field changed and Sprig struggled to run uphill. He glanced over his shoulder to see the engulfing blackness spiral into a hole that had been Kate's impostor. His legs ached as they pumped, trying to negotiate the incline, but the hill became too steep and he fell. The nightmarish world turned around and around as he rolled down the hill into the waiting blackness.

Sprig's uncontrolled tumble abruptly ended when his flailing form slammed against the stump of a blackened shattered tree. His head reeled and he fought the vertigo threatening to make him sick. He rolled over and clamored to his hands and knees. He shook his head to clear it, and regretted doing so immediately. His arms and legs faltered and he collapsed onto the ground with his face buried in the foul muck that was the ground.

A voice echoed in his ears.

"My turn."

Spring lifted his head and propped his torso off the ground on his elbows. He scanned the darkness around him. The field of flowers was now replaced by a charred blackness engulfed in swirling gray shapes. An overwhelming silence filled his surroundings. Sprig pushed himself into a sitting position, trying to clear his head. His heart raced and he tried to sort his thoughts but was interrupted by a low growling sound somewhere in the obscured surroundings.

A set of red eyes appeared in the fog opposite of Sprig. He was unsure how close it was due to the distorting effects of the mist. He did know, however, that whatever was stepping toward him had to be at least ten feet tall and he scooted on his rear, backing away from the creature.

The glowing eyes were set into a frame darker than the surrounding mist. Sprig searched frantically for anything he could use as a weapon. His hands raked across the grounds, sifting through what felt like ash and broken glass. The creature moved slow enough not to disturb the mist around it. Sprig wondered if the creature was doing it just to relish in his terror.

The creature darkened as the mist let it pass, and a jagged set of fangs stretched into a cruel smile on the demon-eyed beast. Two wispy appendages snaked out from the creature's torso, forming elongated arms ending in massive claws that fanned out through the air.

Sprig stood slowly, in awe of the creature, his fear momentarily forgotten. The creature loomed over him. "This has to be a dream," Sprig said out loud to himself.

"Oh, really," the creature croaked out in a deep guttural response. "What makes you so sure?"

Sprig looked around the swirling scene and then back to the creature that was dwarfing him. "You . . . everything . . . all of this. It's not real. This is some kind of a dream brought on by the miserable weather." Sprig's reasoning did little to diminish the creature's presence even though it stopped and smiled as if amused.

"If this were a dream, would I be able to do this?" The creature roared and slashed its clawed hand across Sprig's chest.

Sprig cried out as fire erupted from his chest where the claws raked him. He threw his body to the ground and rolled, trying to smother the flames that licked at his face. The creature's roar changed into a deep chuckle and its form wavered in the mist because of the display.

Sprig's face scrunched into a grimace, and he wrapped his arms around the wound on his chest. A familiar voice sounded in his ears and his eyes opened against the pain to see the lupine form of Sasha standing over him. "I said I would come back for you. I can't wait to see what you taste like." Spittle and drool hung precariously from her lower jaw as if in anticipation. The image of Sasha devouring Jorth while he still lived flashed back into his mind.

Anger blocked the pain and Sprig forced his injured body to stand before the terror that loomed over him. Sprig cradled his chest and stood to his full height. "Do your worst. Everyone I cared about is already dead, you would only be doing me a favor," Sprig said, trying not to show the fear that he knew was there.

Sprig felt something crawling up his leg and chanced a sidelong glance. Several spiders worked their way up his trouser leg. His leg jerked into a quick spasm flicking the arachnids into the mist. Sprig saw that the ground was moving and all he could see was spiders. The glowing red eyes of Sasha receded into the darkness of swirling mists and disappeared. The spiders continued to crawl up Sprig's body. He flailed his arms, trying to rid himself of the conglomerate spiders that raced up his torso.

The shear weight of the crawling creatures locked his legs in place and a conical shape of spiders formed around Sprig's body as they attempted to engulf him.

"Sprig?" Sprig heard the echo of a muffled voice. He covered his face with his hands as the spiders swarmed his body, covering every inch. "Sprig?" The faint voice said again. Sprig made no attempt to reply because he was doing his best to protect his exposed flesh. "What is wrong with you?" the voice insisted.

The weight of the crawling mass forced the air from his lungs and threatened to crush him. "Wake up, Sprig!" the voice in his head insisted. He felt his body convulse and shake, and the spiders fell away from him. He could feel himself being pulled away by unseen hands, and he surrendered to their fate.

"Sprig! Wake up!" the voice said urgently, and it was no longer just in his head. His body shook and his eyes opened to the lovely vision of Kate hovering over him. Sprig recoiled away from her, believing it was another deception.

Kate's green eyes were filled with concern as she watched Sprig's peculiar display. "You were having a bad dream, that's all." Sprig found that he was in the same bed he had fallen asleep in. A candle on the bedside table lighted the room, and Kate stood near him, holding a damp cloth and wearing a belted robe. She had obviously been awakened by his outbursts.

"Wha—what happened?" Sprig stammered in a disoriented state.

"You were having a bad dream," Kate said in a gentle voice. "You're also running a fever." Recollection dawned on Sprig, and he threw the covers off, jumping from the bed. He doubled over in pain and fell onto the hardwood floor. Kate rushed to his side, sponging his head with the cloth, trying to steady him with her other arm.

"Sasha. She tried to kill me," Sprig said.

"It was just a dream, Sprig," Kate assured. Sprig looked down toward his chest and ripped his shirt open. He ran his fingers across the burning raised bruises that stretched across his chest.

"That was no dream," he said looking up at Kate. She gently pulled his hands away from the wound so she could see it. Four bruises ran about fourteen inches in a diagonal, from right to left, across his chest. She also noticed a blue-black circular mark on the back of his right hand.

"It looks like you have a spider bite," Kate said turning his hand over to get a better look at it.

"Yeah. I had a run-in with a few," Sprig said with a sigh, looking into her curious eyes. "I'm sorry for awakening you," he said, "go back to sleep Kate, I'll be fine." Her skeptical look showed that she did not believe him.

"I'm not sure about that, Sprig. You look really pale. I'll stay with you tonight." Sprig's eyebrows shot up in protest, but the scornful look that Kate sent kept him from protesting the idea.

"Lie down," she commanded. Sprig did so to avoid a confrontation, and she pulled the blankets up over him that he had kicked onto the floor. "Try to get some sleep," she said and caressed his head once more with the damp cloth. She blew out the bedside candle and left the candelabra lit on the opposite wall of the room.

Kate lay on the bed on top of the blankets next to Sprig. Sprig stared at the ceiling, feeling nauseous from the spider bite. He refused to close his eyes for fear that the images would return. Eventually exhaustion took hold and he drifted off in an uneasy slumber comforted by the fact that Kate was near to chase the darkness away.

6

Sprig awoke to the smell of frying eggs and sausage. He raised his head slowly from the pillow and righted himself on the edge of the bed. Sunlight filtered through the bedroom windowpanes, cutting harsh lines on the hardwood floors. Kate pushed the partially closed door open and entered carrying a tray of steaming food.

She smiled at him with an obvious sigh of relief. "It's about time you woke up. I was really starting to worry about you. I couldn't tell what was worse, the dreams you were having or how dead you looked sleeping so soundly," Kate said as she set the tray on the nightstand table, and then sat next to Sprig on the edge of the bed. She placed her palm against his forehead. "Your fever is gone. How do you feel now?" Sprig forced a smile even though he felt as though he had just climbed out from under an avalanche. He stared at the wound on his chest. It did not look any better now then it had some hours ago.

"I'm feeling okay," Sprig lied. Kate smiled reassuringly.

"Eat this and you'll feel better," she said, passing the tray from the table to his lap. Sprig's mouth salivated involuntarily as the vapors reached his nose. He smiled shyly and scooped the eggs into his mouth. "Are they good?" Kate said with a look of concern.

"Wonderful!" Sprig exclaimed between mouthfuls. "I've never tasted better." Kate smiled with relief. Sprig had been used to the bland campfire food of his traveling caravan. *Ah, so this is the food of kings*, Sprig thought to himself. The eggs were spiced and the sausage was sweetened with wine.

"I'm not exactly at my best in the kitchen. Mother used to do most of the cooking before she died. The servants do most of it, now." Sprig stopped chewing and looked into Kate's eyes. A fleeting moment of sadness flickered through them and was gone. Sprig was sure he saw something in that instant.

"I'm sorry," he said unsure what else to say.

Kate patted his arm and smiled, "That was a long time ago. I was only five when she died, and I barely knew her." Sprig stared at Kate's face, trying to separate Keltch's features from her own.

"She must have been very beautiful," Sprig said in a barely audible voice of awe. Kate blushed and looked away from his probing eyes. Sprig averted his gaze from her, suddenly embarrassed by his actions. Kate's eyes fell on the boy before her in amusement. Truth to be known, he was probably about the same age as her and an idea popped into her head.

"Would you like to see a picture of her?" she said in an expectant voice.

"Of course," Sprig swallowed the last bite of food on the plate. "I just need a moment to get dressed." He handed the tray to Kate and she exited the room, closing the door behind her.

Sprig stretched his arms over his head and was feeling much better after eating. A fresh linen shirt was draped over a chair, and he felt foolish when it took him a few minutes to figure out how to button it. He tucked the shirt into his trousers and buckled his belt. His bandoleer hung on the arm of the chair and he flung it over a shoulder and worked his arm and head through the opening. Reaching for his hat that hung on a hook near the door, he dropped the floppy thing onto his head and straightened the bandoleer across his chest. And in doing so, he caught a glimpse of himself in the full-length mirror in the corner of the room.

Sprig laughed at the ridiculous sight. A billowy white shirt covered by worn leather bandoleer filled with knives, wrinkled trousers tucked into unpolished riding boots, and a black oversized hat with mite-infested plumage dangling from it. He was a striking image of the romantic heroes that he had read about in so many books; he looked utterly ridiculous.

Sprig laughed again and tossed the hat on the bed and struggled out of the bandoleer that he hung back over the chair. He quickly made the bed and glanced back into the mirror. *More like it*, he thought, but still laughed in spite of himself. *Oh well, it will have to do.*

Sprig opened the door and found Kate sitting on the top step. She looked over her shoulder, hearing the door open. She smiled and stood up as Sprig joined her. They walked together down the stairs and Kate led him through the main rooms and into the rear of the cottage.

Two massive mahogany doors stood before the couple. Kate gently turned the brass handle, and the doors swung effortlessly inward at the touch.

Sprig stood with his mouth agape, stunned. The ornately carved shelves held hundreds, even thousands, of books. The opposite wall was composed of a fireplace made of a strange amber-colored rock. Above the fireplace, like a gem in a crown, was a painting of a strikingly beautiful woman resembling Kate. Through a strange detachment, Sprig entered and walked to the center of the room, his eyes never leaving the painting. "She's beautiful," Sprig heard himself say.

"I wish I could have really known her," Kate said in a childlike manner. "This is my father's study and he spends a great deal of time in here just staring at her. He adored her and still does."

"You look just like her, except for the red hair. No wonder your father is so protective of you. I honestly thought he was going to lure me off and leave me to my fate," Sprig said. Kate smiled.

"His bark is a lot worse than his bite. I know him, and I can tell he likes you," she said reassuringly. Sprig was not so easily convinced and his expression showed it. "I'll prove it," she said taking his hand and leading him out of the study. They walked through the kitchen and outside by way of a side entrance in the cottage.

Kate led the way to a low fence covered in yellow flowering roses. At the center stood a polished marble stone with the word "Mariel" carved on it.

"This is where my mother is buried," Kate said. She knelt down and pulled a weed that was growing up the side of the stone. When she was satisfied with its appearance, she took Sprig's hand and walked past the grave to an area some fifty feet or so away.

A large shade tree blanketed the area. Two rock markers sat on top of the freshly tilled earth. Sprig looked at the graves and back at Kate questioningly. "Your friends are resting there," she said.

"What?" Sprig said, not understanding.

"My father had Mengrig bring the remains of your two friends here to be buried properly away from the corruptibility of the Undead. He has never lain to rest someone close to him so near my mother's grave, let alone a bunch of Stakes. He did so because he knew how much they meant to you. He would have never done so if he did not like you, Sprig," Kate said.

Sprig was astounded. He would have never guessed that the Baron was capable of such generosity. "He did this for me?" Sprig asked, completely dumbfounded. Kate nodded.

"I'm sorry there are no names on them. My father was not sure who they were," she said.

"Do you know which is which?" he asked.

"The one on the left was the priest," she motioned with a gesture.

"Thanks." Sprig knelt before the two unmarked stones. He fought back the attempt his eyes made to cry. Turning around, he said, "You don't know what this means to me. They were the only family I had."

"What about the others? Weren't the others of your band also your family?" Sprig turned away from her, ashamed.

"No, not really. I never really cared for the rest of them. They were mostly mercenaries trying to make some coin. They're a rough lot, but soldiering does that to you. It's a hard road to travel, and an even harder one to come back from. They were not the kind of people I wanted to be around," Sprig justified.

"Your friends were mercenaries, weren't they?"

"They were different," he insisted.

"How so?" she asked.

"Jorth and Simil were commissioned soldiers and only became mercenaries after the war in the East. The others were mercenaries to start with. Jorth said he even fought against some of the very same men that were in our troop. He didn't seem to have any hard feelings toward them though. He said you only hate the enemy when you are at war with them, and love them as brothers when you are at peace," Sprig explained.

Kate nodded her understanding and said, "It was fortunate you were under such tutelage," Sprig stood and turned toward Kate.

"I would like to thank the Baron for this," Sprig said gesturing to the graves, "Is he nearby?" Kate shook her head no.

"He left at sunrise with Mengrig. They were going to the outlying villages to recruit more men. Mercenaries," she said with a wistful smile.

"Does he expect trouble with Flange?" he voiced his concern.

"I think he is just being cautious. He likes to have contingency plans," she explained. Sprig shook his head in understanding.

"So now what?" he asked throwing his arms up in the air.

"We enjoy the warm sunshine while we can, before the darkness comes."

* * *

The Baron and Mengrig rode in together that evening followed by twenty-five men on foot carrying various tools as weapons. Sprig was relieved to see that at least a few men carried swords of different caliber. Mengrig led the men to the bunkhouse while Keltch dismounted from his horse and led it disappearing into the stable. Sprig jogged from the cottage.

Keltch had removed the saddle and hung it over a short wall separating the stalls and was brushing the horse's mane. He nodded to Sprig as he entered. "Are you feeling better, lad? I was going to take you with me, but Kate says you were burning up with a fever all night."

"I'm fine now, sir. I feel much better, and thank you," Sprig said.

"For what?" Keltch said, eyeing him. Sprig shuffled his feet nervously.

"For laying my friends to rest in your garden," Sprig said. Keltch shrugged it off and continued grooming his horse. After a moment of silence he said, "It was necessary. I did not want them up and walking around again. We have enough trouble as it is." Sprig could tell that the Baron was uncomfortable about the subject, so he thanked him again and entered the stall containing his own horse.

Sprig stroked the horse's mane and patted its flanks. The horse was in excellent condition. The stable hands had washed and cleaned the horse, leaving no sign of the nightly excursion just twelve hours before. Not only had its mane had been brushed, but it had been re-shoed also. Sprig smiled at the meticulous care of the animal and felt a twinge of guilt for not taking as good of care of the gift as he should have. Sprig's horse had an uncanny shaped hoof, and he was surprised to notice that the horse's right-rear shoe had been shaped in the gentle curve to match the odd hoof.

Sprig looked over the short stall wall at the Baron. "Your stable hands do wondrous work. I almost didn't recognize her," Sprig said rubbing between the horse's ears. The Baron looked over at the mount.

"Aye. The lads take their work quite seriously. They love each and every animal as if they were their own." Keltch went back to brushing the matted mane of his own animal. A puzzled look crossed Sprig's face.

"If you have stable hands to take care of your horse, why do you always do the work yourself?" Sprig wondered.

Without looking up the Baron said, "Just because I am lord of the land does not exclude me from such duties as taking care of my mount. Besides, it is a bonding experience with the animal. I have to be able to know that I can trust it and vice versa. And you'll never know unless you spend time with it."

Sprig looked at his mount with new insight. He was sure that he had not intentionally neglected his mount in that respect, but he also knew that he did not know it very well. Keltch looked over at Sprig stroking the horse as it nuzzled against his body. He could not help but smile. "Take care of her and she'll treat you right every time," Keltch said, finishing up the maintenance of his mount. The Baron exited the stall and closed the hinged door behind him.

After a moment, Sprig also exited the stall and caught up with the Baron. "Sir, you hired more men?" Sprig questioned.

"That's right," Keltch said.

"It may not be my place to ask, but could you tell me what you are planning to do?" Sprig said, unsure how the Baron would react to his inquiries. Without losing stride, the Baron said, "I want to make sure that my greatest treasure is secured when you and I check out this place called Haven tomorrow night." Sprig was silent a moment in thought.

"You mean Kate, don't you?" Sprig said. Keltch stopped and eyed Sprig carefully. Sprig did not allow his eyes to waver from the scrutinizing stare of the Baron. Keltch nodded.

"You are correct, lad. Katie is my greatest treasure. This land and everything else has little value without her in the picture. I mean to see that she stays safe during this little venture of ours."

"Do you expect Flange to go back on his word?" Sprig asked.

"Just a precaution, lad. I don't see Flange breaking his oath. That does not mean that his siblings won't interfere somehow. I don't like surprises and I'll do what I can to counter any of them that come along." The duo stopped near the entry of the cottage. "Any other questions, lad?" Keltch asked.

"Yes, sir," Sprig looked past the stable to a small building that was jetting a plume of black smoke. "Is that a forge?" Sprig asked. The Baron nodded. "I would like to purchase some silver from you to be forged into a weapon," he said.

"What kind of weapon?" Keltch asked.

"One of my blades is made with a steel and silver mixture. It wounded Sasha when I stabbed her. I only have one blade like that and would prefer to have more made if it is possible."

Keltch stroked his chin in thought.

"All right. Tell the blacksmith what you want, and I'll see to it that you get your silver. Anything else?" Keltch inquired.

"Just the cost, sir. The silver, lodging, and cost to maintain my horse."

"We'll worry about that later. Just get what you need," Keltch said opening the cottage door.

"Thank you, sir," Sprig said turning to stride to the forge.

"By the way, don't let that old scoundrel give you any lip. Stand your ground with him!" Keltch said grinning and closed the door behind him. Sprig could have sworn that he could hear the Baron laughing behind the heavy oak door.

Sprig passed the stable and could hear the pounding of a hammer on an anvil. The shop was small and the opening was dark. Sprig could see the orange glow coming from the fired coals and sparks flying as the hammer struck the heated metal. A blacker shape was outlined in the darkness. "Excuse me," Sprig said loud enough to be heard. The hammering stopped. A set of dark eyes, surrounded by intense whites, focused on him from the head of the dark form.

"Go away, boy. I've got work to do," a gruff voice said. The eyes disappeared and the hammering continued.

"Excuse me, sir, I would . . ." Sprig tried to say.

The hammering stopped and the gruff voice yelled cutting him off, "I said I have work to do, you little bastard!"

An extremely large bare-chested man, covered from head to toe in soot, emerged from the darkness of the enclosed forge. His intense bulging eyes stood out in contrast to his blackened skin. Sprig could not tell if the singed curly hair that was tied back was actually gray-black, or if it was a product of the soot. The smith had a wooden crutch under the crook of his right arm, which he leaned upon heavily. His left hand contained a hammer, which he wielded in a threatening manner. The smith was missing his right leg from just below his knee.

Sprig's first instinct was to roll away and pull his blades, but instead, he stood his ground as the giant loomed over him.

"Don't you got ears, boy?" the smith snarled, rearing the hammer back ready to strike. Sprig's face wrinkled into a scowl and he took a step forward to stand inches from the giant of a man.

"Yeah, I got ears and so do you. Now use them!" Sprig snarled. He pulled his bandoleer over his head and off his shoulder shoving it into the chest of the big man. "I want you to drop what you're doing and forge some more blades like the silver-steel in this bandoleer. Use the steel from my other blades if it is necessary, but I want them before we leave tomorrow."

The smith was confounded by this child that was standing up to him. He lowered his hammer and grabbed the bandoleer that was thrust before him with his open hand. He hung the bandoleer from the top of his crutch and pulled the silver-steel dagger from it. Eyeing the weapon closely, he tested the edge. "It is sharp, but very poor quality. It looks like an apprentice's job," the gruff voice said with less scorn. He looked from the blade to the waiting youth before him. "I don't make weapons anymore, lad," the man simply said.

"You don't or won't?" Sprig said evenly. The smith watched the intrepid youth for several moments, letting his anger simmer. Recognition dawned on Sprig and he broke the silence, "You made my horse's shoes, and I have never seen better. I even noticed the special curve you put in the right-rear shoe. My horse has an unusual-shaped hoof and most shoes give her some discomfort but the one you made is a perfect fit."

The smith shrugged and looked away as if the compliment made him uneasy. The moments passed and finally the smith spoke,

"I lost my leg to a weapon that I made." Sprig could see an intense anger in the man's eyes.

"I don't understand," Sprig ventured. The smith had a faraway look on his face and began speaking more to himself than to Sprig.

"I used to be a field smith repairing armor and creating weapons for the mobile army during the wars in the East. I was also a soldier when not at the forge. I made a double-bladed axe, the like that I've not seen since. I was so proud of my work that I gave it to the General as a gift. You see, it was his weapon of choice, and I believed that only the most worthy should wield such a fine axe."

The smith stopped talking, but held the faraway look as if he was reliving the experience again. After a moment, he continued. "Winter set upon us and a series of snowstorms cut us off from our supplies and reinforcements. We pulled back, trying to hook up with the main army while being chased down by the enemy. They knew we were desperate to get away and constantly harassed us. Eventually, we were backed into a snow-blocked pass and tried to dig our way through to the other side. Those bastards sent charge after charge until they broke through our line. Our men scattered. The General tried to rally around the standard-bearer and I tried to fight my way to him. I cut a path through the savages, but my view was obscured and I lost sight of the General. I could still see the standard and reached the standard-bearer as he was run through with a spear. I charged in and tripped over the slain bodies. I lost my balance and fell hard to the ground. The body I had fallen on was that of the General's. He was dead. I looked up in time to see one of those leering savages hoisting the General's axe overhead. It crashed down and severed my leg. I lost consciousness and woke in the army infirmary. I swore then never to make another weapon again, and I haven't since."

The man's words and the pain they contained moved Sprig. The smith handed Sprig his bandoleer, which he fitted his head through and rested over his shoulder. Sprig nodded to the giant man. "Is it too much to ask for a hammer and a chisel?" Sprig asked. The smith turned and disappeared into the shop, returning moments later handing some tools to Sprig. "Thanks," he said and left the smith standing in front of the forge.

Sprig walked to the shade tree in the garden and sat before the two marble stones. He studied several pebbles and found a suitable one to scratch the name "Jorth" on the first one. The chalky substance rubbed white letters onto the stone. He was not quite satisfied with the drawn characters, and spit in his hand using the moisture to wipe the residue off the stone and made another attempt to write Jorth's name.

He rocked back on his heels and studied his handiwork. He was satisfied with the results and picked up the hammer and chisel. He carefully aligned the chisel matching his markings and gave it a gentle tap. A chip of rock flew away from the stone. Sprig tapped again and he worked for hours until he completed the engravings on both stones.

He stood and dusted his hands. A sense of closure gripped him, and even though he was saddened, he was happy with his accomplishment. He gathered the tools and returned them to the now empty forge.

Sprig closed the door to his room and plopped unceremoniously onto his bed. He let out a deep sigh and closed his eyes. *What am I supposed to do now?* Feelings of uncertainty began to nag at him. There was not much else he could do and eventually he drifted off to sleep.

A gentle knock on the door stirred Sprig from his slumber. He was still wearing his clothes and his knives were in his hands. He had drawn them unknowingly and slipped them back into his bandoleer. "Yes," Sprig said wiping the sleep from his eyes.

The door opened and Kate poked her head in and said, "Hi. Are you hungry?"

"Very," Sprig said stifling a yawn. "Give me a minute and I'll meet you downstairs."

"All right," she said smiling and closed the door. Sprig washed his face and hands in a basin and dried them on the sleeve of his shirt. Slinging the bandoleer over the chair, he ran his fingers through his tussle of hair. Opening the door, he vaulted down the stairs to join Kate in the dining room.

The troubled look on Sprig's face caused Kate to raise her eyebrows and prompted her to ask, "Is there a problem?" Sprig tried to break the mood by smiling.

"I'm just trying to sort my thoughts. Too much going on in my head I guess," Sprig said and smelled his plate of food, bringing a smile. "Did you make this too?" he said.

"No, I tend to stick to the simple things. I hope you like it just the same," she replied.

They both ate in silence, but stole occasional glances at one another. "You know, you can stay if you want to, when this is all over," Kate said, breaking the silence. Sprig was unsure what to say. He had not stayed in any one place for very long since he left his village as a child. The troop was always on the move looking for work.

"I haven't thought that far ahead," Sprig said.

"Just an option," she said, feeling somewhat embarrassed.

"I'll keep it in mind," Sprig said, staring at her. To change the subject he said, "Where is your father?"

"Out somewhere with Mengrig. He said he wouldn't be home for dinner," she explained. Sprig shook his head in understanding and finished his meal. Afterward he said, "Do you think he would mind if I looked at the books in his library?"

"I don't see a problem with it. Sure, go ahead," she said. Sprig grabbed his plate and made to go into the kitchen. "You can leave it for the kitchen staff," she said.

"I can clean up after myself. Besides, it is the least I can do. Are you finished?" he asked. Kate nodded and he removed their dishes and deposited them in the kitchen.

After finishing the task, he entered the library door and closed it behind him. Again his gaze swept the room and settled on the painting of Mariel. He smiled at the angelic image and found comfort in her presence.

Sprig walked to the left side of the room and began browsing the bookshelves. Some of the books were written in different languages and he could not make out the titles. Sprig located a title he could read and gently slipped it from the shelf. He opened the leather cover and read the first page it fell open to. "Tell me of the night and the beauty who walks in it . . ."

Sprig walked to a plush chair and sat. His head rested against the cushion and an odd sensation hit him. He looked up at the image and into the eyes of the woman in the painting. He was aware that the chair had some worn molded contours and realized that this was the Baron's chair. The hairs on his neck stood on end and he quickly stood up. Another identical chair was on the other side of the room. He examined the chair, finding that it did not contain the wear or the contours like the other one had. Sprig felt like he was in violation of a ritual that the Baron had established for himself some time ago. He chose not to sit in either one of the chairs and instead, stretched out in front of the fireplace on the rug.

Carefully, he opened the book and read the first page. About a quarter of the way through the book, Sprig stoked the dying fire and added some more fuel. About halfway through the book, he fell asleep. He dreamed of white chargers and knights rescuing damsels in distress. He dreamed of a world where the weak are protected by the strong, and good always triumphs over evil. His elation ended when he woke in the night and realized that his dreams were just that, dreams.

Sprig pulled himself up into a sitting position and stretched. The fire had died down and he was chilled. He placed another log on the fire and nearly jumped out of his skin when a voice addressed him. "I'm sorry, lad. I would have built up the fire for you, but I did not want to disturb your sleep. Maybe if I had placed some wood on the coals, you would not have been woken now," Keltch said from his worn chair.

"Am I disturbing you in here, sir?" Sprig said his voice filled with concern. Keltch chuckled.

"Actually, lad, I'm sorry to have disturbed you," Keltch said rising from the chair. "I'm going to bed. Good-night."

"Do you mind if I sleep here?" Sprig asked the exiting Baron. Keltch stopped and looked over his shoulder at the youth.

"Of course you can. She brings me comfort too," Keltch said and winked before taking a last glimpse of the portrait. "Good-night."

"Good-night, sir."

Sprig yawned and stretched back out on the rug, closing his eyes. Tomorrow was going to be a long day and he needed some more rest. The heated air struck his face and the sensation felt good. The comforting crackle of the burning wood lulled him into a deep sleep.

Sprig felt another different warmth on his face, and he stretched and exhaled in a deep sigh. It took a moment for his eyes to adjust to the brightness of the room. The sunbeams were filtering through the lead glass windows onto his face. He picked up the book he was reading and stood, stretching his calves and back. He replaced the book back on the shelf after marking the page he last remembered reading with a piece of a leather strip.

Sprig quietly walked up the stairs to his room and removed the shirt he had been sleeping in. A fresh cotton shirt and a soft black leather jerkin were laid on his bed. He slipped into the clothes after washing his face. He was not sure when they were planning to leave and decided to be ready. He worked his way back into his bandoleer and grabbed his hat. Unsure of the hour, he walked quietly down the stairs. The cottage was still and he saw no one until he ventured into the kitchen.

Three women worked with flour-covered hands. Two of the women were silver-haired and plump. The third lady was little more than child doing her best to mimic the work that the others were doing and only succeeding in covering herself in flour. The ladies smiled at the approaching youth. "Good morning," one of them chimed.

"Is it still morning?" Sprig inquired. The ladies smiled.

"Quite early morning to be exact. In fact, the Baron hasn't made it down yet," the other woman said. Sprig pointed to some fresh-baked biscuits and asked if he could have some. One of the ladies wrapped several into the bundle of cloth, while the other lady reached into a cabinet and withdrew a sealed glass jar of sand plum preserves. Both items were presented to Sprig in a small wicker basket with a wooden spoon. Sprig thanked them both and left out the side door for the stables.

Sprig opened the cloth and retrieved a steaming biscuit and took a bite. It melted in his mouth. *Ah that is good,* he thought. Sprig entered the stable and sat the basket down on a bale of straw near the stall where his horse was taking residence. Breaking the wax seal on the jar, he dipped the spoon into the preserves and tasted the sticky contents. The sweetness of the taste left a wide grin on his face. *This just keeps getting better,* he thought.

Two stable boys entered the main doors, both yawning, trying to wake themselves up. Sprig saw the similarities and waved the brothers to him. Both boys approached and Sprig spread two of the biscuits thick with the preserves and handed one to each of them. They smiled shyly and accepted the offerings, eating greedily. When Sprig was sure he had them in his confidence he said in a surly voice, "All right, which one of you worked on my horse yesterday?"

The two boys looked at each other with stunned looks of surprise, then back to Sprig who stood with his arms crossed over his chest and taking a menacing stance.

One of the boys began to stammer, "We, we both did, sir."

"Good!" Sprig said with a smile and reached into a pouch hanging from his belt. He removed two silver coins and handed one to each of them. In a theatrical voice he said, "Thank you so very much for the wonderful care you have bestowed upon my mistreated beast," and bowed. Surprised, the boys stared at the coins. Each boy smiled, thanked Sprig, and ran off to start their morning duties. Sprig smeared the last biscuit with preserves and fed it to his nudging horse.

Sprig had not noticed the silence upon entering the stable. Puzzled, he stood listening, and then recognition dawned on him. It was the blacksmith's rhythmic pounding that was missing. Sprig removed a piece of straw from his horse's mane. A shadow crept into the doorway behind him. Sprig acted as though he was unaware of another's presence and only turned when the figure cleared his throat, trying to get the boy's attention.

It was the blacksmith. Sprig watched the figure approach on his crutches. It was obvious that the blacksmith had been working, but it also appeared that he had wiped the black grime from his face. Though the man was still large, he did not look as menacing without the mask of soot. Sprig's eyes darted to the leather bandoleer hanging from one of the crutches and back to the other man's eyes. The blacksmith removed the bandoleer and held it in outstretched hands to Sprig.

The bandoleer leather was beautiful and it was of extreme craftsmanship. But even more beautiful was the eight silver daggers that were nestled into the sheaths of the bandoleer. Sprig slipped into the bandoleer and removed one of the blades. The silver had black lines running through it in wavy patterns. He had never seen the like before and judged they were perfectly balanced for throwing. The blade felt as if it was made for his hands. Sprig stood with his mouth open, at a loss for words. The smith smiled, showing a wide row of even white teeth. He reached out and removed a dagger from its sheath. "These are called Damascus blades. I have folded steel and silver in layers. It has strength and will keep a keen edge." He slid the dagger back into the sheath.

"I don't know how to thank you. I don't even know your name," Sprig said. The smith slapped the dumbfounded boy on the back.

"My name's Brundle, and you are very welcome, young Sprig!"

7

Brundle left the boy to scrutinize his work on the newly forged daggers. He was still unsure why he had changed his mind. Perhaps it was the way the boy stood his ground. Brundle knew that he was not liked and was only tolerated because of his craftsmanship. He also knew that he carried a lot of anger and vented it on anyone who got anywhere near him. The only exceptions were the Baron and his headstrong daughter. He rarely spoke to either and tried to make himself scarce when he was not crafting at the anvil.

Brundle continued his slow trek to the waiting forge, thinking about the conversation yesterday. He had watched the disheartened boy march into the garden. The blacksmith followed the youth and watched him spend the afternoon chiseling names on two gray stone markers on the freshly covered graves. A deep sadness had filled his heart, pushing through the anger that usually resided there.

Brundle left the boy to complete his task and had returned to the forge to find several bars of silver and steel waiting for him on his workbench. He quickly scanned the area, trying to see who had left the metal. For more than an hour he sat staring at the waiting materials. He rubbed some of the grime from his face and dumped some coal on his dying embers. He vigorously pumped the bellows, stoking the fire bringing a rich orange glow.

Ceremoniously, he lifted one of the bars of silver. The metal was cold to the touch, waiting to be reborn as something new and spectacular. A smile stretched across his face and he closed his eyes, imagining what form the metal would take. He opened his eyes and slipped the silver bar into a set of tongs and placed the bar in the scorching flames. Brundle stretched his arms and removed the hammer from the hook on the workbench. He removed the heated metal from the flames and held it across the anvil with the tongs and began hammering the metal flat. Brundle continued the process with the steel bars and folded the two metals together.

After an hour, the lump of metal began to take the loose shape of a dagger. The smith heard the youth approaching and decided to disappear behind the forge shack. He watched the youth replace the borrowed tools and then leave. The smith resumed his work and created seven more lumps resembling the first. In the hours that followed, Brundle honed the edges and weighted the blades for balance, especially for throwing. The sun was slipping past the trees when he completed the last blade.

He inspected each blade, looking for any imperfections. He was surprised to find none, which was no small task for someone who had not worked a metal blade in nearly a decade. The experience lifted his heart, and for the first time since he could remember, joy and satisfaction filled his well-being. He smiled in spite of himself; it was a wonderful feeling.

Darkness filled the sky and the blacksmith lighted an oil lantern and sifted through an old worn oak chest. He removed some leatherworking tools and a long piece of thick soft black leather. Brundle spent the rest of the night stitching together a bandoleer worthy of holding the newly forged weapons.

Brundle yawned and stretched as his lantern burned low and the first rays of the dawn filled the sky. He blew the flame out and slipped the daggers into the sheaths of the bandoleer. Another smile escaped his face, and he hung the bandoleer on the crutch and leaned it against the wall. He dipped his matted hair and face into a barrel of water and refreshed himself. He wiped his face on a coarse towel and poked his head outside the forge in time to see Sprig disappear into the stable, soon followed by two of the young stable boys. Brundle seemed to recall that they were brothers. He was not sure, for the boys stayed clear of him and with good reason. Brundle furrowed his brow at the thought of how everyone must see him.

Brundle was limping along, searching for Sprig when the two stable lads ran past him with their faces filled with glee. Brundle crept to the stable unsure how to approach the boy that only yesterday he had been so rude to. Sprig was facing the opposite wall, checking his horse. He was glad that the boy was at a loss for words, for it made it easier to present the gift to him.

Brundle shook off his reverie as he returned to the forge. He looked at his workspace with different eyes. There were no pressing matters today, however, he did notice that most of the new men brought in yesterday did not have any decent weapons. He smiled and rubbed his bearded chin at the thought of the blades he could produce for them. Another thought occurred to him. It had been a long time since he had taken breakfast in the kitchen. The way he was feeling, it was about time to make up for the rough treatment he had given to everyone over the years.

Brundle stripped off his leather apron, boots, and britches. He climbed into the cold barrel of water, splashing the overflow onto the floor of his shop. He scrubbed the grime from his face and body. One of the stable boys ran past his shop. "Hey you, lad!" The boy stopped dead in his tracks.

"Yes, sir?" he stammered.

"Is the field still filled with wildflowers?" Brundle asked.

"Yes, sir," the boy said puzzled.

"There's a silver piece in it for you if would gather me a bundle of them," the smith said to the dumbfounded boy.

"Sure. I'll be right back," the boy said, running off to the adjoining field.

"Be sure to get lots of different colors and leave them on me bench!" The smith hollered after the departing boy. Brundle squeezed the water from his hair and beard and climbed down from the barrel. Wrapping a somewhat clean towel around him, he squatted on the floor and removed a brick in the floor. He sifted through his hidden coins and laid a silver piece in plain sight on the workbench.

Grabbing his crutch, he limped from the shop to the small one-roomed shack only twenty paces away. Drying his hair with a flour sack, he fought the tangles in his matted hair with a coarse comb and trimmed his scorched beard. Brundle slipped on a clean wool shirt and britches. Tucking in his shirt and slipping on a riding boot, he tied back his wet hair with a piece of leather and hobbled back to the forge.

An exquisite bouquet of multicolored flowers lay on the bench. Brundle scooped up the flora and buried his face in the fragrant bundle. He inhaled deeply and a sense of peace overcame him. Tears filled his eyes and he wiped them away with the back of his hand.

Brundle carried the flowers and made his way to the side door leading into the kitchen of the Baron's cottage. He poked his head in the door and watched the busy ladies. He cleared his throat and both ladies turned and stared in awe at the smiling man standing in the doorway. "Is it too much trouble for me to take my breakfast here in the kitchen?" he said with his hand outstretched, offering the bouquet. Both ladies gazed at one another and then back to the waiting smith. They accepted the flowers and placed them in a leaded glass pitcher on the table.

"We'd love to have you share breakfast with us," one of the ladies said, helping Brundle to a chair and leaning his crutch against the wall behind them. "Would you like biscuits and some preserves? They're fresh out of the oven." The huge man held a toothy grin and helped himself to the bounty.

* * *

Keltch slipped from the rear door of the cottage, surprised to see Sprig already up. He had made a makeshift target on the side of the stable and was throwing a blade with incredible accuracy into the center of it. Keltch strode to the boy who was retrieving a stuck blade. Sprig saw the approaching Baron and said, "Good morning, sir!"

"Morning, lad. May I?" Keltch said motioning to the dagger in hand. "A mighty fine blade. It is perfectly balanced." He returned the knife back to the youth.

"Thank you, sir. I'm not sure what you said to Brundle, but whatever it was changed his mind," Sprig said excitedly. Keltch stroked his chin in thought then said, "I had nothing to do with it. I did not say a word. I had one of my men leave some steel and silver at the forge, but I left no instructions. Whatever changed his mind came from you. I seriously had my doubts that he would even talk to you. I am truly amazed," Keltch said and slapped Sprig on the back.

"There must be magic in these blades because I haven't missed yet," Sprig said pointing to the knife marks on the target.

"Not magic. Just a well-made blade forged by a master craftsman," Keltch explained.

"Are we ready to go, sir?" Sprig asked.

"Shortly. I am going to get some supplies for the trip and leave some final instructions before we go. Stay close to the stable. I'll be back soon," Keltch said, leaving to return to the cottage. Sprig stepped off twenty paces and spun, throwing several of the blades in rapid succession. Each one hit in a tight bunch in the center of the target.

Keltch entered the side door to the kitchen and stopped dead in his tracks. The smith was sipping a cup of juice and laughing along with the kitchen women. The cooks were having the smith sample everything they had been preparing for the morning breakfast. Crumbs and stains of red jam were clinging to Brundle's beard. One of the round ladies was dabbing the shed morsels with a damp rag.

The laughter stopped as the Baron entered. Keltch hid the smile at the sight under a stoic face. He looked at the trio from one to the other, then said, "I'm looking for the smith, has anyone seen him today?" The giant blacksmith broke the silence with a hardy laugh from a smile that was not unattractive. The women giggled nervously, unsure of the reaction from the Baron. Keltch cracked a grin and added; "I always thought I had a bear for a smith. You clean up nicely," he clasped the smith's forearm in a warrior's handshake. The smith pumped it vigorously.

"Thank you, Baron," Brundle replied.

"Fine job on the Sprig's blades. Are you up to making anything else?" Keltch asked.

"Aye, Baron. I intend to start making blades for your new soldiers after these lovely ladies quit feeding me," Brundle said, exchanging glances with the kitchen help. The women blushed and giggled like young girls.

"You keep this up, and the rest of us may never get fed!" Keltch said goodheartedly and took a bite from a warm biscuit. He smiled and winked at the ladies and disappeared through the kitchen door into the storeroom.

Keltch grabbed some oats and dried fruit from a shelf and put the contents into a burlap sack. He placed some salt and sugar in smaller pouches. Lastly, he stuffed some salted deer meat into the sack with the rest of the items and tied it shut.

Mengrig entered the storeroom. "I almost could not believe my eyes. That was the blacksmith, was it not?" Mengrig asked, wearing a baffled look.

The Baron chuckled and said, "Aye. I almost didn't believe it myself. He's well on his way to wooing my kitchen out from under me." Mengrig laughed at the thought.

"Who's doing is that?" Mengrig wondered.

Keltch smiled and said, "Who else but Sprig. That lad has a strange effect on people."

"Including you, my lord?" Mengrig said with a knowing smile. The Baron just shrugged and grinned.

"Any last words for me to carry out?" Mengrig asked. Keltch swung the sack over a shoulder.

"You know the drill, same as always. Keep my daughter safe and make sure the men stay alert for trouble."

* * *

Kate located her father and Mengrig leaving the pantry. "Papa, how long will you be gone this time?" she said, slipping her long slender arms around his barrel chest and kissing his cheek. Keltch kissed her gently on the forehead and squeezed her in a loving embrace.

"I'm not sure, Katie, but the weather looks fine today and should not slow us down any. I'll be back as soon as I can," he said hugging her again. The trio walked from the house to the stable.

Sprig had increased his distance from the target and was once again throwing multiple blades. Keltch mused at the skill at which Sprig hurled the weapons. Three blades were thrown in a blink of an eye to stab within the coin-sized circle that had been drawn on the stable's wall. Mengrig whistled and shook his head in admiration. Sprig was yanking the blades free from the target when he heard the group approaching. "Pretty fancy throwing there, son," Mengrig said.

Kate shot a quick wink the Baron's way and said, "I don't know. It's easy to hit a target that doesn't move. Are you as accurate with something in flight?"

Sprig frowned. "What do you suggest?" he said, looking around for something to throw at. Keltch tromped up and removed Sprig's floppy hat.

"This is as good a target as any," Keltch said, preparing to toss the hat in the air. Sprig stifled a protest and watched the Baron march off with his hat.

"You know, that is the only hat I have, and I am quite partial to it."

"Quit your bellyaching, Sprig and let's see what you're made of!" Keltch bellowed.

Sprig gave a resolved shrug and watched his hat spiral through the air in an awkward flight. He quickly assessed its movement and streaked a blade to intercept. The first blade pierced the hat knocking it from the air, but a second stabbed into it before it hit the ground. Small applause erupted from the trio as Sprig retrieved his hat and placed it on his head after fingering the holes he had just put in it.

"I'm convinced," Kate said, smiling, and kissed Sprig lightly on the cheek. Sprig flushed, unsure what to do other than stand there, embarrassed. Keltch shook his head in disgust.

"Let's mount up, boy, we've got work to do," Keltch growled. Sprig shook his head and bounded into the stable, grateful to be relieved of the awkward situation. "What am I going to do with you, girl? You keep this up and I'll never be rid of him!" Keltch stormed off in mock-anger after the youth, Kate only smiled, watching her father disappear into the stable to mount their horses. She gave a final good-bye to the two men as they rode off at a gentle gallop toward the tree line.

* * *

Rewella sat at the edge of the etched Circle of Power. She rested her hands on her knees and rocked gently on her heels. The gold and silver lines of the circle reflected light that danced and played across her ivory features. Again she looked for some hidden message in the lines and spirals on the floor. A small crease deepened in her brow and she shook it off, breaking the hypnotic spell the circle held her with. Was it her imagination or did the circle seem to reach out to her before every use? She shook her head, feeling foolish at the thought. *It is only a tool, just like so many other things,* she mused to herself.

Rewella rocked back on her heels and stood facing the circle. A shimmering ripple in the darkened corner caught her eye. Barcus emerged from the darkness and strode purposefully to where Rewella had her back to him. Without turning she said, "I thought I made it clear to you not to disturb me in Haven while I'm preparing." Barcus' tendrils snaked out in her direction, feeling the air around her.

"I have questions that need to be answered, sister," Barcus said.

"They can wait till I'm finished," she said, still not turning to face him.

"No, they can't." Rewella half-turned her body and looked over her shoulder at her hulking sibling. She stifled the smile that threatened to tear at her lovely lips. She had healed the wound in his head, but the crater still remained where the mace had smashed into his face.

"Ask your questions, and be quick. I've much work to do," she said turning around to face him with milky arms resting on her small shapely hips. Barcus hesitated at her shift in tone and mood.

"If you are so sure that Flange will show up here at Haven, why don't we just wait for him?" Barcus said, not sure what she had planned. Rewella let her head drop to her left shoulder and her eyes rolled up, staring at the ceiling. She looked as if she were trying to find the best way to answer a question a toddler had asked. The look was not lost on Barcus and his tendrils darkened and thrashed in anger.

"Barcus, you and I cannot survive the daylight. How Flange and Sasha do is completely beyond me," Rewella said, having prepared to give this speech.

A small flash hit Barcus for a moment; a thought. For a brief instant, he saw himself confronting Sasha about being a creature like them and knowing she was not. *Surely that never happened*, he thought.

Rewella continued, "We are weak and vulnerable in the sunlight . . ."

"But we are not affected that way in Haven," Barcus broke in, cutting her off. Rewella smiled sweetly at him as if he was only an excited child.

"That is true," she mused, nodding her head. "But he can sense when we are near." *And the whole world can smell you, Barcus*, she thought to herself with a snicker. "He knows that we are against him, and he won't chance coming around with us close by."

Barcus stroked his chin in thought and said, "What are you going to do? Sasha says that he is conspiring with that, self-righteous Baron."

Rewella shined with that unnerving smile that always made Barcus uneasy. "I am in the process of setting a trap for him which you have rudely interrupted." Again she smiled but this time it held a hint of danger. "I need time to finish, and you questioning me, Barcus, is wasting it. Any more distractions, and you may not find me so generous in the future," she said, looking at the appalling wound in his head. "Once you leave, do not come back to Haven until I say it is safe to do so. Do you understand?" Her question left no room for dispute.

Barcus shifted uneasily and nodded his head in defeat. He did an about face and strode to the corner, vanishing.

At the sight of his exit, Rewella let her shoulders slump. She had been up most of the night gathering the items needed to prepare the spell in the Circle of Power. Most of the items had been placed except the key components needed to trigger the spell.

Rewella picked up a tray from the table and moved into one of the shadowy corners. Setting the tray on the floor, she removed the lid to a clay pot. Three other identical pots from the tray were placed in various positions in the chamber.

Rewella removed a vial from the tray and emptied the liquid contents into the pot. Replacing the lid, she moved to the next clay pot and repeated the process. She adjusted the last container to her satisfaction and returned to the center of the room, standing before the Circle of Power.

Kneeling, Rewella picked up the final components and slid them into place on the Circle. Blue-black lightning danced across her face as the jewels on the circle flashed with intensity before being used and spent. The once precious stones and metals incinerated, leaving a fine dust on the Circle.

The lightning arced across the room, rebounding off the walls at odd angles. Rewella had a sense that the floor was tilting toward the circle and she scrambled on hands and knees, backing away from it.

A dot of darkness suspended over the center of the Circle and grew larger. Rewella felt a force at work trying to pull her into the void of darkness. Panic welled within her, for she had never tried this particular summoning before.

In fact, this was a variation on the summoning spell that was etched into the wall. She had become aware that the formulas on the walls were not the only possible ones, and began experimenting, creating her own. She also knew that Flange had the same revelation and that had led to her attempts to thwart his return to Haven. She could not watch him all the time and needed a deterrent.

The dot became a large black sphere absorbing the illumination of the chamber. In the swirl of black, what appeared to be a swarm of red eyes darted around the sphere, looking for an escape.

Rewella could still feel the pull on her body, but stood up defiantly anyway. One particular set of larger eyes stopped its attempt to flee the sphere and fixed its gaze on the shapely figure whose silk robe danced from the pull of the orb. A voice that was made up of thousands said, "Who summons us?" Rewella smiled in anticipation, but said nothing.

Again, a multitude of voices came from the flaring eyes. "You are not known to us. Who are you to pull us from our solitude?"

Rewella was ecstatic because the summoning had actually worked. Now if she could just control them... "I am Rewella, Keeper of the Spiders," she said. She knew there was power in a name and knowing that, she would not give her family name.

"You are not known to us. Return us to the Void or suffer a fate worse than death!" the voice of voices shrieked. The sphere wobbled and a pulse of black and red lunged toward her but stopped as if hitting an invisible barrier. Rewella walked around the edge of the Circle, ignoring the failed attack.

"Actually, I had something else in mind," she said, stopping on the opposite side of the sphere. "I have summoned you to provide me a service, and I only need four of you." The voices were silent but their agitation was evident.

"We cannot survive here for long and are already growing weak," the voice said with less of a screech.

"I can sustain you while you are here, but I will hold the others in the sphere as reassurance for your obedience," Rewella said, once again pacing the outer edge of the Circle.

"If we do your bidding, you will return us to the Void?" the voice said, almost pleading. Rewella nodded.

"Yes, but only *after* you carry out my wishes," she said.

"And what do you require from us?" the voice asked. Rewella stopped her pacing and paused for effect.

"I want you to kill anyone or thing that enters this chamber when I leave it. When I return, I will set you and yours free. Agreed?" she said and smiled sweetly.

"Agreed," the multitude of voices said as one.

Rewella closed her eyes and began a chant. A crack appeared in the sphere. Four sets of eyes, and a trail of misty vapor, streaking from the sphere, each drawn to the clay pots. One of the sets of eyes halted above the pot and began to solidify. Rewella gasped as the forming creature fought the spell she had laid.

A bulky mass of claws and tendrils formed in the black matter with red eyes that blazed with hatred. A twinge of fear crept up the Porcelain Lady's spine. She threw her arm out in a halting gesture. "Come any closer and I will destroy the sphere with all of your kind in it." The creature stopped before Rewella as if sizing her up.

"We have an agreement. As long as you don't violate it, we will help you. If anything happens to my kindred, your soul will be mine to torment for an eternity in the Void," the single voice threatened in a deep tone.

The creature gave itself over and was pulled toward the clay pot. Its translucent body changed back into an undistinguishable form and disappeared into the waiting vessel. Relief filled Rewella and she threw her head back and her laughter echoed off the chamber walls. Turning, she walked to a darkened corner and disappeared.

*   *   *

The sun's rays filtered through the trees, and the limbs bent, waving across the ground, pushed in the gentle breeze. Flange stood in the brush near the clearing facing opposite of the fairy ring of mushrooms.

He knew that Haven could be entered from many different areas, but this particular spot posed less resistance and therefore less energy expenditure. Rewella had left Haven earlier before the sun had rose. He sighed and turned his face toward the sun. His skin itched and a burning sensation spread across his gray face. Even though the fiery globe threatened to destroy him, he enjoyed the pain from the desperate attempts to sear him. The discomfort was the constant reminder of being an Undead creature.

Undead. He rolled the word over in his head. *Dead creatures that still live.* Perhaps, but other than the physical changes, Flange never really thought of himself as a dead being. Changed maybe, but not dead.

Birds and other creatures paid little attention to the still figure. A squirrel even ventured to sit underneath Flange's parted feet. A slight shift in his weight sent the rodent scurrying for cover.

Flange scanned the area for any signs of Sasha. He knew Rewella wanted him watched, and Sasha could move around in the daylight. He also knew that she could not go to all the places he had access to. After all, she was not an Undead creature like the siblings. He figured out her secret long ago but never revealed the knowledge.

When Sasha was tailing him, he never let on that he knew he was being pursued. He could sense her presence just as he could any other creature that was near him. When he chose to evade her, he simply disappeared into the earth and reappeared elsewhere.

Today, Flange was somewhat unsettled by the fact that Sasha had not been watching for him. In fact, he had not seen her since his meeting with the Baron. What he had seen was Rewella's many trips to Haven during the last two nights. She kept the place occupied during the night hours and left before daybreak. Flange had decided not to enter until the daylight hours before the Baron arrived. However, he had remained in the woods, watching the main entrance to Haven.

Flange smelled the air and reached out with preternatural senses. Something in the air, or in the shapes of the colors that swirled before him, kept him from moving into Haven. He remembered Rewella leaving before the predawn and the smug look of satisfaction she was wearing like a badge. He knew that Rewella usually hid her emotions well behind a mask of neutrality. It seemed out of character for her to have any other expression.

Flange continued his surveillance of the landscape, aware that Keltch would soon appear on the trail. Again, he reached out with his senses trying to locate Sasha or any other dangers. Nothing seemed out of place, which only made him feel even uneasier.

Gradually, a shift in the radiant colors of energy swirling in the air around Flange notified him that the Baron and another rider were close. One last time he swept the area then let the earth swallow him.

The Baron and Sprig ambled slowly up the trail, ever alert for unseen danger. Both men watched the thick undergrowth warily, expecting an Undead creature to leap upon them at any moment. Sprig held his reins loosely in one hand and the other hand rested lightly on the hilt of a sheathed dagger. The Baron rode more casually, but still held a look of readiness from past experiences.

Keltch's horse's head snapped up with its nostrils flaring and stopped short. Sprig's own horse became skittish and he drew one of his daggers.

A ripple passed across the ground, pushing dirt across the horses' hooves. Sprig's horse reared and took several steps backward. Keltch's mare stood her ground, with her hooves scratching at the displaced dirt.

From the center of the ripple appeared the top of a head. The head soon thrust out of the dirt revealing an attached body that rose and settled over the ground from which it came.

Flange, stood before the two bewildered riders. The looks of astonishment on their faces almost made Flange smile, but he knew better. Instead he nodded to the Baron and said, "Baron Keltch, I'm glad to see that you made it." Keltch nodded in return, but refused to add to the pleasantries.

"It's been two days, Flange. Take us to the place you called Haven so I can see it for myself," Keltch said in a neutral voice.

Flange's pleasant facade quickly changed to a look of puzzlement. He shook his head. "I'm not sure that is a good idea, Baron. I was unable to test whether it will be safe for you to enter," Flange said.

"That is why you gave us two days, remember?" Keltch said, biting back the venom that was rising in his voice. "I'm not here to play games with you, Flange. You either take us to your Haven, or I leave right now and you can forget any treaty," he said gruffly.

Flange shrugged. "As you wish. But I warn you, there may be side effects entering Haven. I have no idea how it may affect your mortal bodies. Just in case, I suggest that your young companion stays behind."

Keltch looked at Sprig for his reaction. Sprig shook off the awe and said, "I'm going with you, sir."

"You heard him," Keltch said, "The Sprig goes too." Again Flange shrugged.

"As you wish," he said, turning and strolling toward the clearing.

The reluctant horses followed at a distance as the Undead figure moved along the path to the clearing.

Sprig watched the back of the receding Undead man as he walked along the trail. Fear plagued him for he could not shake the terror welling up inside. He wondered if Flange could sense his fear and was secretly enjoying his discomfort.

Then again, this creature barely acknowledged his presence and that judgement of not feeling worthy enough for his attention also made Sprig angry. He imagined himself pulling his newly made daggers from their oiled sheaths, and sending them one after the other into the back of the Undead creature just to see if they were effective. A wicked grin crossed his face at the very notion.

Keltch looked over his shoulder as if sensing what was going through Sprig's mind. Sprig had unknowingly pulled a dagger from its sheath and was preparing to throw it. Keltch saw the intent in Sprig's eyes and shook his head "no" vigorously. Sprig shook his head and snapped out of his daydream, realizing what he was about to do. He sheathed the dagger, suddenly embarrassed by his actions. He refused to look at the Baron or the figure leading them through the forest. He let his horse fall back behind the Baron's while he concentrated watchfully on the passing woods.

The trees began to thin as the trio entered a clearing. Flange signaled for a halt as he stopped and appeared to be listening to the surroundings. Sprig also looked around for any signs of danger. Keltch dismounted and slowly led his mount up to stand next to Flange.

Sprig could not shake the sight. Keltch and his mortal enemy standing side by side of each other, wary of impending danger.

How is it that these two can put aside their differences so easily? Sprig knew that the chance of a common danger could very well make allies of enemies, *but these two?* He wondered. Yet both watched the woods as if ready to jump back to back in preparation of a defense.

Sprig shook his head in disbelief and then dismounted. He led his mount to stand off to the side of the Baron, and he stared at the side of Flange's face, taking in every detail. It dawned on him how human Flange looked, even handsome. He could imagine what the Undead creature would look like given some color in his face and hair, easily the face of a young nobleman.

"Is that the fairy ring you spoke of?" Keltch said, barely above a whisper. He pointed to a circle of mushrooms near the center of the clearing.

"Yes, but I feel uneasy about doing this," Flange said, still watching for an unseen danger.

"We'll take our chances," Keltch replied, unshaken by the warning.

Flange took the lead and strode to the center of the ring and turned to face the Baron and said, "You will have to leave your mounts here." Keltch nodded and tied his mount to a low-hanging limb. Sprig followed the example and stood waiting at the Baron's side.

Flange spent a moment sizing up the two men standing before him and said, "I'm not sure what traveling into Haven will do to the both of you. Be on your guard for anything unusual. Anything that doesn't look right, kill it." Both Keltch and Sprig nodded in understanding.

Flange walked to the center of the fungi. The circle spanned a diameter of about sixteen feet. "I'll need a free hand from the both of you," Flange said, holding out an upturned palm to each man. "As soon as you become aware of your surroundings, be ready for anything. The chamber is a large rectangular room that is torchlit. The walls contain pictorial writings, and the center of the room contains an etched circle. Do not step on it. I don't know if it can harm you, but to be safe, stay away from it."

Both men acknowledged that they understood. Sprig shifted nervously as Flange held his hand out. An amused smile crept onto Flange's thin lips at seeing the uneasy look on the boy's face. "I don't bite, boy," Flange said in an amused tone, "At least not without being provoked," Flange added with a mischievous smile that shone with glee.

Sprig refused to succumb to Flange's antagonism and grabbed a dagger in one hand and grasped the reaching Undead hand in the other. The Baron drew his sword and grabbed Flange's other waiting hand.

Sprig felt a cold, charged, tingling sensation. As much as he wanted to retrieve his hand from the phenomenon, he clung to the uncanny embrace.

Flange closed his eyes and began focusing, on what, Sprig was unsure. Sprig felt the earth move under his feet as a wave of vertigo passed over him. He was falling, or so he believed. His grip tightened on the Undead hand as a numbing cold laid siege to his limbs.

The falling sensation, that seemed to last a lifetime, ended as Sprig fell heavily to the ground. He shivered uncontrollably as he tried to make sense of what had happened to him. First he felt the falling sensation, then the extreme cold.

Sprig opened his eyes to find himself curled into a fetal position on a stone floor. He was shivering uncontrollably as a frigid chill spread through his limp body. Sprig pulled his frost-laden eyelids apart to see torchlight filtering through his watery eyes.

Keltch was down on one knee with his sword drawn and shivering. Ice crystals had formed in his beard and over his skin. His teeth chattered uncontrollably as he did his best to prepare to defend himself from an attack.

Sprig tried to uncurl his grasping fingers that were stuck to the frozen blade, but his sluggish body refused to respond to his commands.

Flange seemed not to notice the frigid temperature as the other two men shivered on the floor, and he simply stood in a protective stance scanning the chamber. "What hap—happened to—to me?" Sprig said through chattering teeth.

The Baron was attempting to stand and Flange extended a hand to help the process along and said, "We have to get out of here, now! Something is very wrong." Keltch made it to his feet and then reached down to grab the stricken Sprig.

Sprig's body refused his mental commands to get up and its only response was to continue shaking convulsively on the hard stone floor. "Let's move, boy, if you want to stay alive!" Keltch grumbled trying to control his quaking jaw.

Sprig fought the sensation to just close his eyes and let the cold darkness embrace him. He stood shakily and blinked away the ice crystals that held his eyelids shut. The blurry torchlit chamber swayed before him and he nearly fell. Keltch steadied the youth and scanned the room with his eyes, resting on the Circle of Power on the floor in the center of the room.

The etched lines reflected the torchlight, giving the Circle the eerie quality of a coiled snake wrapped around itself. Keltch shook off the thought as he noticed a black globe that seemed to be floating above the etching. Flange was also staring at the floating black swirl. "What is that?" Keltch questioned.

Flange stroked his chin in thought and answered, "I have no idea, but I'm sure it's nothing good." Flange stepped away from his charges and moved cautiously toward the Circle, trying to get a better look at the swirling mass. He watched the translucent shapes move within the sphere that held them captive.

Flange shifted his focus and knelt before the Circle and ran a slender finger across the depressions of shapes in the elaborate etching. A fine dust clung to his fingers and he smelled and tasted the contents. He continued probing the circle until he was satisfied with the investigation.

Keltch watched in silence, scanning the chamber. Sprig was more alert now and held his blades ready for an attack. Flange stood and watched the blackened sphere. "I thought you said we were in danger," Keltch said, breaking the silence.

Without turning to face the Baron, Flange replied, "You are." The "you" instead of "we" was not lost on the Baron.

"Why are we in danger?" Keltch questioned again while shaking the melting ice crystals from his exposed hairy arms. Sprig turned toward the pictograph-laden walls and began trying to make some sense of the work.

"You are in danger because my sister has taken the opportunity to lay warding spells on this chamber," Flange said looking over his shoulder at the expectant Baron.

"Nothing has happened yet," Keltch replied.

"We haven't set the trap off yet," Flange answered. "My guess is that it will happen when we try to leave."

"So what do we do?" Keltch asked. Sprig was staring at the characters on the wall.

"Hey, this writing looks like some kind of equations for something," Sprig said aloud but more himself.

Flange turned to look in the direction of the youth who had his back to him. "How do you know that?" Flange said in a low menacing tone while wearing a creased brow. The dangerous change in Flange's demeanor set the two men on guard.

Sprig carefully turned around to face the waiting Flange, putting his back against the pictured wall. In an even tone he answered Flange's question, "My mentors had a library with lots of books. I remember reading one that contained pictured art like the ones on the walls. I'm not sure exactly what it says, but my best guess is that each strip of pictographs is a list of items," Sprig finished without showing a hint of the fear he was feeling.

Flange's facial features softened and he visibly relaxed. "You are very right in your assumptions, knife-wielder," Flange said, seeing the boy with new eyes. Keltch exhaled the breath he was holding during the exchange. "What else do you summarize about the carvings?"

Sprig was relieved by the response and turned back to study the pictures before him. He quickly regained his composure and scanned the wall once again. After a few minutes, and no new revelations, Sprig turned around to face the waiting Undead. "If I knew exactly what I was looking at, I might be able to give you an answer. You obviously know what it says, you tell me," Sprig said with bravado that he did not truly feel.

The face of the Undead creature lit up with a mischievous smile. "Okay, young Sprig, I'll enlighten your curious mind. I did not have the luxury of books that covered this type of lore, but I did have plenty of time to learn their significance over the centuries." Flange glided to the side of Sprig, faster then a heartbeat. The quickness of the movement startled the boy, but he kept his cool. If Flange noticed the uneasiness on Sprig's face, he chose to ignore it by staring at a row of pictographs on the wall. He continued, "You may not be sensitive enough to feel this," he said holding his hand over an etched picture, "but this particular glyph radiates a faint power. I knew that they were somehow different but it took a long time to learn how to fine-tune my senses to understand just how it worked."

Flange turned his head slightly and looked into the boy's eyes. Sprig had to fight the shiver that ran down his spine. Looking into the creature's eyes was like staring into a never-ending abyss that he could feel himself falling into.

An even smile tugged at the corners of Flange's mouth. Sprig shook his head to clear it and Flange started to speak again. "Each one of these pictures refers to items that exist somewhere in the world. Some of the items are fairly common, while others are quite unique. The pictographs show what items are needed to do certain things and where they are to be placed on the Circle. Some of these glyphs radiate no power at all, and it can be assumed that they have been used in the Circle, or they have been destroyed somewhere outside of Haven."

Keltch listened intently and cautiously walked over to the conversing men. "So what happens when these items are added to the Circle?" Keltch asked, joining the conversation.

"A power is unleashed and the items are destroyed," Flange said in a nonchalant way. Keltch was convinced that there was more to it then that and pressed further, "What does this power do?"

Flange smiled once more and said, "It can do almost anything. Some of the formulas are for trivial things; while others are so complex that I have yet to figure out their purposes. My task has become even harder since my siblings have banded together against me. My research time has become rather limited."

Sprig brushed his hand lightly across the wall's surface trying to feel any of the power that supposedly radiated from the etchings, but he could feel nothing but the cool damp surface.

"Did your siblings use these pictures to create that globe over the Circle?" Keltch asked, thumbing over his shoulder in the direction of the center of the chamber. Flange's eyes followed and settled on the blackened sphere hanging over the silver-and-golden-etched floor.

"I can almost guess that they did," he said and turned back around to face the wall. He began carefully searching the pictures following the rows, some halfway around the room. He stopped and knelt by a particular row and gently probed the surface with his fingers and mouthing the etched words silently to himself. "This is it," he said aloud poking his index finger into one of the recesses of a picture. "She has opened a doorway to a nether world and summoned some kind of beings. That might explain the globe."

"Did we interpret her work?" Sprig questioned. "Is that why they did not attack on us when we arrived?"

"I don't think they can," Flange said and stood from the kneeling position that he was in and walked to the center of the chamber at the edge of the etched Circle. His eyes scanned the globe and the contents that were held within. Keltch and Sprig exchanged concerned looks and shrugged. Neither one really knew what to think about the whole ordeal.

The torchlight caught a flicker and the blade that was only moments before sheathed at Flange's side suddenly leapt into his hands in a ready position. Sprig brought his own blades to bear on an unseen enemy. Keltch had kept his sword in a defensive position since he had picked himself off the cold floor and only dropped his stance to get better balance.

Flange bought his curved sword up over his head in both hands and slashed the blade forward in a quick downward stroke. The forward momentum slowed as the blade cleaved into the black globe and was momentarily held before it burst through the lower side. Unearthly howls and screams erupted, filling the room in what seemed like unfathomed agony.

"My brethren!" A hoarse, guttural voice roared from the opposite end of the room. An explosion of clay shards pelted the walls, ricocheting and stabbing into the exposed flesh of the three men. Flange did not seem to notice the barrage, but red blots of free-flowing blood dotted the flesh of the two mortal men.

Black menacing translucent forms appeared from the center of the explosions at the four corners of the room. "My brethren!" they roared in hateful voices and streaked through the air to intercept the waiting Flange.

"You could have given us some kind of warning you Undead bastard!" Keltch bellowed.

Flange ran the image of the speeding creatures through his mind. The beasts were enormous! They flew through the air aloft on heavy wings much like bats, with outstretched claws jutting from thick-corded arms and legs. Their flattened faces held chiseled angles that surrounded a deep-set maw filled with jagged fangs. Perhaps the most frightening feature was the red hate-filled eyes that sought retribution. He had no memory of such creatures or the best defense against them, so he braced for the charge.

One of the beasts, even in a corporal form, had enough mass to knock Flange off his feet when the two collided. Flange took the blow and skidded across the Circle and halfway to the other end of the chamber with the creature riding on top of his chest.

Keltch leaped over the Circle and was surprised to see his blade pass through one of the creatures as he struck in a furious attack. The creature ignored the Baron's blow and flew over the Circle where the sphere had hung and was sucked into the swirling mass of darkness. The two other beasts from the opposite corners also hurled themselves into the dissipating black void over the Circle.

The creature, crushing Flange's body, dug its taloned claws into his chest. "What have you done to my brethren?" the creature spat in an unearthly voice with words full of venom. Flange was too busy trying his best to support the overwhelming weight to answer.

Sprig spun and hurled two daggers and struck what would have been lethal wounds on any other creature. Unfortunately the daggers slowed and passed through the creature's shimmering form, clattering against the opposing wall.

Flange kicked and twisted his body in a fitful effort to be rid of his assailant. The misshapen creature was hurled into the opposing wall and the effort appeared to buy some time.

In the voice of a mighty battle general, Flange yelled as he sprang to his feet taking a defensive stance, "Rally to me!"

Keltch leaped forward and stood back-to-back with Flange while Sprig dove forward and rolled across the room to retrieve his discarded daggers.

The creature shook off the stun from the impact of the wall and turned, roaring, full of rage for the waiting duo. Flange stood rigid and began an incantation while the Baron prepared for another attack. Sprig rolled into the corner retrieving the blades and turned, crouched, ready to face the demonic foe.

"I'm sworn to destroy any who enter this chamber," the creature spat with malice. Flange finished his incantation and the floor where he stood seemed to falter and shift. The Baron threw his arms out to keep his balance as he fell through the opening that Flange had created in the stone floor.

Sprig watched as the ground swallowed Keltch and decided this was not a place he wanted to die, so he rolled across the floor and fell into the soupy mix that had been the stone floor only moments ago.

Flange's eyes cleared and he turned to face the creature lurking before him. "What are you and why do you disturb the practice of Haven?"

The creature crept slowly toward the waiting ashen-gray figure. The massive creature sized up the smaller one before him. "You have destroyed my kin!" the creature roared as it sought an opening in the stance of the defensive warrior.

"I do not fully understand the properties of this blade, but I am certain that I did not destroy your brethren. More than likely, they have returned from whence they came."

The creature halted, pondering what Flange had said. "Why should I believe you? You may have destroyed all that is left of my race and trapped me here to boot," the creature said in a rough guttural voice.

Flange beheld the creature and sadness fell on him. "My sister is to blame for your debt. Consider yourself a pawn in her game if you must, but I wish to leave the premises," Flange said watching the creature.

"I cannot let you. I am bound by an oath that must be obeyed when summoned."

Flange nodded in understanding. "I see, but I must leave this place and see to my charges. I too have an oath to keep," and with that said, Flange leaped at the creature and struck it with blind fury.

The creature fell back under the onslaught and Flange turned and dove toward the ripples in the shimmering floor. His outstretched body hit the floor and he slid toward the opening. But just as he reached the edge, the creature's body elongated and lunged with its clawed talons latching around Flange's trailing leg, bringing his forward momentum to an abrupt halt.

Flange twisted his body, rolled onto his back, and kicked at the unyielding creature with his free leg. The creature used the opportunity to grab the other leg and lift Flange off the ground. With a half-turn, the beast hurled Flange across the room to crash into the opposite wall. The impact was so great that the stone wall cracked and portions of the centuries-old formulas fell into debris on the crumpled form of Flange.

Flange lay still as the dust settled on his body. The creature moved cautiously and stood over the fallen form. Flange's face was twisted into a grimace and suddenly his eyes snapped open and a wicked grin stretched across his dust-covered face. "That actually hurt," Flange said as thick black blood ran from his mouth and lips down his chin.

The creature hovered over the sprawled man, just out of sword reach. Flange suddenly rolled away and came up in a defensive position with the sword in front of him. The creature turned with the action and leaped after the evasive figure. Flange parried the striking talons and followed with a slash across the creature's eyes. The blade appeared to pass through the area without apparent harm, but its unleashed cry said otherwise.

Flange used the opportunity to run the other direction. The creature's temporary blindness gave way in time to see the fleeing figure disappear as the floor swallowed it. The creature bellowed in rage for it had failed in its summoned task to keep those who entered from ever leaving.

* * *

Sprig felt himself falling into a darkened gap. Again the numbing cold pierced his body, and he did his best to curl up into a protective ball. The falling sensation turned into one of being flung up into the air, and he landed hard on his side. His body shook uncontrollably and his teeth threatened to rattle out of his head as they hammered together in a violent rhythm. Frost covered his entire body and he fought to pry his stuck eyelids apart.

He was lying on the ground and the darkness refused to leave his eyes, yet he could make out shapes of things around him. "It's night. What happened to the day?" Sprig said to himself through clacking teeth.

The shapes around him began to make sense. He was curled into a fetal position on his side and dry twigs and pine needles poked at his frostbitten skin. Trees from outside of the clearing broke up the darkness in jagged bands.

In an extreme effort, Sprig forced his head off the ground to get a better perspective of his surroundings. "Baron?" Sprig heard his croaking voice say. His limbs were numb and near useless in their current state, but nonetheless, he struggled to pull his uncooperative torso from the dirt. The air smelled of something putrid.

Propping himself on his hands, Sprig bobbed his trembling head, trying to locate the Baron. The rustling of leaves and branches could also be heard about thirty feet away, and he could see some movement of dark shapes against the lighter background.

Sprig pushed himself off the ground and fell forward on unsteady legs. He managed to catch his balance and stumble toward the motion. The clang of steel echoed through the clearing and a glint of light reflected off of swinging blades. Sprig drew two of his own blades and staggered toward the melee.

Sprig could see that one of the forms was definitely the Baron, but exactly what the other was left him for a loss of words. It appeared to be a man surrounded by long waving arms. Sprig had never seen a creature to compare it to.

The arms lashed at the Baron followed by a sword stroke by the man entwined within them. Sprig could see that Keltch was in no better condition than he was. The Baron clumsily deflected the blows and did nothing to counter with an attack. Sprig was not sure how long he could hold out from the assault.

Sprig slowed and steadied his footing. He held out one of his blades in a shaky hand and aimed for a throw. The creature hammered the Baron with a blow that sent his sword flying from his grasp. The Baron fell to one knee and held his arms up to shield his head. The creature stayed the killing blow, but its surrounding tendrils lashed out and grabbed the Baron around the neck.

A blood-curdling scream escaped Keltch's throat and he fought to loosen the creature's strangling coils. The attempt to escape failed utterly, for the more he struggled, the tighter the grip became. Already exhausted from the freezing temperature and the combat, Keltch fell limp with his face scrunched in a grimace, and he dangled from the entangled tentacles.

Sprig panicked, seeing the predicament of the helpless Baron, and raised his hand over his head to aim a shot with his newly crafted dagger. Before he could launch the blade, a crushing grip by an unseen assailant forced him to drop the blade. His restrained hand was twisted and his body lurched around to avoid having his arm broken.

"I told you I would feast on your bones!" croaked Sasha, towering wickedly over the young man. Sprig reached with his loose hand and grabbed another blade from the bandoleer. But as he attempted to stab her, she lashed out with a lightning-fast backhand and struck him across the face. The force of the blow stunned Sprig and his dagger flew from his hand.

Jolting pains brought him to his senses long enough to realize that Sasha was holding him off the ground by his twisted arm. He tried to grab another dagger but she snatched his searching wrist with her free arm and held him off the ground.

Leaning forward, Sasha head-butted Sprig in the face and he collapsed with an open gash across his forehead. Sasha held him up and searched the unconscious face and then tossed his body across her shoulders like a grain-filled sack.

"Drop him, Sasha," a voice said. Sasha half turned and looked over her shoulder. Flange was rising out of the ground with his sword drawn and ready.

"Well, well, hello lover," Sasha said, losing some of her guttural tone. "So you made it out of Rewella's little trap. Somehow I didn't think it would hinder you."

The ground under Flange's feet became solid and he dropped his weight and balanced. "I said drop him," he repeated, and his tone was pure ice.

"Looks to me like you have a choice to make. You might be able to take the boy, or you can have the Baron, but you can't have both," Sasha said, smiling from her lupine face at the predicament.

Flange looked past Sasha and saw the limp form of Keltch being drained by Barcus. Flange had no allegiance to the boy but was certain that he was a ward of the Baron's. He hesitated, trying to formulate a plan to save both but knew it was next to impossible.

Flange's enhanced senses could feel the life forces ebbing from the clutched Baron. He knew that too much time spent sparring with Sasha would only end with Keltch's death.

Flange made his decision and launched an attack at Sasha. She leapt back out of the arc of the sword slash. Sprig yelped in pain as Sasha's movement yanked his arms apart as she used his dangling body as a shield in front of her. Flange's attack was a feint and he rushed passed the retreating Sasha to attack his sibling.

Barcus stood with his arms outstretched and his head rolled back enjoying the ecstasy of the stolen life force. He was oblivious to Flange's charge until it was too late.

Flange's movement was swift and would have been missed in the blink of an eye. His sword slashed in a downward arc and passed through the corporeal tendrils that were wrapped around Keltch's throat.

Barcus screamed and was shaken from his bliss as his multitude of appendages thrashed uncontrollably from the intense pain. Keltch collapsed to the ground as the two severed tendrils released their death grip.

The sword that Barcus held up in his outstretched arm swung around and down to block the blade streaking toward his face. The two swords clashed together in a loud clang that echoed through the surrounding trees. Recognition dawned on Barcus' misshapen face and his expression turned into one filled with unbridled hatred.

"You did this to me, you bastard!" Barcus raged and swung his sword furiously, trying to get through the defense of parries that Flange sent against him. "You tipped off those hunters and look what they did to me," he yelled jerking a thumb toward his cratered head, "and you stole from my lair!"

"I've done nothing of the kind, although you've been deserving of what has happened to you," Flange said deflecting another savage blow.

"Liar! You think you are so full of honor, but you are no better than us. You're a killer and a murderer no matter how much you try to say that you aren't," Barcus spat venomously.

"I get no pleasure in killing babies, and I have never turned the living or raised the dead. There is no honor in it."

"Bah! What about all those mortals you have killed during your little game with the Baron?" Barcus said, jerking his thumb over his shoulder in the direction of the unconscious Keltch.

"I've only killed those seeking my death. They knew what to expect and made their decisions freely," Flange said as he sent a stab to Barcus' midsection. The thrust was parried and a backslash was returned aimed at Flange's head, which he sidestepped easily and took another two steps back away from his brother.

"Bah! Do you think those poor wretches really had a choice? They're only doing what they have to do to survive and feed their families."

Flange had to believe that he was different from his treacherous siblings, but the truth of the words stung. He had killed many men over the past years, and he had enjoyed the sport, but ultimately, he knew he was an exceptional creature and that there really was no challenge killing these mortals, at least those without any swordsmanship anyway. "I have no want to kill you, brother, but I will leave you with a reminder for your audacity," Flange said as he flicked a wicked slash across Barcus' chest.

Barcus was too late to deflect the cut and grimaced in pain as the blade sunk deeply into his flesh and tore across opening a deep a gash in his chest.

"You bastard!" Barcus spat, grabbing at the flesh that spread apart as the blade departed.

Flange stepped back out of striking range and displayed a wicked cruel smile. "Oh, come on, brother, do you think your victims feel any less pain? How many babies and elderly have you turned only so their loved ones could destroy them? Do you think they feel any less pain during their transformation? How about their last moments as they burn in the sunlight?" Flange said, continuing to smile gleefully.

"I need it and you know it," Barcus fumed through gritted teeth. "You know it drives the hunger that threatens to turn us mad."

"I don't need to do that and neither do you," Flange said as the smile disappeared from his face.

"We are all different, Flange. You must satisfy your desire by killing those who oppose you. I've seen the look on your face as you're hacking away at those hapless souls. It is no different for me."

Flange backed another two steps away from his brother although he did not lower his guard. "It is different because I get no enjoyment out of killing those who cannot defend themselves, and you seem to relish on preying on the weak. It sickens me, brother."

"You are in no place to judge. I never asked for this to happen to me!" Barcus yelled and charged toward Flange, slashing furiously.

Flange dropped his stance and prepared for the attack. Barcus' furious charge was textbook of someone who had nothing to lose. His attack may have been furious, but Flange merely sidestepped and sent a thrust to the exposed chest of his brother. The sword passed easily between Barcus' ribs and through his heart.

The brothers stood a breath apart from each other and the look of shock on Barcus' face was evident but anger also filled his features. Flange yanked his blade in an upward motion, tearing it from Barcus' clavicle, and stepped away.

Barcus' look of shock turned to one of incomprehension and his legs gave way as he collapsed to the ground. "I'm sorry, brother, but eventually your actions do catch up to you," Flange said lowering his guard and straightening from his defensive stance.

A long howl pierced the silence and Flange looked in the direction of the shriek. Sasha had the limp form of Sprig draped over one shoulder and she was walking away as she looked over her other shoulder at Flange. A darker shadow elongated and swallowed her and the dangling Sprig before Flange could act on her departure. A sigh escaped his lips and his shoulders slumped.

Flange turned and looked at the sprawled form of the Baron. He wiped his blade on the grimy shirt that Barcus had been wearing and sheathed his sword.

Flange stood over the sprawled Baron and thought, *Here lies the enemy who had spent his entire life trying to destroy me.* A quick knowing smile tugged at the corners of his mouth, and he mused at his fallen nemesis.

Carefully, as through he were picking up a sleeping child, Flange scooped up the unconscious Baron and held him against his chest. A shape on the ground caught Flange's preternatural eyes and he walked to it, carrying the Baron against his body. A filthy plumed wide-brimmed hat lay on the ground. Flange shifted Keltch into one arm and reached down with his free hand and picked up the hat, which he tucked into his belt. Then the ground opened beneath his feet and he slowly sank, disappearing under the earth and the cover of the night.

* * *

"Where's Barcus?" the Porcelain Lady asked as Sasha emerged from the black shadow that had opened in the corner.

Sasha slung the limp form of Sprig forward and dropped him on the ground on the cold stone floor. Without detouring her gaze Sasha said, "Flange killed Barcus, Rewella. I watched him tear the blade from his heart."

"Barcus cannot be dead," Rewella dismissed the idea, for it was simply an impossibility. "Flange would never kill his own blood."

"Oh really? I saw it with my own eyes, Rewella. He killed Barcus and would have killed me if I had not escaped with this bag of bones," Sasha glared at the unconscious man, "I want this one dead, Rewella, and I don't appreciate you insisting that I bring him back alive. He's a threat and deserves death like any of those who hunt us," she said and gave a swift kick in the ribs of the unconscious man. A groan escaped Sprig's lips and he instinctively curled into a ball for protection from any future blows.

Rewella spoke an incomprehensible word and a candle sparked to life on a nearby table. "Go get Barcus and meet me at the entrance to Haven," she said, turning away from the dumbfounded woman in lupine form.

"What if Flange has him?" Sasha said with concern.

"He doesn't. Now go before it is too late," Rewella said not turning to face her protégé.

Sasha reluctantly walked back to the corner she had appeared from and felt the cool grip at her being as the surroundings blurred and changed to the darkened woods that she had left only moments ago.

She crouched down and sniffed. Barcus' smell was heavy in the air but the scent of Flange was fleeting and she knew he had disappeared shortly after her departure. She smelled the air again just to be certain.

The tension left her shoulders and she sighed heavily. Carefully she stalked toward the position where she knew Barcus had fallen. His slumped form lay on the dew-filled grass and she crouched over him and gazed at the terrific wound in his chest.

A twinge of fear sent a chill down her spine. She knew what Flange was capable of once he set his mind to a task. Again she shivered. She bent over the massive form of Barcus and slipped her furry arms around his waist, hoisting his remains over her shoulder.

Sasha smelled the air and peered around cautiously. There still was no scent of Flange, but that did not mean much of anything. Flange had a knack for disappearing when he did not want to be found. For all she knew, he could still be right under her nose.

Sasha decided that the path to Haven was clear so she leaped a fallen tree trunk and bounded into the clearing containing the fairy ring.

A shadow lengthened and a gigantic spider appeared and strode into the meadow carrying a webbed bundle on its back. The enormous spider stopped in the center of the patch of mushrooms and Sprig tumbled from its back onto the ground. The spider disintegrated into smaller ones that scurried to form into Rewella.

Rewella searched the unconscious face of the boy who lay on the ground before her. She knelt down before him and caressed his cheek. *Other than the bruise on his forehead,* she thought, *the youth is quite handsome.* Her hand moved across his cheek to the ugly bump that she gently probed.

Sprig grimaced at the inquiring touch, a moan escaped his lips, but he remained unconscious. Rewella shifted her hand from the bruise in favor of running her fingers through his tussle of hair.

Sasha ran into the clearing and stopped short of the Porcelain Lady who was seated on the ground with Sprig's head cradled in her lap. She hurled Barcus to the ground and in a hurtful tone demanded, "What are you doing to him, Rewella?"

Rewella smiled up at the jealous she-wolf and carefully removed Sprig's cradled head from her lap, stood up, and said, "How would you like a companion, Sasha?"

Sasha's hurt turned to rage. "You can't be serious! You wouldn't dare make him like us!" Sasha fumed.

"Like you," Rewella corrected, "You may be immortal, but you are not an Undead being."

Sasha stood in surprise with her jowls hanging open. "Why would you do that to me?" Sasha said with a throaty growl. Rewella smiled at the lupine that towered over her and said, "I'm offering you a unique being like yourself." Rewella looked down at the unconscious man. "He is quite handsome, Sasha, and you could do far worse."

"He tried to kill me! How could you even consider that I would want someone like that as a companion?" Sasha howled.

"For starters, you might actually respect him because he did manage to hurt you. He would be a worthy equal for you," Rewella reasoned.

"I don't want him, Rewella. I have you, don't I?" Sasha croaked.

"Yes, my pet. But if you refuse, I may not offer this opportunity ever again. Are you sure this is what you desire?" Rewella questioned. Sasha stared down at the unconscious man with a look of disgust.

"Yes," Sasha growled. Rewella nodded and began chanting. Sprig's body began radiating an unnatural heat, and then the group wavered into a mist and disappeared into the ground.

The trio appeared on the stone floor in a corner of Haven. Sasha immediately reared up and leaped in front of Rewella. A low warning growl escaped her throat as she prepared for an attack.

An enormous winged creature stood near the center of the room looking at the etched Circle. Without turning, the creature spoke in a very deep voice that resonated off the walls, "I have failed and my brethren are destroyed." The hulking creature slumped onto the stone floor and its wings folded around it.

Rewella placed a hand on Sasha's shoulder to stay her and then walked around her protector. At the gesture, Sasha visibly relaxed, but nevertheless stayed on her guard. Rewella walked from behind the slumped beast and moved around the edge of the Circle of Power until she was facing opposite of the beaten creature.

Yellow eyes rimmed in red glared at her from across the Circle. Rewella folded her slender arms across her chest and watched the creature in silence. "Tell me what happened," she asked in a polite manner.

The creature's harsh glare did not soften but its taloned wings unwrapped, rising slowly off its plated shoulders as it sat up straight. "This place holds great power. I have seen very few Power Points that are able to hold my kind. Time is eternal in the Void but I know that it has been centuries since a summoning of our race has happened and not by creatures such as yourself," the beast said in a hoarse whisper.

Rewella felt a tremor race down her spine and it had been centuries since she had felt such a sensation. She kept the surprise from her face, steadied her voice, and said, "Power Points? You are referring to the Circle before you?" The creature held its gaze on her and nodded slightly. "There are others? How many? Where are they located?" The questions spilled from her mouth rapidly in the excitement.

A deep chuckle rumbled from the creature, booming off the walls, and its scaled body shook with the motion. "You may have ended my life by trapping me here, but I don't have to answer your questions, Keeper of the Spiders."

Rewella composed her face once more into a mask of neutrality and said, "Your life is not forfeit, yet," she added as a thin smile traced her lips. "I can still save you."

The creature broke his gaze and looked at the Circle. "It does not matter. My brethren are destroyed and I long for no other purpose," it said with a sigh and slumped to the floor.

"Your kindred are not destroyed and I can return you to them once you have completed your summoned task," Rewella lied rather nonchalantly. She had no idea whether his kin were destroyed or not, but a plan formulated in her mind.

The creature shifted and his eyes fell on her once again and it said, "You can do nothing to save me other than sending me back to the Void. I am growing weaker by the second. My form is already dissipating."

Rewella knew he was speaking the truth. The brilliant colors of red and orange were turning grayish in tint, and the creature's own weight seemed to be crushing its corporeal form.

"I can save you and will return you home after you have killed Flange," Rewella said, watching the behemoth before her for any signs of its thoughts, "but you have to tell me exactly what happened in this chamber before I can do anything for you."

Again the creature laughed, "I fear you are lying but I will tell you what you ask," the creature said and attempted to sit up again before he spoke. "Three beings entered the chamber," the creature smelled the air and turned and looked over its shoulder at Sasha and the unconscious man at her feet. "That boy is one of them. Another man and a creature like yourself," the winged beast said looking back at the waiting Rewella.

Rewella nodded and said, "The being like myself is Flange."

"This Flange opened a portal and the two men escaped. I fought him but he fled after them," the creature said with some effort as its form began to shimmer, becoming more translucent, and then toppled forward to land on the outer edge of the Circle. Its eyes rolled to the back of its head and the body twitched and convulsed.

Rewella knew that time was of the essence and barked a command to Sasha, "Quick! Move it to the center of the Circle!"

Sasha had been listening to the exchange in silence and leaped to Rewella's side at the command. "Hurry! It is almost too late," Rewella said and spoke a word of power causing a box to appear in the shadows of a corner. Rewella ran to the chest and opened it. While she was doing that, Sasha reached around the torso of the mighty creature and strained as she pulled the massive creature into the center of the Circle. Sasha's arms seemed to pass through the body, but the creature eventually slid across the floor.

Rewella hastily grabbed items from the chest and ran to kneel before the Circle. She placed several gems and objects of gold and silver into the slots and etchings of the Great Circle. Rewella looked up from her task and said, "Now grab Barcus and that whelp of a boy and put them in the circle."

Sasha stopped and stared at her mentor and said, "What are you going to do, Rewella?"

"There is no time to question me, Sasha, do what I said!" Rewella yelled.

Sasha was surprised by the usually composed woman and stared at her tutor.

"Do what I say, child! I fear it is already too late!" Rewella yelled.

Sasha leaped over the Circle and grabbed both of the still forms and slid them across the floor into the Circle, one in each arm.

The three bodies rested with each piled onto the other in the center of the Circle of Power. Rewella leaped from her position and sank to her knees on the other side of the Circle dropping more of the items into the etchings. She leaned back and sighed, putting her hands on her hips.

Sasha leaped from the Circle and landed behind Rewella, taking up a protective stance.

"I'm not sure this is going to work, but it is worth a try," Rewella whispered.

Blue-black lightning sparked from the etching on the floor and coursed into the bodies lying on the Circle. The unconscious forms twitched as the arcs of electricity entered them, and then fled back into the gold and silver etchings of the Circle.

The crackle and charged energy burst into a white flame, engulfing the occupants of the Circle. Sasha threw up a furry arm to block the brilliant bright light and Rewella closed her eyes for only a brief moment.

Barcus seemed to incinerate into ash, and the summoned creature changed into a translucent mist that surrounded Sprig's body and then disappeared altogether.

Sprig was alone on the Circle, convulsing as his body swelled and took on a reddish tint. The spasms stopped and he struggled to raise himself from the floor. "What's happening to me?" he tried to say in a voice that was not his own, and collapsed to the floor.

"What have you done, Rewella?" Sasha whispered from behind her mentor. Rewella smiled and watched the floundering boy.

Sprig pulled himself from the floor and tried to sit up on the Circle. He then stood up and starred at his arms in wonder. He took in every detail, inhaling heavily as he stared at his form. His muscles bulged, filling out his once-loose clothing.

"What have you done, Rewella?" Sasha hissed again. It was evident, she was becoming extremely agitated by what was happening. She grabbed Rewella's arm and turned the raven-haired woman to face her.

Even in lupine form, the shock was apparent on Sasha's face. "Are you out of your mind? What could you possibly be thinking to do that?" Sasha howled.

Rewella flashed a knowing smile, not unlike Flange's own and said, "You had your chance, my love, and squandered the opportunity. I only took advantage of it." Rewella's smile faltered and her eyes took on a sinister cast as she intentionally led her gaze to the furry arm that was clutching at her own, and Sasha immediately let go.

Rewella's smile slowly crept back to her red, perfect lips. She turned from Sasha and walked to the edge of the Circle. Lost in the moment, Sprig continued staring at his altered body. "Do you like your new form?" Rewella questioned.

Sprig broke from the wonderment of his body, and he looked over at the waiting woman. Rewella could see that his eyes were yellow, trimmed in red, and the crimson tint seemed to be slowly disappearing from his muscled skin. "What have you done to me?" Sprig spoke in a voice deeper than normal. He rubbed his right wrist absently and was not sure why he was doing so.

"I have kept you from perishing just like I promised," Rewella stated. "Now tell me what happened here, and I want all the details."

A smile spread on the handsome face of the young man and he threw his arms up and stretched. After finishing, he purposely strode from the Circle and stood before the Porcelain Lady. "Show me my brethren. If they still exist and you have not lied to me, then I will tell you everything you want to know. If not, I will tear your head from your body," Sprig threatened. A smile grew on his face as if relishing the thought.

Rewella stood locked in his gaze, and her mind turned circles trying to come up with a plan. After several tension-filled moments, she smiled back at the youth and said, "I do not have the components with me to duplicate the summoning spell. I must go back to my lair first."

"Unacceptable. You can send your pet after the items," Sprig said and grabbed her wrist as she tried to turn away from him.

A roar echoed through the chamber and a lightning flash of a furry shape sailed through the air toward Sprig. Sasha's slavering jaws opened and she tried to bite at the arm that held Rewella.

Sprig turned loose Rewella's arm in favor of using the same hand to grab Sasha by the throat. The lunging she-wolf was stopped dead in her tracks and she let out a stifled yelp as Sprig hoisted her off the ground. He stared into the feral eyes of the shaggy beast and smiled. "You hate this boy, don't you? His memories are of terror and hatred for you too. He was intent on killing you for some reason."

Sprig's grasp nearly choked the life from Sasha. Her eyes bulged and she raked her claws repeatedly across Sprig's arm in an attempt to escape. "I see it now. Oh yes. You killed his mentors. I see fear in your eyes, she-beast. Is it because I'm about to squeeze the life from you or is it because this boy was capable of killing you?" Sprig asked.

Sasha struggled desperately in a last attempt to free herself. Her eyes rolled to the back of her head and her great pink tongue loped from her massive jaws. Her body shook with a spasm, and her resistance began to falter as her arms slipped clumsily from Sprig's choking grasp until they hung limply at her side.

Sprig smiled at the unconscious she-wolf. "Your growl is worse than your bite." With that said, Sprig hurled the were-creature across the room.

Sasha sailed through the air, crashed into the opposite wall, and crumbled to the stone floor in a twisted heap.

Sprig's laughter bellowed off the walls, echoing throughout the chamber. The creature that now inhabited Sprig's body watched

Rewella intently for a reaction, but she stood quietly, with her arms crossed over her chest.

"Impressive," Rewella said calmly, watching the exchange. "I'm glad that the abilities I gave you won't go to waste."

Sprig stared at her with those unearthly eyes and smiled a slow cruel smile. "You have no idea what you have done for me, do you? The ancients were never foolish enough to give us physical form. It shows me how inept you truly are," said the creature that had been melded into Sprig.

Rewella smiled and placed her hands on her petite curvaceous hips. "I made you this way for a reason. You still have the task to complete that I summoned you for. I spared your life so that you may avenge any wrongdoing that Flange may have done to you or your people."

Rewella sank behind a mask of neutrality and then her face took on a hard edge as her eyes narrowed in anger. She said, "You will obey my commands or you will never see the Void you came from or your kind again."

Sprig laughed and said, "You have never summoned a creature such as me before, and you know nothing of what you are trying to do. You put my form in the flesh and in so doing, you freed my will." Again Sprig laughed and closed his eyes, taking a deep breath and then letting it out as a sigh. His eyes opened and settled on the opposing form of Rewella. "You cannot control me now to do your bidding. This body's will is combined with my own. I can and will oppose you."

"I knew that would be one of the byproducts of the gifts I have lavished on you," Rewella lied, "I thought you would have sense enough to see what I did for you, but I may have been wrong," she said nonchalantly and shrugged her shoulders. "It matters not, for if you won't do my bidding, you have trapped yourself in that body and this room. So either way, your existence is a prison."

"Wrong!" Sprig bellowed, "I also have the memories of your brother, and his abilities."

"You fool. Why do you think I put Barcus' body on the Circle? I knew my spell would combine you all. I felt it was necessary for you to complete your task, for Flange is a powerful enemy," Rewella added.

"Yes, I see him now. He is also your brother," Sprig said as if in a trance.

"Yes, then you know of his treachery," Rewella spoke hopefully.

"I know of yours," Sprig said and smiled, revealing his handsome features, "You speak of treachery, yet you would try to have your own sibling killed? What has he done that would warrant his death?"

"He may have destroyed your kind," Rewella interjected.

"Only because you summoned us and trapped my brethren within the Power Point," Sprig countered, "If they were not held, he would have never been inclined to bring action against us."

"Think what you will about me, but that does not change the fact that you are trapped here without my help to leave," Rewella said.

Sprig smiled and said, "Are you so sure about that? I have your brother's memories and abilities. I can leave this place you call Haven. I can move through its walls as if they did not exist."

"I wasn't talking about Haven. I was talking about this world. You can't go back home without my help," Rewella insisted.

Sprig's smile grew even wider. "I have no intention of going home," he paused for effect, "but I do intend to bring home here."

Closing his eyes, Sprig tilted his head back and raised his arms up over his head. Luminescent strands snaked from Sprig's body, casting an eerie glow on the etched stone walls. The strands danced and popped in electrical excitement and grew brighter in the passing seconds.

The sparkling filaments expanded into a blinding light that surrounded Sprig's body. Rewella could barely make out the outline of the figure buried within the thrashing radiance. The silhouetted form looked very much like Barcus before it was enveloped and disappeared completely.

The supernatural light flickered across Rewella's face and faded away. A frown creased the forehead of her perfect features. She exhaled a deep sigh. Her attempt had been to save the summoned creature so that he could seek out and destroy Flange. Throwing Barcus on the Circle had been an impulse. She had no idea exactly what to expect, but she was sure that she would be able to control the creature and the volatile situation. Now the creature had escaped her control and fled from Haven. Another sigh escaped her lips as she replayed the unfolding events back in her mind.

A moaning growl broke her reverie and she turned in Sasha's direction. The she-wolf was desperately trying to raise her body from the stone floor. Rewella covered the distance quickly and knelt down beside the sprawled form of Sasha and caressed her thick coarse hair of her head. "Are you all right, my pet?" Rewella whispered.

Sasha's head lolled over so she could see Rewella's face. Sasha glared at her with contempt. "What do you care? You caused this to happen to me, Rewella. Why did you do it? Because I refused to have that boy made into my companion?" she pleaded. Sasha's eyes rolled to the back of her head and she faltered and collapsed to the ground. Rewella continued to stroke the coarse fur and then she kissed Sasha's head tenderly.

Rewella smoothed some more of the stray strands and then spoke a string of magical words. The corner's shadow stretched and encompassed the two and they were swallowed within it, disappearing from Haven.

8

Mengrig paced nervously around the outskirts of Keltch's grand cottage. It was well after curfew and the Baron had not returned from his meeting with the evil one known only as Flange. The scouts that Mengrig had sent out to follow the Baron had found no signs of the Master's whereabouts and he feared the worst.

Mengrig eyed the lighted silhouette of Kate, who was watching and waiting for the return of her father through the leaded glass window of the cottage. Mengrig turned from the window and scanned the blackened undergrowth. His eyes were sharp, but he could make out nothing of the ordinary. A sigh escaped his lips but the uneasiness in his shoulders refused to allow them to relax.

A movement out of the corner of his eye caught his attention and as quick as lightning an arrow was notched and drawn. Mengrig stood with his bow drawn to his cheek as the ground thirty paces away seemed to ripple and shimmer. A head popped out of the ground and a body rose up attached to it.

Mengrig watched in horror as a figure appeared from the ground with a body sprawled across its shoulders. As the rays of moonlight filtered down to reveal the angular features of the rising figure, recognition dawned on Mengrig at the limp form of the Baron in Flange's arms. Reacting instinctively, Mengrig loosened the shaft, sending it flying toward Flange's moonlit eyes.

Flange shifted the Baron's weight to is right side and snatched the arrow approximately an inch from his eye with his left hand. A wry smile filled his face. "Nice shot. I almost did not see it coming until it was too late," Flange said. He turned the arrow over and looked at the fletching. "Beautifully made. Is this your workmanship?"

Mengrig was startled, but not unresponsive, as he pulled another arrow from his quiver, notched it, and drew the bowstring back for another shot.

Flange watched the display with an amused smile. Mengrig sent the arrow streaking in the same path as the first, aimed at his target's head. Flange snatched the arrow easily from the air and said, "We could be at this game all night and accomplish nothing. Lay your weapon on the ground and let me approach."

Mengrig was aware that he was in a situation that he could not handle alone. He was the only thing that stood between this evil creature and Keltch's daughter. "To arms! To arms! Form on me! Form on me! To arms! To arms!" Mengrig yelled into the still night.

Torches and lanterns flickered to life in an instant as men ran from the barracks and nearby woods toward the summons. In the few seconds that it took for the men to clear the distance to form up, Mengrig had notched another arrow and was prepared to fire it.

Several dozen hired soldiers surrounded the Undead creature with swords and spears. Flange only stood still and waited, holding the Baron with one arm and grasping the two arrows in the other hand.

"Lay the Baron's body on the ground and move away from him," Mengrig ordered. Flange's smile grew wider and he said, "The Baron is not dead, but he has been injured and not by me."

"Lay him on the ground and move away," Mengrig repeated, not lowering his aim.

The cottage door burst open, and Kate ran out, carrying a short sword and a small buckler. "What is going on?" she shouted at the gathered crowd.

"Get her back inside!" Mengrig bellowed without taking his eyes or aim off of Flange. A handful of men broke off from the crowd and barred Katie's path, forcing her to retreat to the entryway of the cottage.

Flange gingerly took a step toward Mengrig, then another, and another until he was standing before the bowman. Flange turned the fist full of arrows with the points facing down and extended his arm slowly toward Mengrig. Mengrig did not lower his aim nor did his locked gaze waver from the Undead man's eyes. Flange dropped the arrows over Mengrig's shoulder into the quiver from which they had come.

"You know that I could have used the Baron as a shield if I wanted to. You also know that if I can snatch arrows mid-flight, then surely I could have placed the Baron in harm's way if that were my intention. Would you not agree?" Flange said, staring at the bewildered yet brave man.

Mengrig loosened the tension on the bowstring and lowered the bow. Flange let his smile stretch and then it faltered as he spoke, "Keltch was attacked by my brother. I could not get to him in time to prevent the outcome. He is unconscious and may yet survive if properly attended to."

Mengrig searched Flange's eerie smoke-colored eyes for any hint of deception. The creature's presence filled him with a horrible dread and a terrible fear tugged at his heart. He could tell that those eyes held all the elements of inexplicable danger, but he also believed none of that menace was being directed at him. "If your intentions are not ill toward the Baron then set him on the ground and step away," Mengrig said with a confidence that he did not feel.

"I held no ill will toward him when I gave you the parley message and I still do not."

Kate stood in the entryway of the cottage, trying to see through the crowd at the exchange. The hired soldiers had turned around trying to keep an eye on Mengrig and Kate took the opportunity to bolt past their haphazard blockade.

Before the men could react, Kate covered the short distance and shouldered past the men standing behind Mengrig. "Father!" she yelled, seeing Keltch cradled in Flange's arms.

Flange caught the movement from behind Mengrig and his gaze shifted to the newcomer. His impassive face changed to an expression of utter astonishment. He said in a soft, questioning voice, "Mariel?"

Kate was startled by the use of her mother's name. "How do you know my mother's name? What have you done to my father?" Kate burst out.

"You're her daughter? You look so much like her," Flange was mesmerized as her words sank in, "I never knew," Flange mused. He shook his head, and gently handed the Baron over to the waiting men. He shook off whatever thoughts he had been having and his face returned to the neutral mask that had been present just moments before. He said simply, "Keep him warm and he may survive this ordeal."

The wonder of this supernatural creature seemed to be lost on Kate as she stepped in close and grabbed his arm. The hired soldiers huddled in closer in an attempt to protect her from any repercussions of such a rash action. "What happened to my father tonight and where is Sprig? Answer my questions, damn you!" Kate yelled, sinking her fingernails into Flange's arm. If he felt any pain, he did nothing to show it.

Flange reached to his waist and pulled the tucked-in worn floppy hat from his belt and held it up before the bewildered girl. "Take care of your father," he said, his gaze lingering on her tear-filled eyes. "Some things are best left unanswered during the hours of the night. I'll answer your questions in the morning."

Kate released Flange's arm and received the misshapen hat. Concerned hands gently grabbed her arms and shoulders, guiding her from the presence of the supernatural creature and ushered her and the unconscious Baron into the cottage.

Flange turned back to Mengrig and said, "You have served your master well, and I will be sure to pass that along when he's feeling better." With that said, Flange allowed the soil to waver below his feet and he sank downward as it swallowed him. The ripples where he had been standing subsided and the ground appeared to be solid once again.

The dazed crowd stood around soaking up what had happened. Mengrig broke the silence, "All right everyone, to your posts. The night is far from ended." The hired men slowly dispersed to take up their positions and digest the night's happenings.

Mengrig continued staring at the spot where Flange had disappeared as if by doing so he might reappear again. Mengrig shook off his daze and trotted off to the cottage entrance.

"What's the ruckus, Mengrig?" a baritone voice hailed. Mengrig turned to see the blacksmith hobble up on his crutch.

"The Master's been injured. I need to go inside and see how bad," Mengrig said in a tone that was meant to end further conversation. As he turned to go into the cottage, Brundle was not finished and said, "What about the boy? How is he?" Mengrig stopped and took a hard look at the colossus of a man.

"Just because you made a few blades for the new men means nothing to me, blacksmith. Your sudden concern for the Master or even Sprig, for that matter, makes me sick. Why don't you go back to your shed and continue hating the world for its wrongdoings," Mengrig spat venomously, and his eyes blazed.

Brundle stood quietly, watching the infuriated man. At any other time he would have jumped at the chance to exchange insults or punches, but the anger that he had been holding inside had abated. He really was quite sincere about his concern for both men. "I know we have had our differences in the past, Mengrig, and for that I am truly sorry, but I *need* to know what happened," Brundle said in an unusually yielding voice.

Mengrig had known this man for years, or at least he thought he did. He could not remember ever hearing the likes out of this man's mouth before. Brundle rarely spoke, but when he did, the comments were always rough and negative with a fierce temper to back them up.

Now here the man stood before Mengrig, meek as a lamb, and with an apology thrown in to boot. Mengrig shook his head and sighed. "You know as much as I do, Brundle. Let's get inside and find out for ourselves." Mengrig hammered on the thick oak door. A slat in the door opened and a pair of eyes stared out and shortly thereafter the door opened. Mengrig waited for the blacksmith to make his way through the entry and then he closed the door, setting the locks. "Where is he?" Brundle inquired in the empty entry.

"I would imagine he was taken to his room upstairs," Mengrig replied, making for the staircase. Brundle followed as best he could and by the time he had cleared the last stair, Mengrig was not to be seen.

Brundle felt uncomfortable and somewhat embarrassed. He had only been in the kitchen of the cottage and nowhere else. He heard an exchange of voices from an open doorway and moved in that direction.

Four men, Mengrig, and the lady of the house were undressing the unconscious Baron on a huge oak-framed bed. "He feels so cold," Brundle heard the young lady say.

"What've you 'spect from that bloodless bastard!" a man exclaimed.

"He should have never believed that there would ever be a truce," another man said pulling off the Baron's muddy boots.

"That damned creature-thing led him into a trap and then tried to kill 'em," the first man spat.

"I'm not so sure of that," Mengrig said, feeling for vital signs on the Baron's neck and wrists.

"How can you say that, sir!" the first man exclaimed in anger, "Just look at 'em!"

"Yes, I see him. I also know that the Baron has enough sense to avoid a trap. I'm not convinced Flange did this to him," Mengrig said, examining the numerous circular wounds surrounding Keltch's throat.

Kate had been dabbing the Baron's head with a warm wet neckerchief and stopped, looking expectantly at Mengrig. "What do you think happened, Mengrig?" Kate asked.

Mengrig shook his head and said, "I'm not sure, Miss, but I know that Flange did not have to bring the Baron here alive if he only wanted him dead. What would be the point in that? He could have killed me for shooting those arrows at him, but he chose not to. There is much more to the story than what we know."

Brundle had moved into the room, listening to the exchange. All eyes fell on him when he cleared his throat. "What about the boy? Do you know what happened to him?" the blacksmith asked.

Kate stared at the huge man and picked up the discarded hat from her father's side on the bed. "I don't know," she spoke quietly. "He would not tell me. He said he would tell me in the morning." Kate barely kept her composure as tears rimmed her eyes, threatening to cascade down her face.

"He's coming back?" Brundle inquired with some surprise.

"That is what he said, and I believe him," Kate said with resolve.

After Keltch had been undressed and placed under the down blankets of the bed, the hired men left the cottage to resume their duties. Kate could see the blacksmith shift uneasily on his crutch and immediately offered him a chair. He propped the crutch against the wall and sat gratefully in the cushioned seat and said, "So what happens now?"

The blacksmith looked at Mengrig and both men shifted their gaze to the young woman who sat on the bed next to her father.

Kate was aware that the question had been directed to her and the wheels of her mind turned. She pursued her lips and thought in silence for a few moments and then said, "We wait. We wait and see what Flange has to say about what happened. There is nothing else we can do."

"What about Sprig?" Brundle said, "He did not bring back his body. If he's on the up and up, why didn't he bring the boy back as well? Even if he was dead?"

Kate bit back the urge to cry and shook her head. "We don't know enough yet. Our questions will have to wait until morning." Then, taking an air of authority, she spoke. "Mengrig, you are my father's Captain. Continue to carry out your duties as the Baron would see fit. Keep everyone on alert till the dawn breaks."

"Yes, Miss," Mengrig answered and performed an about-face and left the room.

"Do you have any requests for me, Miss? Is there anything that I could do to help out?" Brundle asked.

"Yes, there is something you can do," Kate said.

"Anything," Brundle replied.

"Stay here with me and my father. I do not wish to be alone tonight after what has happened. I can have a bed brought in for you," Kate offered.

"Of course I will stay if you would like, but Mengrig would be a better choice at protecting you, Miss," Brundle stammered.

"I would feel more secure if you were here, blacksmith. I know you and Mengrig have a history with my father, and though I do not know you well, my father trusts you and so do I. Please, I am begging you to stay with us," Kate pleaded.

"Of course, Miss, but I don't need any bed though. This chair is fine enough for my old bones," Brundle said.

"Thank you," Kate said and lay next to her father, putting her head on his slowly rising chest.

Kate faced away from the blacksmith, but knowing he was sitting behind her gave her some comfort. This was really the first time she had ever had a conversation with the man. She had feared him as a child although he had never said anything to her, not even in a hurtful tone.

The children of the kitchen staff told stories about how the blacksmith had lost his leg. They swore that he had cut it off himself trying to take a swat at a sleeping stableman and missed. That story and the many others never really sat well with her. When she inquired to her father about them, he set the record straight. Keltch told her that Brundle had been injured in a war and the amputation did not sit well with the man and hence that is where his anger came from.

When she asked why he would tolerate such a sour man, Keltch replied, "Katie, circumstance may change a man and not for the better, but I know that deep down under all that anger is a good man." Her outlook had changed that day, and she forbade any more stories about the man to be circulated in her presence.

Kate turned her attention back to her unconscious father. She rested her head on his barrel chest and felt its gentle rising and the shallow breath on her cheek. Kate would have been sure that he was just sleeping if not for the icy feel of his skin. Fear gripped her heart at the prospect that her father might never wake up. She tried to push the thoughts from her mind but her unanswered questions kept coming back to haunt her.

What happened to Sprig? A pang of hurt shot through her at the question and she realized just how much she liked the boy, even loved him. *Love him?* She almost laughed out loud at the thought. *I don't even know him, how can I love him?* But she knew that she did and losing him would hurt almost as much as losing her father. Kate could feel tears streaming down her face, soaking her father's chest.

Brundle heard the gentle sobs but made no move to comfort her; he was not sure how to do so. Instead, he did nothing but let her cry herself to sleep. He stayed the night in the chair keeping vigilance over parent and child.

The hours passed quickly and morning came with a gentle rap on the bedroom door and a round face poked its way through the crack. "Is the Master still asleep, Brundle?" the plump woman from the kitchen asked.

Brundle stretched and pulled himself from the chair, grabbed his crutch, and moved to the side of the bed. Keltch was still breathing and some of the color had returned to his flesh. Kate slept heavily and had snuggled next to her father and was clutching his arm. After completing his check, he hobbled over to the waiting woman, "He still lives but I doubt if you can get any food down him," he said, eying the breakfast tray sitting next to the door. "It's best to just let them sleep, Danya."

Danya fidgeted and Brundle could see the concern on her face. "I'm sorry, I don't know what else to do," he said and moved out into the hallway. She gave his hand a gentle squeeze as he passed and closed the door behind him.

Brundle knelt down, picked up the tray, and handed it to Danya. "These are dark times," she muttered. Brundle had never known of any other and bit back a cynical retort. Instead, he smiled and gave her own hand a tender squeeze and said, "Yes, they are, and we need to make the best of them. And I am going to do so by eating this wonderful breakfast so it don't go to waste." He smiled cheerfully and bit the corner off of a piece of hot buttered toast. His actions brought a quick grin to Danya's pudgy face and her worried eyes sparkled. Brundle replaced the toast on the tray and followed Danya down the stairs.

* * *

Kate awoke to gentle rapping on the bedroom door. She yawned, stretched her arms above her head and then remembered her father's state. She could see his chest gently rising and falling in a slow but steady rhythm. "Papa?" she said, placing her hand against his neck and face. His body still felt unnaturally cold, but some of the color seemed to be restored to his face. "Papa, can you hear me?" Kate asked again but the only response was another knock on the door. Kate turned and said, "Come in."

Mengrig opened the door a crack and poked his head in and asked, "Has he wakened yet, Miss?"

Kate shook her head and said, "Papa is still alive but he won't wake up. His skin is still icy to the touch," she broke off, on the edge of tears.

Mengrig nodded and his already solemn face grew longer and he said, "Miss, he's back."

"Flange?"

"Yes, Miss. I was walking around the outskirts of the cottage and he came out of the ground and stood before me. He said nothing and just stood like a statue."

Kate could hear shouting voices outside and she ran to the leaded glass windowsill and saw the bustle of activity. The hired soldiers had loosely surrounded the Undead figure, but Flange seemed to take little notice of the armed men. Instead, he shifted his head and locked his gaze with Kate's as she was staring from the upstairs window.

Kate seemed mesmerized by his presence and her heartbeat quickened. Even from this distance, Kate could see his eyes clearly as if he was standing a breath away from her. His eyes were the color of iron gray coldness but their insides held the fire of fierce determination and intellect. She felt herself willingly falling into the soft gray that seemed to be enveloping her.

"Miss?" Mengrig said in a voice filled with concern, "Miss, are you all right?" When she did not answer, Mengrig ran to her side to look out the window and then gently grabbed Kate's arm and said, "Miss, tell me what's wrong!"

Kate shook her head as if clearing it. She looked at Mengrig as if seeing him for the first time. "I'm fine," she said in a soft voice that was barely audible.

Mengrig rubbed his chin and shook his head. "You sure aren't looking it," he said, unconvinced.

Kate's face seemed to clear and then took on a hard edge and she said, "Let's find out what that bastard has to say." Mengrig seemed to relax at her change and he moved to the door. Kate stopped at her father's bed and piled the covers on him, kissed his head gently and whispered, "Get well, Papa." She grabbed Sprig's hat from the bed and balled it in one hand.

Mengrig retrieved the bow left resting against the wall next to the Master's bedroom door and moved to the staircase. Kate followed quickly on Mengrig's heels as he hurriedly cleared the landing and made for the entryway door.

Mengrig stopped suddenly as he grabbed the doorknob and turned to look over his shoulder and said, "Do you have anything in particular you want done, Miss?"

Kate stopped short of the door and looked at Mengrig in thought. Finally she shook her head and said, "Let's hear what he has to say, but stay on your guard. Most of all don't let the men do anything foolish. I have no doubt that he could kill them all if he wanted to." Mengrig nodded in understanding for he had no doubts of that possibility.

The front door opened and Mengrig stepped out, followed by Kate. She moved to his side and both walked together toward the gathered group. An aisle opened in the mass of men as they parted, allowing the two newcomers to pass.

Mengrig had notched an arrow to the bowstring and held his bow at his side in a loose manner. He worked his way through the men that he commanded and stepped clear of the group. Mengrig was less than twenty feet opposite the supernatural creature when he stopped.

Kate continued past Mengrig and stopped just short of sword striking distance from Flange. The spell she seemed to be under only moments ago was forgotten and her eyes were hard and relentless. "All right. The sun is up. Now tell me everything that happened last night," she said in a less-than-cordial tone.

Flange started to smile but thought better of it. Instead, he looked past her shoulder at the gathered men and said, "I would prefer to recount the night without this hostility surrounding me. I can see by their faces that these men already think the worst of me."

"Why shouldn't they? You've managed to kill their family members or someone who meant everything to them," she said in a hateful tone.

Flange stared into the woman's eyes before him. *So much like her mother,* he thought, *filled with passion and determination.* Yet, he could see that the woman before him was little more than a young girl. Correction, she was very much more than a young girl. After a few moments of silence, he said, "You are quite right in many respects, but I did not come here to harm anyone, including yourself. I need to talk to you but what I have to say is not for everyone's ears. Please allow me to talk to you alone."

Kate shook her head and said, "No, that is not all right. Anything that you have to say to me can be said before these men."

Flange watched her determined look and said, "If protection is what you are seeking from these men, then you know that I am capable of negating that possibility."

"I thought you were not here to harm anyone?" Kate interjected.

"True, but if I am left with no choice, I will defend myself to the last one of your men," Flange said matter-of-factly.

"I have no doubt about that," Kate said, "Are you a man of honor, Flange?" Flange watched in silence, looking for some sort of hidden meaning in her words. "My father believed that you are, or he would not have trusted you or your truce. Mengrig also believes that you are a man of honor and were not responsible for my father's injuries."

"My word is always good unless circumstances keep it from being so," Flange replied.

"Do you swear that if I talk to you alone that no harm will come to me?" Kate asked.

"Of course, but if you prefer that someone is with you," he raised his arm and pointed a finger at Mengrig, "he may accompany us," Flange said.

"And me," a deep voice interrupted. Kate turned to see the blacksmith hobbling through the crowd with a crutch under one arm and an axe in the hand of the other.

Kate looked at Brundle and a smile filled her mouth. She looked back at Flange with a questioning look. Flange nodded his approval. "Mengrig, order the men to go about their duties."

Mengrig nodded and said, "You heard her, lads, to your posts, it's business as usual." The soldiers muttered to themselves, but eventually broke rank and went about their dealings until only the four remained standing together.

"Okay, Flange, tell us what happened," Kate said, becoming impatient.

Flange looked past the waiting trio and then back to them.

"I met up with the Baron and the boy you call Sprig. I took them into Haven as planned, but my sister had laid a trap. She summoned creatures that I have never seen and we were attacked. I opened a portal to allow the Baron and Sprig to escape while I fought the remaining creature. I did not know that Barcus and Sasha were waiting for them after leaving Haven. The fight with the creature lasted longer than I hoped for and when I was finally able to follow, Barcus had attacked the Baron and Sasha had run off with the boy."

"Was Sprig still alive?" Kate questioned.

Flange nodded and said, "Yes, but he was unconscious from injuries."

"Sprig told me that he had injured the she-wolf and that she had threatened to kill him when she found him next," Kate said out loud, remembering the whole ordeal.

"Maybe so," Flange said, "but she seemed intent on keeping him alive, if only to prolong his pain."

Kate shook off the thoughts that were forming in her head. There were just too many possibilities to think about. "What happened to my father?" she asked, trying to shift her focus.

"By the time I made it out of Haven, he was already unconscious from being drained by Barcus," Flange responded.

"How did you manage to rescue my father?" Kate questioned.

Flange hesitated and his lips pursed together. Finally, he said, "I killed Barcus."

Silence filled the air and Kate questioned, "Did you really kill your own brother to save my father?"

"My brother deserved a fate far worse than what I provided for him. He was so full of himself and lived only to kill and destroy for his own pleasure. I should have ended his miserable existence long ago, but I honored the agreements made in the past and that is the only reason that I had not slain him," Flange spat in an angry spill.

Kate watched the spasm of anger move across Flange's face and she was filled with an undeniable fear and heard herself ask, "What happened to the agreements? What exactly were they?"

Flange's angry mood seemed to pass as his eyes locked with Kate's own. "It was a long time ago," Flange seemed to say to himself, "after the change. We knew we were quite extraordinary creatures and that we were very different from each other. We had been in life, why should it be any different in undeath? We knew that our paths would cross in conflict if certain arrangements were not made. We decided on some ground rules that we would never traverse under any circumstances. I should have known better of the outcome, however, I was surprised that it managed to last some four hundred years.

"Our abilities made us very different, and my sister insisted that we share Haven for a month at a time to research and use of the Circle of Power would not be interrupted. We shared the cycles for hundreds of years. We also agreed on other more personal terms." Flange's eyes took on a more sinister cast and a crooked smile worked its way on his face.

Kate knew that there was more to the story than what Flange was telling and she waited silently for whatever fleeting thoughts that were running through his head to finish. The moment passed. Flange shook his reverie and then continued speaking, "I left for a time and returned to find that my siblings had made a new pact and that I had been excluded from it. Sasha ransacked my lairs and stole my belongings."

"And Barcus raised those you slew," Kate said thinking aloud.

Flange's gaze intensified and his lips drew taut. "How do you know about that?" Flange said barely above a whisper. The change in tone sent a chill down Kate's spine and she struggled to keep the fear that she was feeling from showing on her face.

"My father said that you made a stand against his men in a clearing and the bodies were gone when they returned to retrieve them. A woodsman found the corpses scattered nearly a mile from where they fell. My father believed it was Barcus' doing because you do not have the ability to create others like yourself," she said.

A thin smile formed on Flange's handsome face and he said, "Oh, I have those abilities too, but I have chosen not to use them. Besides, there is enough of my kind around as it is. I have no need to teach another Undead how to survive."

"Survive?" Kate questioned in a baffled voice, "Undead creatures are stronger and have powers beyond any comprehension. Your kind preys on humanity, why would they need to learn to survive?"

Flange took a long hard look at Kate and then at the two men who were acting as her escorts. "If your questions and tone are meant to be sarcastic, I choose not to be offended. Instead, I will try and explain what it is like being Undead," Flange said and his gaze swept the trio once more. "I know that none of you trust me, and I do not blame you. I would not, being in your boots, yet I am here on good faith and my actions should prove it. If I did not want peace with the Baron, I would not have brought him back. I could have left him for dead wrapped in my brother's embrace and more than likely he would have been raised."

"You could've saved his life only to prolong the agony you've enjoyed causing him over the years," Brundle said. Again, Flange ignored the venomous stab of words. He only nodded and said, "That is a valid point, blacksmith. If Keltch died, I would no longer have a worthy adversary."

"If he dies, I'll take up his sword and you can measure my worth," Kate said in a dangerous tone. Flange could see the fierce determination in her eyes and knew she would be as good as her word. *So much like her mother,* he thought.

"I know you would, but that is not my intention. I have no quarrel with you, and I would like to resolve the one with your father," Flange said.

"You killed his father, my grandfather! Do you think it would be easy to forgive something like that?" Kate fumed.

"I'm not asking for forgiveness, and I'm not asking for any of this to be forgotten. However, I am tired of the senseless killing and so is your father," Flange said with a sigh.

Kate knew the truth of the words but her anger continued to brew. "My father trusted your parley and you nearly allowed him to be killed. And as far as I know, Sprig is dead!"

Flange could see another flame in her eyes at the mention of the young man. And then he understood; she was in love with Sprig. Flange could not bear to meet her hurt-filled eyes and he turned his back to the group.

Brundle griped his axe in both hands and stood calculating what kind of swipe he could make that would take the head off the creature. Mengrig knew exactly what the blacksmith was thinking and thought better of it. He shook his head enough for Brundle to see that he did not want him to try anything. Brundle relaxed his grip but stayed wary.

"I am truly sorry, Kate, about what happened to both of them," Flange said and turned back to face her, "I had to make a choice, and I chose the life of your father over the boy's because I have more invested in Keltch. If you think that was an unfair decision, then realize that they could have both been killed."

Kate somehow knew that Flange was being sincere, but his insight only made the hurt feel worse and she balled Sprig's hat in her hands in frustration. She had so many questions about what had happened the night before but one suddenly stuck out and leaped to her lips, "How do you know my mother's name? Did you read it on her stone?" Kate questioned.

Flange was silent as he pondered the best way to answer her queries. "Your mother was a sell-sword and was hired to try and slay our kind," he said.

Kate burst out laughing and said, "My mother was never a Stake!" An uneasy glance passed between Mengrig and Brundle and they shifted slightly. Kate caught the motion and the laughter died as a serious expression set on her face. "Is there any truth to what he is saying?" she questioned. Again a nervous exchange was made between the two men.

"Yes, Miss," Mengrig stammered, "your mother was a mercenary."

Kate nearly fell over from the shock. She remembered very little of her mother and she had never been told any of this history. As far as she knew, her mother was like any other, but a warrior mercenary? The thought was unbelievable.

Kate turned to her would-be protectors and said, "I want to talk to Flange alone."

"But Miss . . ." Mengrig interjected.

"If he wanted to harm me, there is nothing you or anyone else could do to stop him. If we are to have a pact, then I need to show that I can trust him," Kate interrupted.

"Miss, I will not leave you alone with this creature," Brundle said, taking up his axe.

"Is this really what you wish to do, Miss?" Mengrig asked.

"It is," she answered.

"I give my word that no harm will come to her from me. I am at her service," Flange said and executed an elegant bow.

Mengrig nodded, "All right. You heard her, blacksmith. The Miss wants to talk to our new friend, so let's go." Mengrig searched Kate's eyes one last time before turning around and walking away. The blacksmith stood baffled.

"It really is okay. Now please go," Kate said in a softer voice, followed by a reassuring smile.

Brundle shifted the axe to one hand and stepped away, leaning heavily on his crutch with the other arm.

Mengrig had slowed until Brundle caught up with him and then the two men walked together toward the cottage and only took occasional glances over their shoulders at the two figures. "The Baron would have your head if he knew you left his daughter in the hands of that butcher," Brundle fumed.

Mengrig nodded and stroked his chin in thought. "I know, but she's the one in charge now, and I have to follow her orders as if she were the Baron himself," he justified.

"Bah, I know how you follow the Baron's orders," Brundle grumbled. "He tells you that he's going alone somewhere and wants you to stay put, but you send men to shadow his every move."

"That may be very true in some cases, but I react to my instincts. And my instincts tell me that she is not in danger," Mengrig defended.

"I don't believe it. He has something up his sleeve. He's been killing too long to do anything else. He has an ulterior motive to all of this and shouldn't be trusted," Brundle insisted.

"That may be true, but he gave his word, and for that, I will give him the benefit of the doubt. I have never known him to break it, and I don't expect him to do it now," Mengrig said.

"I still don't trust him. So what do we do now?" Brundle asked as they neared the cottage.

"We keep our distance, but we also keep a wary eye out," Mengrig said and stopped. He turned back to face the conversing couple. Brundle let out another growl but held his tongue.

Flange beamed a smile. "They are arguing about your decision to talk to me alone."

"You can hear them all the way over here?" she said with some surprise.

"Yes, I can hear quite well in fact."

"One of your Undead traits no doubt."

The smile faltered and Flange's face became quite somber. "Yes, it is. It seems that for all the amazing things we can do, there is a tradeoff of a weakness of some type. Sunlight and fire seem to be the most damaging."

"But you seem to me to be able to handle the daylight just fine. After all, you're standing here talking to me right now."

"That wasn't always the case. I built a resistance to it over a period of years. I stayed in the scorching sunlight for as long as my body could stand it. I have been burned severely on many occasions. There have been many times that I wondered if I would ever fully recover. My efforts seemed to be futile but my strength grew and eventually my body could tolerate the light. My siblings believed that I had used the power of Haven to gain the resistance, for they had been using Haven to change and enhance themselves from the very beginning."

"What enhancements did you gain from using the Circle?"

"None," he shook his head, "I never used it that way."

"Why not?" she asked.

"I started with most of my abilities already intact, but over the years they have been fine-tuned. We knew next to nothing about Haven and learned as we studied the place over the years. In truth, we still know very little, but we did manage to learn how to unleash some of its power.

"The walls are covered with pictographs that are a sort of formula and each formula is made of individual items that mimic power that is locked away in the actual items. If the items are arranged on the floor of the Circle, the power is unleashed and the items are absorbed and destroyed. If the item was unique, then the representation of that item in the pictographs no longer radiates power," he explained.

"How did you ever find that place?" she asked, suddenly absorbed by the idea of Haven.

"Actually, I came to my senses there after the change."

"Were you created by the Circle?"

Flange stared at the ground, stroking his chin in thought. Finally, he looked up into her waiting eyes and said, "I'm not sure. I feel that I was somewhere else before I ended up in Haven, but those memories are a blur to me. All I truly remember was feeling an overwhelming sense of terror and bloodlust. Haven drew us to it and somehow calmed the madness that was consuming us. Something about the place allows us to keep the cohesion of our minds, because if we stay away from Haven for too long, the madness tears on the fringes of our sanity.

"So, to answer your question, no, I do not believe that the Circle was responsible for my creation, however, I have no doubt that there is some correlation between the power that it dispenses and the negative life force that flows through this body of mine. I have spent the last few centuries trying to unlock those secrets."

"And during all that time you never once considered using the power from this place you call Haven?" Kate asked.

"I cannot say that I have not considered it; I just choose not to use it. You have to understand; I have seen the effects from the Circle on my siblings. And for every expenditure and alteration, there seems to be a downside as well. I know for a fact Barcus' use of the Circle made him more susceptible to the damage done by sunlight. I am sure the same goes for Rewella. They both have become sluggish and weak during the daylight hours, more so than when we were first created."

"You say created. Who or what created you?"

"I have never spoken about this subject with a mortal before. Most of the history surrounding my family has been forgotten and very few have even heard of our House. But at one time, it was the most powerful and envied House in the country. I was very young when my father was killed during a war with the Eastern counties. He was an explorer and a General; a great man who was known to me by deed alone. I remember seeing the painted portraits of him hanging in the great hall, but I have no memory of ever actually seeing him in person. How he sired three children is beyond me," Flange said and grinned in spite of the insinuation.

Kate smiled and found herself searching the eyes and face of this creature, who was once a man, trying to place who he once was before the change. A twinge of guilt washed over her. She knew her feelings were in conflict with the feelings she had for Sprig. She decided just to try and listen to the information of the stories Flange was presenting but nothing more. Unfortunately, this was extremely hard for her because Flange seemed to emit a fascinating and very real charm.

"I was nearly seventeen when the suitors began courting my mother. Several rival Houses sent emissaries to convey their intent and affections for her. She was very reluctant to allow a marriage for only political means and she turned away the advances.

"Eventually, she became enamored with a man who came calling from a country located far to the West. From the very start she seemed a changed woman. My mother became a recluse and completely disappeared from the daily social scene, preferring to spend all of her time with Duke Leonine.

"I had always wondered why I never saw him more than a few times," Flange mused and his eyes narrowed, "I assume he was an Undead creature and made my mother in his image. She decided that she wanted her children to become as she had. The Duke was more than happy to oblige and he used his abilities to change us into Undead. My siblings and I woke up in Haven nearly as the creatures you see now," he said without emotion.

"What happened to your mother and the Duke? I have never heard anything about them before," Kate said.

A crooked smile stretched taut on Flange's face. The smile sent a chill down Kate's spine and she tried not to visibly shiver. "The Duke set about changing everyone in our household into Undead.

It was only a matter of time before the family members of our staff caught on and formed a mob to attack our estate. My mother and her changed servants were burned to death when our house was set on fire by those seeking vengeance."

"And the Duke? What happened to him?" Kate asked, knowing the answer by the smile on Flange's face that grew wider in anticipation.

"I killed him," he said. "I hid away, growing more powerful. Our estate was demolished, and he had returned to his castle in the West. I sought him out, destroying his skeletal servants. The Duke had no real knowledge of Haven or the power it contained, nor had he exploited it. I attacked him during the hours just before daylight. I could feel his powers ebbing from him. He became weak and I carried his body to the courtyard and impaled it on the iron fence that surrounded his castle. The sun rose and I watched him scream in agony for nearly six hours before his body finally succumbed to the burning light and was destroyed. I then took the liberty of burning his castle and killing his servants; after all, it was only fair."

Kate blanched. She was appalled by what Flange had told her, but could also relate to it. If the situation had been reversed, she could not say that she would have done anything different. She knew she would have been out for revenge just as Flange had been. "Did your siblings participate in the actions of killing the Duke?" Kate inquired.

Flange shook his head and said, "No, they did not. At that time, they were too fearful of leaving the vicinity of Haven."

"How does my mother fit in all this?" Kate asked. Flange looked deep into Kate's eyes and said, "You look so much like her. I honestly thought that you were she. I had no idea that she had died," Flange said and could say no more as his gaze fell to the ground.

Kate reached across and placed her warm hand on Flange's frigid one and said, "How did you know my mother? Please tell me. I need to know," she said in a pleading voice.

Flange looked back into those familiar yet unrelenting eyes and said, "Mariel nearly managed to kill me," Flange said without an ounce of scorn. "Your mother hunted me because she was paid to, not because she feared or hated me. It was only a job, pure and simple. I was impressed with her physical prowess and her skills with a sword were untouchable. She was the most beautiful woman I had ever seen. You have all her stunning features except for her red hair," Flange said and seemed suddenly embarrassed by his words.

Kate was flattered by his actions and a smile danced across her perfect lips.

"Your father was still quite young and extremely intent on killing me. I had been testing him and allowing him to hone his skills for the hunt. At that time, I still considered our actions a game. I was extremely bored and this helped pass the time."

Kate's smile faltered and slipped from her face.

"Your mother was part of a band of adventurers who were hired to help your father to rid the countryside of the Undead. They were actually quite successful in killing the lesser Undead that Barcus had created over the years. However, most of the warriors died while fighting my brother."

"And by you," Kate interjected.

"Yes, and by me. I admit that I killed those seeking my death," Flange said, "And I have no regrets in doing so. Mariel had been able to track me to one of my lairs. She found me in the morning hours and was intent on destroying me.

"I fought her blade to blade for many hours. Neither one of us had gained ground against the other. I must admit that I was rather winded and that fact exhilarated me. It had been centuries since I actually feared for my life, and I truly believed that this woman was going to kill me.

"Fortunately for me, I was able to disarm her. We both sat on the stone floor panting from our excursions. She was not afraid and waited silently for me to kill her, but I chose not to. In fact, we had a wonderful conversation and found some common ground. She left with her life and the understanding that she would not hunt me in the future," Flange said as the two strolled past the flowerbeds of the garden.

"If she wasn't afraid to die, why did she agree to your terms?" Kate wondered.

"Because it would have been a stupid waste and she knew it. I thought she would return home, and I would never see her again. I had no idea that she would end up staying and marrying the Baron," Flange said and a strange sadness filled his unearthly eyes.

Kate could only imagine what was going through his head. Before she could stop herself, she said, "You were in love with her."

Flange's head snapped up and he focused his eyes on hers. On his somber face grew a slow smile. "I'm not so sure that I was in love with her, but I do know that I respected her more than any other creature. She was an incredible person and left a lasting impression on me," he reminisced, but then his expression turned dark, "If I were mortal, I could have loved her."

Kate turned away from the Undead man and tried to soak up what she had learned. *My mother was a warrior. I never knew or would have guessed,* she thought. Her mind drifted off to the possibilities, and she caught Flange staring deep into her eyes. She felt herself squirm under his scrutiny. "What?" she questioned.

Flange shook his head. "I'm sorry. You remind me so much of her and it has been so long since I have seen her," Flange said and regained his composure. He tried to alter his thoughts and the melancholy that threatened to absorb him. "I wish your father was conscious so you would believe what I am telling you," he said and stared at the blooming flowers.

"I believe you. I'm sure you're telling me the truth. At least as much as you'll allow," she said and followed the response with a reassuring smile.

Flange's face became even more serious and he said, "I never lie. I may only tell as much as I want known, but I never lie."

Kate nodded, "I believe you and so does my father. So what do we do from here?"

Flange came to a sudden halt outside of an arch surrounded by rose bushes. "I cannot enter here," he said.

Kate looked through the opening seeing the stone that marked her mother's grave and the two newer stones with the freshly tilled earth. "Why? Are the memories too painful?" Kate asked, stopping short of the courtyard.

"To some extent that might be true, but I cannot physically enter this place," Flange said looking at the markers. "Your mother was buried with a silver necklace with an black oval medallion hanging from it?" Flange asked, already knowing the answer.

Kate shook her head, "Yes, I believe so. She never took that necklace off and my father thought it was only proper that she was buried with it. How do you know about it?" Kate questioned in wonder.

Flange was silent as if he was reliving a memory of the past. "The necklace she wears radiates a protection from Undead creatures like myself. An unbearable discomfort keeps my kind away from her. I can feel the power of the necklace from here," he said.

"How were you able to get close to her when you fought?" she wondered.

Flange smiled and said, "She did not have the necklace when we fought. I gave it to her that night."

Kate stood in awe. After a minute of hesitation she said, "That beautiful necklace was given to her by you? She said that she would not hunt you, why would you give her something like that?"

Flange cracked a charming smile and said, "I knew she would not hunt me, but I was not sure of what my siblings would do if they learned of our encounter, and I felt obligated to protect her if they should come after her. In fact, Barcus did make an attack on the cottage and was driven away by the amulet."

"Did she know of its power?"

"No, not really. I never told her what the amulet could do. I just told her to keep it close always, but I believe that she knew that the necklace held special properties."

"Did you ever talk to her again after the original encounter?"

Flange shook his head. "No. I did not. I did my best to avoid her and anything to do with the Baron. I tried to spend my time researching the Circle. But restless nights in thought, I would end up leading the Baron and his men on a chase through the forest. I usually spent the morning tearing through his men like paper," Flange said in a less-than-enthusiastic voice, "I always felt the elation but also the remorse for killing mere mortals, but in the end I would do it all over again on another night."

Flange spun suddenly and walked away from the courtyard, leaving Kate standing in place. He turned sharply and stopped. "I need to find out what happened after I left Haven. I will return when I have some information," Flange said as his body sank quickly into the ground.

Kate ran toward Flange, as his head was the only thing sticking above the ground and said, "When will I see you again?" Kate yelled at the disappearing figure.

"Soon," Flange said as his eyes sank beneath the ground.

The earth settled as though Flange had never even been there, and Kate had to replay the whole incident over in her head just to be sure that it had even taken place.

Kate turned around and walked purposely through the courtyard and stood before her mother's grave. "Were you really a warrior, Mother? Did you hunt the creatures that plague the countryside?" Kate yelled at the grave, and then stormed away toward the cottage.

Mengrig and Brundle had watched the exchange in wary silence. When Flange had disappeared into the earth, both men had begun their march toward Kate, but both stopped when she rushed to her mother's graveside and began shouting aloud.

Both men looked at each other in puzzlement and continued their trek toward her.

A strange light shone in Kate's eyes and she turned toward the intruding men. "You knew my mother was an Undead Slayer and you kept it from me? What else do you know that's been kept from me? Is there anything else that's been left out that you want to tell me now?" Kate yelled as tears welled in her eyes and streamed down her face.

When no answer was forthcoming from the two bewildered men, Kate pushed past them both and ran into the cottage.

"We best let her calm down for a while. She has her father's temper after all," Mengrig said, scratching the stubble on his unshaven chin.

Brundle nodded his approval. Mengrig left him standing there and walked around the outskirts of the cottage glancing over the surrounding countryside for anything trivial. After a moment, Brundle hobbled toward the forge, trying to absorb the happenings from the last few days.

Kate threw open the cottage door and ran inside. She raced into the center of the cottage and then to her father's study. She scanned the walls and the arms that it held. Her eyes quickly searched over each weapon and she dismissed them all. "It's not here," she said and bolted from the room.

Kate ran up the stairs to her father's room and threw the door open. She was angry and nearly out of breath. She slowed her hectic pace as she approached the pillared oak bed.

Keltch continued to sleep, unmoved by the intrusion. Kate stood over her father as if seeing him for the first time. She felt as if this person were a stranger. Her father had an extraordinary temper that he tried, for the most part, to keep from affecting her. Kate knew what would happen if her father's limits were pushed and the outcome was evident in the way he had dealt with the priest Iesed.

A partial smile formed at the corner of her mouth at the thought. She disliked the priest and always had. His condescending tone and pompous attitude had never sat well with the headstrong girl. To her, Iesed was nothing more than a charlatan just like the majority of Stakes.

"Stakes," she mused to herself, "My mother was one and so is Sprig. And my father might as well be."

Kate leaned across her sleeping father and kissed his cool forehead. The color seemed to be returning to his face. She pulled the heavy woolen blankets up to this chin, took one last look, and left the room.

Kate headed for the stairs but stopped. At the end of the corridor hallway was a ladder that was built into the wall. The rungs were being used as shelf space and were loaded with heavily bound leather books. The ladder stretched to a trap door in the ceiling, and a dangling leather rope, ending with a wooden knob, was attached to the door. "The attic," she said aloud and clawed the books from the shelves, sending them plummeting into a heap on the planked floor.

Kate climbed the ladder and grabbed the rope, pulling the attic door open with a resisting creek. It had been years since the squeaky hinges had been moved, but the door opened fairly easily.

Dust smoked the air and Kate covered her nose and mouth as she coughed. She leaped lightly from the ladder back to the floor and picked up one of the discarded candles that had fallen from the shelf. She lit the wick from the oil-burning lantern in the hall. The stirred dust settled and she worked her way slowly up the ladder into the attic, using one hand.

The dim candlelight cast stark shadows on the dark wood walls. Kate stood on the last few rungs of the ladder and stared at the trunks, shelves, and sheet-covered antiquities. She finished her climb and circled slowly, eyeing each of the stored items. She stopped as her eyes fell on a battered trunk with a broken hinge.

Kate moved before the trunk and wedged the candle in a peg hole on a broken armor tree. She tried to open the lid but the lock held fast. She looked around the room and found a bust of possibly an ancient god or a forgotten bearcat. She brought the stone statuette down with a crash, smashing the brittle lock and crumbling the bust.

Kate clapped the dust from her hands and kicked the broken shards away from her. She kneeled reverently before the chest, and placed her slender hands on the lid, carefully opening it.

Even in the darkened room, Kate could see the gleam from the links in a set of chain mail armor. She grabbed the chinking armor and held it up in the waning candlelight. The shining links glistened and looked as if the metal garment had been well oiled before being stowed away. She felt the cold steel links and then laid it carefully next to the chest. Kate removed a steel helmet with ancient red plumage and laid it carefully on top of the chain mail.

Next, Kate removed a black leather corset that seemed to be made to fit around her lithe and curvy form. A pair of black gauntlets, with chain mail fringe, and soft leather boots were the next items removed from the chest. Each inviting piece looked as though it had been made specifically for her. The leather was worn but had been cared for meticulously.

An object lay in the bottom of the chest and was wrapped in an oiled leather cloth. She lifted the item in both hands and held it before her. She grabbed the bound cloth and pulled it loose. The hilt of a sword appeared.

The hilt was wire-wrapped with pure silver in an exquisite pattern, and doe skin leather had been wound over the silver for a softer more comfortable grip. The rest of the cloth fell away, exposing the steel blade. She hefted the long-sword with her right hand. The weight was misleading for she noticed that the blade felt lighter than it looked and was perfectly balanced. She ran her fingers across the edge with her left hand. A crimson line formed on her fingers; she had not even felt the blade make the cut.

A strange familiarity came over her. Her father had taught her to use a sword and ride a horse. She believed that her father had always longed for a son. After her mother died, Keltch had taught her everything that he would have taught a son. In fact, it dawned on her that her father was treating Sprig as though he was his son.

She also knew without a doubt that was the reason her father had become distressed when the two had taken an interest in each other.

Kate felt inside of the chest and removed the leather belt and scabbard made for the razor-sharp sword and buckled it around her waist. She slid the blade home, gathered the items, and descended the ladder, closing the attic door behind her.

Kate closed her bedroom door, unbuckled the sword belt, and laid the items on the bed. She stood before a full-length mirror and undid the buttons on the front of her dress, letting it slip off her shoulders, down over her hips, and onto the floor. She stood in front of the mirror and looked at her nude body.

Kate had always been mentally mature for her age, but her body had only just recently caught up with her mind. Now she looked every bit the woman she always imagined herself to be. She turned from the mirror and opened a dresser drawer, removing a pair of soft black leather leggings.

Kate sat on the edge of her bed and slid her limbs into the leggings. She pulled the leather corset over her head, shrugged into it and fastened the silver clasps. She was unsure if the boots would fit her and was surprised when they did.

Kate stood and walked around the room in her new attire. Her mother must have been the same size because a custom tailor could not have made a better fit. Kate donned the chain mail shirt, buckled the sword belt around her trim waist, and slid the gauntlets over her lovely hands.

When she was finished, she took a hard look at herself in the mirror. *So this is what my mother looked like,* she thought, *all but the brown hair.* Kate flexed her hands, getting used to the feel of the gloves. Then she drew the sword and moved it through the air in gentle arcs. As she became more comfortable with the blade, her strokes became quicker and the movements more intense.

After a flurry of moves she sheathed the sword. Stepping before her dresser, she picked up a strip of leather about six inches long and tied back her hair. Kate took one last look at herself in the mirror then grabbed the silver helm and settled in the crook of her arm, and left the room.

Kate moved toward the stairs but decided to check on her father one last time. She opened the door and strode to her father's bedside. She grabbed his hand in her leather-covered one and held it against her cheek.

Keltch inhaled deeply and his head moved slightly. Kate gasped and could see a flickering motion with his eyes. Barely audible, she could hear her father say, "Mariel, you swore that you would never pick up a sword again."

Keltch's eyes fluttered for a second and then closed as he fell back into the oblivion of sleep. Kate squeezed his hand reassuringly and then placed it back under the blanket.

"Father, I am taking up where you and Mother have left off. Today, I become the hunter," she vowed, leaving the room.

Danya was on her way up the stairs and gasped at the spectacle that stood at the top. Kate stood with her left hand on the pommel of her sheathed sword and she walked down the stairs to meet the stunned Danya halfway. "My father's health seems to be improving. He was conscious for a minute or so and even spoke to me. Keep a close eye on him and make sure he stays warm. I'll return as soon as I can," she said slipping past the puzzled woman.

"Miss?" Danya said. "Where are you going? Shouldn't you be here when your father wakes?"

Kate stopped and turned toward the befuddled woman and said, "I don't have a choice. I need to find out what is going on and time is short." She finished the inquiry by turning and stepping quickly down the stairs and out the front cottage door.

Kate stopped and eyed the surroundings, looking for Mengrig, but he was nowhere in sight. Kate marched around the cottage toward the stable.

Brundle heard the clink of the chain mail and poked his head out of the shack that surrounded the forge. "By the Gods!" he swore and hopped to a metal chest, throwing open the lid. Brundle fished out a metal prosthetic leg and buckled the straps around the nub of his calf muscle. Grabbing the axe that he had been carrying earlier and throwing a satchel over his shoulder, Brundle limped away from the forge to the stable and on the way saw Mengrig appear from the nearby treeline. He waved to get his attention and then limped inside the stable.

Kate was filling a satchel with grain and oats for her horse. She had already spread a blanket over her mount and a saddle rested on top of it.

A stable boy ran in from the side door and said breathlessly, "Here you go, Miss," and he handed her three leather flasks of water. Kate thanked him and hung the flasks over the saddle horn.

"Lad, bring me a few as well," Brundle said to the young boy who nodded and ducked back through the door.

Kate stopped her preparation and watched the giant of a man. Brundle did not meet her eyes, and instead, limped to a stall containing a chestnut gelding. He stroked its muzzle and patted its neck, then stroked the side of the horse and hugged it affectionately.

Kate watched as the smith bridled and saddled the horse. Finally she said, "Just what do you think you're doing?"

Brundle did not look up and continued making adjustments to the saddle and then said, "I'm going wherever you've decided to go." Brundle leaned over a barrel of oats and began scooping the content into a saddlebag.

Kate buckled the strap, pulling the saddle taut and then adjusted the stirrups to fit her legs.

Mengrig stepped through the stable door and stopped with his mouth agape. "Miss?" he questioned.

Kate strode to him, her expression serious and almost menacing. Before he could say another word, she said, "Listen to me, Mengrig. I'm going to go to Klevia to seek some information about what has been going on."

"Miss, I can send riders to find that out . . ." Mengrig started but was cut off.

"I said listen to me," Kate said in a stern tone, "I am going to the village and Brundle is accompanying me. I want you to do exactly what my father asks you to do when he leaves the estate."

"Your father's orders were always to make sure that no harm came to you," Mengrig answered.

"Well now I am asking you the same for my father. Keep him and everyone here safe. You are my father's trusted Captain and I expect you to do as I ask."

Mengrig nodded in understanding. "When do you plan to return?" he asked.

"I'm not sure yet. If darkness falls before I can get back, we'll stay in town and head back in the morning," she replied.

"What if Flange returns? What do I tell him?" Mengrig questioned.

"If Flange is such an extraordinary creature, he'll know how to find me." Kate put a leg in the stirrup and hauled herself into the saddle.

Mengrig marched over to Brundle and eyed him suspiciously. "You aren't responsible for this are you?" Mengrig whispered in a hiss.

The blacksmith shook his head and said, "No, it must have something to do with that getup she's wearing. I'm just glad that I got here in time to go with her. Now give me a hand and get me on this horse."

Mengrig grabbed Brundle's foot and hoisted him into the saddle. Brundle shifted until he was comfortable. The stable boy returned with two leather flasks and tossed them up to the waiting blacksmith. "Thanks, lad. There is another silver piece in it for you and your brother if you pick another bouquet of flowers and leave them for Danya in the kitchen," Brundle said to the child. The boy nodded, smiled, and waved as the two riders trotted from the stable.

Mengrig placed his arm on the boy's shoulder and said, "If you do leave the grounds with your brother, come get me first. I'll go with you. I don't want anything to happen to either of you."

"Yes, sir," the boy chimed.

"Good lad, now get back to your chores," Mengrig smiled and saw the boy off but his smile faltered after the child was out of sight. "The Baron will have my hide when he hears about this."

Mengrig left the stables and whistled. Four men appeared from the nearby trees dressed in various colors of brown and green. When the men had assembled, Mengrig said, "Listen up. Kate has decided to go to the village with the blacksmith. She made it clear that she wants to go alone. I want you four to shadow them all the way to town and stay where they cannot see you.

"The Baron is still unconscious and we are taking orders from the Miss until he awakes. I want someone to have an eye on them every moment. Anything goes out of the ordinary; send a runner back to me. Notify the pickets on the outskirts of the grounds as to what is going on. Hurry up, or she'll get too far ahead of you." The men nodded without a question and disappeared back into the forest.

Mengrig watched them leave and the crease in his brow advanced as he let out a long deep sigh. "That girl is going to be the death of me," he said and continued on his duties.

* * *

A shimmering ripple passed and for a brief instant, the pictographs became distorted and unreadable on the ancient stone wall.

Sprig appeared suddenly in the corner of Haven. His form solidified and he took a quick look with his new eyes. A slight smile tugged at his mouth as his body took a breath of air. "How long has it been since I actually breathed air?" he wondered. The creature stood and stared at the fleshy human form that he was now attached to. His smile widened. To be in the physical world once again and not be a summoned slave, the thoughts were almost inconceivable.

Sprig moved to the Circle and looked at the details of the etchings. He held his hands out and certain spaces on the etching glowed. Sprig's eyes closed and the glowing spaces on the Circle darkened and the recesses were filled with newly arrived objects. Sprig opened his eyes.

Blue-black lightning arced from the Circle's etching and cast dark flickering shadows on the walls. A black globe appeared suspended over the Circle. Sprig starred intently, trying to see the contents within. *Curse these mortal eyes,* he thought, *they are far more limited than my own.* "Drafkris! Do you hear me? Come forth so that I can see you," Sprig demanded.

Images swirled in the globe and a set of eyes formed and focused on the man before the Circle. "I feel your presence Daekrey. You are bound to the flesh? How is this possible?" a disembodied voice asked.

Daekrey sighed in relief and said, "I thought you'd been destroyed when the globe vanished."

"No, Daekrey, we merely returned to the Void without you. How did it happen? Who melded you?" Drafkris asked.

"Someone very foolish and not versed in the ancient histories," Daekrey said, "It has been so long since we were flesh. I thought that we would never be that way again. I am going to open a gateway and free our kind into this world."

"We can't survive there for long, Daekrey, what do you intend to do?" Drafkris wondered.

"I am going to graft every one of us to flesh so we can stay in this world indefinitely," Daekrey stated.

"How is that possible?" the bewildered voice wondered.

"A foolish creature melded not only my flesh with a mortal, but also with that of a powerful Undead being. I have his power and abilities in addition to this physical body. I can bring all of you back into this world as whole beings and not as shadow slaves," Daekrey said raising his arms. His eyes fluttered as they rolled to the back of his head.

"Yes, I can feel their presences mingled with your own," the voice said and its eyes became lost in the churn of the black globe.

The inky sphere swirled and began to change, radiating the light of a miniature golden sun from within. The globe shot upward and the ceiling shimmered and bent. The globe passed through and disappeared from the chamber.

Sprig opened his eyes and a mirthful smile spread on his face. He stepped away from the Circle, shimmered for a moment, and vanished.

* * *

Kate's horse cantered through the trees on the winding trail with Brundle riding next to her in silence. Neither had said a word since leaving the estate. Every once in a while, Kate could feel a presence and she would look into the surrounding countryside but would never catch a glimpse of anyone. "We're being followed," Kate said barely above a whisper.

Brundle nodded. "I know. It's Mengrig's doing. He always sends men to shadow the Baron when he insists on leaving the estate alone."

Kate's brow furrowed. "I told him to watch out for my father," she said in an angry voice.

"Miss, he always sends someone to follow the Baron whether he wants them to or not. Your father knew they were there but let it slide only as long as he never saw them. I had no doubt that Mengrig would do the same for you," he explained.

Kate reined her horse and stopped. She scanned the area, "Whoever is following us, show yourself now," Kate hollered through the trees, all the while searching through the underbrush for any sign of the pursuers. Silence echoed through the trees as she waited.

Kate looked at Brundle, who seemed to be amused by her actions. She looked back into the trees and said in a commanding tone, "I know that there are at least three of you following and if you do not show yourselves this instant, I will dismiss every retainer my father has when I return."

"I'd do what she says, lads. She already knows you're here," Brundle's deep baritone voice boomed.

One figure appeared from a nearby clump of bushes dressed in greens and browns with a fur cloak draped around his shoulders, and on his back was a quiver of arrows. The huntsman held an unstrung longbow in his hand like a walking stick.

The man's hair had been red but was now peppered with silver strands and his beard was thick, coarse, and unkempt. He smiled nervously and shuffled his feet like a child who knew he was in trouble but was unsure of what the punishment was going to be.

Kate hid the smile that she felt on the inside and decided to play it tough. "Where are your companions, Landon?" she said in a neutral tone.

The man stammered for a second and then placed two fingers in his mouth and made a call whistle.

Two men appeared from different sides of the trio and joined the group. Kate knew of Landon because he had worked for the Baron for nearly four years now, but she did not know these two men. By the looks of them, they were brothers because of the shared hawk-nosed features, thin dark hair, and brown hooded eyes.

"I've seen you both before, but have never met either of you," Kate said, keeping her tone neutral.

Neither man smiled as they introduced themselves, "I am Wendon and he is my brother, Wells." The other man nodded but said nothing.

"Okay. Now that we all know each other, we can go about our business. I'm giving you two choices. You can go back to the estate where you will stay or you can continue with us to the village," Kate stated.

The three men agreed that they were sent as protection and would stay with Kate for the duration of the trip. The men stood in silence waiting for her orders.

Kate eyed the trio and her gaze fell on the two brothers. "Wendon, Wells, I want you two scouting ahead for us. Keep yourselves hidden and stay alert for trouble. If anything looks awry, get back to us immediately," she commanded and turned in the saddle to focus on the third man, "Landon, you get the rear-guard. The same goes for you. Any trouble, get back here immediately."

The two brothers disappeared into the undergrowth almost instantly. Landon hung his unstrung bow over his shoulders and walked along the trail in the opposite direction of the riders and was soon blended into the scenery of the forest.

The time was nearly noon when the riders cleared the forest and met up with the two waiting brothers. Kate climbed from the horse and stretched her legs. The burly woodsman Landon soon caught up with the group and then they continued the last few miles together into the village of Klevia.

9

Seth leaned against the rough bark of a drooping oak tree looking down at the blue and green tunic that covered his simple clothes. He kicked at the exposed roots absently as he cursed under his breath. "It's not fair. I drew lot last month and again for this one," he complained aloud.

Three other men, dressed in the same heraldry, stood off away from Seth, conversing. One of the men turned at the gripe and chided, "What are you complaining about? At least you don't have to be with that nag of a wife of yours." The three men laughed.

Seth nodded in agreement. "Too true, but these patrols don't pay enough for what we have to do," he protested.

"Quit your bellyaching. Your lot covers the shift during the day and nothing ever happens until the night falls," one of the men scolded.

"Yeah, but I did have the lot for night last month, and I was there when the Undead Slayers were killed," Seth justified, "and it is just not fair that I have to take another turn so soon."

"Well, take up your grievance with the Magistrate. Maybe he'll transfer you to his private guard," another man noted, his voice full of sarcasm.

"Or maybe he'll be sure that you are drawn from next month's lot as well do to your unending complaining," another man chided. The three men laughed in agreement.

Seth kicked at the base of the tree and continued grumbling to himself.

Klevia's guards were simply the townsfolk who had the unfortunate luck of being chosen by a mandatory monthly drawing of lots. The chosen wore the tattered tunics and carried the communal weapons from the public armory. Each man had the option of being paid in silver for his shift or having the amount deducted from what was owed in monthly tax. Only those who were in serious debt ever considered taking non-mandatory shifts; the pay did not justify the risks. Those looking for gold coin ended up working for one of the Barons and at an even greater peril.

One of the men could hear the sound of hoofbeats coming down the path and got the attention of the others. "Someone's coming," he said.

The four guardsmen straightened their tunics and spread out, blocking the incoming trail leading to the village. Two horses with riders and three following footmen appeared around a bend in the trail surrounded by trees.

"Hail!" one of guardsman shouted. The lead rider was a dark-haired woman dressed in black leather armor, glinting chain mail, and a silver helm. The rider spurred her mount ahead of the entering group, drawing rein in front of the four guardsmen.

Recognition dawned on the face of the lead guardsman and he said, "By order of the Magistrate, I am to keep the ex-Baron Keltch and any of his retainers from entering the town. That includes you, Miss."

Kate edged her horse closer to the men and said in a stern tone, "By what right?"

The four men shifted uneasily and eyed each other as the approaching woodsmen spread out to take up positions on either side of Kate's horse.

The lead guardsman spoke up and said, "Keltch was supposed to pay his mandatory share for the services of a group of Undead Slayers hired by the Magistrate and he refused to do so. His actions indirectly caused their deaths."

Kate laughed and threw back her head. "You must be joking. My father's lack of payment was not the reason those men were killed. The outcome would still have been the same no matter what the payment would have been," Kate reasoned.

Seth concurred with her assessment, and he caught himself nodding in agreement.

"Wicked creatures outmatched them and they paid for it dearly with their lives. Now, we are going to enter the town regardless of your bogus charges," she said in the most serious tone, nudging her horse forward, causing the men to step away or be trod on.

One of the men drew his sword and prepared to make a strike at the passing girl. Kate's own sword sprung from its sheath and intercepted the blow, knocking the guardsman's blade clean out of his hands.

Kate reversed her swing and held the point of her sword just under the man's chin. "Don't be stupid. I don't want to kill you, but I will if you force me too," she warned. The man stood rigid. "You heft that blade like a hoe. You're not a soldier are you? Just a farmer?" Kate questioned.

The nervous man nodded and said, "Yes, Miss, I'm just a farmer. So are these men. We are taking our turn in the lot and trying to do what we were ordered to do."

Kate lowered the blade and said, "Are you making enough to have your life end in this manner?" The man lowered his eyes and said nothing. "I thought not." Kate sheathed the sword.

"There is no dishonor in being a farmer, nor was I implying anything of the kind. I am here to request an audience with the Magistrate to help clear up any wrongdoings that he believes my father to have committed. Is this an acceptable reason for being allowed into town?"

The lead guardsman stroked his stubbly chin in thought and nodded, "Yes, Miss, that is acceptable. We need to disarm you though. Is that a problem?"

Brundle had been watching the exchange and his admiration for the girl was growing. However, he was sure that Kate might give in to their demands so he walked his horse next to Kate's and said in a menacing tone, "There WILL be a problem if you decide to try and disarm us!"

Kate exchanged glances with Brundle and said, "We keep our weapons, and I give you my word that we are here on the best of intentions."

"I don't really have a choice, do I?" the man questioned, seeing the seasoned men ready to repel an attack.

"Afraid not," Brundle grunted.

"All right, Miss, will you at least allow us to escort you through the town so it looks like we're doing our job?" the guardsman said with a yielding sigh.

"Of course. Lead on," Kate said.

Seth gave a toothy grin and took up the rear. Suddenly, he felt safer than he had in months. The four guards took up a diamond formation around the party and marched into town.

* * *

"That is not the point, young lady," Burgman said with a sigh. It had been nearly two hours ago when Kate's group was first led to his office. Actually, it was more like she was leading the guardsmen instead of the other way around.

The Magistrate had glared at Quin when the lead guardsman opened the door for Kate and petitioned for an audience on her behalf. Burgman sat in silence, letting his eyes bore into the guardsman as he stammered the request. Burgman gave only the slightest nod and the man took the opportunity to disappear quickly out the door, closing it behind him.

Kate had unbuckled her sword belt and leaned the sheathed blade against the side of the desk. He had looked to the blade and then back to her. She ignored his gesture and sat ramrod straight in the chair opposite his desk.

She started the conversation explaining some of the happenings and the fact that her father had been injured. The Magistrate knew she was purposely leaving out details and in doing so, only fanned the flames under his anger. Her pleas soon turned into the argument that her father always had the best intentions for his actions whether the Magistrate considered them right or wrong.

"The fact of the matter is that even though we live in dark times, the laws must be obeyed by all of the citizens. Your father broke those laws and is subject to its penalties just like anyone else."

Kate sat flustered across the Magistrate's desk and said, "That should not even be an issue right now. He has been injured fighting these creatures. Sprig is missing, probably dead, and Flange said that some kind of demons had been summoned . . ."

"Flange said?" Burgman interrupted, "You have been conversing with one of those creatures? Did it ever occur to you that Flange might have been responsible for your father's injuries?" Burgman could not hide the anger from his voice as he leapt from his seat and pointed an accusing finger at the woman seated across from him. "Your father has been waging war with Flange for decades and now you are taking his counsel? What has gotten into you, girl? Are you possessed?"

The thought took form in Burgman's mind as he spoke the accusation, and he instinctively took a step back from his desk, putting some distance between himself and the armor-clad woman.

Kate's face filled with shock and horror at the claim of such a thought. "How dare you even consider such a thing?" Kate whispered.

Burgman moved his right hand over the hilt of his cavalry saber and said, "I'm sure of nothing at this point, but you did just admit to being in league with an Undead creature. Your men are to put down their arms and will be taken into custody until I get the answers to the questions I'm looking for."

Kate watched as the Magistrate slid his hand over the hilt of his sword, preparing to draw it. Kate let her shoulders slump in resolution, and Burgman relaxed his stance at her gesture.

Kate lunged for he resting blade as Burgman drew his saber and slashed out at her. She was barely able to block his strike away from her face with the clutched sword scabbard, and the blow sent her tumbling over the chair she had been sitting in.

Kate quickly leaped to her feet, drawing her own blade and tossing the scabbard aside. "You're making a big mistake, Magistrate. I'm not possessed, and I'm not Undead. Put your blade up before either of us get hurt," she said, trying to reason with the enraged man.

"Lower your blade and allow yourself and your party to be detained. If you're telling me the truth, you have nothing to fear from me. If you don't surrender, I will take that as an admission of guilt and you will be dealt with accordingly," Burgman gave his ultimatum while searching for an opening in her defensive stance.

Even if she surrendered, Kate was sure that the Magistrate would be biased on the grounds of the recent happenings with her father. "I'm sorry, but I can't do that. You are not being reasonable, and I can't trust any of your decisions."

"So be it," Burgman said, and feigned a stabbing attack, following it with a backslash toward the face.

Kate blocked the feint and still managed to raise her sword in time to protect her face from the wicked slice intended for her slender neck.

She leaped back and took several more steps backwards toward the door. The Magistrate followed her movement, closing the distance that Kate was trying to put between them.

"If you step through that door, I'll see to it that you don't get out of this town alive," Burgman spat.

"You sound like the one who is possessed," Kate said, sending two quick slashes to the Magistrate's midsection. Burgman knocked away the first blow, but the second scratched across his hip.

A red line appeared at his side and the crimson stain enlarged, spreading across the starched white shirt.

Burgman grimaced and slapped his left hand over the seeping wound. "I will cut your heart out, bitch!" he snarled and threw himself at her.

Kate was quick to drop to the floor, causing Burgman to trip over her sprawled form, crash through the oak doors, and drop heavily onto the stone-cobbled street outside.

Kate leaped to her feet following on the heels of the stricken Magistrate.

Burgman was trying to pick himself up off the street when Kate sent a kick into his ribs, sending him rolling across the ground. She stepped on his hand, forcing his fingers to relinquish their grip on the sword handle, and then kicked the loosened blade, sending it scurrying and clattering across the street.

Kate backed away from the fallen Magistrate as he began yelling for his personal guard. Several guardsmen appeared from a nearby structure that was being used as a makeshift barrack, and drew their swords.

An arrow streaked past Kate and stabbed into a rotten beam of wood, just missing the first guard by a mere inch. The first guard leaped back, knocking three of his compatriots from their feet.

Kate turned to see Landon notching another arrow with his now-strung bow. "The next one kills the man stupid enough to try and stop us," he shouted with a growl of certainty.

Brundle appeared atop his horse from the stable doorway and was leading Kate's own. Wendon and Wells followed in his wake, surveying the nearby buildings.

The two brothers stopped short of Landon and took up a defensive position around him. Wendon drew his bow and aimed a shot at the new group of guards that were running up the street from behind. Wells drew his long-sword and dropped into a lower stance, ready to fend off a directed charge.

Brundle rode past the defending men and tossed the reins to Kate, who vaulted into the saddle.

"Kill them, you cowardly bastards! I want their heads!" Burgman shouted as he regained his footing and his displaced saber.

Brundle kicked his horse's flanks and ran his mount though the regrouping men, causing them to scatter for cover. One sluggish guard felt the swat on his backside by the flat side of the blacksmith's axe as Brundle rode past.

Kate turned to the three defending woodsmen and yelled, "Run for the woods. We'll meet you there soon enough!" She spurred her horse to clear a path for them and then wheeled about, preparing to fend off any attack.

Brundle also yanked the reins and veered around to stop short of Kate.

The confused guards, unsure whether to regroup, either stood in place or ran for cover.

When the woodsmen were out of sight, the two riders turned their mounts and fled down the street toward the outskirts of town. "I take it that the conversation didn't go in our favor?" Brundle shouted.

"You could say that," Kate yelled back over the rushing wind of the speedy ride.

Burgman's nostrils flared and his eyes stared wildly, standing in the street watching the horses disappear around the bend. He slapped the saber blade against his side in frustration, ripping an opening in his now-dirty blue leggings.

Burgman's rapid breathing began to slow and he absentmindedly scratched at an itch on the back of his neck. Unknown to him, a spider fell from his shirt collar and scurried to hide under a displaced cobblestone in the street.

* * *

Kate and the blacksmith drew rein about half of a mile into the woods. A few minutes later the three woodsmen appeared stealthily from the foliage that had concealed them.

"What do we do now, Miss?" Landon questioned.

Kate's horse shifted nervously, and she fought the reins to keep it calm. "I guess we go home and prepare for the worst," Kate answered, "There are only a few hours of daylight left and I don't want to be caught on the trail after dark." The men nodded in agreement.

Brundle's horse startled, made snorting noises, and pawed heavily at the ground. Both horses clung to the edge of panic, extremely fearful of something terrible. "Steady boy," Brundle said, leaning over the saddle and patting the horse's jaw.

A heavy dread hung in the air, thicker than any fog. No one was spared by the sinister cling that seeped through their skin and settled deep in the bones like a wet drenching in the dead of winter.

A chilling gust moved through the trees, causing branches to creak and leaves to stir. The temperature dropped noticeably in only a few moments. The horses were near panic and fought the reins in an attempt to flee.

The filtered blue sky, seeping through the treetop canopy, quickly diminished as a fading gray swallowed it.

Kate yelped as her horse reared on hind legs while kicking wildly at the air with its front legs. Kate held on for dear life.

"Look!" Wells shouted and pointed down the trail.

A fog rolled through the trees with the speed of a great hunting cat. Kate's horse reared again and she was thrown to the ground.

"Kate!" Brundle bellowed, trying to control his own frightened mount.

The fog swirled around the ancient gnarled trees as if sentient. Tree trunks warped and moved in a contorted dance, and the coarse bark took on the look of faces twisted in fury with huge gaping maws. Branches swayed and creaked, becoming multifaceted arms with thousands of misshapen raking fingers.

Kate's horse, free of a mount, tried to bolt, but a nearby tree turned about and stabbed a jutting limb into the side of the hapless terrified beast. The horse neighed with pain and kicked about furiously as it was hauled from the ground. The tree-creature twisted its barky trunk to one side and then hurled the horse several dozen feet to crash into another tree-creature.

The affected trees pulled their roots from the ground and stomped in a wide circle that surrounded the party. Another branch batted at Brundle's horse sending him from the saddle to land heavily on the ground.

Brundle fished his axe from the ground and took a wild swing at the overwhelming tree-creature that loomed before him. His axe bit deeply, tearing away a fleshy chunk from the trunk of the tree-creature. A blood-like substance sprayed from the wound, splashing across Brundle's face. The taste was extremely bitter and he spat it from his mouth.

Wendon drew his bow and sent an arrow into the creature lurking over Brundle. The arrow struck but appeared to do no other damage.

Wells drew his long-sword and hacked at a seeking limb, lopping the appendage off. The creature roared and its bulk twisted around to face the attacker. Wells swung his blade again as several limbs snaked out to entangle him, but his swipe was deflected and the sword bounced harmlessly off the bark.

The tree-creature's limbs first clubbed Wells about the face then wrapped its branches around the bewildered woodsman, hoisting him off of the ground.

Brundle spun clumsily on his prosthetic leg, trying to balance himself for an attack on the creature hefting Wells. Before he could take a swing, the tree-creature yanked Wells in close and repeatedly bashed his head against its trunk until it cracked open, splattering the contents on the rough bark. Then the creature stuffed what was left of the dead man's head into its jagged maw and crunched on the battered flesh.

Kate had been stunned from the fall, and she rolled to her stomach, trying to raise her body off the ground. Her quivering arms almost would not allow her to, and she nearly collapsed back to the ground. Her head swam with strange images only to find that the images were very real; the forest was actually attacking them.

Kate drew her sword and tried to piece together what was happening. Brundle was hacking at a tree, Wendon was screaming fitfully, and Landon was swinging his bow like a sword, deflecting branches that reached out trying to ensnare him.

Kate staggered and placed both hands on her knees waiting for the nausea to pass that had rushed up over her.

Something grabbed her leg and yanked her feet out from under her. She hit the ground with a crash and stars exploded in her head once more. She lashed out angrily with her sword, severing the branch wrapped around her leg, and kicked it away.

Something else grabbed her arm and she reacted with a blind stab in the general direction. "Damn it, girl! I'm trying to help you!" Brundle yelled, barely dodging the point of the blade that streaked past his face.

Kate allowed Brundle to pull her to her trembling feet. She did her best to try and clear her head, but the warm soft inviting darkness threatened to engulf her.

"Pull yourself together, lass, or we all die right here!" Brundle shouted through the haze.

Kate opened her eyes and nearly fell. Her head swam and she fought desperately to get her bearings.

The surviving four stood huddled back to back. The tree-creatures ringed around the defending group, blocking any avenue of escape. The creatures made a few feeble attacks but kept their distance outside of sword range.

"They're herding us," Brundle said.

"Herding us? What for?" Landon said, and smacked away a branch that crept too close.

"For *who* would be my guess," Brundle murmured.

"We're not going to stick around and find out," Kate said, regaining her senses, "Where's Wells?" Kate wondered aloud. If she could have seen the look on Wendon's face, she would have known the answer, but he was standing behind her, facing the other direction.

The temperature continued to fall and frost was forming on the fallen leaves on the ground. The defenders' breath could be seen in the air, and they shivered from the bitter cold. The tree-creatures lifted their roots and inched toward the huddled group.

Landon turned, throwing off his satchel, and dropped to his knees. He scattered the contents on the ground and sifted out his tinderbox and a corked vial. He tore a strip of cloth from the hem of his shirt and wrapped it around a dead branch lying near him. He uncorked the vial, dumped the oily contents on the cloth, and struck the flint from the tinderbox. The makeshift torch lit up, and he spun around to face the tree-creatures.

Landon waved the torch as the leaves and branches of the opposing creature burst into flames. The tree-creatures howled in pain and backed away, breaking the circle that confined the defenders.

"Make a break for it now!" Brundle bellowed.

Landon led the way, waving the torch wildly before him. Wendon followed, ducking under the swinging branches. Kate lopped off a limb blocking her path and Brundle took up the rear, limping along on his good leg.

The group bounded from confinement but the creatures turned about and lumbered after them.

"We have to make it back to town!" Kate yelled and chanced a glance over her shoulder.

A root exposed itself, tripping Landon, who sprawled face first into the soft earth and was followed by Wendon who was right on his heels. The torch rolled away out of reach.

More roots and vines burst from the ground, snaking around and engulfing the two fallen men.

Landon struggled wildly, trying to rip the vine loose that had wrapped around his neck, cutting off his airway.

Wendon yanked out a knife hidden in his boot, slashing at the entwining vegetation. As soon as one root would be cut away, three others grabbed him until he was immobile.

Kate slashed furiously at the roots that choked Landon but found herself being engulfed as well. She was temporarily relieved when Brundle's axe crashed through the vegetation that snared her. But soon he too was knocked from his feet and restrained by the leafy vines.

Kate swiped feverishly and leaped back away from her companions. She could see the ground churn in front of her and she leaped back again to crash into a tree-creature that had crept up behind her. The creature's branches wrapped around her and she was lifted from the ground.

A ripple passed across the ground, like a stone thrown in a still pond, between the tree-creature and the three entangled companions. The soil parted from the origin of the ripple and a head popped out, followed by an attached whole body.

Flange stood above the ripple with his feet resting lightly at the center. His left hand rested on the pommel of the sword hanging at his side. He took in the surroundings, bearing a mask of neutrality.

To his left, Kate was hanging from the ground wrapped in branches and to the right her companions were trapped under strangling vines on the forest floor.

His sword flew from its sheath into his hands and over his head faster than the human eye could follow. In a single leap, Flange flew through the air, bringing the slightly curved blade down in an arc that sliced through the confining limbs.

Kate fell to the ground, throwing the severed limbs away as she fought to get to her feet.

The tree-creature roared and lumbered at the intruder. Flange stood his ground, waiting for the colossal tree to cover the short distance. The tree-creature lunged out with its branches, trying to snare the newcomer.

Flange dropped his stance, and then leaped past the tree, bringing his sword down in a diagonal arc. The trunk split and the crown of the tree-creature toppled to one side. The weight of the falling foliage carried the tree over, causing it to crash heavily to the ground.

Flange grabbed Kate by the hand and said, "Let's go."

She stood looking at him, dumbfounded. "I'm not leaving without them," she said and yanked her hand free of his.

Flange watched her turn away and run back to her struggling companions. She hacked furiously at the vile vines and branches. He observed her determination and a smile crept on his face. "Oh, you are so very much like your mother," he said aloud, but to himself.

Kate saw a quick flicker of a sword blade and the creeping plants she was hacking at parted and fell away.

Flange stood next to her and with the skill of a surgeon, sliced away the seeking undergrowth. The three men struggled to their feet, pulling away the still-clinging vines and roots.

The lumbering tree-creatures had cleared the short distance and were attempting to confine the escapees. All the trees of the forest seemed to have been turned into the tree-creatures, for Kate could see nothing else. The ground continued to freeze over as the temperature around the defenders dropped.

"Who's doing this, Flange? Is it your siblings?" Kate yelled as the group went back-to-back in defense.

"I don't think so. There is some greater power at work here," he said, sizing up the creatures, "And these are lesser beings being controlled by something else."

"We need to get out of here," Kate said hacking a limb that tried to grab her.

"That is probably a good idea," Flange said looking over his shoulder in the opposite direction.

Kate followed his gaze and saw the swirling fog condense to become translucent creatures with raking claws, huge bat-like wings, and unforgiving eyes.

Flange turned back to the defending group. "I'll buy you some time. Get as far away from here as you possibly can. I'll catch up with your later," and with that said, Flange turned and strode to the nearest tree-creature and unleashed a swift swipe that split the tree down the middle.

Three more attacks and a hole opened wide enough for the defenders to escape. "Let's go!" Kate yelled and led the way through the opening with her companions in tow.

Flange leaped through the opening and then stopped, blocking the way of the pursuing tree-creatures.

"All right, shall we hear the sound of the mighty oak crashing to the ground?" Flange said, twirling his blade expertly in a whirl with one hand. A deadly smirk spread over his handsome face.

The humor was lost on the advancing creatures and they struck out with every flailing branch. Flange hacked and cut, but his inhuman strength had fled with the daylight. The shear numbers of tree-creatures began to overwhelm him.

The tree-creatures packed around the Undead being until he had no room left to move. Flange flipped the sword back into the sheath and used his bare hands to tear the branches from the trunks of the surrounding trees.

Eventually the trees were trunk to trunk and Flange had his arms pinned against his chest. He relaxed, smiled and said, "You can't kill what is already dead. You waste your time by keeping me here."

"Is that so?" a heavily accented voice said, "I feel your negative life-force, and you are quite alive. Maybe not for this world, but you are very much alive. I could feed off of you for days."

"Who are you?" Flange inquired to the disembodied voice.

"It doesn't matter. You won't be around long enough to care," the voice promised.

A rush of panic began to work its way inside of Flange. The reaction not only scared him, but amused him as well. It had been centuries since he had felt anything of this magnitude. He was actually enjoying the sensation.

The tree-creature stretched Flange's body out, lifting him from the ground. Flange was suspended between the trees being pulled in opposing directions.

Some of the tree-creatures parted and a demon that had formed from the condensed fog stood looming over Flange. The demon reached out with a taloned hand and placed it on Flange's chest.

Flange had not felt cold or warmth in over four hundred years, but now he felt the most intense frigidness that he could ever remember.

Flange became aware that he could hear the sound of a high-pitched shrill and realized it was coming from his own mouth. He quickly clamped his jaw shut cutting off the howl. *I sound like a wailing woman,* Flange thought to himself as the demon inflicted intense pain on his body.

The demon seemed to solidify and what passed for eyes rolled to the back of its head. Flange noticed the similarities to the ecstasy that Barcus seemed to share with this creature and an intense anger stirred from somewhere within him.

Flange stopped struggling and became limp, allowing the tree-creatures to suspend him. Without flexing or showing any resistance, Flange rested his left hand over the pommel of his sword. In a flick of motion, Flange drew the sword blade across the demon's arm.

The blade passed though the forearm with little resistance and the loosened appendage lost its form and changed back into fog that rolled away joining the surrounding vapors.

The demon howled and recoiled, its severed arm close to its body. "Who's screaming like a girl now?" Flange said and followed the cut with a backstroke that slashed through the tree-creature's limbs that were holding him suspended in place.

Flange dropped to the ground and was swallowed by the earth leaving the miffed creatures to howl alone in distress.

* * *

Kate ran from the woods with Landon and Wendon hot on her heels. Brundle brought up the rear, limping on his bad leg.

A low fog had settled along the ground and Kate eyed it warily as she stopped to catch her breath. At first the town appeared deserted, but the frantic screams that could be heard coming from it soon put an end to that idea.

"Come on, we have to help," Kate said and charged in the direction of the shouts.

"Hopeless girl, wait for us!" Brundle yelled. The force of the exertion on the crippled leg was obvious by the painful grimace on his face.

Kate ran ahead, regardless of danger, and straight into an ethereal creature standing over nine feet tall. The creature had wrapped its enormous arms, ending in taloned hands, around a woman. The terror-stricken woman screamed and was silenced just as suddenly as her body convulsed under the frigid grasp. Blisters formed on her skin where the demon held her as the life force fled from her body; she was being frozen to death.

The demon seemed to solidify before Kate's eyes and the hulking creature threw the husk of the dead woman away and stood searching for another hapless victim. Its eyes settled on Kate, and a wicked grin stretched across its crooked grotesque jaws.

The horrific experience terrified Kate. Nonetheless, she dropped into a ready stance and distributed her weight evenly between each leg and waited defensively for the attack.

The demon seemed to be amused by the action and crept purposely to stand menacingly over her. "I can smell your fear, human. Yet your life force is strong so I will prolong your agony and savor it for as long as possible," the raspy voice croaked. The creature lunged for her.

Kate leaned from leg to leg as the demon rushed her. Kate feigned an attack to the face but followed it with a backslash across the midsection. If it had been any other creature, its ingestions would have spilled to the ground. However, the demon barely noticed the blow and continued forward with its great arms outstretched, ready to engulf her.

A battle cry sounded from behind Kate and a silver axe sank deeply into the muscular scaled chest of the solidifying demon.

Brundle wrenched the axe free and hoisted it over his head preparing for another cleaving attack. "Get back, girl!" Brundle commanded.

Kate did not fall back but instead made another attack with her long-sword. The thrust stabbed the creature through the mouth, tearing away its translucent cheek. The flap of skin hung from the side of its mouth, which seemed only to enhance the maw of jagged teeth. The creature howled in pain as its taloned hands flew to cover the wound in its face.

Brundle grabbed Kate's arm and tried to drag her back from the furious demon and shouted, "Use your head, girl, or you're going to get yourself killed! Our weapons have little effect on these creatures. We need to find a place to hole up until we can get some help!"

The demon surged forward, using its wings to buffet the two, knocking them from their feet.

An arrow stabbed into the demon's head followed by a second in its neck. Landon and Wendon both notched arrows and drew back, prepared to fire a second shaft each.

The demon hulked over the two stricken forms, ready go render them apart. The gleeful savage look was replaced by a mix of curiosity and surprise as a sword blade jutted out from its chest. The demon could only watch in grim fascination as the blade was ripped downwards tearing through what passed for the groin.

The creature wobbled unsteadily on its misshapen legs and then doubled over, collapsing with a crash to the ground.

Flange stood behind the stricken demon and sheathed his blade with an expert flick. "You have a knack for finding these kind of creatures, do you not?" Flange chided.

The demon lost cohesion, becoming more translucent until it was nothing more than the fog that surrounded it.

Flange stepped around the wispy strands of the disappearing demon and helped Kate to her feet, followed by Brundle, who took his hand reluctantly.

The blanketing fog continued to thicken over the town's streets and the temperature plummeted drastically. The sounds of splintering wood and desperate screams echoed off the buildings. The wary group pivoted and spun about, trying to locate the many sources of distress.

"Where are they coming from? It's so hard to tell!" Kate questioned aloud, searching the deserted streets and alleyways in frustration. Her companions sought through the haze that obscured view.

"I can sense several more of those creatures nearby," Flange said as if in a trance. He shook it off and said, "Are there any buildings made entirely of stone near here?"

Kate shook her head. "There are a few," she said, not understanding the relevance of the question.

"Any of great size?" Flange questioned.

"I'm not sure. I think Iesed's church is probably the largest. Why?" Kate wondered.

Flange rubbed his chin in thought, nodded his head and said, "It will have to do. Get everyone you can in there and barricade the doors. Once inside, do not open it for anyone."

"You're not going with us?" Kate said, searching the Undead man's iron-gray eyes.

"No. I need to find out where these creatures are coming from and how to stop them. I need to find Rewella and get some answers from her."

"I thought you said that your siblings weren't behind this?"

"They could be indirectly responsible if the power from the Circle was misused. You have to admit, this is all very unnatural compared to the norm," Flange said.

"Unnatural?" Brundle grumbled. "You have a lot of room to talk."

"You will have to keep yourselves safe until I can get back with some answers," Flange said ignoring the jibe.

"If you do come back," Brundle said not disguising his mistrust.

Flange smiled amusingly and said, "How many times do I have to save your hide, blacksmith, before you show some trust?" None of the defenders answered. "I owe you nothing, blacksmith, and I could just leave your carcass here to rot," Flange paused for effect, "but I swore an oath to your Baron and would prefer that you all come out of this situation alive or as close to it as possible. Now you are going to have to trust me, or you can take your chances on your own." Flange folded his arms around his chest, waiting in silence.

Kate broke the lingering silence saying, "People are dying while we stand here arguing over who can be trusted or not. I trust your word, Flange, as much as I do the blacksmith's own. We're all friends here even if it's by necessity only. The truce still stands. Do what you have to do, Flange, and then get back to us. We're going to need your help and so are these people."

Flange looked at Brundle with a half-smile on his face and asked, "Are the terms acceptable to you, blacksmith?"

Brundle gave a slight nod and said, "They are."

Flange turned back to Kate and said, "Help those you can, but don't be foolish. Not everyone can be saved and there is no sense in getting killed because of false bravado. I will be back as soon as possible." He turned his gaze from Kate to let it fall on the rest of the group and then said, "Keep yourselves alive until I get back." Flange leaned in close to Brundle and whispered, "Keep her safe, blacksmith, or the demons will be the least of your worries." With that said, Flange flashed an evil smile that made Brundle's blood run cold.

Flange's eyes fell back on Kate's wondering face, and he smiled charmingly at her. He took an exquisite bow and let his body sink into the earth until his form disappeared under the swirling fog.

Brundle could not hide the next shiver that overcame him from the display. "That creeps me out every time he does that," he muttered trying to excuse his action.

"You're telling me," Landon said in agreement.

Screams and shouts continued to echo off the buildings. Everyone looked around, but no one moved.

Kate realized that everyone was waiting for orders. She cleared her throat and said, "We make for the church and get as many people as we can to go with us along the way. Everyone stays together and if we encounter those creatures, we spread out enough to fight but not enough that we get separated. Got it?"

Everyone agreed and walked cautiously through the deserted streets. Landon tripped and fell heavily to the cobblestones under the ankle-high layer of fog. "By the Gods!" he yelled scrambling to his feet.

"What is it?" Kate questioned ready for another attack.

Landon regained his composure and probed through the soupy murkiness to the ground in front of him with the end of his bow. He fished around and hooked his bow onto something. He slowly raised the bow and the mist parted, revealing a shriveled hand caught in the crook between the bow and where the string attaches to it. "Poor soul," Landon said allowing the hand to slip away back under the obscuring fog.

"There are probably more people like that all along the way. We'll have to slow our pace," Brundle said.

"I think that is a great idea. I prefer not to fall face-first onto any more corpses," Landon said.

"I wish that was the case," Kate said with detachment. Then she yelled. "Everyone run!"

The low-lying fog swirled violently as a demon dropped from the sky, using its enormous beating wings to slow its descent to the ground.

Kate could see that this creature was dark and held none of the translucent properties that the other demons that they had faced. This one was stained in blood and entrails hung from its mouth as it chewed on the remains of one of its hapless victims. She knew without a doubt that this creature was much stronger and that they would not have any defense against it. "Don't try to fight it, just run!" Kate yelled and led the way.

The band of defenders fled from the main street into the nearest alleyway. "Where are we?" Landon questioned aloud.

"Somewhere in the Merchants Quarter," Kate shouted back, "but I'm not sure exactly where."

"Keep moving east and we'll eventually be in the Temple Quarter where Iesed's church is," Brundle said between breaths as he scanned for the pursuing demon.

"Yeah, but how can we even tell which way to go with all this ungoldly mist?" Landon questioned as he looked for a familiar landmark.

"Well, we're not going to find it standing here," Kate said as she edged her way against the wall to the other end of the alley. "Brundle, keep an eye on our back while I check this out."

Brundle grunted but allowed her to scan ahead. Refuse was scattered on the ground and she crept forward cautiously to keep her footing. She kept to the side of the building, her back against the cool but reassuring bricks.

Landon covered Kate with his bow from the end of the alley. Wendon stood next to him in a daze of incoherency. Landon understood the man's condition, for his brother had just been killed and great sadness filled his heart. He had known these men for only a short time, but they were both good loyal men and neither deserved the events of the day.

Kate peered cautiously around the corner. Demons were in the streets, killing everyone they ran across. And with each killing, they became more substantial; more powerful; more blood-thirsty. Kate looked past the massacre and could see the masonry work of Iesed's church nearly three blocks away. "I can see the church. I also see several of those demon creatures but they look preoccupied," she said as the group moved to the end of the alley to join her. "We head straight for the church. Avoid a fight if you can. Go! Now!" Kate nearly yelled as she leapt from the cover of the alley to run into the street.

The defenders ran in a jagged line for the church. Demons, too concerned with their current victims, ignored the fleeing party. The group ran up the short flight of steps to the church doors and tried to open them, but they held firm.

"Open up!" Brundle bellowed and beat the broadside of his axe on the closed doors that were barred from the inside. The group waited for a response and for the doors to be opened.

"Open up, damn you, Iesed! Open these doors or I will smash them down!" Brundle bellowed hefting his axe up as if for emphasis. Only the surrounding screams of agony were there to answer him.

"Break it open," Kate said when Brundle looked her way.

Another cry echoed off the stone buildings. A child had wandered into the streets looking for its missing parents only to find the bloodthirsty demons destroying everything in their paths. The child cried out in terror.

Echoing thuds sounded as Brundle used the end of his axe to repeatedly ram the church doors. Kate heard the child's screams and barely saw her standing a head above the mist. "Get that door open, blacksmith," she yelled and bolted for the distraught child.

Kate ran down the steps past a demon caught in the ecstasy of killing an ill-fated townsman. She did not stop to help that person for her intent was spent entirely on the child. Kate covered the distance quickly, scooping up the frantic child with her free arm and than ran back toward the church.

Three demons materialized from the frigid unnatural fog, blocking access to her friends standing on the threshold of the church steps. Kate held her position, with the child dangling under her left arm and her sword outstretched in the other.

Brundle pounded on the doors with his axe and then started chopping at the wood.

Landon had been watching Kate as she ran from the steps and his heart nearly stopped when the demons appeared in front of her. He loosened a shaft at the demon in the center. The arrow streaked and struck the muscular neck. The creature swatted the back of its neck, breaking the shaft of the arrow. It lumbered around to search for the assailant.

Kate took the opportunity to run past the distracted demon. Landon sent another arrow at the creature that was searching for the attacker. The creature held up its hand and the streaking arrow pierced the translucent flesh between the thumb and finger of its left hand.

Kate ran up the steps to the protection of her waiting companions. Brundle hit the door again and one of the doors jarred open under the impact. He shouldered the battered door and wedged himself between the two entrance doors of the church. The wooden beam keeping the doors shut splintered, and both doors swung open on bent hinges.

"Come on!" Brundle yelled and hopped into the entryway of the church. The group followed hurriedly into the stone structure. "Quickly, find something to bar the doors," Brundle hollered slamming the battered doors shut and putting his weight against them.

Landon and Wendon both rushed through the hall, grabbing heavy furniture and sliding the pieces in front of the doors. "We need more!" Brundle yelled as he leaned against the makeshift barricade.

A powerful blow thudded against the door, nearly knocking Brundle from his feet. "These doors won't hold for long! I did too much damage to 'em trying to get in," Brundle growled as another jolt shook the doors.

Kate ran to the interior set of doors recessed down the hallway and rattled her sword against them hollering: "Iesed! Please open the doors! If not for us, do it for this poor child." Silence. Kate looked helplessly at the frightened child and then to Brundle who was wedged against the exterior doors joined by Landon and Wendon in a desperate attempt to keep them closed. Another thud hammered the doors jolting the three men. Silence. Kate looked at the child, who was looking back at her.

A bolt slid open revealing a removed slat about a two-inch wide and about six inches long. A set of squinty eyes looked into the foyer. "Iesed! Please open the door," Kate pleaded.

The set of eyes looked from Kate to the child held in her arms, and then to the men trying to hold the entry doors shut.

"Please, Iesed. Regardless of what you think about me or my father, please let us in," Kate begged. The eyes looked again at the men holding the door.

"If you don't open the doors, Iesed, I'll hack them down and the situation won't be any better for the both of us," Brundle said in a steely voice. The eyes moved back to the child and settled on Kate. Then the slat closed. "Damn him!" Brundle hissed through his teeth as the doors bounced into him from yet another assault.

A scraping noise could be heard on the other side of the interior doors and one of them opened. Iesed poked his head through the crack and said, "Hurry up before you get us all killed!"

Landon and Wendon both looked at Brundle. He nodded and both men leapt from the door following Kate and her charge behind the interior doors.

Brundle waited until another thud jarred the doors and then hobbled down the hall to the interior set of doors. He slammed the open door closed behind him and then Landon and Wendon grabbed the heavy oak beam and lodged it into the iron holdings on either side of the doors.

Brundle limped forward and said, "We need to re-enforce the doors. Find anything not fastened down and get it over here!"

The quartet scattered in different directions for the task. "There's a bookcase over here!" Landon yelled, grabbing an end. Wendon changed his direction and scurried to grab the other side of the heavy bookcase.

Books toppled to the floor as the bookcase slammed against the barred doors. Kate followed up by dragging a piece of statuary of an alabaster child. Landon helped her secure it against the bookcase.

Brundle had slipped into a side passage and was returning with a wheelbarrow filled with cut stone. "There's a fountain being built in here," he yelled through the entryway, "plenty of rock to seal the entrance." Brundle limped forward, straining under the weight, and dumped the wheelbarrow contents on the floor in front of the interior doors.

"I'll get it," Landon said and grabbed the wheelbarrow handles. Brundle glared at the younger man. Landon saw the look and what it might imply. "We need you to guard the door in case they come through," Landon blurted quickly. Brundle nodded and let the younger man continue the venture.

Kate ran ahead of the trio into the fountain room and had already picked up a piece of stone and dropped it into the wheelbarrow as Landon came to a halt in front of the incomplete fountain. Quickly the cart was filled and dumped at the foot of the interior doors. Brundle hefted the loose pieces and tossed them on the growing pile.

On the third trip Brundle said, "They've come through. I heard them hit these doors but they didn't budge. A few more loads and we might be able to ride this out." Kate nodded and followed after the two men, returning for more stone.

"This is the last of it unless we're to chisel apart what's been mortared together," Landon said, rushing the half-filled cart and dumping its remains on the floor. The four quickly tossed the stone on the pile before them and rested, breathing sighs of relief.

Kate panted heavily and then noticed, as if for the first time, the priest standing very still so near to them. She had completely forgotten about Iesed. From the time when he had let them in to now seemed like an eternity. His silent face held a look of controlled contempt. "What are you doing here besides vandalizing my church?" he questioned in a low, even threatening, voice.

"Iesed, the demons . . ." Kate started.

"The demons that you brought here!" he said heatedly and jabbed a gnarled pointy finger at her. "All because of your sins against me and especially of those of your father!"

Kate's look of astonishment turned to a murderous one. Her sword flew from its sheath into her hands and began a stroke destined to cut Iesed from shoulder to groin.

"Kate!" Brundle yelled and raised his hand to try and stay the blow. The sword stopped just above the old priest's collarbone on his right shoulder. "If you do this, you are no better than the murdering demons outside these doors," Brundle finished, looking into her anger-filled eyes.

Kate breathed heavily and struggled with the side of her that wanted to kill the producer of those hurtful words. Her nostrils flared and her arm ached to bring the blade down on the cretin of a man.

Her steel eyes hardened with determination. The silvery blade streaked toward him and stopped just short of its mark. Did the blacksmith say something? He must have, for her eyes softened and the blade flashed away from him and back to the sheath hanging at her side. A long sigh escaped the old man. He knew that someday his bold bluffs were going to be the death of him.

The words of the blacksmith hit Kate like a ton of bricks. *I am no murderer!* She heard the words resound through her head. And just as quickly, her sword was in the worn scabbard at her side. She turned from the infuriating priest and stalked to the far corner of the room, followed by the child she had rescued.

For a moment, Iesed saw what he had only seen in Keltch himself. He felt the fear run down into his quivering limbs. For a moment, he thought she was completely capable of killing an unarmed man in anger, or at least one she could hold a grudge against. He saw the fury and the fire that resided in the eyes of a driven woman. *Oh yes,* he thought, *very much a woman.* He believed that his earlier mistake of calling her a child was going to be his bitter end.

Brundle exhaled the breath that he had been holding and watched the girl walk away. He then turned his attention to the priest. Iesed had lost some of his color and looked visibly relieved at the outcome. "Your eminence," Brundle said, trying to sound humble, "we are not responsible for the cause of the demons, but were only caught up in their devastation to your faithful servants."

The reverent tone of the blacksmith snapped the shaken priest back to his centered self. Iesed felt more in control and relaxed his angry demeanor. "No. Forgive me, good man, for my outburst," Iesed said as he placed a hand on the head of the now-kneeling blacksmith, "These unfortunate circumstances have made me terse and forward."

The child grabbed Kate's hand and held it close to her side. Kate heard the words but in her heart she knew the priest was being callous and wordy; she could see through his façade. She exhaled slowly, trying to regain her composure before turning to confront the priest. She stared hard at the old man and finally said lamely, "I am sorry for my actions, Iesed." She refused to apologize further and crossed her arms, turning to face the opposing wall.

Iesed took this as a small victory and began questioning. "What is it like out there now?" Brundle sat on the pile of stones against the door to take the weight off his bad leg and said, "Creatures have started appearing with the fog. They're killing everyone they find."

"Some claim they've seen demons," Iesed said.

"Aye. That would be the only way I could describe them."

"Will they be able to get in?"

"We have been told that stone may protect us," Brundle said with a quick sidelong glance toward Kate. The subtle action was not lost on the priest.

"Who said that?" Iesed questioned.

Kate turned suddenly and said, "A friend who is trying to help us." Iesed held her gaze and waited for an explanation. None was forthcoming. Iesed looked back to the exhausted blacksmith for his answers, but Brundle changed that subject, "Are there others in here?"

"A few, mostly children and some adults. I was in my study when the creatures attacked and my congregation fled here for protection. We bolted the doors and ushered everyone into the chapel."

"What about the rest of your congregation laying dead in the streets or even right outside your door? What about her mother?" Kate said gesturing to the child against her side.

"I don't need to justify myself to you chi . . . , Kate," he corrected. "People were scared and dying. If we had not bolted the doors, we'd all be dead now. Now excuse me while I help those still living." Iesed excused himself and walked through the adjoining corridor.

Kate smiled down at the clinging girl. The hesitant child half-smiled back in uncertainty. "Are you hungry?" The child just stared back. "Do you have a name?" Kate wondered. Again she just looked up at her. "Come on then," Kate said and lead her through the foyer into the main chapel.

* * *

The mist swirled and parted as a form soundlessly rose out of the ground to stand on the edge of an obscured clearing. Flange hesitated about going into the clearing containing the fairy ring of mushrooms, for this seemed the source of the mishap that had befallen the area. Streams of cold air and fog blasted from a spinning vortex stationed over the entrance to Haven.

The event itself was strange, but creatures even stranger seemed to materialize from the vortex emerging into the clearing. Flange could feel lines of powerful energy streaming from the spiral in what he believed could only be a form of sorcery. And that magic was having an effect on the surrounding countryside.

Flange closed his eyes and concentrated. He began to see the area using his extraordinary senses. The lines of magic emanating from the vortex grew stronger and more defined. Blurs of colored forms streaked from the nexus exiting into the countryside.

Flange took note of one in particular that seemed to be absorbed into a nearby tree. The colored energy seemed to expand and radiate more as the tree stirred with animated life. The twisted form yanked its root from the ground and shambled off out of the clearing. The tree-creatures, which had attacked Kate's band, had been the direct result of the entering magic.

Other forms of colored energy emerged from the vortex in search of life forms to corrupt. Flange felt the pull as if a world was being turned inside-out and dumped into this one. He shook the trance-like concentration and moved to the fairy ring. The ground began to ripple and he sank to his ankles and stopped.

A frown creased his forehead. He began concentrating harder. The ground continued to ripple but he moved no further into it. He could feel a resistance to his presence and wondered if Rewella had found a way to keep him out of Haven. He knew of other ways to get in, but they were strenuous and sometimes left him weaker than he would ever prefer. He decided to try a different approach and allowed himself to rise out of the ground and blend with what was left of the unchanged trees.

A spider scurried across the ground and stopped short of the turbulent vortex. Multifaceted eyes drank in the swirling maelstrom before it.

Another unwordly tree roared to animated life as a spirit form corrupted it. Roots were torn from the ground as the newly formed creature attempted to lumber from the formerly anchored spot.

The spider scurried out of the way, sensing the impending danger as the tree-creature ambled past out of the clearing. A shadow detached itself from the nearby woods and blended with what little outline the spider's legs produced on the ground by the heavily diffused sunlight.

10

A cut-crystal representation of a huge clear spider sat upon an ornately carved oak table. The hexagonal-cut surfaces of the multifaceted eyes of the scurrying arachnid projected images that hung about the air of the darkened room. All of the projected hexagonal images held multiple copies of the same image and each hexagon beheld a different scene.

The sheer volume of the cascade of images would have confused most anyone, but Rewella drank them all in at a glance. Each of the hundreds of hexagonal images came from the viewpoint of the surveying army of spiders the Rewella held in service.

Rewella mused at the scenes of destruction that she had inevitably unleashed by merging that troublesome Undead hunter with the summoned creature of the Void and throwing the corpse of Barcus in to boot. A frown creased her perfect brow as she stared at one particular hexagonal image, one that was completely black.

The wall shimmered and the lupine form of Sasha stepped into the room. Her wolfish features softened as she reverted to human form. She slipped her naked body into a neatly folded silk robe and tied the belt in a loose knot about her waist. She noticed Rewella's furrowed brow and intense concentration. She waited for the other woman to acknowledge her presence, but when she did not, she spoke, "I'm sorry to disappoint you, Rewella, but I can't locate Flange. He's not at any of the locations where I would normally find him."

Rewella still seemed in contemplation and did not respond or react in any way. Sasha stood fidgeting. She wondered if Rewella's silent treatment was due to her lack of locating the ever-elusive Flange. When no answer was forthcoming, she looked to where Rewella's gaze was fastened and asked, "What's wrong with that one?" Sasha pointed to the black hexagonal image floating above the crystal spider. "Is that spider dead?" she wondered aloud.

Rewella stirred from her observation shaking her head. "No, it's not dead," she said still eyeing the puzzling image. "Not dead," she repeated, "but somehow blocked from my view. If it was dead, the image would not exist at all."

"Let me guess, it's the one left in Haven," Sasha reasoned.

"Yes," Rewella whispered, still intent on the image.

"Flange's doing?" Sasha speculated.

Rewella shook her head again. "No, my spiders were in the clearing when the summoned creature opened the vortex. It may be its doing."

"The summoned creature that you gave power to," Sasha interrupted with a snicker.

"Yes, the creature that I unleashed on the unsuspecting world," she said with a hint of sarcasm.

Rewella broke her gaze from the images and turned to face her protégé. "You will never grow unless you try new and different things. Experimentation is the key to unlocking the universe or even the multiverse, Sasha," she said as if talking to an inexperienced child. And in most ways Sasha was just such a child.

Sasha's face hardened as she placed her hands on her hips and straightened into a menacing pose. "Look at those, Rewella," she said jabbing a finger at the images of death and destruction suspended in the air. "You *do* realize that you brought something into this world that you have no control over?"

Rewella cracked a bit of a smile on her perfect red lips and thought of how Sasha could easily be referring to herself just as easily as the summoned creature. That interpretation was not lost on her in any way. She let the smile bud into an alluring grin.

Sasha broke her menacing gaze, shaking her head in frustration, and began pacing the room in a looming circle around the centered table. Rewella smiled all the harder, watching the predictable display. How many times had she seen Sasha vent in such a way? More than she could remember and she knew what was coming next.

As if on cue, Sasha stopped her pacing and posed a question. "What about that spider?" she said looking at the black hexagonal representation looming in the myriad of swirling images. "What happened to it if it is not dead?"

Rewella watched her closely from a careful neutral mask of alabaster porcelain. After a few lingering seconds, she shrugged her shoulders dismissively. That action sent Sasha fuming back into a pace about the room.

Rewella hid her smile and then responded to the questions. "Something blocked the connection to the spider in Haven. I am planning to do a little reconnaissance, but I am waiting for night to fall so my powers are at their peak."

Sasha halted the pacing and pondered the delayed response. She stood for many moments, turning the information over in her mind. Her gaze intensified and she said, "What if it is not just the connection with the spider that is blocked? What if this creature is so powerful that it permanently closed Haven to us? What if we could never enter again?"

Rewella understood the underlying words that were not spoken. What if she was blocked permanently? Would the madness that the siblings so feared creep into her being? Would her mind lose cohesion and she'd become like those bound creatures that she and Barcus were so fond of creating? A visible involuntary shudder passed through her that was not lost on the she-wolf. Sasha caught the gesture and barely suppressed a shiver of her own.

Rewella recognized the look on Sasha's face and expected the woman to come to her in an embrace of sympathy. She was extremely surprised when Sasha did an about-face and strode from the room. Rewella sat and pondered the action. Maybe her protégé was not as predictable as she expected her to be.

The myriad kaleidoscope of hexagonal images shimmered in the air about the room. Rewella, lost in contemplation, failed to see her own multifaceted image in the mix as one of her spiders stared at her from a darkened corner. The spider's shadow detached itself and became one with the shadow cast on the wall from the dim illumination. The spider scurried away, wondering what brought it so far away from the area it was supposed to be watching.

* * *

Sasha stormed from the room, stomping through the decorated halls filled with massive woven tapestries depicting mundane scenes of noble life. She stopped short of a set of double doors, clenching the handles tightly in her hands. Instead of opening the doors, she leaned forward, placing her forehead against the cool oak wood. She held herself there deep in thought about the transpiring events.

She had always thought it intoxicating terrorizing the townspeople and then sucking the marrow from their bones. She could smell the fears of her victims and did her best to extract as much anguish from them as possible before finally killing them. Her belief that she was practically invincible furthered the notion of her dominating lesser beings.

Then comes along a boy that manages to strike a near-fatal wound with a silver dagger. *Why would Rewella create me with such a flaw?* she wondered. *Was it intentional or just an oversight on her part? Is it her way of always having control over me?* The same boy that Rewella had every intention of changing into a lupine companion for her, but Sasha had angrily refused. *Why would she do that to me? Does she not feel the same way that I do about her?* Rewella instead used the boy to create a creature that she had no control over and is responsible for ravaging the countryside with demons, spirits, and other creatures from the Void.

Sasha lost herself in thoughts of those presumed implications and the possible "what ifs." She repeatedly slammed her fists in frustration on the heavy doors, rattling the wrought-iron hinges.

A shadow in the stone corner lengthened and Flange materialized in the hallway. He brought his right hand up and stroked his chin in reflective thought as he eyed the surroundings. Sasha continued to bang and rattle the doors, unaware of his existence.

After a few moments, Flange decided to announce his presence, "Funny—I thought this place had been destroyed several hundred years ago, but yet surprisingly, here it stands," he mused.

Sasha's head snapped up and she spun around into a defensive crouch. Thick coarse hair enveloped her body and jowl, and her claws lengthened as she changed into lupine form. She settled back on her haunches, ready to spring forward in an attack.

Flange watched her with an amused look but did not move into an offensive position. "You're getting slow in your old age, Sasha. I figured you would have at least smelled my scent by now. I've only been shadowing your every move the whole while you've been searching for me," he said, showing his attractive smile to her.

Sasha said nothing but continued her crouched stance gauging the Undead man carefully. She knew that Flange held no love for her after the ruse that she and Rewella had perpetrated against him so many years ago. Thoughts of that time filled her head to near panic.

Flange had entered Haven to find a beautiful naked woman lying near the Circle in what seemed to be a state of bewilderment and confusion. He approached her cautiously, feeling the radiation of Undeath about her.

Sasha had looked at him pleadingly, very afraid. "Where am I?" she stammered, "Who are you?"

Flange watched her for a moment and then said, "You are in Haven. My name is Flange."

Sasha looked around her setting as if seeing the place for the first time. "What's happened to me? How did I get here?" She stared at her obviously changed body.

Flange took a moment to ponder her predicament. After making a decision, he knelt before her and asked, "What is your name?"

"Sasha," she mouthed more as a whisper.

Flange paused again, thinking over his course of action. He and his siblings had determined a set of governing rules and guidelines for not tripping over each other. And in those rules, they created an allowance for such a case.

It had been decided that if a sentient Undead could make it to Haven, without being destroyed in the process, then it would be spared from being destroyed by the siblings. Sasha seemed to be just such a case.

"Sasha," Flange started, "you have been changed into a creature not unlike myself."

She had watched him as if not understanding. "What do you mean?" she asked quietly.

"I am an Undead being. You have been drawn to this place that you see before you because you are Undead too. We call this place Haven. It is a sort of sanctuary for our kind. That spot with the etching that you are laying next to is what we call the Circle of Power. That Circle has tremendous power that can be unleashed under the proper circumstances."

After a long stretch of silence, "You said our kind and we, are there others like us?" Sasha queried, her expression filled with awe.

Her uncanny reaction and questions set Flange rolling back on the balls of his heels. This was not quite the response he had expected out of a newly changed Undead. Pondering left him somewhat cautious in answering right away.

"Some, though each person changed seems to be unique with unusual abilities. My experience leads me to believe that each changed person's abilities are reflected by personality. Each of my siblings are completely different with exceptional powers, so to speak."

Flange paused, eyeing the slightly pointed ears and lengthened canines. "I'm sure your abilities will be quite interesting," he finished, reaching out to the waiting woman. Sasha slowly accepted the offered hand and allowed herself to be pulled gently to her feet.

Flange and Sasha spent the next year together as he trained her to survive against humankind and taught her of his studies of Haven and the Circle. Sasha pretended to learn as a fledgling Undead companion and even acted as if she had fallen in love with the Undead man.

When Rewella was ready for her return, Sasha left Flange with a few of his secrets and the knowledge that he too had fallen for her. Flange was nearly devastated to learn that Sasha had been one of Rewella's henchmen all along. He felt angry and foolish for being blinded so.

Sasha broke her reflective trance as Flange took a step toward her. She crouched even lower, anticipating a forthcoming attack. Instead, Flange stopped and looked around the room again, reminiscing.

"Interesting," he uttered, "either Rewella is an incredible architect with abilities I've never dreamed of, or we're indeed in the past." Flange's wandering eyes settled back on Sasha as if waiting for confirmation to his query.

Sasha held her silence. She gauged the distance to the other set of doors at the opposite end of the hallway, located behind Flange, leading to where Rewella was.

Flange read the expression and said, "I wouldn't even think to try it, Sasha. I'll cut you in two before you even make it halfway there." Sasha glared at the notion, but Flange just smiled all the wider.

Sasha prepared to dash, but Flange's next words held her in place. Flange motioned to the handle of the sword waiting in his scabbard. "This blade is made of a silver alloy. I understand that you had an adverse reaction from an attack by a young man using a dagger," he said allowing his smile to widen.

Sasha looked visibly shaken at the proclamation. She let her shoulders slump somewhat and lessened her stance. Finally, in a guttural voice she asked, "What do you want with me?"

"What makes you think that I want anything from you besides your furry head?" Flange smiled in glee at the possible outcome.

Sasha reverted back to human form in an attempt to show that she was not going to be a threat. "I'll give you back the items taken from your lair," she said in resignation.

Flange held the mirthful smile. "Do you honestly think I would have left anything of value behind for you to loot? How stupid do you think I am, Sasha?" he questioned.

"Stupid enough to take a fledgling Undead under your wing for guidance and mentoring," Sasha spewed hatefully.

"Touché," Flange consented, "I would like to think that I have grown since our short stint together." Flange took another step toward Sasha. "I would like to think that I have grown beyond revenge, but you and I both know that I never will." Flange's eyes narrowed into a dangerous glint.

Sasha tensed for an attack as Flange crept ever closer, beaming that unnerving smile the entire time. Sasha's nervousness caused her to change back into lupine form. Her tongue lolled and she began to pant in anxiety.

Flange glided ever nearer until he was standing just before the unsure she-wolf. The charge in the air between them was more than Sasha could bear. With a low growl, Sasha sprung forward and leaped over Flange in an attempt to flee. Flange simply ducked and allowed her to hurtle over him and bound down the corridor.

When Sasha disappeared through the double doors, Flange slowly followed, quite happy with the alarm imparted in Sasha. He emerged through the double doors in time to see another door slam shut near the end of the hall. Flange glided along in anticipation.

Sasha stormed into the room and slammed the door shut, leaning heavily against it. Sasha barked out something in a less than understandable guttural voice.

"What's wrong?" Rewella questioned, knowing Sasha was visibly shaken as fear radiated from her trembling shaggy body.

"Rewella! Flange is in the hall!" Sasha managed to blurt out somewhat coherently.

Rewella kept her neutral mask of composure even as she heard the new voice, "It's true, sister, but I am no longer in the hall," Flange said, appearing from the shadowy corner behind her.

Rewella spun about, seeing her younger sibling as the projected images tracked across his face as he moved past the table toward her. Rewella backed toward the door and nearly tripped as she collided with Sasha.

Flange stopped short, watching the startled women. His alarming smile spread again in delight. "So what do we have here? It looks like the two of you have been busy. I would say very busy by the looks of the destruction around the countryside. Of course you do not have to worry about that here, do you?" He let the accusations hang in the air for a moment.

Neither of the women said a word with the exception of Sasha who was inadvertently allowing growls to escape her throat as she panted in a state of near panic.

"Let me guess, you somehow managed to use the Circle to transport you back in time to escape from your wrongdoings. I would have never ventured that it was even possible. The Circle seems to be filled with surprises," he wondered.

"Wrongdoings?" Rewella spewed, breaking her mask of neutrality. "You have yourself and our brother to thank for this mess. He opened that world and you killed him before he could close it," she lied. "Now look what has happened! I have no way to close it in our time so I am searching for a way to do so here in the past.

"I don't think so," he scoffed, seeing the lies for what they were, "Barcus had nothing to do with this unless you used him for such a purpose. You are the mastermind and have always been so." He glared at the two women, barely able to control his building rage. "I supposed Barcus was also responsible for summoning those creatures that attacked me in Haven."

"Attacked you and that miserable Baron," Rewella cut in, "You who brought the enemy to our very place of sanctuary! You who deserved our wrath for consorting with those humans!" she spat venomously.

"I need not remind you that *we* were once human too," Flange replied. "Although your sensibilities seemed to have fled along with your humanity."

"Don't try to patronize me, Flange. You talk of us losing our humanity? What about you, dear brother? You killed your own flesh and blood and you think you have the right to chide me about humanity!"

Silence hung in the air for a long while. His smile lessened into a grim expression as he shook his head. "No, not flesh and blood. Not anymore. We are not the same persons we were while still living, not since the change. We should have parted ways on that same fateful day we discovered that we were monsters. We stopped being siblings then and there, but it has taken me centuries to realize the error of our ways.

"Barcus was a bully who preyed on the weak during life and continued to do so even more in undeath. His actions led to his final demise. He deserved something far worse than the swift death I provided for him. I only wish that I had ended his reign of terror centuries ago."

"He was your brother, regardless!" Rewella shrieked, "and you had no right to kill him!"

"But I guess it was okay for you to use him for your own means?" Flange snickered.

"I never did!" she fumed. "We were partners trying to secure goals for our very survival."

"Just like Sasha is your partner?" Flange queried.

"She is my partner, you fool."

"Really?" Flange said, sounding nowhere convinced, "I figured she is just another pawn in your rise to power just like your last 'partner.' You did tell her about your last 'partner' didn't you?" He let the smirk creep back onto his lips.

"What's he talking about, Rewella?" Sasha questioned in a hurtful tone as she reverted back to human form.

"Nothing," Rewella spat dismissively, "he's making it up trying to turn you against me."

"Really?" he said, folding his arms across his chest. "Why don't you tell Sasha about your first attempt at creating a 'partner'? Or would you rather that I be the one to tell her?"

Rewella glared at the man as her luscious mouth pursed together into a scowl that seemed out of place on such a perfect face. She held her ground not giving an inch. "You're making it up and you know it," she said through gritted teeth.

Sasha had always known Rewella to hold a controlled composure no matter the adversary, and it was unnerving to her to see it slip away with the accusatory banter. "Is he?" Sasha blurted. Rewella turned her glare on the she-wolf but held her silence.

Flange watched the exchange between the two women and the wedge that he had driven amidst them. When Rewella refused to impart any information to the questioning she-wolf, Flange decided to, "You see, Sasha, you were not the first."

Both women turned his way, with Rewella becoming a rigid porcelain figurine and Sasha looking more like a child who had just witnessed the fall of someone placed upon a towering pedestal.

"I never put it together until recently enough, but they say that hindsight is perfect vision," he said allowing an alluring smile to spread across his handsome ashen face. "You see, Sasha, I found another sentient Undead creature in Haven nearly fifty years before I found you there."

Flange let the smile widen as the look of shock registered on Sasha's face. "Yes, this creature was actually Undead and had not been provided a mask such as you have. Rewella had planted this creature in hopes that I would see to mentoring it."

"What happened?" Sasha heard herself say, completely enraptured by the findings.

Flange was quite happy to see that he had her complete attention. His smile twisted up on one side of his face into a tugging smirk. "Why, I killed it of course," he said letting his eyes move from Sasha to settle on Rewella's fuming countenance. "I saw no reason why I should share the sanctuary of Haven with any other Undead, even if they were sentient.

"When Rewella found out about what transpired, she called a meeting of the siblings to discuss future actions against sentient creatures that might be drawn to Haven. She pleaded her case that we were just such creatures that had awakened in Haven, and what if someone had been there to attack us in our own state of despair and confusion?

"At the time, it seemed like a logical conclusion that we should leave well enough alone any sentient Undead who made it through the barrier into Haven, and so we came to an agreement. No others have ever been found in Haven until I stumbled upon you, Sasha, and I have not seen one since."

Flange paused, letting Sasha soak up the information. "It took quite some time before I realized exactly why Rewella wanted such an agreement. I started questioning her intentions after the little ruse that you both managed to pull over on me. Eventually I uncovered some evidence that linked Rewella to the Undead creature that I slew in Haven."

Rewella had not moved during the entire delivery and her lips stirred only a bit as she said, "You have no evidence for anything, merely wrongful speculation on your part."

"Really?" Flange said for the third time during the exchange, with a knowing smile. "You are not the only one who can use the Circle, Rewella. I have created items that you have no knowledge of. If fact," he paused dramatically, flashing an acorn-sized gemstone between thumb and forefinger, "this gem detects truths and lies. It changes colors depending on the response, and I have caught you in more than one lie. In fact, I have not seen you tell the truth about anything as of yet," Flange revealed happily.

Rewella's face held a momentary lapse of her careful facade, started to respond, thought better of it, and closed her mouth tightly.

Sasha slipped from Rewella's side and moved away from her, keeping her eyes on both the siblings. The tension continued to mount as the three stood roughly in a triangle with each sizing up the other.

Sasha's gaze fell back on Rewella and she broke the silence. "Is that what I am to you, Rewella, just a tool in the grand scheme of things?" she asked in a hurt tone.

Rewella started to respond, but Flange held the gem up before him, pointed in her direction. The action was not lost on Rewella as she glowered at him. Rewella could not get the nerve to refute the claim.

"I guess there is little point in using this anymore," Flange tucked the gem back into a pocket. "It seems you have little credibility, Rewella. Now, why don't you start at the beginning and tell me the truth?"

Rewella tried to compose her neutral mask, but she was not fooling anyone. Perhaps for the first time in centuries. The moments passed, but she refused to offer up any information.

Sasha edged around Flange, and when he made no move to stop her, she marched to the corner and stood facing the wall with her arms folded across her chest. Flange held Rewella's gaze, waiting for a reaction. Sasha half-turned toward Flange, "What do you want to know?" she said with a resolved sigh.

"Sasha, no!" Rewella blurted, hearing the resignation and knowing that the tables were turned against her. Flange ignored her outburst and focused on Sasha.

"First of all, tell me how is it possible that we are in the past?" he asked.

"Do not Sasha or I will . . .," Rewella started to threaten. But quicker than thought a resounding cling filled the room as Flange's sword leapt from its sheath, blurring in a streak that stopped suddenly, resting against her throat.

"If you are not going to offer up any information, and you want to keep your pretty head intact, I suggest that you stay very still," Flange said in a menacing tone of voice that left no room for discussion.

Sasha had blinked for only a second. And in that second Flange seemed to blur with a sword appearing in his outstretched hand, slashing out. Sasha gasped, for she thought Flange would lop Rewella's head clean off, but the blade stopped short. Sasha's heart was beating so fast that the blood rushed into her ears, keeping her from hearing the exchange between the two.

Flange tilted his head and said, "Continue, Sasha. There will be no more interruptions if she knows what's good for her."

Sasha paused, waiting for a response or some sign from Rewella on how to proceed. When nothing was forthcoming, she decided to tell the truth as she knew it. "Put up your sword, and I will tell you everything I know."

Flange regarded Rewella with a quick smile. "I take it that you will cooperate enough to keep quiet?" he said more as a statement then a question. Rewella made no move or sound, so he took it as acknowledgment. The curved blade ended up in the sheath nearly as fast as it had come out. Flange stepped back and gave a mocking bow to his fuming sister then turned to give his attention to the she-wolf. "I say again, how is it possible that we are in the past?"

Sasha exhaled the breath that she had been holding. She took a final look at her defeated mentor and said, "We are in a pocket, or at least that is how Rewella explained it to me. We are in a set diameter or a sphere that we can move about in, but it has its limits."

"I suppose so, only because she has not found a way to widen the area," Flange speculated.

Sasha shrugged her shoulders, no longer wanting to look directly at the stricken Rewella, knowing that things would never be the same between them. "I don't know specifics, only that she was able to open a door to this place."

"Can you get to Haven inside of this pocket?" Flange asked.

"No, I don't think the sphere can go that far. We can enter only a few rooms in the castle. Rewella chose the ones that no one ever goes into."

Flange's face lit up with thousands of questions. Although Sasha was narrating, his next questions were aimed at Rewella. "Have you found a way to widen the range?" he questioned.

Rewella held her silence.

"Are we back before we changed?" he wondered aloud in a somewhat softer voice. A slight smile crept to the corners of Rewella's luscious mouth. "Yes," she decided to answer. "Yes, we are in pocket of sorts," she said throwing a glare Sasha's way. "I was experimenting while you were away. I utilized the Circle in your absence. There are no formulas on the walls of Haven for this particular enchantment, but I was able to create it through trial and error."

Sasha was particularly glad that Rewella had decided to cooperate even if she was unsure to what extent. Anything was better than the betrayal she felt.

"The same way you were able to summon those creatures by opening a portal," Flange reasoned.

"No, I told you it was Barcus who—" she started to say, shaking her head.

"No more lies, Rewella," Flange interrupted, "I know what things Barcus was capable of, and summoning was not one of them.

Now quit wasting my time. Tell me what I what to know so I can try to stop this."

Rewella searched the smoldering eyes of her sibling, unsure of his ultimate intent. She knew that her rash actions of late were the cause of his intervention. She had always believed that she was the strongest of the three, but seeing the unyielding look of determination in his steel eyes, made her recant such thoughts.

She had summoned beings that she knew nothing about and even managed to merge one with a boy and the carcass of her brother, giving it powers that even she could not dream of. She was responsible for the mayhem caused by the opening of a plane of existence that was emptying into the world. If Flange had a way to stem the destruction and possibly even end it, why not let him?

Rewella's face softened a bit, something even Sasha had rarely seen, and her statuesque posture relaxed a bit. She even managed a bit of a smile as possibilities formulated in her head. "Okay, "I'll tell you what we know. Yes, this is a pocket located in the past. I originally built it as a place to store my treasures. Of course then, it was only a sphere about three feet round."

"So you did manage to increase the size of the sphere and it in turn became your lair?" Flange queried.

"Yes, but only to the size that it is now," she answered. "Trying to make it any larger would cause it to collapse in on itself."

"Have you tried to penetrate outside of the sphere?" Flange wondered, taking the next logical step. Rewella's smile faltered.

"No. Everything that I have learned shows that it would be detrimental to do so."

"Kind of like opening a world into another one?" Flange said with a hint of sarcasm.

"I did not open that portal!" she said slowly, trying to control her anger. "The summoned creature did."

Flange eyed her with open suspicion. He had assumed that the demon opened the portal, but he also knew that Rewella was more than capable. "Do you know how to close it?" he asked.

Rewella averted her eyes and gave a noncommittal shrug. "I'm not sure if it is possible. I would need to get into Haven to even try to stop it and the way had been blocked by the energies of the outpouring portal," she explained.

Flange rubbed his chin in thought. "We're going to the clearing where the portal is," he said decidedly.

"It is still daylight there, we cannot," Rewella refused, shaking her head.

"You can take your changes in the sunlight or you can be cut down right here. I could care less, but either way, that is where I am going."

A stricken look of utter terror filled Rewella's face. "The burning sunlight will kill me! I do not know why it does not affect you, but I cannot."

Flange let his unnerving smile tug at the corners of his mouth. "You're already dead so what is there to worry about? You spent so much time using the Circle to enhance your looks and powers that you had no idea of the tradeoffs."

Rewella looked stricken. "What do you mean? Are you saying that the Circle is responsible for the reaction to sunlight?"

"All newly created sentient Undead seem to be affected by sunlight. I chose never to use the Circle on myself. My resistance to sunlight grew as I got older and stronger. You on the other hand used the Circle to enhance yourself and now suffer from the side effects. Receiving vigor from Circle increased your sensitivity to sunlight," Flange said letting the revelation sink in.

Rewella seemed to be focused inwardly. Sasha listened to the exchange in a state of awe. Rewella shook herself from the trance and stared intently at Flange and said, "We need to catch the summoned creature and return to Haven. I might be able to break the merging effect and banish it back to the Void."

Flange shook his head and said, "I believe the Void is what is being emptied into this world. We must close that rift first, then nab the demon."

"We need to get into Haven, regardless, in order to succeed. We need the Circle," Rewella said, "but I must wait until the sun goes down."

Flange watched her carefully and said, "I do not trust you, sister. You would find a way to save yourself and flee this godforsaken place. I dare not let you out of my sight."

"You need my help to get into Haven. I have many items that can be used on the Circle but I have them scattered about. I need time to prepare. I'll meet you, no, the both of you at the clearing at dusk," she said.

Sasha and Flange exchanged looks of doubt, neither seemed thrilled at the prospect. "I'm not your slave, Rewella, and I am not taking orders from you anymore," Sasha snarled, pointing a clawed finger her way.

"Sasha goes with me," Flange interrupted. Sasha glared at him.

"I don't take orders from you either," she growled, changing into lupine form.

"Sasha," Rewella said in a cooing pleading voice, "you do not have the means to transport yourself from this bubble, nor to walk the shadows without help. Please, go with him as a token of my good faith," and after a pause added, "you were never my slave."

The two women exchanged a lengthy stare. Sasha broke the silence, "Let's go, Flange," she growled turning for the door but stopped short to face the Porcelain Lady, "Be at the clearing at dusk, or I'll hunt you down myself," and that said, Sasha was through the door.

Flange started to speak, but was interrupted by Rewella saying, "Save your speech, brother. I will be there." Flange gave an exaggerated bow, followed by a knowing smirk, and he too was through the door.

Rewella exhaled a deep sigh. She walked to the crystal spider and waved a hand over it. The projected images faded as the refracted light dissipated. A deep frown set on her perfect features as she tried to think of a plan that would eliminate the demon threat and possibly her sibling in the process.

Rewella's body fell apart into a tumbled mass of spiders that scurried to the four corners of the room, melting into the shadows.

* * *

Kate sat on the corner of the fireplace hearth as the child sat on the floor next to her, with small arms wrapped around both of Kate's calves. Kate stroked the sleeping child's hair as she clung for security.

Brundle stoked the fire with an iron and carefully dropped a seasoned log into the center of the dying embers. He nodded Kate's way as he lowered his tired body to sit on the opposite corner of the hearth. He fumbled with the buckle on the leather strap holding the metal leg to the nub of his stump. The prosthetic leg fell away revealing an ugly purple-black bruise from the cinched strap and a track of congealed blood. Brundle massaged some life back into the sore extremity with relief openly evident on his burly bearded face.

Kate disengaged herself from the sleeping child, laying her down on the floor at the foot of the hearth. She opened a waterskin pouring some of the contents on a clean cloth from her pack and knelt before the hefty blacksmith in an attempt to clean the irritated wound.

"Thanks, Miss, but I can do that," Brundle said taking the cloth gently from her hands. Kate looked at the man for any hint of meanness and decided there was none. He caught her questioning gaze and said, "I'm not used to anyone caring for me but me," he said with a wink and bit of a smile as he dabbed the raw nub.

"And Danya," Kate said with a teasing smile. Brundle's bearded mouth stretched wide, showing huge white teeth. Kate was a bit surprised and quite happy to see such a hearty grin on the normally ill-tempered man.

"Aye, and Danya," he managed to say, placing the wet cloth over the stump.

"She's taken a shine to you," Kate prodded. Brundle pretended not to hear as he took an immense interest in doctoring the rubbed irritation.

Kate moved back to the hearth near the sleeping child. She stared down and watched the rising and falling of the girl's chest.

"Has she said a word?" Brundle wondered.

"No. Poor thing. She finally fell asleep although she fought it all the way."

Landon entered the room and leaned in closer to Kate as to not disturb the child's slumber. "Miss, we are still holding the door. Our barricade seems to be keeping them out. We'll stay out here just to make sure," he said.

"Thank you, Landon. Make sure the men get some food and sleep."

"Yes, Miss. We have already set a watch." Landon saluted her as if she were Mengrig and marched back into the other room passing Iesed as he left.

Iesed stood in the doorway studying Kate as she covered the sleeping child with a discarded cloak. Kate had the sense that someone was watching her and she turned quickly to see the priest enter the room.

Iesed sat his old body into a cushioned chair just to the other side of Brundle. After sinking into a comfortable position, he said, "Everyone that can be tended to has been, but I fear that we shall be killed by those creatures long before the supplies run out."

"That's a cynical view for a priest, Brother Iesed," Kate jabbed.

Iesed, too tired to take the bait and get angry, shrugged his shoulders and slumped further into the chair exhaling with a deep sigh. "Dark times," he muttered barely above a whisper, "I remember when I was strong enough to turn one of those cursed creatures with only a prayer and a slight gesture. It has been too long since those days."

Brundle stroked his chin in reflective thought after discarding the soiled doctoring rag next to him on the hearth. He felt pity for the aged cleric and understood the source of resignation in the man's voice. He had been in that same dark place for too long. Brundle's thoughts were broken up as Kate spoke.

"What made you lose your faith, Iesed?" she questioned with no hint of malice. Her query seemed genuine.

Iesed stared hard at the young woman and stayed silent for what seemed an indefinite stretch of time. Again he shrugged, breaking his gaze with her, and focused instead on the flickering flames of the fire. "I've seen nothing but devastation and death in my lifetime. I've lost count of the number of children that I've given over to the sun's consecrated rays. I have tried to share the word of the Tome and preach its message of love and peace, but this land is foul and corrupted and seems to be more so now than ever before," Iesed said looking back at the expectant woman. "How would you feel knowing that everything you stand for seems to be a lie? That everything that you were taught to believe is nothing more than a flight of fancy?"

Kate shook her head vehemently, "No, I do not believe that, Iesed. I *cannot* believe that."

"Regardless of what you believe, the fact remains the same. Evil has crept into our lands and we are helpless to do anything about it other than suffer it," he interjected.

Kate continued to shake her head. "No, not while there are men like my father here to defend what is right and what is good."

The priest laughed mirthlessly. "My dear lady, your father may have the right ideals, but his quest to rid the land of Undead has led to the wholesale slaughter of the majority of the young men in this community. Who will protect the women and children when there are no of-age males left to do so? To me, that crime is nearly as bad as the babes lost to those Undead fiends."

"How dare you!" Kate spewed hatefully, launching herself from the hearth.

Brundle interceded by hopping up on one leg between her and the sitting priest. He clamped vise-like hands on her shoulders, stopping her momentum dead in her tracks. She glared at the blacksmith. His eyes held only gentleness. "Easy Miss. Remember, you asked the question first. He was only answering. Leave it at that."

Kate dropped back to the hearth, sending a murderous glare back at the unmoving priest. Brundle held his place for a moment to make sure that it was not a ploy and then sat back down gingerly.

The priest continued as if the interruption never happened. "You asked what made me lose my faith? It is seeing a good man like your father, having to use young men to try and stem the flow of evil and never really making a difference in the overall scheme of things. You asked me what made me lose my faith? How about a good woman cavorting with one of those foul Undead beings, Flange, the bane of our young men? Where is faith in such a union?" the priest said and was silent.

Kate held his gaze, clenching and unclenching her jaw. Finally, she said, "Maybe sometimes you have to trust an enemy to bring about the greater good."

"So it seems that every man must, and in the end, bring about his own doom." With that said, the old priest raised himself with effort from the chair and exited the room.

Kate fumed and stared into the fire. "I'm not selling my soul by receiving help from Flange," she muttered aloud.

"No one is saying that you are, lass," Brundle said in a low voice, "the priest is dealing with his own ghosts. I understand what he means. You have to look at it from his side of things. Here is a man who is supposed to lead by the examples of his book, and I'm sure it is disheartening for him to have to compromise those principles in the face of Undead adversaries. He believes that no good can come of evil, but here we are trusting one of that bunch." He held his hands up to stay her intended outburst.

"I'm not saying that what we are doing is wrong in any way. Under the circumstances, we don't have any choice but to trust in Flange. The priest sees and understands that, but he has to question what goes against his beliefs. Is he happy about it? Absolutely not, because he does not see any end to the vicious cycle. Don't hate him for his despair, Miss. He already hates himself for it."

Kate was astounded by the insight. She nodded in understanding and let the anger melt away. Brundle hobbled from the hearth and sat in the recently vacated chair. "Oh, that feels good on me old bones," he said sinking into the plush cushions closing his eyes.

Kate lost herself in thought stroking the sleeping child's hair as Brundle dozed in the chair.

* * *

Daekrey, in the guise of Sprig, placed the last gem in the recess on the Circle of Power and stepped back near the waiting winged form of Drafkris. "Drafkris, it is time to locate a suitable choice for melding," Daekrey said, staring into the heart of the Circle. The enormous winged demon-like creature stretched its jagged maw in delight as blue-black lightning arced amidst the Circle, destroying the placed items sending fine powdered dust to hang in the air.

The air shimmered and the gelatinous appearances of blocks of a mortared stone wall formed from the floating particles over the Circle. The apparition of the wall, with its transparent quality, framed the outline of a room formed on the other side, containing furniture and three figures.

Daekrey/Sprig stepped through the suspended image of the wall and as he did so, the hazy decor and persons in the room solidified as the image rushed into focus.

Kate looked up to see Sprig suddenly appear in the room. "Sprig!" she shrieked, springing from the hearth to dash and embrace the missing man. She sobbed, burying her head into his chest wrapping her arms tightly around his waist. "By the Gods, I've missed you! You had us so worried!"

Brundle jolted from his uneasy sleep at the hysterical declaration in time to see Kate leap into Sprig's arms. The bemused look on the boy's face seemed out of place for such an emotional reunion.

The likeness of Sprig wrapped an arm around the woman's trim waist and brushed against a familiar item. He pulled the plumed crumbled hat from the belt that it was tucked into. "What do we have here? Oh yes, I believe the boy has missed this item very much," the voice of Sprig said, mesmerized by the battered item.

"Sprig?" Kate said, confused by the manner that he was presenting. She thought it very peculiar under the circumstances. "Sprig?" she said again, taking a step back away from him.

The image of Sprig plopped the furrowed hat onto his head, smiled as if seeing the woman for the first time, and said, "Yes . . ." his smile changed to a leer. "He has very strong feelings for you."

"You're not Sprig," Kate said, horrified at the sudden insight, for Sprig's eyes were yellow and rimmed in red. Her hand went for the hilt of her mother's sword only to realize that she had laid the scabbard on the hearth. She backed away from the impostor.

Brundle, up the instant Sprig had appeared, hopped to the hearth, grabbing his axe in one hand and Kate's sword scabbard in the other. "Landon! To arms! Bring the men and form up on me!" he bellowed, echoing through the halls.

A silhouetted winged hulking creature solidified as it passed through the wall, stopping short at the side of Daekrey/Sprig.

Kate backed up to the hearth, taking up a defensive position after catching the retrieved blade. Brundle did his best to keep balance on one leg while hefting the axe, ready for a swing.

Landon, Wendon and several refugee men burst into the room with weapons drawn, ready to fight.

As the door was flung open, the winged demon Drafkris surged forward into the incoming men. Landon was swept aside with a wing buffet slamming him into the wall. The dazed man grimaced at the pain and held his hands over the gashed wound in his head.

Wendon hurled himself with full abandon and hacked mercilessly at the demon threat. The few swipes that managed to get through the stone-hard skin left only shallow nicks and barely a trickle of blood.

The demon seemed amused by the effort on the desperate man's part and sent him crashing to the ground with a backhand across the face. Wendon fell heavily on the already wounded Landon. The other refugee men fled the room in terror.

Drafkris' mouth opened, jutting razor sharp teeth in a semblance of a wicked smirk. Then a sickening crack sounded as Brundle sank the double-bladed axe into the back shoulder of the gloating demon. It howled out in pain and surprise, spinning around to confront the new attacker. The axe was wrenched away from Brundle's hands in the process. The man stood his ground as best he could on one leg and sent a rocketing punch into the side of the demon's skull.

Drafkris staggered under the powerful assault, but still managed to lunge out, clamping a taloned hand around the neck of the blacksmith, hefting him from the ground. Brundle fought desperately to break the iron grip about his throat as the threatening darkness from the loss of air began to engulf him.

Kate started a sword swipe at the outstretched demon's arms, but was intercepted and deflected away. Daekrey/Sprig had parried her sword with two daggers pulled from the shouldered bandoleer. Daekrey/Sprig watched the woman as she calculated her next move.

"I want this one for the melding!" Drafkris snarled. Brundle's body shuddered and went limp from the lack of oxygen. "He has strength and spirit, but we will have to do something about that missing leg."

"No!" Kate raged, sending a rushed slash toward the demon. Drafkris lowered a scaled wing, bringing it forward over its corded shoulder to absorb the glancing blow. Daekrey/Sprig reversed a dagger and clubbed Kate in the back of the head as she passed him, sending her sprawling to the floor.

"Hurry, the opening is starting to fade!" Daekrey/Sprig said seeing the translucent wall shimmer and quiver. Drafkris flung Brundle through the gelatinous membrane and made for the opening.

Kate, still dazed from the blow, pulled herself onto her hands and knees. She looked up in time to see Brundle hurled through the wall and could see his distorted form slide across a floor on the other side of the gateway. She grabbed her sword and fought the agonizing pain to get to her quivering feet. Drafkris, followed immediately by Daekrey, passed through the wall and became somehow obscured by the magic used. Kate shook off the dizziness and staggered unsteadily toward the shimmering barrier.

The sensation of passing through the wall for Kate was like swimming through icy water. She could feel the freezing substance pressing in all around and she was unable to breathe the frigid air. Panic welled inside and she fought the sensation desperately, seeing that the creatures were so near to her on the other side and apparently all right.

A jolt from behind found her through the membrane and onto a stone floor. Kate looked to see the frightened little girl beside her. Apparently she had awakened and rushed into the portal to keep from being left behind. The semitransparent shimmering of the wall behind her winked out, leaving her standing at the end of an unfamiliar chamber.

They were no longer in the church of Klevia, but in some sort of ancient room setup for alchemy and the walls were covered in strange diagrams. Recognition dawned on Kate as she saw the etched Circle in the center of the room. This had to be the Haven that Flange had told her about. The towering demon discovered her as she backed away with the girl until she bumped into the adjacent wall.

"Daekrey, we have visitors," the demon said, motioning in her direction as it wrenched the colossal axe from its back, tossing it to the floor with an echoing clatter.

Daekrey/Sprig turned from the Circle, sizing up Kate and the trembling child clinging to the nape of her neck. "Persistent, I have to give you that," he said with a hint of admiration, "she would be a good candidate for melding as well."

"Maybe for another of our kin, but I want that one," Drafkris growled, pointing to the unconscious man on the Circle.

"Suit yourself. Keep an eye on her while I prepare," Daekrey/Sprig said and walked to the only table in the room. He closed his eyes and held his hands before him. A silent moment passed and a black box appeared on the table. Daekrey/Sprig opened the box removing various articles including colored gems, pearls, clear stones, and a hard leather-bound book containing a strange clasp.

Kate sat herself on the dusty floor and the child went straight into her lap. The demon seemed to be watching her but made no move toward her. She cupped the sword in one hand, with the blade resting on the ground next to her. Her throbbing head ached and she fought to regain control as swimming darkness threatened to envelop her. The strength had fled her limbs as she stared at the spectacle laid out before her.

Daekrey/Sprig, kneeling before the Circle and the unconscious blacksmith, set the retrieved items into various cracks and recesses. Satisfied with the placement, he stood and took his place next to the sentinel demon.

Kate could feel the charge in the air as the child's hair began to rise and stick to her face. A flash burned her sight as lightning leaped from the floor, arcing above the Circle to come back down, coursing through the body of the blacksmith.

Brundle yelped and convulsed as the lightning crackled around and then coursed through him. He screamed and grabbed at the stump of his calf where the concentration seemed to be focused. The energy dispersed, leaving the room smelling of ozone and singed hair and smoldering flesh. Brundle's eyes were squeezed shut as he grimaced at the receding pain, and his thick hair and beard stood straight out away from his head. Uncontrollably, his body twitched intermittently on the Circle.

After the process subsided, Drafkris easily hefted Brundle and removed him from the Circle, laying him not unkindly on the stone floor.

Daekrey/Sprig nodded his head in approval and said, "We are going to need some time before finishing the melding process. In the meantime, I need more components that cannot traverse so easily. We must go and bring them back."

"What about her?" Drafkris asked.

"What can she do? Where will she go? They do not have the means to leave on their own, and if we leave them here, they cannot cause trouble elsewhere," Daekrey/Sprig reasoned.

Drafkris scratched his chin in silent understanding and followed Daekrey to the center of the Circle. Daekrey/Sprig closed his eyes in concentration. The two began to shimmer, blurring as they slowly vanished from the room.

Kate let go of the sword and slipped the girl from her lap. She crawled near the Circle and placed the palm of her hand on Brundle's cheek.

He winced and slowly opened his eyes not sure what to expect. He stared up into concerned teary eyes. "Me rattled teeth hurt," Brundle managed to slur out, "I nearly bit me tongue off."

She smiled and sobbed in relief that the blacksmith had survived whatever it was that had been inflicted on him.

"Oh, that hurts!" Brundle gritted his teeth and groaned still clutching his calf stump, "Miss, it feels on fire! Like it is burning from the inside!"

Kate could see that an angry-red swollen protrusion on the end of the stump had replaced the purple-black bruising from the irritation of the prosthetic leg. She touched the spot, gingerly testing the swollen tissue. Brundle winced and bit back his curses.

She helped Brundle to a sitting position. "We have to find a way out of here," she said looking about the chamber, "I don't see a visible door anywhere."

"Probably not any," he said looking at his stump.

"We have to find a way out before they come back," she said in desperation.

"They didn't kill us. Maybe they need us for something."

"They need us all right. You missed the part about us being melded, whatever that is."

"I remember, that thing said it wanted to be melded with me. Do you suppose that's what happened to Sprig?"

"*If* that was Sprig. I don't know what we can do about it now other than try to get out of here," she said leaving his side to examine the walls. "Maybe we can use the Circle to get out of here?"

"If you please, Miss, I have used the Circle and prefer not to do so again," Brundle said not at all in jest.

Kate stomped to the waiting table and examined the contents left in the box sitting atop it. "They left behind some things. Maybe we can put them on the Circle and get out of here," she wondered.

Brundle grabbed his stained axe and scurried far from the Circle to pull himself up next to the bewildered child. He turned himself over and plopped against the wall, laying the weapon next to him. "I've no intention on being near that cursed thing while you experiment," he chided while still rubbing the inflammation on the stump.

Kate removed the box from the table, placing it near the edge of the Circle. She eyed the various pieces and tried to match the shapes to the recesses on the Circle. She placed all the items, stood back away from the circle, and waited.

After several minutes, nothing happened. "Damn it!" she shouted kicking the items from the Circle and scattering them across the floor. A motion caught her eye in the corner where it began to darken. "Oh no!" she said and raced to the waiting pair, scooping up her sword and taking a defensive position in front of them.

The shadow lengthened in the darkened corner and jutted into two forms that began to solidify in the room. The creatures had returned.

11

Darkness settled as the trace of the sun's final glow fled from the sky. Flange and Sasha stood in the clearing near the fairy ring of mushrooms. Neither spoke, as both were lost in silent contemplation as they watched the spiraling otherworldly vortex empty its contents into this plane of existence.

"There may be a finite amount of beings because there seems to be less and less of them entering," Flange said, barely above a whisper. Sasha, even in human form, had exceptional hearing and only grunted in response. "You better hope your mistress has a way to close that fissure."

"She's not my mistress," Sasha said trying to keep the quiver from her voice and adding, "not anymore."

Flange smiled but did nothing else to encourage the already distraught she-wolf. Instead, he focused on the stationary vortex and the occasional energy forces that streaked from it to violate the land.

A single spider crept to the edge of the clearing, taking in the swirling spectacle. Another spider joined the first, and then followed by yet another. The forest floor seemed to come alive with movement as thousands of types of arachnids converged on one another at the edge of the clearing.

The spiders merged into the form of Rewella carrying a small ornately carved chest. She had looked upon the vortex from every angle in the guise of the spiders and was now seeing it with her own eyes. She suppressed a shiver at the magnitude of power necessary to create, or close for that matter, a rupture so enormous. She was startled out of her contemplation by a hand suddenly grasping her shoulder from behind.

"Did you bring everything necessary?" Flange said without preamble.

"That depends on what you plan to do," she said shrugging his hand loose from her shoulder when he did not remove it right away.

"I plan, with your help of course, dear sister, to close that opening into this world. Can you get me into Haven?" he stated more than questioned.

"I've been studying the barrier erected around Haven and I think it is possible to get around it. I can create a temporary disruption but you will have to act fast to get through it., The barrier can be disabled once inside of Haven," she stated.

"Your disruption will have to last long enough for two, because I'm taking Sasha with me," he said studying for a hint of a reaction.

Rewella stared hard at the Undead man. After a few moments of silence, "I'm not sure that's going to be possible even for one, let alone two persons," she said maintaining her composure but only just.

"I think I have some say so in where I go," Sasha said heatedly to both of the siblings.

Flange ignored the outburst. "When I get through, I will need her to guard my back until I can get the barrier down," he said turning to the indignant she-wolf. Both women stared defiantly at him. "This is not open for discussion from either of you. You will do as I tell you. If you will not be part of the solution, I will remove you as part of the problem."

Sasha visibly shuddered under the intense scrutiny aimed her way from the Undead man. That, and the fact that his hand crept to the hilt of his sword, stifled any protests. She issued a low throaty growl as her only disgruntled response.

"We're wasting time. Now open the way into Haven," Flange commanded.

Rewella opened the small chest that was resting under the crook of her arm, handing several objects to the Undead man. "When you get into Haven, use these items and the corresponding formula on the wall to break the barrier. I'll enter when the obstacle is removed."

Flange nodded in understanding and walked for the fairy ring in the clearing, careful to avoid the hovering vortex and the entities that spewed sporadically forth.

Sasha hesitated for a moment, searching the eyes of her former master. Rewella only nodded for her to go into the clearing. Sasha's shoulders shrugged in indifference, and she leapt deftly, bound for the ring of mushrooms. Rewella followed at a slower place preparing herself for the ordeal yet to come.

Flange held a hand out toward Sasha who took it reluctantly. Flange enclosed his arms around the she-wolf's slender waist, pulling her close in an intimate embrace. The resentment was evident by the scowl Sasha sported. "It's a necessary evil," Flange mused, "just like you."

Rewella closed her eyes and let the surrounding energy flow through her. In her inner mind's eye, she saw the vortex as a funneling whirlwind jutting through an upsetting rupture in the physics of this world.

As intrigued as she was by the new insight of the phenomenon, she instead searched through the earth into the magnet lines of force locating a pocket of an enclosed universe surrounded by pulsing energy bands. Rewella knew this area to be Haven.

She focused her will at deflecting portions of energy making up the barrier away from the entrances into Haven. The task strained her being to the core, and at one point, she could feel herself become absorbed into the protecting energy bands as they fought back at their would-be attacker.

Rewella had the fleeting sensation of Flange's presence near her and then was gone. She fought for as long as she could before trying to remove herself from the draining embrace of the shielding barrier. The entangling energy held firmly, trying to absorb her essence adding it to its own.

Panic swept through her and she nearly gave in to the force threatening to engulf her, but her resistance pulled her further from the influence of the barrier and eventually far enough away to allow her consciousness to return to the waiting, perfect shell of her porcelain body.

Flange pulled Sasha closer than was actually necessary so that his chin rested snuggled against her cheek. Sasha's intended protest was stifled as her feet fell out from under her and she clutched Flange in a tighter hold as the ground suddenly swallowed them.

* * *

Kate brought her sword overhead preparing for a striking blow. A shadow in the corner lengthened into two separate forms that began to take shape and solidify. She struck at one shadow with her blade only to have it intercepted and blocked by a dancing sword, that seemed to appear out of thin air, in defense.

"Kate? How did you get in here?" Flange questioned in wonderment as his body solidified. He lowered the blocking sword, returning it to the sheath with a blurred quick flick. Kate stared hard at the Undead man, not lowering her own blade.

Brundle, curled in a fetal position holding the throbbing stump, groaned and grimaced with eyes squeezed tightly shut against the searing pain.

Flange broke his gaze with Kate and knelt before the stricken blacksmith. As he did so, Kate watched the she-wolf congeal in the corner of the room.

"You!" Kate shrieked, lunging for Sasha, slashing the blade in an arc that nearly took off one of the lycanthrope's ears. Sasha dropped to all fours and sprung over the Circle to the other side of the room, trying to put as much distance between her and the sword-wielding woman.

Kate administered a swipe in passing, just missing the exposed ribcage. Kate pursued her intended prey, circumvent the Circle, intending to corner the fleeing she-wolf at the other side of the room.

"Flange, tell her I am not the enemy!" Sasha croaked during the transformation, as a coarse mane covered her body and her maw jutted forward, baring sharp fangs.

"You're sure not a friend," Kate spewed, taking another stab at the shaggy-furred woman. Sasha nimbly moved out of range of the repeated attacks, putting the only table in the room between the two flailing women.

"Flange! Call her off, or I will tear her still-beating heart from her chest!" Sasha threatened.

"It would not be any more than you deserved Sasha," Flange said aloud, but not paying any other attention to the feuding females. His focus instead was on the distressed man and the angry swollen stump. "Tell me blacksmith, was the Circle used on you?" Flange said in a softer voice as he examined the nub.

"Aye, they said something about melding me," Brundle hissed through gritted teeth.

Fascinated, Flange studied the tissue, poking and prodding in places. The blacksmith sucked air through his teeth but did nothing to hinder the examination.

The table at the end of the room landed with a loud crash as Sasha kicked it over, using it as a shield from the furious woman.

Flange pulled a small sharp knife from his boot. "This may hurt a bit, blacksmith, but surely not more than you are already suffering." With the care of a surgeon, Flange sliced open the tender flesh at the end of the nub and peeled back the skin.

There was very little blood from the cut, much less than Flange would have expected. As the flesh parted, fresh pink skin, like that of a newborn, showed in the center of the nub. Flange saw with great surprise, that the new soft tissue had five digits attached to it.

Flange stood up, smiling broadly down at the behemoth of a man. "This could very well be your lucky day, blacksmith."

"Flange!" Sasha bellowed as she bolted past the Undead man. He grabbed her protruding tail, yanking her off her feet. Kate was hot on her heels when she crashed over the sprawled form of Sasha, causing her sword to clatter out of reach across the stone floor.

"Enough, both of you!" Flange hissed sternly. Both women stopped struggling and turned their attention to the Undead man whose focus was on the blacksmith.

"What did you do to him?" Kate questioned when she saw the tender exposed flesh.

"If I did not know any better, I would say that the blacksmith is growing a new leg," Flange responded appreciatively.

Kate's shock and awe was more than apparent at the realization. "We have to get him out of here now! They're coming back for him!"

"Who is coming back?" Flange asked.

"A demon that wants to meld with Brundle and something posing as Sprig. They said they needed some items to complete the melding, whatever that is," Kate explained.

"How did you get in here?" Sasha questioned.

Kate glared at Sasha and picked herself off the stone floor. She retrieved the lost sword and held it in a loose grip. "Since when are we working together?" Kate said challenging the she-wolf.

"Kate, I need you to tell me what has transpired since I left you at the church," Flange said interrupting the heated exchange.

Kate shifted her glower from the she-wolf to Flange. "What are *you* doing here with *her?*" Kate questioned with an accusing glare.

"I came to get rid of the barrier surrounding Haven and to close the portal letting the demons into this world," Flange said and thumbed over his shoulder, "She's here as insurance."

"What?" Sasha growled. "I came here to help protect you while you worked on the barrier!"

Flange spread a slow knowing grin. "Believe what you want to believe, but I brought you here so I could keep an eye on you and your *mistress*." Sasha let out a low growl, spun on her heels, and plodded to the opposite corner in a huff. Flange let the smile slip from his face as he turned to face Kate. "Now tell me what has transpired."

Kate eyed the man, gauging his intentions, and after a moment said, "They did something to the church wall that allowed them to move through it. They attacked and brought us here."

"Straight here?"

"Yes. Then they placed some things on that circle over there and lightning struck Brundle. Then they left saying they needed more items to finish the melding. They left us here knowing that we could not get out."

"Well, they were right about that. Without any help you would be stranded here. How did they leave?"

"They vanished," Kate said shrugging.

"I need you to be more specific, Kate. How did they vanish?"

She thumbed a motion at the Circle and said, "They stood on the circle and slowly vanished."

The exhilaration could not be contained on Flange's handsome ashen face. "Was there lightning as was before?" he questioned excitedly.

"No. They simply vanished," was her only response. Flange mulled over the information in silent thought. He walked to the Circle, seeing the loose items and gems scattered about. The items and the locations they had been placed made little sense to him. Kate followed him, seeing his deliberation.

"Were these placed by the demons before they left?" he asked Kate.

"No. They were left over on the table. I put them on the Circle, hoping it would open a way out of here," she said.

That answer satisfied Flange and seemed to fit the situation. He knelt, picking up five gemstones. Three of the stones seemed to be near identical in the power they radiated, while the others seemed to be different and lesser in vivacity. The three gemstones were unlike anything he had ever seen or felt before. The closest item, near as he could tell, was the ancient and unique blade hanging at his side.

Kate watched the silent contemplation as Flange examined the gemstones and three in particular. Flange opened a pouch and placed all of the gemstones, except one, into it. He held the gem up to the undisclosed light sources looking into and through it.

Something about this stone tickled a forgotten recollection of thought. Flange brought the gem very close to his eyes. In the attempt, he unintentionally touched the stone to his forehead.

A vivid rush of flamboyant colors and vibrant energy rushed into his mind, forming a mental picture. The picture was of a room very similar to this one, including an etched Circle of Power surrounded by pictographs of formulas on the walls.

Flange could see his perspective move with him as he scanned the Circle presented to his mind. He took in every detail. Yes, the Circle was similar to the one located in the room, but had varying differences.

Flange felt his viewpoint move as he scanned the represented walls. Every pictograph was present as if the walls had just been created with each radiating the mimic vibe of the items necessary to perform an enchantment on the Circle.

The implications almost overwhelmed Flange. He had located another Circle of Power thousands of miles away. The reason for his disappearance for so many years was the search for another Circle. His siblings had stayed in the area only out of fear of losing the cohesion of their minds. It had always been necessary to return to the chamber containing the Circle of Power frequently, to stave off the attempted madness that always seemed to be lurking on the fringes of the mind.

Flange had challenged the continual lure of the Circle by trying to move beyond its reach even if it drove him to be a mindless zombie like the lesser kin of Undead. The attempt to pull away by traversing the many thousands of miles nearly caused the madness to overtake him. On the brink of mindless disaster, a tingle of another lure could be sensed as the known one began to recede.

Flange followed the growing sensation, even traveling to another continent to find its source. In an unnamed desert filled with desolation, and as the madness having nearly torn away the recesses of his mind, he sank into the forgiving ground, locating another Haven, another Circle of Power. Immediately his mind regained the needed cohesion for staying a sentient Undead being. The experience was invigorating, for the presence of the Circle restored mind and the deterioration of body.

The newfound Haven was more intact than the one he had known for centuries, with a slightly different Circle, and a horde of pictograph formulas that he would have never imagined existed, including the very special one starting the quest that had brought him back to the land of his siblings. Yet, the image that his mind was seeing through this stone was not the one he had found! It was a completely different Haven!

Flange removed the stone from his forehead and excitedly grabbed another of the three gems from the pouch, placing it to his brow. The sensation flooded his head once again as another pictograph-walled room and an etched Circle appeared. He quickly scanned the room's contents, realizing that this was yet another Haven.

Curiously he held the third stone to his head, seeing the presentation of the Haven he had located in the desert. "Four of them," he muttered under his breath, dropping the gem into the pouch.

Kate watched the display in silence as Flange investigated the gems. "Five," she corrected, not understanding.

Flange decided not to tip his hand in the present company of the she-wolf and only nodded and said, "I need to get the barrier down." He marched to the center of the room, placing the items retrieved from Rewella's box into the crevasses of the silver-etched Circle.

Lightning arced, temporarily blinding most everyone in the room, as the items were consumed in the reaction. "That should do it," Flange said.

"By the Gods!" Brundle exclaimed, "Would you look at this!" Brundle's eyes were wide in disbelief. The agony that he had most recently suffered was no longer evident on his face. Instead it was filled with child-like wonderment as he flexed newly grown toes on the fully restored leg.

Everyone in the room, including a naked reverted Sasha, stood in amazement over the blacksmith and his new appendage. "Miss, would you help me up?" Brundle asked in bewilderment. It was Flange who grasped the blacksmith's forearm, wrist to wrist, as is the warriors' way, and easily hefted the huge man to his feet. Flange released the man's hand as Brundle tested his weight and balance.

Tears of joy flowed freely down the burly man's face, dampening his unkempt beard. The anger and resentment that had amassed over the last unforgiving years dissipated with the cleansing sob. Brundle was at a loss for words, but felt no shame in the unleashing of emotions or in the release in his very soul that it had given to him.

"How touching," a voice said from behind the group. Kate spun about, ready for another attack. Brundle swept the axe from the ground, the exalted expression disappearing from his face at the approach of danger.

Kate saw one of the most beautiful women she could ever remember seeing before standing in the corner of the room. Even rivaling that of her mother. The woman's face seemed to be carved from living alabaster and her raven-black hair shone silkily in the gleaming phosphoric light. The contrast of hair and features complemented each other perfectly. Kate was surprised by the twinge of jealousy that ran from one end of her spine to the other.

Rewella took the scene in at a glance and walked to the further wall studying a pictograph formula. Without preamble she said, "This is the one needed to close the rupture."

"Is there a way to reverse it first before closing it?" Flange questioned.

Rewella tapped her cheek with a lithe digit, still facing the wall. "I suppose it can be done with an alteration. "Why?"

"Those creatures will need to be forced back through before we seal the rupture," he said.

"Eventually they will run out of substance and simply die," Rewella stated, "so why worry about it?"

"Not before they have killed everyone in the land," Kate spat.

"That's no concern to me," Rewella said nonchalantly in dismissal.

"It should be," Flange said angrily. "You are the primary cause for everything that has happened here."

"And so what?" she challenged, "They are mortals, dear brother. They are fodder to be lost in the greater game of our lives. You know that, so why the sudden change in heart?" Rewella chided.

"Not anymore. Reverse the flow from this world so I can clean up your mess," Flange said. His eyes and tone held no room for any argument.

"I cannot do exactly what you want. I can seal it shut right now, or I can reverse the flow and cause the rupture to eventually seal itself. You will have limited time to do whatever it is you are planning to do, brother," Rewella said.

Flange glowered as he thought about it. "How long will I have?" he finally questioned.

"My guess would be two days at the most if you are lucky," Rewella said.

"Do it now," he commanded. Rewella shrugged, walked to the Circle and began placing items from the small chest into the recesses on it. Kate watched, trying to discern any pattern that may be useful at some later date. Rewella dusted her hands, got to her feet, and backed slowly from the Circle.

Lightning once again filled the room, sacrificing the precious items to unleash the terrifying power of the Circle. Rewella pointed to the opposing wall. "That formula is 'dead' now Flange, and I know of no other that will reverse or close another rupture should they open one."

Flange knew that she was right. The mimicking vibe from the pictograph formula was gone with the usage of the items. He shrugged in reluctant acceptance. "It will have to do. Can you open a gateway back to the church?" Flange questioned.

Rewella looked as if he had slapped her in the face. "You're joking." Realization occurred to her, "The demon opened a gate using the Circle. That is how they got here unharmed," she guessed.

"And in even better condition if you're the blacksmith," Sasha piped in.

Rewella held a mask of neutrality seeing the "too pink" unmarred flesh of the blacksmith's leg. Her mask slipped a touch to let out a quick glare at her brother. The fleeting glance was quick enough that only **Flange and** Rewella were aware of the exchange.

Flange decided not tell her that he was not responsible for the regenerated appendage, and instead was happy to let her stew in unfounded anger. "Open the gateway," he commanded.

Rewella stood staring defiantly, her eyes ablaze in fury. "I could, but the items that would be expended are priceless and irreplaceable," she said, her words dripping with venom, "and I am not about to waste them on an exit passage for mere humans. If you feel the need, *you* can take them out one at a time."

"If you refuse to open a gateway back to the church, I have no further use for you," he spoke in a dangerous tone. The ancient sword leapt from the sheath to his hands as he stormed toward the porcelain woman.

"No!" Sasha cried out, lunging for the Undead man. Kate's sword arced down between Sasha and Flange, stopping the naked she-wolf short. Kate's smile showed that she would like nothing more than to lop this woman's head clean off.

Apparently Rewella understood this as well for she stretched an upraised hand, "Stop!" She sighed in resignation, "All right, I'll open a gate for them."

Flange stopped short, but did not put away his sword. "No tricks," he said emphasizing with a flick of the blade reminding her of what would happen otherwise.

Rewella stormed to the center of the room, placing the last of the precious items from the small metal chest onto the Circle. Lightning forked through the chamber settling on an area suspended in the air forming a smoky picture of a tiled room with an unfinished fountain in it.

Rewella glared at Flange, "There, you have your gateway for your little friends. I am finished here with or without your consent." She rose and moved toward the corner, sending a quick glance Sasha's way.

On cue the naked woman changed back into lupine form and bound for the corner, intercepting Rewella. Both became like the shadows and disappeared from the room.

Flange shook his head and considered whether letting them go had been the best decision. Instead, he shifted the focus to the task at hand.

The gateway waved and shimmered in the air. "Go, before it closes," he said to the waiting companions. As he spoke, two forms began to take shape on the Circle.

"They're coming back!" Brundle bellowed, hefting his axe in both hands. Daekrey/Sprig and Drafkris' wavering forms solidified, and they stepped from the Circle.

Brundle bellowed a war cry, made entirely of pure rage, and charged the hulking winged demon. A loud sickening crack echoed off the chamber as Brundle's axe head sank deeply into the skull of the creature that had chose him for melding.

The demon shuddered under the impact but seemed as if he would recover, but just as suddenly, the creature's legs buckled, and it crashed to the stone floor in a heap.

"We have to go! The gateway is closing!" Kate yelled grabbing the little girl's hand and pulling her in tow. Brundle tore his wicked axe free and dove through the fading portal after the fleeing woman and child.

Daekrey watched the portal expire from the room. He could sense that the barrier that he had erected surrounding the Power Point had been compromised and removed. He also knew that the opening he had created into this world had been reversed and that the demons and spirits that were not lucky enough to survive in this world would soon be drawn back into the safety of the Void.

Daekrey stared hard at his unmoving companion on the floor, and then shifted his hateful glare to the waiting Undead man. Daekrey backed away a step and then another. Flange followed, keeping the distance the same between them. Daekrey stood over the very center of the Circle and a slight smile tugged at the corner of his youthful mouth. He closed his eyes, lost in concentration.

Flange could feel the charged energy that hung in the air about the enigma of the creature in the guise of Sprig, and lunged for it. The melded being began to fade away immediately as Flange crossed the Circle in a flying tackle. His senses became distorted momentarily in a swirl of vertigo, but then he felt his body land hard on the sprawled form of Daekrey as they slid across the floor.

Daekrey managed a kick that sent Flange in a roll ending with a thud against one of the walls. Daekrey was on his feet running back to the Circle. Flange pursued but was too late to reach the creature as it disappeared from the room. Instead, he passed through the air just missing his prey and fell sprawled onto the floor on the other side of the Circle.

Angrily he picked himself off the ground and stared at the metallic etchings. Suddenly his head snapped up and he took the whole room in at a sweeping glance. This was not the same room he had just been in! In fact, this was another Haven altogether and not the same one that he had located in the desert.

* * *

Daekrey shimmered and reappeared on the Circle in the room with his fallen comrade. Pools of moisture formed in the eyes of the melded man and fell in a cascade of heavy drops over the crumpled form sprawled on the cold stone floor. Daekrey felt the warm flowing streaks on his face, surprised by the emotional response from his newly acquired body. His kind had been far too long outside the world of flesh and blood. He had nearly forgotten the effects and feelings that only the flesh seemed to provide. He had known Drafkris even before the thousands of years of exile that they had shared together with the last of their kin.

He carefully hoisted the hulking form with an easiness that would have shocked any spectator that would have stumbled upon the awkward scene. The leathery wings hung draped across the melded man's shoulders and dragged across the stone floor as Daekrey moved to the shadows of the far corner.

As he stepped into the corner with the massive bundle of his former friend, he turned and glared toward the Circle. "You will pay for the loss suffered today," he spat, and with that vowed to his unseen enemy, Daekrey vanished into the shadows.

* * *

The silhouettes of two shapes appeared in the center of the fairy ring of mushrooms. The moon's eerie light fell on the emerging women, bathing them in ghastly monochrome blue luminescence.

Sasha and Rewella stared intently in silence at the opened fissure suspended overhead. The turbulent flux of the vortex shimmered gossamer threads in the reflected moonlight. The flow of the energy had been reversed back out of this world, leaving the wind to stir in an unnatural way.

Rewella could see that the rupture was closing at a minute rate. Even so, the anomaly reached inside and pulled at her very essence, beckoning her to surrender into what waited in the Void. She shuddered fearfully under the unfamiliar dominating sensation.

Sasha interrupted the silence with a guttural growl, breaking the attempted spell woven by the vortex. Rewella sensed it too. Both women fled from the fairy ring into hiding in the surrounding woods.

A blast of air surged forth as a winged demon fluttered past the wary women. The demon appeared to be in a weakened state, its skin completely translucent. It seemed to be answering the summons as it dove straight into the heart of the spiraling vortex vanishing from the night and from this world.

A shadow seeped from the ground, emerging before the maelstrom of the extra-dimensional gateway. Daekrey held the colossal form of Drafkris and raised it over his head. Limp leathery wings flopped about as the vortex yanked at the creatures. After a few moments of silence, Daekrey hurled Drafkris' body back into the waiting Void.

Rewella watched in grim fascination, for the being that she had melded had emerged only minutes later than she from Haven and with a dead minion no less. "Go back to the lair and wait for me," Rewella said without preface, as she moved from the place of hiding amidst the trees. She gave no chance for a retort as she strode purposely for the clearing.

Sasha sank back on her haunches, clearly conflicted by the hurtful treatment from her former mistress. She decided that Rewella had deceived her for far too long, and that their relationship would have to be completely overhauled if she was to hang about. She watched curiously through the interlaced branches, trying to hear any of the forthcoming conversation.

Daekrey stood staring at the entrance back into the Void as the ethereal winds stirred the plumage of the worn ridiculous hat that Sprig was so fond of.

Rewella glided soundlessly over the grass near him. "Your brother is going to suffer for my mentor's death," Daekrey said aloud, giving the only hint that Rewella's presence had been detected. She halted suddenly but said nothing.

Daekrey half turned his body and fully turned his head to look at the Porcelain Lady. "Where is he?" she asked. He watched her for a moment in silence.

"I trapped him in another place far away," he stared for a moment before continuing. "However, he seems to be a cunning individual and my trap may only keep him busy for a short time. But then again, time is not really a true factor," he finished cryptically.

Rewella was more than intrigued. "Tell me more," she said expectantly. A scowl creased his face as he glared intently at her.

"What do you want?" he asked as if she were a blackmailing child.

"Your secrets. Haven's secrets. I want to understand the workings of the Circle," she said vehemently. The melded creature stared at her intently. She held her ground with his unrelenting gaze boring into hers.

"You closed the vortex," he stated flatly.

"Yes, it is slowly closing," she confessed knowing that he could see through any of her lies. "My brother forced me to do so."

He sized her up once again and nodded, having made up his mind. "Come, I have lots to show you," he reached out for her hand, which she took without hesitation.

Sasha spied from the confines of the trees. She caught only a glimpse of a word here and there. She watched the melded creature reach out a hand that her former mistress took willingly and the two disappeared from sight.

"No!" Sasha growled, bursting through the underbrush, skidding to a halt helplessly before the shrinking vortex.

12

Rewella held the gem before her, studying the eddy of power that radiated from it. She had been led back to Haven to begin her tutelage from the melded creature. "Place it on your brow," she heard a detached voice say.

In all the centuries that she had been studying and experimenting with the Circle, she had never ran across such a magical vibration from an artifact before. Upon further thought, that really was not so surprising. The negative energy that linked her kind to Haven had also made the local land a kind of prison to her. The constant fear that her mind would lose cohesion, causing her to turn into a mindless lesser Undead being, had limited her intended research. She had been forced to create the likes of Sasha to carry out any tasks that would normally lead her away from the nurturing replenishment of negative life-force from Haven.

And yet, Flange had managed to leave the known confines of Haven for several years. There were so many things she had yet to discover, and now a chance had finally presented itself in the form of a melded, conjured demon.

Rewella's reminiscing thoughts vanished when she placed the gem to her forehead. A burst of energy coursed through her head as a picture took form of Haven. In her mind's eye, she could look and see every pictograph etched on the wall and feel the mimicking vibrations given off by each one.

She opened her eyes and matched the overlaid image from her mind onto the walls that surrounded her. "Some of these images no longer exist," she said excitedly, "Some of the pictograph etchings have been destroyed on the walls, but this gem shows me what they were!"

Rewella pulled the gem from her brow, severing the mystical connection. She stared expectantly in wonder at the melded man. "What is this?"

"It's a memory stone. Think of it as a place marker of sorts. That one was made over a thousand years ago from this very room," he said pointing to the gem Rewella still held reverently between the thumb and forefinger of her elegant alabaster hand. "And this one has an image of just over four hundred years ago," he said showing a similar stone, "and this one was created just after you first summoned me," he said holding up yet another stone.

"What's their purpose?" she queried excitedly. Daekrey smiled wistfully. Rewella suppressed a shiver that threatened to race down her spine. Instead of answering right away, Daekrey moved to hover over the silvery etching. Rewella followed around the other side of the Circle to stand opposite of the summoned being. The silence built into an electric charge, not unlike the released byproduct of the blue-black lightning from the Circle's use.

"You see," he started, "you have discovered one of the minor properties of the Power Points. They have many other uses rarely dreamed of."

If his tone was meant to be condescending, Rewella forgave it immediately with the sudden knowledge of his words. "You said 'Power Points' and 'they'," she murmured in an astonished voice, "There are more than one?"

The wistful smile stretched into a full-blown grin. "That's right," he said nodding at her comprehension.

"How many?" she queried after a long moment of contemplation.

"Four on this world," he replied.

"Four, on this world? How many worlds could there possibly be?" she said as her legs gave out beneath her. She plopped unceremoniously onto the stone floor before the Circle.

Daekrey also sat on the stone floor, but with much more grace. He could see that she was running the possibilities through her beautiful head. After a few moments of introspective silence, he removed a four-sided stone from a pouch on his belt and began to explain. "Do you see this stone?" he asked. She nodded in return. "Each of the four sides is a perfect equilateral triangle. Do you know what that is?" he asked as if talking to a learning child.

"Yes, the three sides for each triangle are the same exact length and the angle where each of the sides join have exactly the same angle," she replied in understanding.

"Good. Now imagine that this four-sided stone has a sphere surrounding it so that each of the four points of the stone intersect and touch the sphere, creating four points on the sphere. Do you understand?" he questioned.

"I think so," she said shaking her raven locks.

"Each one of these points on the sphere is equal distance apart from each other," he said.

Rewella lit up in understanding. "Each of the four points is a type of Haven!"

"Yes, and different worlds are stacked on top of each other into infinity," he added.

"That's how Flange was able to stay away for so long. He found another Haven and it kept his cohesion together," she said in wonderment at the revelation and surfacing possibilities.

Daekrey's smile vanished at the mention of Flange. "Yes, and I am going to use these stones to hurt your rather resourceful brother," he glowered.

The resentment was not lost on Rewella in any way and she suppressed a shudder. "How do you intend to do that?" she wondered.

An edge of a smile crept to his face. "Why, with the help of these stones," he said in a melodious voice as he clacked the gemstones together in the ball of his fist. He stretched out an upturned palm, waiting for Rewella to deposit the stone she was holding, which she reluctantly did. They both stood and Daekrey stepped onto the Circle with Rewella following suit.

Daekrey held one of the stones to his forehead and closed his eyes in concentration. The silver lines of etching on the Circle began to blaze in an unearthly light. Rewella found herself moving from the Circle only to have Daekrey's free hand snake out and grab her wrist, locking her in place. A feeling of vertigo swept through her and she feared that she would fall. The sensation passed and she opened her eyes. The room looked exactly the same, except for one thing; the table that she had placed in the chamber was no longer there.

Daekrey steered her from the circle and over near the corner of the room. Without another word, he moved back to the Circle and knelt before it. Rewella's view was blocked and as she moved forward, Daekrey backed away toward her, further blocking the view.

The familiar blue-black lightning washed the walls of the stone chamber. A black globe hung over the Circle. Daekrey's voice echoed through the room in a shrieking vocal of an unrecognizable dead language.

The black globe elongated and changed shape, turning into the likes of a winged translucent demon. Daekrey smiled and tossed a gem at the demonic creature that snatched the jewel from the air in a closed-taloned fist. The creature stared at the duo in angry silence. With a wave of dismissal, Daekrey watched the creature disappear and the globe fade away.

Rewella watched the exchange, waiting for an explanation as Daekrey turned a deceptively handsome smile her way. "You see, I recognized you when you summoned me and bound me to your service," he said as if amused by some inside joke she was not privy to.

"What?" she said, not understanding.

"I did not recognize this form until after you had melded me with the boy and your recently slain brother," he said with an unnerving smile.

"I don't understand. What do you mean recognize me, from where? I had never laid eyes on you until I summoned you," she said, completely bewildered.

"Exactly, but today was the first meeting for me and your second," he said enjoying her confusion. Rewella stood and stared as she mulled the information over.

She finally came to terms with what she had been told and had experienced. "You're telling me that the demon you just summoned was you," she stated. "When?"

"Just over four hundred years ago according to the timetable of your world. I used the memory stone to bring us to this particular point in time according to your world. The Void has no such timetable. Each summoning seems back to back. From the time that I summoned myself here to the time you summoned me was just a blink of an eye in the Void."

"So this has already happened," she tried to reason.

"Yes. I did not understand why the summoning stranger had given me a memory stone and asked for nothing in return. It was not until you summoned and melded me to the mortal that I understood what was happening," he mused.

"Why did you give yourself a memory stone?" she was almost afraid to ask.

"So that I would have the means to go back to this point in time in your world," he answered.

"But why? What could you possibly want here?" she wondered. His grin unsettled her.

"Revenge. I am going to make your brother pay for his crimes against my kin," he said coolly.

Rewella stood open-mouthed at the sheer volume of the happenings. If what he was saying was true, then she was in the past, and what was still yet to come chilled her Undead bones.

* * *

Flange fumbled for the pouch containing the gemstones and poured the contents into his hands. He sorted through them until he located one in particular. Holding it to his brow, the image appeared in his head. Flange opened his eyes and could see a perfect overlay of the room presented before him by the jewel.

It had taken him years traveling across the open land to locate another Haven, and now he had traversed from one to another in the blink of an eye. The implications were astounding. The fact that he had been duped into following, and then subsequently being stranded, possibly thousands of miles away, left him unsettled.

He removed the stone from his head and sighed. Somehow the creature had used the Circle without adding items to trigger an effect, to transport him to this location. Flange replayed the scenario over in his head. He remembered that the melded creature stood in concentration on the Circle and that somehow produced the transport.

Flange moved to the center of the Circle and closed his eyes. He began using his preternatural senses to search the Circle. The gold and silvery lines seemed to come alive with a dormant energy that held the potential for some kind of action or reaction but some kind of catalyst seemed necessary to ignite the spark.

While still concentrating on the energy of the metallic lines, Flange held one of the gemstones to his forehead. A surge of power jolted through him as any fleeting sense of up or down went missing.

The gem had fallen from his hands and rolled haphazardly away as he fell to the stone floor. Flange pulled himself up onto his elbows. A horrible ringing in his head kept his movement to a minimum. As the thrum died away, he sat on the Circle taking in his new surroundings. He recognized this room as the one he had found in the desert.

He picked himself up from the floor and staggered to the opposite wall. One of the pictograph formulas caught his eye. He was sure that that particular one had been extinguished by his own use. He knew that the items he had used were unique and that the mimicking of power that the walls radiated had died away.

He turned around and ran to the far wall. He stopped near the corner and stared at a pictograph formula that had made his initial journey here the most rewarding. This particular formula was also the main reason that Flange had called a truce with the Baron. This intended procedure was one that would change everything for him if only he could find the other missing item.

The pictographs had a representation of a sword and a blue gem. It was a fairly simple combination, but one that would grant the ultimate power. Flange pulled the ancient ornate blade from the scabbard at his side and held it before him. Using his extraordinary senses, he felt the singing vibration of the sword and all it stood for. The same unique pattern was reflected in the mimicking pictograph displayed on the wall.

The other item displayed in the formula was a blue gem that radiated the essence of life creation. Flange sheathed his sword and ran his hand over the depiction of the gem, absorbing every detail. He knew without a doubt that this formula would change an Undead creature back to a mortal one again. This knowledge had become his driving mission. He longed to be a living being again, and when he finally located the missing piece, he would be so again. He ran his hand over the formula one last time and then walked purposely to stand near the Circle.

Flange picked up the fallen gem and placed it back to his forehead. The image of the room came to life as it overlaid the existing one. He had not been certain which stone he had put to his brow during the experimentation on the Circle, but now he knew. He removed the stone and placed it in a pouch hanging from his belt.

Flange stepped gingerly onto the center of the Circle, closing his eyes. He searched out the power in the silvery lines. Again, he could feel the energy, poised and ready to be controlled and directed. He allowed his essence to reach through the lines to trace their path along every inch of the Circle.

When he was satisfied with the results, he reached out further seeing where the lines would go if they could. To his surprise, he felt his sense of being moved along the lines outside of the chamber of this particular instance of Haven. He had the sensation that the Circle was a focal point and that he was traveling through a conduit moving away to another focal point.

He could feel the presence of another Circle as he traversed the coursing energy. He opened his eyes to see himself on another Circle in a different chamber. He smiled broadly at his newfound revelation. *No pain this time,* he thought to himself.

He stood staring at the covered walls, and using a memory stone, confirmed that this chamber was one he had not visited before. He was becoming aware of the slight differences of each of the chambers and the Circles they held.

Confident that he could traverse from chamber to chamber, he moved to the center of the Circle, concentrated on his target, and vanished from the room.

* * *

Kate stood atop the clutter in the entryway, blocking the front door of the church. She pressed her frame against the door straining to hear. The blacksmith stood near, axe at the ready, balanced on his newly grown leg and wearing a found mismatched boot. The rest of the wary party had opted to stay clear of the man since his return.

Kate and the little girl seemed to be the only ones not disturbed by the abnormal transformation. "I don't hear anything," she said after a few minutes of intense listening.

"Don't mean there's nothing out there," Brundle was quick to add, shifting his axe from hand to hand in anticipation. He could see a couple of men looking from the foyer who were careful not to meet his eyes. Brundle huffed under is breath. It was bad enough when no one would talk to him because he had lost a leg only to find out now that none of them wanted to acknowledge his presence because he grew one! *You can't please anyone,* he mused inside of his head.

Actually, he was not upset at any of the men who deemed fit to ignore him. He felt sorry for them and their mistrusting dispositions. In fact, it was hard to keep the toothy grin from his face even under such dire circumstances. *Maybe that's what unnerves them the most,* he thought.

His pondering was broken as Kate said, "I want out of this place. They could come through the walls at any time again, and I don't want to be here when it happens." He could not agree more, but abandoning the church to those creatures bothered him.

"What about the church? What about those people taking refuge in here?" Brundle questioned.

Kate jumped down from the rubble and dusted her gauntleted hands together. Her brow furrowed as she thought about the question for a moment. "We take anyone who wants to go," she replied firmly.

"And the children? Who's going to carry them so that we can fight our way out?" Brundle asked, trying to show her the necessary logistics of such an action that fleeing would cause.

"We'll have to manage. It's been quiet for a while now; maybe they've gone away. It'll be light soon, and we can make it back to the estate before dark," she said with her mind made up.

"All right, Miss. We do it your way, but it will be slow moving," Brundle said stroking his shaggy bearded chin in furrowed thought.

"Landon, Wendon," Kate yelled to the doorway. Both men poked their heads through the interior double-doors. "Get some men in here and start clearing the debris. I want those doors open by daybreak."

Both men nodded, but were careful not to make eye contact with the blacksmith. The action was not lost on Kate. "And the problem is?" Kate asked as the two men fidgeted in the doorway.

"We would prefer to work in here without the blacksmith's help," Landon muttered. Wendon nodded in agreement. Brundle rolled his eyes in defeat.

"And why is that?" Kate pressed. Wendon took a quick glance the blacksmith's way and then back to Kate.

"It's not natural," he muttered. Kate's response was completely short of what the blacksmith had expected. She burst out laughing in an uncontrollable fit.

When she could catch a breath, she added, "And anything that has happened recently is natural?" She continued her sporadic laugh. Brundle chuckled at her overly done hysterics.

Both the accusing men exchanged embarrassed glances with one another and waited for the two to finish.

Kate wiped the tears from her eyes. The look that she took on was all business. In a serious tone, she said, "Gentlemen, we have all suffered losses recently due to the most unnatural of things, including demons and Undead. What *would* have happened to the blacksmith is the same thing that *did* happen to Sprig. He was melded to a demon, and if we had not escaped, it would have happened to us as well. Now get over your narrow-mindedness and clear the doorway!"

"Yes, Miss!" they said in unison, scrambling to clear the debris. Brundle could not help from chuckling as he followed her into the foyer.

"Well done, Miss," Brundle said jovially.

"That's not anything we need right now," Kate voiced angrily.

"They'll get over it, Miss. It just takes a little time to do so," he stated. Kate shrugged nonchalantly.

"So I take it now that you have put all of our lives in danger that you are going to cut and run," a sarcastic voice uttered from the other hallway. Kate rolled her eyes and spun on the priest.

"I'm taking everyone out of here at daybreak," she spewed. "It is not safe to be here anymore."

"This church stopped being safe when your party stepped foot inside of it," Iesed accused.

Kate wanted to retort to the comment, but she knew there was truth in it. Instead of firing back angrily, she stated calmly, "We are leaving at daybreak with anyone who wants to go with us. That includes you too, Iesed."

Iesed stared at the woman. Her audacious nature drew a cold response. "I will stay with my church and with anyone who wishes safety outside of your group," he stated flatly through clenched teeth. Kate crossed her arms and shrugged dismissively. The priest stormed from the room in a huff.

"We leave at dawn," she said aloud. The blacksmith nodded.

* * *

The torn garments, disheveled raven hair, and the smeared

muck covering the majority of her petite body marred Rewella's normally pristine appearance. She glared at the amused face, struggling to pull her captive wrist free.

Daekrey held her fast as she thrashed about. The realization that the melded creature had no intention of bestowing his tutelage upon her was infuriating. Insatiable lust for power had blinded her to the trap that had been set. And when it sprung, she fell deeply into it.

Rewella dropped heavily, skidding across the ground as Daekrey suddenly released her flailing arm. *The Porcelain Lady looks more like the Muddy Madame,* he mused in thought. He smiled wider, reveling at her predicament.

Rewella's glare changed to one of fright as the start of flamboyant colors edged into the receding night sky. She felt numbing weakness settle in her limbs followed by an incessant itch that compounded and crawled across her skin. "I . . . have to . . . get away . . . before . . . sun rises," she sobbed frantically, curling into a ball on the leaf-littered ground.

Daekrey's face lit with glee at the pathetic sight. He had lured her into the chamber housing a Power Point with false promises only to drag her through to this world's past as an unwitting pawn. *Serves her right,* he thought at the irony, *she summoned me into service as a slave and now she will pay the price for doing so in full.* His expression faltered at the sound of an approaching carriage on the nearby road. He left the quivering woman on the rain-soaked turf and approached the muddy-tracked thoroughfare.

A two-horse-drawn carriage, displaying a royal seal of some kind on the doors, trudged through the muck around the bend in the road. Daekrey moved to the center of the avenue and halted before the listing coach.

The coachman pulled the reins, causing the carriage to slide to the side and eventually draw to a sinking halt. "You had best have a good reason for making me stop. I damned near ran you over in this dark," the man grouched, throwing the reins around the brake and reaching down between his legs under the buckboard. "If you're a robber, you'll be getting yours," the coachman aimed the fished crossbow at the waiting man. "I've killed many a highwaymen in my day," he finished boldly.

The gesture caused a look of amusement to pass over the melded creature's face, but the lack of fear and wistful smile from the impeding man ran the coachman's blood cold. He was just about to shoot the eerie man wearing the floppy hat with dropping plumage, when the right door of the carriage opened.

"What's the problem, driver?" a regal voice commanded, dropping to the muddy ground and latching the just-closed door behind him. Despite the man's posh cut, he emitted unquestionable authority. His soft leather riding boots were lacquered in beeswax polish and were more than likely buffed to a glaring sheen. Daekrey was unable to tell because of the lack of light and the newly acquired cake of mud that had just soiled them. The man's black woolen pants were tucked into the boots and a frilly white silk shirt was in turn tucked into the pants. A dark coat covered the shirt, stopping just over the knees. A red ascot, looking nearly black in the absence of light, was tied properly around his neck and a jeweled badge of office bounced lightly from side to side against his chest. A decorative belt held an ornately carved sheath housing a cavalry saber that rattled regularly against the hip with the rhythm of his stride.

The imposing figure stopped standing near the guarding driver. He grabbed the lapel of the dark woolen coat with one hand and tugged one side of the curly end of his wax moustache. His piercing ice-blue eyes and brown manicured hair shone brightly even in the encompassing darkness. He stared silently at the impeding figure in the roadway including the shouldered bandoleer full of daggers.

"I am Duke Leonine and if this carriage has become stuck because of your impudence, I shall tie you to the rear axle and have you dragged for your efforts," the Duke said in a thick, almost cruel voice, "Now why are you in the road?"

Rewella had told the melded creature all she knew about the circumstances leading to the betrayal of her family by the Duke who had courted her mother and was ultimately responsible for changing the siblings into Undead. Of course, Rewella revealed this information only because she believed that Daekrey was to be her mentor. Had she known it possible to travel back to the days before the change, she would have never have told him the truth.

Daekrey continued a pleasant smile and said, "Ah yes, Rewella told me of your courtship with her mother."

A confused look knitted the Duke's brow. "Rewella? How are you acquainted with that child?"

Daekrey ignored the question and continued speaking as if to himself, "She told me you were solely responsible for the change, but you are not Undead."

"Not Undead? Are you mad? Who are you and why are you rambling as such? Are you possessed?" the Duke said heatedly, placing a hand on the grip of the saber and preparing to use it.

The melded creature held a sardonic reflective thought. "No, you're not Undead. Not yet, anyway," Daekrey said letting his lofty tone change to a malevolent one.

The coachman fired the crossbow, just missing the man as in a blur of motion, two throwing daggers sped through the air striking the driver in the throat and in the left eye socket as the impeding man sidestepped the bolt. The old man dropped the discharged weapon and tumbled from the carriage, plopping onto the saturated ground.

Angrily, the Duke's sword cleared his sheath as he tromped through the bogging mud toward the melded being. Daekrey closed his eyes in concentration and the Duke stopped short as if struck by a giant's hammer.

Unseen tendrils snaked from Daekrey, working their way into the Duke's essence, tearing away at his will. Leonine collapsed to his knees in agony as the negative life force flowed into him from the lashing tentacles, replacing his own living essence. The man cried out, fighting for control of his very existence. Daekrey snickered as the anguished man lost the short-lived battle for his soul.

Leonine collapsed forward into the mud. Daekrey knelt before the newly formed creature. "Do you feel the coming sun? Does it threaten to incinerate you, Duke?" he asked playfully.

The Undead man pulled his hateful face from the mud and scowled. "Yes," it murmured though gritted teeth, "something beckons... a hunger..." The changed man convulsed on the ground.

Daekrey stood over the quivering mass of the formidable man. "I suggest that if you want to survive, go to what calls you," he said and left the Duke to his own means of survival. Daekrey walked back into the woods to the location to find that Rewella was no longer present. The only trace was the last of a scurrying spider that hid from the approaching dawn. He shrugged at the loss for it was inconsequential in the grand scheme of things.

He moved back to the road, not surprised to see that the Undead Duke was also gone. After retrieving the thrown daggers from the dead coachman's body, he leaned over the dead man, watching the blood pool across the ground. Closing his eyes in concentration, the unseen tendrils whipped out, settling across the corpse. The body jerked in spasms and an eerie red glow filled the empty socket and glazed orb.

With a lurch, the coachman climbed from the mire and stood before its new master. With a nod from an unheard command, the coachman climbed onto the buckboard and flicked the reins. The spurred horses caused the carriage to move with a slow start as the traversing wheels sucked through the grabbing mud. Eventually, the carriage picked up speed as it followed the mucky road.

Daekrey resettled the floppy hat on his head, cleaned the soiled blades on the grass returning them to the waiting bandoleer, and followed the receding coach as it disappeared around the bend. Daekrey smiled in appreciation of good irony.

* * *

Flange stood on the outskirts of the village of Klevia and scowled. He had returned to the Haven, under the fairy ring in the clearing via the transporting Circle, and knew immediately that something was not quite right. The chamber was the same, but it was missing the table that Rewella had provided many years ago. His suspicions were further aroused when he exited the chamber into the clearing.

The underbrush growth and the surrounding trees were smaller. Not smaller, he realized, but younger. Also, there were no signs that the adjoining trees had been animated by the invading spirits, and had rampaged through the countryside.

Klevia's roads were no longer paved cobblestones. Instead the roads consisted of churned mud covered in loose straw. The buildings were mostly wood instead of stone or brick. The village looked as it had when he was still a living being, before the change. "How was this achieved?" he wondered aloud, fumbling with the memory stones. "Was it the Circle or the stones? Both? Maybe it was the demon who stranded me here."

He placed the jewels back into the pouch and moved deftly through the woods, being careful not to reveal his presence to any anyone. *Am I too late to save my siblings or myself from the fate presented to us?* The thoughts were overwhelming. He had every intention of finding the appropriate items to reverse the curse of undeath on himself. Being back to the point in time when the situation happened altered his whole train of thought. Too many questions had to be answered before he could even think about that hopeful solution.

Flange moved fleetingly through the forest, moving parallel to a road he had not been on in a score of years. In fact, in the present, there were no signs that this road ever existed. He stopped sniffing the air. *Blood.* Turning toward the direction of the road, he walked steadily from the trees.

The black muck was stained with crimson in a thick pool. Flange touched the blood, feeling the texture and found part of a ruined eye. He flicked the mud from his soiled fingers, and began studying the tracks on the ground. It was easy enough to see what had happened. Someone had stopped a wagon or a carriage and managed to kill the driver and or passengers.

Someone else had climbed from the wagon and approached the attacker with a drawn sword and then fell to the muddied road. Flange could not see the cause or injury for the bodies were gone from the ground.

Another scent caused Flange to freeze in his tracks. He knelt over the patch of ground that the Duke had fallen to. A fetid stench hung over the spot. He had smelled that same odor hundreds of times before. It was Barcus' signature scent.

How is that possible? he wondered. *Barcus is gone.* Was he too late? Had the change already happened and his brother was about terrorizing the land? "No, can't be," he said aloud, "those powers came later. It took years before we had that much control over them and besides, it's daylight." Flange needed answers, but he filed away his questioning thoughts. He wiped his hands on the grass, trying to remove the clinging stench. He finally gave up trying, and melted into the ground.

13

The speeding coach raced around a corner of what passed for a street in the village of Klevia. The rear wheel caught a post of a building causing the rear axle to tear free, spilling the carriage onto its side.

The manic driver tumbled from the buckboard, falling clear of the overturned rig as it skid to a grinding halt. The tangled fallen horses screamed in agony as they fought to stand on broken legs.

Several townspeople rushed from their homes to investigate the unsettling noises in the street. Two men used knives to cut the tackle away from the struggling horses, while several others ran to the aid of the driver.

An anguished cry rang out as the limp-lying driver suddenly burst forward, grabbed a helping passerby and sank his teeth into the side of the would be helpful man's head. The captive man shrieked for help as the stunned populous finally acted by beating the animated Undead man away with pieces of lumber and tools from the nearby stable.

Eventually it took six men to stay the Undead man with pitchforks, pinning it to the ground. A severing axe blade chopped the creature into numerous writhing parts. The shook-up crowd watched it squirm in horrified awe.

"It was the Duke!" a voice yelled echoing off the buildings, "I saw it with my own eyes!" The crowd searched around and found that the voice belonged to a young man staggering through the mucky street. He stumbled, nearly out of breath, and almost fell. Bystanders in the crowd steadied the young man as he sucked great gasps of air.

"Tell us what you know, boy," a man commanded after a silent moment of hesitation. Daekrey eyed the man, knowing he was with the town watch.

"I saw Duke Leonine attack his driver turning him into that—that creature," he said pointing at the still-writhing limbs.

"He sent it to attack the town and said he would be back with others. I fled for my life! I tried to get back in time to warn you, but I guess I was too late."

The guard patted the young man on the shoulder and said, "You did good, lad. You did your best. Now, run home. I'm sure your parents are worried about you."

Daekrey nodded and worked his way through the throng of people. With his back turned to the crowd he let a knowing smile slip. "All too easy," he muttered under his breath.

"Get me a flask of oil and some kindling," the guard said gesturing at the Undead man. "We need to burn this abomination."

"What about the Duke?" someone in the crowd yelled.

"We go to the Magistrate and let him decide," the guard answered as he doused the coachman's bloody limbs in oil before setting them ablaze.

Several angry men broke from the group to dispatch the news to the Magistrate. Others went door to door spreading the word about the tragic afternoon's happenings.

* * *

A shadow lengthened in the corner of Haven as Flange solidified with sword in hand. A gentle sobbing echoed through the chamber. Flange pinpointed the origin of the sound from a crumpled form in the opposite corner.

Flange, ever wary of danger, covered the distance cautiously. He sighed heavily, sheathing his sword as he knelt before the form of Rewella. Her milky flawless skin was like flaking ashes of spent cinders from a burned-out hearth. Her body was seared to the bone in many places. Her formerly black shiny hair was singed and matted and the color seemed drained away, leaving only murky gray strands.

"Rewella," Flange said, resting a hand against her cheek. The brittle flesh came away with his gentle touch, floating slowly down like a leaf spiraling from an autumn tree. He jerked his hand away in shock.

Rewella opened her eyes into crescent moons. "Flange?" she mouthed. "How did you get here?"

"Rewella, do you know where you are?" he questioned.

"He left me to be burned in the sun . . ." she stated with a touch of anger in her crackling voice.

"Do you know *when* we are?" he said insistently.

Her eyes seemed to clear a bit. "Yes, Daekrey had a stone that transported us here," she said in a clearer voice.

"Had?" he questioned. "Where is it now?"

"He summoned his past self and gave it to him," she whispered in a halting breath.

Flange mulled over the information. He thought perhaps that Rewella had gone mad, but quickly dismissed the notion. He nodded in understanding and said, "I have some of those stones as well. Maybe I can use them to get us back to the present, but I need to stop him first. Can you set up a contingency spell using the Circle? Something with a delayed reaction?"

Rewella's face looked vacant. He shook her shoulders, causing more of the cracking skin to shake away and fall off in clumps. She winced, but shook her head in understanding.

"Can you break apart the meld?" he asked.

"Yes, I think so," she said hesitantly, "but it will probably kill the boy."

"At this point, I don't care. That creature is too powerful to deal with on his level. I need him knocked down a notch or two. Get the Circle ready, I'll lure him back to Haven."

Rewella nodded and pulled herself across the floor. Flange spun heading for the shadowed corner.

"I'm responsible for what happens to us," he heard her soft voice admit. "I melded Daekrey and he changed the Duke into a greater Undead being."

Flange stopped dead in his tracks and turned back around staring in shock. "What?" he questioned, but already knew the answer.

"Daekrey is responsible for our creation and I am responsible for his. I didn't know . . ." she began to plead.

Flange glared at her. "Just have the Circle ready when I get back," he spewed. "This is the past, Rewella, it has already happened," he paused, and then vanished from the corner. As he disappeared, Rewella also thought she heard him say, "Maybe we can still save ourselves."

* * *

"I thought I might find you here," Flange said conversationally as he stepped from a shadowy corner of the stable. His dark look was anything from conversational. Daekrey spun around, hurling two daggers faster than the blink of a mortal's eye.

Flange swept his sword even faster as it leapt from the sheath and into a defensive position blocking the first blade. With a slight shift of the sword's angle, the deflection sent the second blade whirling harmlessly away.

The sullen face that Daekrey sported was replaced with a wistful smile. "You are full of surprises, Gray One," he chided. Daekrey straightened from his offensive posture, placing his hands on his hips.

A meaningful smile spread on Flange's face. "You don't know yet, do you, demon?" he said, stretching wide an unnerving smile.

Daekrey held a slight look of amusement but did not respond to the bait. Flange lowered his sword, but did not sheathe it. He began to slowly pace in a circle around the melded man. Daekrey was confident that he could handle anything the Undead man could throw at him and showed it as he stood his ground, even letting Flange move out of his range of vision behind him.

Flange stopped and stood directly behind the melded man. "I expected a different response from you," Flange continued to chide.

Daekrey ignored the banter and started some of his own, "I am impressed with you inventiveness, but under the circumstances, I figured you would be at your mother's castle." It was Flange's turn to ignore the attempted jibe. Daekrey turned his head to look at Flange. His body followed just a step behind. "Haven't you heard? The village Magistrate is in the process of leading a mob of people to burn your mother's castle to the ground. It appears that a certain Undead Duke has gone on a bloody rampage," he said, thinking to dishearten the Undead man.

Flange's smile only grew wider. The gesture seemed to annoy the melded man and a slight crease furrowed his brow. He held the gaze for a long moment before going back to his original tactic. "You've been so busy playing out here trying to ruin lives, that you haven't been back to the Circle to see that I've ruined yours. Or I should say, your kin's." Flange flashed a wry grin, careful not to show the anguish that he was feeling.

Daekrey's mild temperament slipped as he scowled and said, "You've done nothing to my kin, Gray One."

"Don't be so sure. I can remember when we first met and you thought that I had destroyed your kin by banishing the globe," Flange reminded.

"True enough, but I have since learned that you and your kind don't have the capacities to use the Power Points to their full potential," Daekrey said dismissively.

"Really?" Flange said in mock amusement, "I managed to return to the past just as you did. I even knew what you would be doing here, so I summoned your kin from the Void and have been punishing them for your activities ever since."

A ripple of unbridled anger passed over the melded man's face. His hands clenched and unclenched almost uncontrollably. Slowly he began to shake his head back and forth. "I don't believe you," he said as if in denial, "you have more honor than that."

Flange kept up the untroubled persona, flashing an even more cynical smile, "This is the past to me, demon. All of this has already happened to me. If I had really been concerned about what came about to me in the past, I wouldn't have spent all my time here torturing your kin for pleasure for days on end."

Daekrey roared a throaty howl and lunged for the Undead man. Flange sidestepped and sent a slash toward the melded man's face, which Daekrey barely avoided. The follow-up kick that Flange threw at the passing man connected, sending him sprawling to the ground.

Daekrey quickly recovered into a defensive crouch. "I have all the time in the world, demon," Flange said grinning and added, "thanks to you." The look that passed across Daekrey's face was full of doubt, but he had to be sure. He feigned a dagger throw and then bolted out of the stable doors.

Flange's smile dropped like a sinking stone. It took all his determination not to show the demon what he was really feeling. His resolve nearly broke at the mention of the mob's intentions. Flange retrieved the two thrown daggers and tucked them into his belt. He only hoped that his plan worked and that he was not too late to change the past.

* * *

Rewella had recovered somewhat from her scorching ordeal.

She sat kneeling at the edge of the Circle, flicking chunks of her burned flesh onto the stone floor. She had placed a contingency spell on the Circle and had just completed the third dry run of testing. She removed the gems from the shallows of the Circle placing them on the outer edge.

She climbed to her feet and nearly collapsed. After steadying herself, she took another quick look at the black globe suspended over the Circle and hoped that it would pass for genuine. She hobbled along into the corner and sat carefully against the wall. She closed her eyes and willed for the pain to go away.

How many centuries has it been since I felt physical pain? she thought to herself. It felt like a new experience to her in a way, and an almost welcomed one. She had thought herself invulnerable to most things and this had been a good reminder that she was not.

A shadow darkened in the corner and a blur of movement streaked forth, coalescing into the shape of Daekrey. He glared at the globe hovering over the Circle. His eyes scanned the room and rested on Rewella, trying to look as inconspicuous as possible in the opposite corner.

In an instant, Daekrey sped across the room to loom menacingly over the debilitated woman. "I'm going to finish what the sun started!" he spat.

Rewella cried out as Daekrey grabbed her wrists in both hands, yanking her to her burnt feet. The rough handling by the melded man broke loose the charred skin from her arms and ash scattered as it fell to the floor. "My kin will feed on what's left of your soul, Keeper of the Spiders," Daekrey said vehemently and flung her, sending her to soar across the floor toward the Circle.

Rewella fought the slide landing just short of the metallic etching. She sighed in relief, unsure what would have happened to her had she triggered the contingency spell that lay dormant and ready for activation. She only had enough components to make one attempt and after that, nothing.

Daekrey marched before the Circle, staring at the globe. A look of puzzlement passed over his face. "That's not from the Void . . ."

The melded man suddenly lurched forward, stumbling over Rewella's sprawled form and landed hard in the center of the Circle.

The contingency spell was triggered. The gems, placed on the outer edge of the Circle, leapt into preordained recesses on the gold and silver etchings releasing the black lightning, which arced wildly, filling the chamber with stark contrasts and leaving a heavy smell of ozone.

Flange glared at the screaming melded man convulsing on the metallic etchings. He had arrived and tackled Daekrey just as he was realizing the globe was a ruse. The lightning continued to course through the man, even after several minutes. Flange could only remember the lightning lasting a few seconds at the most.

Sprig's body lurched into the air, suspended above the Circle and dissipating the bogus globe. More lighting raced into the air arcing from the lines flooding the already battered man. The charged energy caused the body to glow with a pale blue light. An outline of thrashing tentacles surrounded the flailing man followed by a silhouette of hulking wings that beat the air viciously.

The lightning disappeared leaving harsh afterimages in the air. Sprig's limp body dropped heavily onto the Circle with an echoing thud. A fist-sized gem spilled from a pouch, skipping across the stone floor. A hulking translucent shape also fell onward outside of the Circle.

The weakened demon struggled to rise. Flange was there waiting with sword in hand. The demon froze, looking into the eyes of his executioner. He saw no mercy and no quarter. Flange's enchanted sword cleaved through the transparent membrane of the demon's neck, lopping the head clean off. The body gave a quick spasm and slowly began to dissipate into a clear jelly-like substance, leaving a slick stain on the stone floor.

Flange heard a groan come from the Circle. Sprig stirred and let out another grunt. His hair stood on end and blackened areas covered his body where the coursing bolts had discharged. He grimaced in pain and tried to pull himself to his unsteady elbows.

"Who are you?" Flange said, posing his sword for a strike.

Sprig looked up from swollen eyes. "It felt like a dream," he stammered. "It was as though seeing through someone else's eyes." Realization dawned on him that the dreamed events had led right up to where he was now, and were actually no dream at all.

Flange sheathed the sword and reached a hand out to the battered man. "I have to get to my mother's castle and try to stop what's about to happen." After helping the young man to his feet,

Flange marched for a corner, stopping short to scoop up the fallen gem.

"That's mine, and I'm going with you," Sprig said, picking up his burnt hat with singed plumes, and settling it over his frizzed hair.

Flange tossed the retrieved daggers to the insistent man as he staggered forward, catching them deftly in spite of his past ordeal. He added them back to the empty spots on the shouldered bandoleer.

Both men moved to the corner where Rewella had scooted during the lightning display. "You!" Sprig bellowed at the recognition and reached for a dagger.

Flange stayed his hand. "No! This gets resolved later. Right now we are going to the castle and try to stop this madness." Rewella nodded and Sprig glared but made no move to disobey. The trio moved to the corner, blending with the shadows, becoming one with them, and vanished from the chamber into the clearing in the fairy ring.

The residue from the melding seemed to protect Sprig from the shadow walking. The trio moved into the shadows of the night using the trans-dimensional paths of the shadow world until they ended up near the castle.

* * *

The twilight hours left the few burning torches held in sconces near the castle gates, casting wavering shadows on the stone walls. A shadow split apart into three separate forms. Flickering light showed the three beings standing on the mud-trekked road before the moderately sized castle.

Summer filled the air and torchlight burned through the lingering fog of the advancing road. The mob, incited by Daekrey, had massed and lurked angrily along the muddied road.

"Who are they?" Sprig said, seeing the mass that had thrown aside its fear and was intent on dispensing frenzied justice.

"The townsfolk of Klevia. Daekrey tipped them off that the Duke is Undead and they are here to burn the castle to the ground," Flange said as the trio moved through the lowered drawbridge and raised portcullis. The servant guards were nowhere to be seen.

"I don't like this," Rewella said, "my mother had guards posted in the entryway and on the outskirts of the castle at any given time."

"Of course she did, you idiot," Flange snapped. "Leonine killed everyone that got in his way when he returned to the castle."

"What do we do?" Sprig questioned. Flange left the question unanswered as he rushed through the entryway. He stopped short in the foyer and eyed the gatehouse.

"Sprig, lower the portcullis. When you've finished, meet us in the main entryway," Flange said bolting away. Rewella was at a loss for words and followed him reluctantly.

Sprig grabbed the brake, loosening the catch, sending the portcullis crashing down and blocking access to the castle.

"Someone's closed the gate!" a voice yelled from the massing crowd. "Get the oil and arrows ready, we'll burn it down," another voice issued the order.

Sprig watched as the mob made preparation. He decided that it was time to fly from the gatehouse to the entryway as flaming arrows streaked through the iron gates.

Running into the entryway Sprig looked left and right for the siblings. His pulse fluttered as the empty hallway sent a cold chill down his spine. *Where had they gone?* he wondered, looking around. "Flange! Where are you?" he yelled.

The dimly lit hallway flickered reflection of two shadowy forms. Sprig drew two daggers and lowered into a crouch, ready for a considered response. He prepared for an attack, waving the daggers in an aggressive pattern.

The two figures emerged from the hallway and Sprig sighed in evident relief. "We're too late," Flange said remorsefully, "we've already been changed by the Duke."

Sprig was startled by the response. Already changed? What the hell was he talking about? "Changed? You mean into Undead? Shouldn't we do something to help them?" he questioned, not sure what else to say.

Flange stood thumbing his chin in thought. "This is the past and all this has already happened," he said as if finally accepting the fact as the truth. He let out a sigh of resolution. "We somehow survived this night and will do so again. I have no memory from the time of the change until I awoke in Haven," he said. Rewella nodded in agreement. "I have no wish to know what transpired during that state. We stopped the demon and it's time to leave. We need to get back to the present."

A loud explosion and the grinding of metal sent the trio scurrying to the ground. Oily smoke rolled through the room as orange flames licked at the fixtures and furnishings. The ancient tapestries that hung on the wall fed the blaze, spreading to the massive dry wooden rafters overhead.

"We've got to get out of here! Stay close to me!" Flange shouted over the split and crackling of the burning castle.

Panic swept Rewella. The exposure to the morning sun had nearly ended her unnatural life and left her in the most weakened state she had ever been in. She knew that the present condition of her body would be completely destroyed by the fire. She had to flee to survive, even if it meant staying in the past. Rewella bolted.

"Damn it!" Sprig heard Flange spew angrily. He could see neither of the siblings through the choking smoke that scorched his eyes. He felt a chilling hand squeeze his arm and yank him forward. He stumbled, trying to catch his balance and keep pace with the Undead man.

Flange led the coughing Sprig through the maze of hallways and up a winding staircase into numerous other hallways and past a set of double doors. For the moment, the smoke was not quite as thick here, but they knew that would soon change.

Sprig closed the double doors and pulled a tapestry from the wall to throw against the base of the doors in a feeble attempt to block out some of the suffocating smoke. Water from his teary irritated eyes ran down his cheeks, making black tracks through the soot. "Where is she?" he croaked.

Flange continued down the hallway to another set of double doors that were slightly ajar. Sprig was quick to follow as the smoke billowed around the makeshift barricade against the doors. Flange slipped past the doors and Sprig followed stopping short.

Rewella was at the other end of the hall before another set of double doors that were opened. She seemed to be pounding the air with fists, shaking loose ashen flakes from her charred arms. "I can see my lair! There has to be a way through!" she bellowed in what could pass for irrepressible sobs.

Flange walked over and stood next to Rewella. He reached out his palm and placed it on the invisible barrier, running it back and forth. Rewella continued to pound her fists in frustration against it.

Sprig covered about half of the distance between the two sets of doors and stopped. After a moment of silence, "How do we get out?" he questioned softly.

Before Flange could offer an answer, the walls around them split apart, bursting into hungry flames. The blast flung Sprig headlong into the barrier. Scorching heat belched into the hall, stealing the breathable air. The flames spread quickly toward them. Sprig gasped and shielded his face with his arms.

Flange knew they were doomed unless he could think of something fast. He stepped back away from the barrier. He looked at the sheath hanging from his hip. The sword housed there was one of the most powerful weapons that had ever existed. He also knew that he had barely scratched the surface of the sword's capabilities.

The sword sang from its sheath with firelight dancing in reflections on the length of the mystical blade. In a graceful, almost reverent motion, the sword raced from overhead in a downward stroke. The blade struck the barrier and passed through it as if it did not exist at all.

Flange completed the stroke and immediately felt the rush of wind as he and his companions were sucked through the rupture in the barrier.

Sasha stood flabbergasted as a burst of boiling air rushed in from nowhere, followed by the unexpected appearance of Flange, an unrecognizable Rewella, and the demon in the guise of the human man Sprig.

The whole background area around the lair seemed to shimmer, twist and distort. "Get to the corner!" Rewella yelled. "The pocket is collapsing! We need to shadow walk out of here!" The quartet hurriedly obeyed, moving to the shadows as the room simply shrank in on itself by the release of the forced torture of physics.

The group separated from the shadow of a grove of twisted trees that danced about in the gentle breeze. Sprig moved from the group stepping toward the husk of a burned-out castle overtaken by trees and plant growth. A large owl watched him from a stone opening in what had once been a window. It was obvious that whatever happened to the castle was done ages ago.

He turned back to face the siblings, hands crossed over his chest. His filth-covered face added to the grim expression. "As far as I'm concerned, my temporary truce with you two is now over," he stated looking directly at Rewella and Sasha. "I will be hunting you both after sunrise. I suggest that you get as far away from me as you possibly can," Sprig said in a low dangerous tone.

Sasha started to snicker, but changed her mind after seeing the man's hands move over the hilts of the silver daggers in the bandoleer. A chill ran down her spine at the sudden fear of what those weapons could do to her. She visibly shuddered under his stare and intended threat. Rewella was in no shape to retort his words. She just stared numbly.

"Does our bargain still hold?" Flange asked, secretly reveling in the fact that this young man had intimidated his sister and her she-bitch servant.

Sprig eyed the man, weighing his response. "Does your bargain still hold with the Baron?"

"It does," Flange said, nodding.

"Then so does mine," he stated.

Rewella watched the exchange and decided it was best to slip away while she still could. She knew the sun would be rising soon and that she would not survive its deadly rays. She needed to make it to one of her other hidden lairs and begin the slow healing process. Sasha followed her lead and disappeared through the thick trees.

"I have another deal I would like to make for this stone," Flange said, holding the recovered blue gem in his hand.

Sprig reached for the gem, taking it into his hand. He looked the gem over in silence. After a few moments, he said, "This is the only thing I have left of my mentors."

Flange watched as Sprig mulled over unheard thoughts. After a minute or so, Sprig looked into the eyes of the Undead man and pitched the gem to him. He easily caught it and watched the man expectantly.

"You saved me from the demon, and you saved me from the flames. It's yours," he said.

"You want nothing in return?" Flange questioned with a look of surprise.

Sprig shook his head and said, "No. I would just ask that you stop killing for pleasure."

Flange searched the young man's eyes. "Agreed," he said, nodding. The moment started to linger. "We should get back to the village and make sure Kate is all right," he said changing the subject.

Sprig still held the memories of Daekrey from the melding and knew that Flange was absolutely right.

"Are you ready for a shadow walk?" Flange asked.

"It doesn't seem to bother me," Sprig replied evenly.

"Probably a residue of the melding," he wondered. Sprig shrugged and the two men moved into the dark woods, disappearing with the shadows.

14

"Kate! Kate!" Keltch bellowed into the night as he reined his horse and squinted, trying to pierce the surrounding darkness. Several armed men holding torches fanned out around the Baron through the mist-filled streets of Klevia. "Katie!" Keltch called again, stepping from the stirrups to land heavily next to his mount.

A hulking demon feasted on the remains of a towns person that was unfortunate enough not to get away from the vicious creature.

"Kill that damned thing!" Keltch commanded and led the charge against the beast, sinking his sword deeply into the putrid scaled flesh. The creature shrieked in surprise and lunged out with a smacking backhand that flung the Baron through the air.

Even from the prone position on the cobblestone streets, Keltch stabbed up with his sword. The demon shuddered as the sword pierced through the ribcage and out of its back. Keltch rolled the demon off his chest and wrenched his sword free. The Baron and the closest hands fell on the stricken creature, hacking it to pieces.

The rest of Keltch's men fanned out, surveying the obscured streets of Klevia. The group had been fighting an assortment of demons and other creatures, never seen to man, on the trek to locate Kate and the missing men. They had burned several of the possessed tree-creatures that trudged aimlessly across the landscape.

Keltch had awakened from his near-death experience, furious to learn that Kate knew the truth about her mother Mariel and that she had decided to take up her sword and mantle.

The hidden runner from Landon's party had made it back to the estate and told Mengrig of Kate absorbing the shadowing party that was sent to protect them, and took them into the village as her escort. His report was just about the same time that Keltch had waked from his feverish slumber demanding to know what had transpired in the last few days of his absence.

The Baron was still extremely weak from his harrowing ordeal, and against Mengrig's better judgment, had rallied the hired help forming a search party to find his beloved daughter.

In the places where the fog was not nearly as dense, Keltch could see the remnants of dismembered bodies littering the blood-slick streets. A cold fury built in him as he searched for any telltale signs that would prove that one of these hapless souls was his own daughter.

Clenching his teeth tightly, he cried her name once again, "Katie!" In a lower tone, and more to himself, he said, "Where are you, girl?"

He grabbed the horse's reins, leading it through the deserted streets. The hooves clopped on the cobblestones, sending muffled echoes off the nearly obscured walls of the surrounding buildings.

A scout worked his way quickly around the obstacles in the street and stopped before Keltch. In a low whisper, he said, "Baron, we found Magistrate Burgman's body in his office . . ." The man faltered and left the details unsaid.

Keltch nodded in understanding, not needing the extra information. "What about the priest Iesed? Have you run across him?"

"No, sir, but that doesn't mean anything. In some places it's just pools of blood and no bodies at all," he replied with a sigh.

Keltch clapped the man on the shoulder. "Get back to your position and tell any of the others that you see on the way to keep a list of any of the recognizable dead. I want to know immediately if my daughter is found; dead or alive."

The scout nodded grimly, not savoring the idea should it fall to him to deliver news of that magnitude. He feared for any who should. The scout disappeared into the fog leaving the Baron with his dismal thoughts. *I guess no news is good news,* he thought trying to shake the sinking feeling in the pit of his stomach.

He continued walking his mount, fearful that it would stumble over something unseen in the dark, cluttered, fog-blanketed streets. The horse whinnied in panic and tried to pull away. "Easy!" he whispered repeatedly in a cooing tone.

Keltch could not see the immediate danger but knew it was close. He stared intently into the surrounding dark. He cursed under his breath. If only it was daylight! The morning was still several hours away.

He tossed the reins aside, crouching into a defensive stance as a shadow blacker than the others lengthened and stretched apart very near him. He started a sword swipe at the insubstantial shapes forming.

The ring of metal against metal echoed off the stone structures and Keltch took several retreating steps, putting some distance between him and the anomaly.

"It's good to see you alive and well, Baron!" a familiar voice said with genuine enthusiasm. As the shapes solidified, Keltch could make out Flange holding a sword that had blocked his blow and the unmistakable silhouette of Sprig wearing his gods-awful hat.

"Kate left the estate to try and find you. Have you seen her?" Keltch asked. An uneasy silence stretched between the three men, making the Baron extremely nervous.

"Baron, there is a lot that needs to be explained to you, but now is not the time," Flange stated, "I left Kate in the church while I retrieved our missing friend here." It was not quite the truth, but Flange did not want to spend the time explaining now when so much was at stake.

Sprig made no attempt to supply an answer. Ever since his reversal, he felt the weight of Daekrey's actions and the burden left on his heart.

"Baron come quick!" a shout echoed from around the corner. The three men spun about and rushed toward the source. An eerie shriek filled the night, mingled with the sounds of clanging metal and random shouts.

The assembly rounded the corner in time to see a small group fending off a demon and two of the tree-creatures. Keltch's heart sank at the realization of the image. Kate stood with someone or some thing clinging to her leg a she fought off the wing buffets of a cruel demon. Keltch realized the buffets were really a feint as a tree-creature swung its barky limbs around her waist, lifting her from the ground. A man, more than likely Landon, sent arrow after arrow into the creature to no avail.

"No!" the three men yelled in unison, trying to reach the fight in time to try and change the outcome. Flange saw the whole scene slow to a crawl as his preternatural abilities kicked in and he moved to intercept the tree-creature. He saw Kate's limbs flail as the interlocking branches first stretched her body out and then brought her crashing down against the trunk of the creature. His movements were fast, but not fast enough to stop her body from being broken and flung away into the hazy street.

An underlying rage broke the surface spilling a dam of uncontrollable energy that flowed through Flange's body to be unleashed into the air in a crackling burst, not unlike a fork of lightning filling the night sky.

He was too late to save Kate, but his enchanted blade cut from one side of the trunk to the other splitting the tree-creature in two. A reverse stroke lopped off the head of the ravenous demon.

Orange streaking light illuminated the sky as several of the Baron's men shot lighted arrows into the remaining tree-creature, setting it ablaze. It shrieked and howled as the burning sap burst into flames, further intensifying the raging inferno. The creature writhed in the streets for a moment and then ceased its death struggle.

Flange stood stunned, looking at Kate's still form and the small body clinging to it. A throaty growl escaped the little girl's mouth. Flange felt the aura of undeath about the girl and knew he was responsible for her change. His momentary lapse in control had unleashed a power that he had yet to use in four hundred years of his undeath. And now, through carelessness, he had changed a child. The remainder of the differences between himself and his sadistic brother was no longer a reality. Flange had just proved that he was no better than his hated brother. He staggered away from the child and the still form of Kate in a state of shock.

Sprig and the Baron raced to the fallen love of both men. Keltch pulled the clinging hissing child from Kate's leg and tossed her away from the group. Tears streaked down both of the men's faces as they held Kate's crumpled form.

The streets were eerily silent with the exception of the two sobbing men. Sprig finally looked up at Flange who was staring at the newly created Undead. "Flange! Please help Kate," he pleaded between sobs, "Please, you must help her."

Flange half turned, with his eyes following to the scene left before him. He and his siblings had been responsible for every evil thing that had transpired over the last four hundred years. He himself had crossed a line that he had drawn in the sand even before becoming an Undead creature.

"Flange," Sprig tried again. "Please, help her."

"I can't," he said softly, letting himself slip between the cracks of the cobblestones into the yielding oblivion of the earthy soil. He could hear a muffled throaty curse and then he could hear nothing else.

"Damn you, Flange!" Sprig cried out in exasperation.

Keltch had been numbingly quiet through the whole ordeal. Every day he had spent his life trying to make a world safe enough for his daughter to live in without fear of Undead creatures. Now she was gone. His whole quest in life seemed so shallow now after the fact. His blurry eyes streamed tears.

The slight tap of someone walking down stairs almost did not register at first. The entire surreal scene seemed to blur together. He shifted his gaze from his daughter to the weeping young man holding her hand ever so gently. His gaze moved to the figure moving down the stone steps of the church.

Iesed took in the scene at a glance. The crumpled form of Kate being held by Baron Keltch and the young man who only hours ago was their enemy. Landon and Brundle both stood reverently next to the Baron and his fallen daughter. At this moment, everyone else who had fallen seemed to be forgotten.

In a soft voice that seemed to carry to everyone, Keltch said, "My father told me when I was a lad, that the priests in his day had so much faith in their gods, that they could heal the sick and dying." His voice trailed off as he stared at the priest.

"She's already dead," Iesed said in almost a whisper.

The Baron shook his head. "No, she still breathes, but not for very much longer."

Iesed knelt before the battered girl and moved a blood-matted clump of hair from her closed eyes. Iesed felt completely helpless in the face of the surrounding disarray. The facade he had carried for the majority of his life as a religious icon cracked, and he wept tears of woeful shame.

There was once a time when I truly believed in the words of the Tome, he thought. *I did believe that good triumphs over all evil and that every man should love and respect one another.*

Calmness fell over the old priest as if he was seeing the situation through someone else's eyes. His hands moved of their own accord, radiating a pulsing faint blue hue.

The visible wounds on Kate's face closed, leaving no scars. Her broken bones moved and reset themselves. Pale cheeks flushed with healthy color and her breathing became steady and even.

Everyone stared in stunned silence, including Iesed. "By the Tome!" he exclaimed as the tranquility subsided, followed by extreme exhaustion as his withered hands returned to their normal coloring and function. The silence continued to linger, broken only by the hissing growls of the newly turned Undead child writhing on the cobblestones.

Kate was unconscious but whole. Keltch stared at her serene face unable to speak, even unable to thank the priest and his gods.

"What about the child? Kate is quite taken with her," Keltch heard Brundle whisper to no one in particular. Keltch looked at the priest who gave a slight nod.

"There is nothing we can do for the child. Her soul has already fled from her body. That creature is not her," the priest said, reverting back to his former stern manner.

Sprig felt like he had been punched in the face. Her soul had fled her body? He had spent enough time with Flange to know that the Undead man still had a soul. Or did he? The confusion spread through him, pulling his sorrowful heart apart. He did not know what to do. Too much had happened so fast and his mind and memories were a tempest awhirl.

Iesed moved to the child, lifting it from the ground and held it well away from his body. She ground her teeth and snarled like a wounded animal. The display was more for show, for she did little to try to injure the priest. Iesed carried the child to the town square and the ancient erected gallows.

He did not impale her on the rusted spears as he had done to so many in the past. Instead, he carefully tied the child's hands to a wooden post and stroked her silken hair.

The sky was already becoming a dingy gray as the sun threatened to burn away the fog. Sprig had retained the musculature given to him during the melding, and he easily carried the sleeping form of Kate as the group followed the priest into the square. Keltch held her outstretched hand, giving it a caressing squeeze.

The white globe of the sun pierced the shrouding fog and the child screamed in terror and agony as her skin began to crack, seeping tiny curls of wafting smoke.

Sprig could do nothing but stand and stare numbly as the frightened child wailed. He held Kate all the closer for comfort.

The cobblestones before the platform exploded from the ground, sending shards pelting the battered onlookers. Flange burst from the ground with sword drawn and covered the distance to the burning child in a blink of an eye. His sword slashed out severing the bonds as he swirled a cloak over and around the child. Just as fast, he had sheathed the sword and plucked the child from the raised stage. He landed onto the hole of the vacated cobblestones and let the earth swallow him and the child.

As the ground fast approached his eyes as he sank, he fastened a quick look at Sprig and the bundle that he was carrying in time to see Kate's eyes open wearily and lock with his own. She mouthed the questioning word of his name before he lost sight of her as he was submerged under the saving ground.

* * *

Flange was back in Haven in the dim light, carefully removing the wound cloak from his Undead charge. She had stopped crying, though her skin was cracked and bleeding. He stared into those hateful malicious eyes and wondered why he had saved her. Was she not better off destroyed, no longer a threat to anyone? She would not be in this position if he had kept control of his abilities.

He sat her on the wooden table as she glared, hissing at him. Was he like this when he had been changed? He had no memory of the event and had no real wish to know.

He moved to the center of the Circle and closed his eyes in concentration. The metallic etchings brightened as Flange's form merged with the lines and he disappeared from the room.

The room shifted slightly as Flange moved from the Circle. He had focused on the Haven located in the desert and was transported there. He walked to the corner, looking at one particular formula on the wall. He drew the sword, feeling the magical emanation and compared it to the pseudo-vibration from the formula. He then removed the fist-sized blue gem, given to him by Sprig, and held it before him.

A shudder of anticipation passed through him. The magical aura matched the one presented on the wall in every detail. Now he had the items necessary to make himself mortal again. He turned, eyeing the Circle and the necessary recesses to be used to alter his Undead state. He sighed in relief knowing that his long search was finally over. He spread a handsome smile showing even white teeth. He was to be a mortal . . . again.

* * *

Baron Keltch and his hired men had flushed the remaining demons and tree-creatures from the town and surrounding countryside and destroyed them. The otherworldly portal in the forest clearing, suspended over the fairy ring, had slowly closed, leaving a scarred landscape in its wake.

Every available man in town carried out the sullen duties of burning the dead in hopes that none of them would rise again from their graves. Iesed had assumed the mantle of leadership, after the knowledge of the Magistrate's death, and coordinated the day's activity. His pompous attitude had been replaced with compassion and a sense of spiritual fulfillment. In short, he had regained his lost faith.

With the grim tasks completed, the Baron's party started home before dark, yet none feared the coming night. Sprig had carried Kate back into the church and laid her on a pile of cloaks on the floor before helping in the necessary tasks of putting the town back together.

Brundle was more than happy to use his newly grown leg in any way possible to help heal the strife. His jovial presence, so uncharacteristic of him, helped boost the morale of the working population as they tried to put their shattered lives back together.

Even the Baron was surprised by the turn of events. Although tragedy and death had happened, some good had managed to survive and flourish. His daughter was alive and healed of her grievous wounds. Iesed's faith in his gods had been restored. Brundle had a new leg and a new lease on life. The only one that still seemed to be troubled was Sprig.

Even though he refused to show it on the outside, the boy had changed. He was no longer the innocent young man that he had been before the melding. The memories of Daekrey still mingled with his own and the physical alteration made him look more a man than boy. In some ways that could be a blessing, but the mental images of the long-lived creature kept invading and blending with his own.

He had decided that he would help with the tasks within the town, see Kate home safe and sound, and then start the hunt for the two responsible for killing his mentors and melding him with a demon.

Kate had awakened as the group prepared to leave town. She insisted on riding her own horse and refused help from anyone, including Sprig.

Keltch suppressed a shiver seeing Kate dressed as her mother had been when he first met her nearly twenty summers ago. She was still angry at the fact that her father had never told her the truth of her mother's past. Keltch shook off another shiver knowing that his daughter was the spitting image of Mariel. He also knew that her anger would pass as it always did. She just needed time to sort things out.

Mengrig and his scouting pickets met the party halfway through the forest and ushered the weary men and woman home.

Sprig had stripped to his waist, wearing only his boots and bandoleer of daggers, not unlike the Baron had done several nights before from returning from the arranged meeting with Flange. After seeing Kate off, he strode straight to his room, locking the door behind him. He spoke very little to anyone on the journey back to the estate.

Epilogue

The morning came and Sprig was up before the household staff saddling his mare and checking his gear. "You don't have to go, Sprig," a soft voice said from the stable doorway. Sprig turned to meet Kate's sorrowful eyes.

"I have to," was all he could say as he led the horse from the stable. He passed by Kate, not wanting to yield to the yearning to grab her in his arms and kiss her passionately.

She stopped him with a touch on his shoulder, yet he refused to meet her gaze. Instead, he said, "I have a promise to keep." Kate grabbed his free hand in both of hers.

"We'll go together then," she offered. He looked into her loving eyes. Her gaze shifted over his shoulder and a wrinkle creased her brow. Sprig dropped into a defensive stance, pulling two throwing knives from the bandoleer and spun on his heels to meet whatever was behind him.

Flange stood barely ten feet or so away, wearing a tattered old cloak covering his frame. A child stepped out from behind him and ran to Kate, grabbing her around the waist, hugging her fiercely. Sprig stared in awe at the child. She was not Undead anymore and altogether very human.

"How?" Sprig stammered. "Is this a trick of some kind?"

Flange smiled that unnerving smile and let it falter. "Let's just say that I found a way to bring her back thanks to the help of that gem you were kind enough to give me."

"And the sword," Sprig said, seeing the Undead man for the first time without it. Flange gave a slight nod as the smile disappeared completely from his face.

Kate hugged the girl tight and kissed her face and the affection was returned tenfold. "It seems that you have a family to look after now, Sprig," Flange stated. Sprig stared, uncomprehending.

"No, I have some Undead to hunt," he said, realizing what Flange was implying. Flange let the smile creep back onto his face.

"Fear not about keeping your promise. I am already in the process of ridding this land forever of Undead," Flange pledged.

"Including yourself?" Sprig added. A moment of silence followed.

Flange looked directly at Kate and said cryptically, "I cannot make any promises regarding myself, but any who are a threat will be gone. Also, I have another gift for you," he added, tossing a gem through the air. Kate deftly caught the token and looked at it and Flange with a puzzled look. "It's a memory stone," he said simply.

Sprig shuddered at the thought of Daekrey using one to move to the past. Flange caught the concerned gesture and smiled. "Have no fear. I learned how to replace the stored information with something a little more practical," and after a small pause added, "and personal."

Kate held the gem before her between thumb and forefinger. "Place it on your brow," Flange directed. She did so and was amazed to see the memory representation of her mother, Mariel; the image created was she in her prime. "It's wonderful!" she voiced, tears welling in her eyes. "Thank you."

"She was a wonderful woman, and so are you," Flange said with a knowing sad smile.

Sprig nodded and Kate flushed at the lingering look of the Undead man, but managed a grateful smile. Flange executed an exquisite bow and sank into the earth, leaving little ripples in the soil that subsided shortly after his absence.

Sprig smiled at the scene of Kate holding the girl and the weight of his thoughts was suddenly lifted. He sheathed the drawn daggers and walked slowly to the two of them, placing his arms around them both. If this is where he was wanted, then this is where he would stay.

About the Author

Jackson Compton was born in Dallas, Texas and lives in Edmond, Oklahoma.

E-mail: jacksoncompton@gmail.com
Photo credit: Shaun Angley